Praise for *Asperfell*

"The wonderfully inventive first installment in Thomas's debut trilogy winningly combines the comedy of manners found in Regency romances with the high spirits of magical school adventure fantasies. [...]

The charming characters, understated romance that simmers between Briony and Elyan, and easily graspable politics are all well-rendered, but the true star here is the strange, mystical setting of Asperfell. This promising adventure has crossover YA appeal and is sure to win over fantasy readers."

—PUBLISHER'S WEEKLY
(starred review)

Explore the world of Asperfell:
ThatJamieThomas.com

Follow the author:
Facebook.com/ThatJamieThomas
Twitter.com/ThatJamieThomas

For more great science fiction and fantasy novels:
UproarBooks.com

Follow the publisher:
Facebook.com/UproarBooks
Twitter.com/UproarBooks

Publisher's Note:
*If you enjoy this novel, please leave a positive rating
and/or review on Goodreads, Amazon, or other similar
websites to let other readers know. Reviews work!
Support your favorite authors.*

JAMIE THOMAS

Uproar
Books

1419 PLYMOUTH DRIVE, NASHVILLE, TN 37027
UPROARBOOKS.COM

ASPERFELL

Published by Uproar Books, LLC.

Edited by Rick Lewis.

Cover illustration by Khristian M. Collins.

Printed in the United States of America.

ISBN 978-1-949671-06-3

First paperback edition.

MIX
Paper from
responsible sources
FSC® C005010

*For every woman who has yet to discover
the power in her own voice*

1

I remember a little about the night the king was assassinated.

I was only eight years old at the time and cared not at all for life beyond my own nose, but some things can never be forgotten.

I was pulled from the deep, satisfying sleep of one who had spent the day climbing the rafters in the west turret to avoid my odious tutor by my older sister, Livia. She smothered my groan of displeasure with her hand, and in the stillness of the room I stared at her wide eyes and disheveled curls as she raised a finger to her lips, then slowly removed her hand from my mouth. Livia was the very soul of decorum. Her reasons for waking me in such a state must've been very urgent indeed.

"There are men below," Livia told me in a breathless whisper, as I struggled to free myself from the bedsheets tangled around my skinny legs. "Men from the Citadel."

"What time is it?" The sky outside the window told me nothing with its darkness. I could've just fallen asleep an hour ago or it might be near morning. The late autumn night guarded her secrets carefully.

"Just after midnight."

With a grunt, I turned my back on her and flopped down into my pillows, my hand groping for the blankets. "Go away."

Livia shook my shoulder, her fingers gripping me so tightly that I yelped. "Get up, Briony," she hissed into my ear. "I think it's bad."

"Men from the Citadel come all the time." My voice was muffled by the pillow, and I shrugged my shoulder in an effort to be rid of her. She only dug her fingers into my skin farther.

"Mother and Uncle Geordan are below with Lord Falstone," Livia said. "And there are guards."

At this, I perked up. "Guards?"

"Yes." Livia pulled my blankets off of me and I gasped at the sudden shock of the cold air of my bedchamber. The little fire that usually burned so merrily in my grate was a dull smudge of blackened coals with very little living inside to stoke.

"Come on," I whispered to her, suddenly eager. "We can listen at the top of the stairs."

We walked down the darkened corridor, our bare cold feet padding silently on the rich, hand-hewed wood floors until we reached the landing that overlooked the grand foyer of our Iluvien townhouse. We crouched together, Livia and I, in our long white nightgowns and pressed our faces as close as we could to the ornately carved railing.

There were six people clustered in the foyer. I immediately recognized the broad, stalwart figure of my Uncle Geordan, and my mother beside him. My mother was still wearing the russet gown she'd had on at dinner, which meant she had not gone to bed. The tall man with a sallow face and hair the color of metal was Lord Falstone, whom I disliked. He was as stern as his countenance and, when it came to children, a traditionalist. He only marginally tolerated my sister Livia because she was twelve and had learned the intricacies of interacting with adults. Which was to say, she sat demurely with her fine white hands in her lap and said nothing at all. Me, he did not care for. I was, as my father affectionately referred to me, a whirlwind.

There were two palace guards on either side of the door to the courtyard, resplendent in black and silver livery and utterly still.

The sixth person I did not know at all. He was an unremarkable man; he was neither short nor tall, broad nor thin, and his face was quite ordinary. It was the sort of face one would forget entirely without frequent exposure. He looked to be in his middle years, younger than my father, but not by much. He hung back from the others, but his eyes were watchful.

"Who is with him now?" My mother's voice, usually melodic and rich, was hushed and pitched low.

Lord Falstone replied, quieter even than she had been, and I could only make out two names of the several he listed: Aeneas and Magnus. The first was one of the king's Mages. The second was my father.

"And the traitor?" my uncle demanded.

"In the Tower," was Lord Falstone's response. "The Guard is with him, and four Mages."

"Has he said anything?"

"Nothing at all."

My uncle snorted in disgust, the sound echoing in the vast open space. Mother laid her hand on his arm. "The girls are abed."

My uncle ignored her. "Tell Magnus to send another detachment to the Tower. The filth killed his own father."

I gasped out loud.

The unremarkable man, who had until this point remained utterly still and silent, turned his gaze to the column where we crouched, and Livia gripped my arm. He must've seen us; we were hardly concealed in the shadow of the column. But if he did see us, he said nothing.

"We should go back to bed," Livia whispered to me, her hand on my arm. "I don't think this is something we should hear."

I shook her off. "You go back to bed, then."

My father, a great friend and councilor to the king, was often at court and shared absolutely nothing about what he did there with Livia or myself. Had the news delivered to our home that night by Lord Falstone been of the mundane sort, I still would've been mad to hear it, mad enough to risk a sound whipping should I be discovered. But my uncle had just pronounced King Gavreth dead, and at the hand of his own son. No power in all of Tiralaen could've sent me back to my cold bedroom. I would hear it never mind what it cost me.

"The bells have not rung," my mother said below. "The news has not spread beyond the palace, then. How long can they possibly contain it?"

Lord Falstone frowned. "Not long, I'm afraid. The court was gathering as I left."

"Will there be a trial?"

"It would be unprecedented if there were not."

My uncle made a vicious gesture with his hand. "A waste," he spat. "He was found with the body, Sabine. The king was killed by magic and we all know his wretched son is a proficient."

Livia's wide eyes met mine, and in the dim light of the hall I could see her face was as pale as I imagined my own to be. To cause another human being harm by magical means was sacrilege.

"He is also only sixteen years old—not even a man," my mother reminded him.

"He is man enough to use his magic to kill," my uncle replied sourly.

"It troubles me greatly," Lord Falstone agreed. "Prince Elyan is arrogant and he has a sharp tongue besides. But to kill his own father? He has nothing to gain from it. The throne was already his birthright."

"No doubt the old man wasn't aging fast enough for his liking." My uncle's tone held none of the doubt in my mother's voice, or even in Lord Falstone's. "He'll go through the Gate for this, though I would rather see him hanged."

At this, the sixth man stepped forward and placed his hand firmly on Uncle Geordan's arm. "I fear your conversation is no longer your own," he said, and he tilted his gaze up to the upper floor where we crouched.

Livia shrank back into the shadows, likely terrified that our clandestine eavesdropping would anger and disappoint our mother. I did not. I gripped the bars of the railing in my small hands and met the faces below with a child's brash confidence.

In the distance, the bells began to toll.

It was still dark when I woke to the sound of the hinges on my door creaking in soft protest. A thin shaft of light fell across my bed and I sat up, fully intending on telling my sister to leave me alone, when I saw it was not Livia's hand that held the lantern aloft: it was my father's.

I said nothing as his tall, broad form crossed the room and set the lantern on my bedside table—had it only been a few hours since Livia had done the same?—and the wood of my bedframe creaked as he lowered himself onto it. In the lantern light, I could make out the proud, handsome planes of his face, the auburn curls shot with gray that spilled onto his forehead. I had inherited the color of his hair, but very little else from him. My brown eyes were my mother's, and far too big for my face. I was a tiny thing like her. Livia was almost as tall as Mother even at thirteen, and bonny like my father. She had already begun her bleeding and was filling out her dresses while mine hung off of me like sacks.

"Is the king really dead?" I whispered into the darkness between us.

My father sighed heavily, inclined his head toward me. "I am afraid so."

"Uncle Geordan said the prince killed him."

Beneath his beard, the ghost of a smile tugged at my father's lips. "Told you that, did he?"

"No." I swallowed. "Livia and I were listening." Then, because I could not discern if he was angry or not: "I'm sorry."

"It would've come to you eventually." My father's voice was so very sad, and I reached out impulsively and grasped his giant hand with my much smaller one.

"Is it true?"

He took so long to answer that I wondered if he'd forgotten me there. "Yes."

When my mother and uncle had spoken of it, it seemed too shocking to be believed, a story that had come from an overactive imagination in the palace kitchens, a fantastical distortion of an event that would eventually turn out to be quite ordinary. Hearing my father confirm it now, it became horribly real.

"But why," I said, aghast. "Why would he kill his own father?"

My father's eyes met mine in the dim lantern light. "Murder has many motivators, none of which are meant to be understood by a child." He sighed deeply and looked down at our clasped hands. "Whatever his reasons, the king is dead, and the prince…"

My uncle had said the prince would go through the Gate for his crime. All children in Tiralaen knew what the Gate was, and knew what lay beyond it: the ancient fortress of Asperfell, a prison created to hold Mages.

Magic was said to have been given to humankind by the goddess Thala, and the taking of a life in which the gift resided was considered the deepest blasphemy. The trouble was, there was not a prison in Tiralaen that could hold them, their power was so great. Many fools had tried and failed spectacularly, and so an alternative was sought: a bargain between death and freedom. The Gate was this grand compromise, and it had done its job for five hundred years. No living being had ever crossed the threshold and returned.

"Will he go through the Gate, father?" I asked in the silence that stretched between us. "To Asperfell?"

"Undoubtedly." He lifted his head and looked at me. "Briony, I must ask something of you. Something of great importance."

I sat up straighter, eager to show that whatever it was that he wanted, I could be trusted to do it.

"Our family is about to see a great change." The way he said it made me feel as though this change was not something he took any pleasure in. "And I fear there may be difficult times ahead."

I nodded, though I had little idea what he meant. Difficult times for a child of privilege meant no pudding at supper, or an early bedtime.

"You have always been a strong-willed child." My father chucked me under the chin gently, and I smiled at him sheepishly. "With a certain, shall we say… proclivity for shirking the rules."

I believe if he could've seen me that morning in the rafters, he wouldn't have put it quite so delicately. "I don't mean to be a burden," I said.

"I know you don't." He smiled ruefully. "And I have always loved this about you, my little whirlwind. But where we are going, the life we will live, you must try your hardest to behave. To play the lady."

My tiny hand found his and I squeezed his fingers in the dark. "I promise to be better, father."

"Just so." He nodded and helped me snuggle back into my blankets, tucking them around me. "Briony, there is one more thing you must promise me."

"Anything," I said. My eyelids were growing heavy.

"Have courage. And no matter how dark the world seems and how much you'd like to darken with it, find whatever light you can wherever you can, and help it grow."

"I will," I murmured.

"Help it grow," he repeated. Against the sweet pull of sleep, his voice sounded very far away. "For that is the only way we can defeat the darkness."

* * *

In the end, it was decided that Livia and I should be permitted to attend the administering of the prince's punishment. My mother protested, believing we were far too young to witness something so somber, but my father prevailed. He was adamant that we begin to learn the intricacies of court life, even those as ghastly as this.

The sentence was carried out on a frigid morning five days after the king's death.

Livia and I were trussed up into our finest gowns, our cheeks rosy and pink after a thorough scrubbing from Augusta, the maid we shared between the two of us. Her deft hands braided our hair into coronets atop our heads and fastened our fur-lined cloaks under our chins and sent us out into the blustery gray to meet my mother and uncle.

I was used to seeing my uncle in his court attire; he did not often change between the palace and our townhouse when he came to call. But the sight of my mother draped in rich silk and dripping with jewels was a rare one indeed. If the gravity of what we were about to witness had not set in for me before, it certainly did then.

We rode in silence to the palace. Bored and uneasy, I sat on my knees on the carriage seat and pressed my face to the glass, watching the grand stone residences of the city's wealthy and influential gradually give way to rows of neatly kept terrace houses and shops in the bustling heart of the city and, farther still, the ramshackle tenements where the poorest lived. I wrinkled my nose at the sudden onslaught of smells, a pungent intermingling of roasted meats, wood smoke, and feces, both horse and human. It was not a smell I cared for.

For those who worshiped the new god, today was a holy day and crowds of people swarmed the gleaming temples, seeking the promise of salvation. Their prayers were sung with reverence, but they were not beautiful; always mingled with the holiness was fear, and fear and love were not easy company.

The places where the Old Gods were venerated were far more ancient, and to worship them was to worship the moon and the sun, the stars, the earth, the water. To worship them was to worship magic, for it was from the Old Gods that magic had first come to humans.

The Father is Coleum, who rules the heavens, and the Great Mother is Sator, whose realm is the world itself. Between them they bore three children. Bellus, who loves discord and strife, is jealous of humanity and petty; thus, we are tormented by his spirits, though such abominations have not been seen for centuries. Mor, whom we simply call Death, cares little for anything living at all.

It is Thala, born of water and stars, who loved the poor creatures her parents had made, and in her love had blown softly against the skin of the first people and woken the light within them, stirred the magic in their blood. Her temple by the sea was said to be made of white stone shot through with silver that gleamed when the sun rose over the sea and bathed it in light. I'd never seen it; only Mages were permitted within its sacred walls.

Like his father before him, King Gavreth honored both the old religion and the new, believing them capable of living side by side, and so families worshiped as they chose, an anathema to the lands to the north and east where the religion of the people was determined by the religion of the crown. There, the monotheistic teachings of the new religion reigned.

Iluviel, the Shining City, capital of Tiralaen, known for progress and enlightenment and culture and learning, had gradually come to embrace the new god as they might a new fashion, but outside of the city the Old Gods still held sway, even amongst the wealthy, where shrines to Coleum, Sator, and Thala could be found on the grounds of most country estates.

Still, there was an uneasy truce between the Old Gods and the fashionable new, though the former thought the latter prudish and insufferably smug and the latter found the former strange and wild and savage.

My own parents had taken their vows of marriage before the Old Gods in the Temple Sol Eternum, but they did not practice the way some families did, particularly families with Mages. They observed only the two most important of the sacred holidays, Serus in the winter and Solarium in the summer, and only occasionally placed offerings at the foot of a statue of Sator in our garden, bunches of herbs and bowls of milk for the faery folk that were her pages and handmaidens.

They did not keep the long vigils, did not know the old stories and songs, did not make pilgrimages to the shores of the Lucet Sea.

"Why do mother and father never take us to the temples?" I asked Uncle Geordan above the rattling of our carriage wheels on the cobblestones.

He smiled. "Perhaps they are waiting until you are grown, so that you may better understand the choice you make when you worship the Old Gods. Or the new, for that matter."

"Which do you worship?"

Uncle Geordan snorted. "I have love for neither, really, but if forced, I would throw in my lot with the Old Gods. This new sort has far too many rules for my taste."

In the distance, the spires of the Citadel rose in the dull morning fog like fingers pointing toward the heavens. Beyond it, I could just make out the Tower Maer. An ancient fortress, the Tower was the original seat of the royal family before the Citadel and the sprawling palace within its walls were built as a gift from a king to his Yalanese bride, who had lived in an exquisite palace by the sea and wept upon seeing her new home. It was now a prison, and a place of execution and banishment.

The poor and wretched, whose crimes were those of desperation and passion, were not kept in the Tower Maer. They were either condemned to hard labor in the east or sent to Vraith off the coast of

Cyr, where they died quickly and were forgotten. If their crime was particularly heinous, or they had some notoriety amongst the rabble, they were executed in Iluviel's main square, but this practice had fallen out of fashion with the rule of King Gavreth and his father before him.

No, it was men and women of wealth and influence who lived out their days within the small rooms of the Maer or were executed within its walls, along with Mages waiting to be banished beyond the Gate to Asperfell.

I had never been to the Tower before, and my eyes drank in the imposing slabs of stone that rose into the sky as we passed under a portico. The outer vestibule of the Tower was a gloomy business, made gloomier by the grim presence of Lord Falstone, who had been sent to collect us in my father's place. He said nothing as we stepped down from the carriage, but gave my mother a stiff bow and offered her his arm.

Uncle Geordan did the same for Livia and me, and I was grateful for his solid, warm presence as he guided us through an archway where two palace guards stood unmoving. We passed into a long corridor lined with ornate sconces holding glass spheres full of Magefire. The effect was quite breathtaking, and I could not help but gasp in delight at the sight of it.

"Are we almost there?" Livia asked Uncle Geordan, her small voice echoing around us.

So enraptured was I by the magic before me that I did not see his smile, but I heard it in his voice. "Very nearly."

"Will they have pies?" I asked, as my stomach rumbled loudly in protest. "The cook's boy said they have pies at executions, and cider."

Livia looked horrified, but my uncle chuckled indulgently. "There are food and drink carts at the executions of commoners in the streets, Briony, but not here. Not at the Tower. Executions here are a serious affair." His smile faded. "And today's most serious of all."

I was highly disappointed by this turn of events. I'd purposefully only eaten half a sweet bun at breakfast in anticipation of the bounty I was falsely promised.

I shielded my eyes from the sharp, cold morning sunlight as we emerged from the passage into the inner courtyard. My first thought of the courtyard where Tiralaen's most noble criminals were executed or exiled through the Gate was that it was much smaller than I had imagined. I could not help but stare openmouthed at the walls of the Tower that rose into the sky, punctured here and there by uneven windows with filthy, warped glass, or by clumps of green growing stubbornly in the fissures in the stones. I began to count the windows, if only to figure out how many floors high the Tower was, but I stopped when I realized there were faces staring out at me. They could've been male or female, young or old, for all I could see of their features. They floated in the panes, smudges of white with sunken eyes, and I shivered at the hopelessness I saw within their depths.

There was a wooden scaffolding in the center of the green, and surrounding it on three sides were benches three rows deep, each raised higher than the one preceding it. Though the benches could've held at least a hundred spectators, I counted only a few dozen men and women, all members of the king's court, hunched in their cloaks against the chill. I could see no children among them. On the fourth side of the scaffolding, there was a dais that held two thrones, one large and one smaller. Two palace guards flanked the thrones, and I realized that must be where the new king would sit to watch his brother's eternal banishment.

As my uncle guided us onto the bench beside my mother, I tugged on his sleeve. "I don't see the Gate. Where is it?"

"The king's Mages will open it when it is time. You cannot expect that they would leave it open with such impish girls running around, now can you?"

I stuck my tongue out at him. "We can't cross through the Gate. We're not Mages."

He meant to abate my worry, I was sure of it, but I honestly had no idea what to expect. My childish mind could not conceive of a gate that could appear and disappear at will, as this one must've done, for I simply could see no evidence of a gate anywhere.

"Look!" Livia whispered. "There's father!"

Sure enough, my father had emerged across the courtyard with two men familiar to my eyes though I could not name them. They each bore the gilded chains of members of the king's privy council, and behind them strode a youth close in age with my sister. Behind them were three very somber men indeed, Mages wearing sweeping robes, and last of all came a constituent of palace guards in black and silver livery emblazoned with the sigil of House Acheron: a raven and a branch of thorns. A murmur rippled through the small crowd at their appearance, and I understood this meant the dreadful thing we had all come to witness was soon to begin.

As the Mages ascended the scaffolding, Uncle Geordan whispered to me, "The young man with the fair hair is the king's cousin, Macon Eleutheris. He has been a ward of Gavreth's for some time, but now I imagine he will return to his family's estate in the south. The other two men with your father are members of Gavreth's privy council."

"Will they serve the new king now?"

"It would be terribly unwise of them not to."

"Where is the queen?" I craned my neck, hoping to catch a glimpse of her. I'd seen her twice before, on Solarium of this year and last, when my father had finally relented and allowed me to attend the palace festivities, however briefly. She was the most beautiful woman I had ever seen—tall and lithe, with a perfect oval face and hair as dark as a crow's wing—and she had the loveliest laugh, like the tinkling of bells. I did not imagine I would hear that laugh today.

"She will accompany the king," Uncle Geordan said.

I couldn't quite remember the faces of Keric, now king of Tiralaen, or his brother, now condemned. I'd caught only glimpses of them at Serus during the feast, before my father had sent Livia and me home in a carriage, determined that we should not see the court descended into what he described as the "less-than-savory activities that typically follow a night of drink and revels."

He'd smiled at me, the younger of Gavreth's sons, when our family approached the throne to wish the royal family health and well wishes for the season and to present our gift: a magnificent hand-painted globe my father had commissioned from an artist in Minn, awash in gold filigree. Likely, he thought me quaint in my best dress and pinned curls, a court lady in miniature. I know King Gavreth certainly had; his booming laugh and pleasant voice had made me blush.

I remembered very little about the king's eldest son and heir, other than that he was tall and had dark hair and a sharp expression. He'd spoken little, and smiled not at all.

Once my father and the king's cousin were standing on the dais, the small crowd on the benches rose to welcome the new king and his mother. Both Livia and I were far too short to see them, so my Uncle let us stand on the bench. Beside Livia, my mother pursed her lips in disapproval, but said nothing.

"Oh," Livia exclaimed quietly. "He is very handsome, isn't he?"

The young king of Tiralaen, resplendent in his fine black velvet trimmed in silver, was indeed a handsome boy with the rich brown hair of his late father and a pair of fine eyes that looked as though they often sparkled in merriment. At only fourteen, he was a strapping lad, and would likely grow finer still. Beside me, Livia gazed at him enraptured.

On his arm, his mother was weeping. If I had not known her to be made of flesh and blood, I might've thought her a statue of the finest porcelain. Her face was deathly pale, and she was shrouded in black veils that billowed around her face.

As the king and his mother approached the empty thrones, the court bowed as one, deep and low. Of course, I had no idea I was supposed to do this, and Livia had to shove my head down.

Once we were seated again, I pinched her leg.

King Keric saw his mother seated in the smaller throne before he took his own. Then he nodded at his Mages.

We did not rise for the prisoner.

Like all of those unfortunate souls condemned to death or banishment through the Gate, he wore no ornaments, only the simplest garments of pale gray: the color of the lost. He bore no chains but walked freely between two members of the king's personal guard and mounted the scaffolding alone. He was a tall, thin rail of a boy with skin so pale it was almost translucent and a shock of overgrown black curls that fell over his forehead. I did not care overmuch for the sharp angles of his face, but he had the most extraordinary pair of eyes I had ever seen: the palest shade of blue, so pale they were nearly clear, the color of summer rain, and of ice.

Those extraordinary eyes slowly swept the court and finally landed on his brother. His expression held nothing but cold contempt, and even from where I sat, I could see the muscles of his jaw tighten.

This was the boy who had murdered his father in cold blood with magic? Even though he was twice my age, he seemed so impossibly young. The anger that thrummed through his taut form was the helpless rage of a child, a throaty scream, hot, furious tears. I could not believe this boy, no matter how proficient a Mage, could take a life.

I knew from my Uncle Geordan that his trial had been swift and attended only by a handful of people at court. He must've had the chance to defend himself then, or at least someone should've done, but I wondered why he said nothing now as he stood in front of us all, facing his terrible fate.

As if he'd understood my distress, Uncle Geordan whispered into my ear: "He'll have been spelled into silence. It would be unwise for the king to allow one smack of perceived martyrdom."

I did not know what martyrdom was, but two of the three Mages were moving toward the young prince and Uncle Geordan's words fell away as they raised their hands and touched the tips of their outstretched fingers to one another's. I had seen magic worked before, of course; everyone in Tiralaen had, but the spells had been simple. Nothing like what I was now witnessing on the scaffolding. Very slowly, the Mages drew their hands apart and between them blossomed a glittering circle of silvery light, as if the sky had been cut open to reveal it. The farther they moved away from one another, the circle grew until it was the height and width of a person.

It became clear at last. "The Gate," I whispered.

"Elyan, son of Gavreth of House Acheron," the third Mage intoned. "You have been found guilty of the murder of your father, the king, by magic and sentenced to eternity through the Gate to the prison of Asperfell, never again to walk this world. May you find solace in the ancient gods, and may they grant you mercy."

Prince Elyan's piercing gaze had not left his brother as the Mage pronounced his fate. Now, he spared a brief glance for his mother. Tears were streaming down the queen's pale cheeks, dripping freely onto her hands, and she made no effort to wipe them away.

"Oh, Briony," Livia whispered, her voice quivering. "To lose her husband must hurt beyond all imagining. But to lose him to her son, and to lose that son as well..."

I glanced up at her and was shocked to see her eyes rimmed with red, the streaks of moisture on her cheeks already drying in the cold wind. Perhaps it was her words, or the distress in her distraught face, but I felt the hot sting of tears in my own eyes. Ducking my head to hide my face in the hood of my cloak, I dashed them away quickly.

Beside his despondent mother, King Keric's face was pinched and pale. He had, up until that point, held his brother's malice-filled eyes. As Prince Elyan's sentence and final benediction hung in the air between them, Keric cast his eyes down. Shock blossomed in Prince

Elyan's face, mingling with the anger, followed by something that almost looked like regret.

Face him, I willed the king, and my fists clenched at my sides. *You'll never see him again.*

But he did not. And Prince Elyan turned his back on him.

Then he strode across the scaffolding and disappeared through the ring of light.

A sharp gasp arose from the crowd. The silvery lines of the Gate seemed to pulse and, with a shudder, collapsed upon themselves until nothing was left but a pinprick of light that blinked once and disappeared, leaving the air exactly as it had been only moments before.

Prince Elyan was gone.

2

In the days that followed, the change my father had warned me about that fateful night began to take shape around me.

Our belongings were borne away from our townhouse by liveried attendants and placed in a suite of rooms in the palace. A furious fight ensued between Livia and myself over the largest bedroom, which she wanted because it was pink and I wanted because the bed was the highest and, therefore, the best for jumping off of onto an enormous pile of pillows. Age prevailed, and I was relegated to the blue bedroom, which I also liked though I did not admit this to anyone out of sheer stubbornness. The walls were a rich cobalt trimmed in gold, and the ceiling was a mural of the heavens: the sun, moon, and stars, gilded and gleaming.

There was a splendid parlor at the heart of our suite with an enormous fireplace surrounded by richly appointed couches, where our family gathered in the evenings to play cards, read, and, in the case of my mother and sister, embroider and darn. My uncle, who had been newly named a member of the King's council, was often with us, which pleased me greatly. I did not acclimate to court life quite as well as Livia, and, knowing this, he went to great lengths to make me laugh. Many evenings we sat around the fire trading stories and playing cards and chess. I was absolute rubbish at the latter;

while my uncle was calculated in his moves, I blundered ahead with single-minded determination only to realize with dismay that had I paid more attention to what was happening on the board apart than my own bold maneuvers, I could've prevented my figurines from being snatched up by my chuckling opponent.

We saw very little of my father, consumed as he was with the young king's initiation into the intricacies of rulership. I longed to know what it was they discussed in the privy chamber. No doubt it was vastly more entertaining than what awaited me as a daughter of a nobleman at court.

Livia and I began lessons under the tutelage of a master for our academics and a mistress for our etiquette. This I did not enjoy because, unlike old Master Robar, the new master, Omerus, was considerably younger and considerably faster. My efforts to escape him were embarrassingly unsuccessful.

Mistress Precia was worse.

She rapped my knuckles with a willow branch if I dared to show less than the most intense concentration in her lessons. I did not mind music, I was fairly good at drawing, and I thoroughly enjoyed dancing (although I think I did it with far more enthusiasm than Mistress Precia believed was warranted), but I loathed table manners, the art of using a fan, and anything having to do with needlework. Livia, of course, was perfect at nearly all of it, and Mistress Precia absolutely adored her. Me, she barely tolerated.

"Your father will expect to make excellent matches for you both in only a few years' time," she said one afternoon, as Livia and I sat side by side in front of the fire, sketching a vase full of flowers that Mistress Precia had set on a low table. Livia's version was true to life, of course, but I'd taken liberties with mine; I'd made my flowers slightly wilder than our model, adding thorns here, tendrils there. Mistress Precia was bound to find fault with it. "You are not likely to do so if you are thought to be an embarrassment to his household."

This, she directed at me. There was no chance of Livia being an embarrassment to anyone.

Mistress Precia made mention of our future prospects no less than three times a day, sometimes more when I was particularly unruly. I thought us both far too young to be anything to anyone's household for quite some time, but Livia, nearly fourteen, listened intently, nodding in agreement. She had begun to copy the women of court of late, wearing her hair pinned in elaborate curls studded with ornaments and carrying a fan around her wrist. The youngest of Queen Alenda's ladies-in-waiting was a mere two years older than Livia, and my sister made no secret of her desire to join their ranks until she made a match among one of the nobility.

"What if I don't *want* to get married?" I lowered my sketch pad and fixed Mistress Precia with the most stubborn look I could muster.

Mistress Precia pursed her lips disapprovingly. "My dear, even you will find marriage a great deal more suitable than the alternative."

"You mean become a governess like you?"

This was, evidently, the wrong thing to say, and my knuckles paid the painful price.

"She's wretched," I told Uncle Geordan that night, as we sat together in front of the fire. I would not have spoken thus had there been anyone else in the room; my sister and mother had retired earlier, and my father was shut away in his study, as he so often was. "And her lessons are boring."

"Are they really? No. Surely not?" Uncle Geordan raised an eyebrow at me. I was too little and inexperienced in the intricacies of conversation to know that he was playing a game at my expense.

"Yes!" I exploded passionately. "It's all curtseying and which fork to use and ever so many dance steps that I can never remember. I nearly fell asleep yesterday while we were practicing embroidery and she pinched my ear!"

"The nerve!" Uncle Geordan feigned outrage, and when I scowled at him, he burst out laughing. "Briony, every man and woman living in this palace has endured the wrath of a master to varying degrees of severity. A rite of passage, if you will, for noble stock."

"Maybe I'll just stop going." My mood was sour, and I sounded petulant even to my own ears.

My uncle faced me then, with a serious look on his handsome face. "I know this has not been easy for you, and you may think me cruel when I say this, but you must learn to think beyond yourself now. Your father is one of the most important men in Tiralaen. He has been tasked with guiding a young and inexperienced king through a difficult time. A great many eyes are on him now, and everything he says and does is scrutinized to an unbearable degree. Do not add to his burden by making an embarrassment of yourself at court."

The words stung, and I felt a hot flood of shame wash over me. He'd been as kind as he could've been in the telling of it, but I still felt as though I had committed a grievous sin. My father was beloved to me. I could not bear the thought of causing him pain. After all, hadn't I promised him on that terrible night that I would try my best to play the lady?

I applied myself more studiously after this, though I still resisted any talk of marriage. Once I overcame my indignation at having been thwarted in my attempts to escape Master Omerus, I realized his lessons were quite fascinating. He loved history and was all too happy to indulge my desire for celebrated battles, magic, and court intrigue. I still did not enjoy Mistress Precia's lessons, though I reminded myself as my hands moved, laboriously at first and more deftly as the time passed, over the strings of my lute that I was helping, even in my own small way, to lighten my father's worry.

And Uncle Geordan was right: he did have much to worry about.

The new king was not as experienced as my father had expected him to be in matters of state. Unfortunately, little thought had been given to what should happen if Elyan did not succeed his father, so although Keric was an intelligent young man, of good humor and charismatic, his knowledge was woefully inadequate. Prince Elyan had been a scholar, rarely seen in the yard practicing at swords and war games. Like all men of royal birth, he'd been a skilled swordsman, or so they said, but he took little pleasure in it, preferring to study politics and languages and history in addition to his magical aptitude.

Keric preferred hunting and gaming to policy, and though there was a modicum of intelligence behind his laughing eyes, he relied upon his charm and good humor to shape his rule.

He gifted lands and titles to his friends, young men he had come up at court with, and wanted to give them positions on his counsel. My father managed to subvert at least some of these impulses, convincing Keric that experience, like youthful vigor, had its advantages. Harder to convince him of was the need for frugality. Keric loved opulence almost as much as his father had, and feasting and tournaments were absurdly abundant in the first year of his kingship.

Keric was also deeply paranoid when the eyes of the court were not upon him. I did not blame him. His predecessor had been murdered by his own brother. Within days of his coronation, he doubled the size of the palace guard, insisting they be trained harder than any before them. He also commissioned a contingency of Battlemages for his own personal protection, who never left his side.

They terrified me. Their black armor and obsidian swords had been created by Alchemists and were imbued with the most terrible of spells. The little of their faces I could see behind their helms could've been carved from stone for all the life in them.

This did not stop me from being deeply fascinated in what they were, what they represented. We all were, if we were honest, those of us not able to do magic.

There were three children in the palace who studied magic, and I was envious whenever I saw them climbing the stairs of the South Wing to their lessons with Master Aeneas, a jovial Elemental Mage with a long silver beard and a hearty laugh that he used liberally. Two of them were the children of a nobleman on King Keric's privy council: a brother and sister near Livia's age. The other was the son of the Head Cook, who was a Hearth Mage herself. Older than the other two, he had already been through his Trial and, unsurprisingly, shown himself to be adept in Hearth magic like his mother. It was assumed he would take over from her when the time was right. I wondered if this pleased him or if he'd been hoping for a life different than the one he was born to.

Of course, I'd never actually seen a Trial as they were private affairs attended only by the adolescent Mage and the Masters he or she studied under, but from what I understood, it was a ceremony of the utmost sacredness involving relics of some kind, enchanted with powerful spells to reveal the true nature of the Mage in question.

Every Mage could, of course, with proper training, bend magic to their will, though some were decidedly better at it than others. But more than that, within each of them was a singular gift, an affinity for a particular branch of magic that they were destined to master.

The most common were the wielders of the Arts of the World, those talents that directly influenced that which surrounded us all: Animalis, Naturalist, Hearth, and Healer. Under their hands crops flourished, animals thrived, and, for those who could afford it, the banalities of everyday existence were lessened.

The Arts of Might were rarer, and concerned physical manipulation of the elements and brute force magic. Keric's Mageguard was comprised mostly of this sort, and he'd had to scour the very corners of Tiralaen to find so many.

Though the spells they employed were fierce, Mages who boasted this aptitude were not always so; in truth, I suspected Keric only selected men and woman of brawn to fulfill his own notions about what strength must be. During a feast at court, a diplomatic envoy from the eastern lands brought a contingency of Battlemages with

him, and they were absolutely nothing like the black-armored figures
hovering on either side of Keric's throne.

Rarer still, and little valued because their enigmatic nature was so
little understood, were the Arts of Truth. There were quite a few aptitudes that fell under this classification, but only two were mentioned
outright in Master Aeneas's books—Dreamwalkers and Alchemists,
though many argued that Alchemists, because of their ability to forge
the fiercest weapons Tiralaen had ever known, were better classified
as Mages of Might. The Arts of Truth were considered that of scholars:
magic of the mind, meant to understand and shape in a far more subtle
way than the conjuring of flame or wind.

And then there were the Mages of the Arcane. These were rarest
of all, and rightly feared for their awesome power over the darkest and
most dangerous sorts of magic. Their ranks included Prince Elyan's
aptitude, Siphon, as well as Necromancers and Blood Mages. If there
were others, I knew them not.

Mages of the Arcane were, in fact, so rare as to be infamous when
they did appear, and often, in the cases of Necromancers and Blood
Mages, engendered such fear that they of necessity lived apart from
the society of men. Had Prince Elyan not killed his father and instead
succeeded him on the throne, he would likely have been an unpopular
king simply by the virtue of his aptitude, his reign perpetually threatened by those who'd have preferred one of his non-magic kinsmen.

I would've given anything to escape Mistress Precia and join
Master Aeneas's students in their dusty tower full of old tomes and
candles, but, to my great disappointment, I was not a Mage. At least,
not yet. Magic was in the blood, and it followed families, though not
always directly. Sometimes two Mages produced perfectly ordinary
children, and a family who had an Animalis several generations back
had children full to bursting with rare magic. My mother's family
tree was dotted with Mages here and there, though no one of note,
and no one within the last four generations. Magic usually appeared

in children by the time they were five or six years of age, so I doubted my mother's bloodline would reveal a Mage within me, ancient at nearly nine years old.

I liked Master Aeneas very much and used any excuse I could think of to visit his rooms at the top of the tower and pepper him with questions. He was possessed of so many delightful things; I could've spent hours poring over everything he kept on his shelves and staring at the images depicted in stained glass in his windows. They told the story of King Soteris, Keric's twice great-grandfather, who was known by all accounts as a bringer of peace and enlightenment to Tiralaen after he took the throne from his tyrannous father in a Mage's duel. King Soteris was an Alchemist; his father, Harpax, a fire-wielder. They clashed in glorious color in glass panes more than three times my height: father throwing Magefire, son turning it to rivers of gold. According to the songs, the son began at his father's feet, encasing them in gold that slithered slowly up the tyrant's body and hardened, all the while begging his father to cease his attack and abdicate the throne. The king refused him, and, with tears in his eyes, for there were always tears in his eyes in the songs, he swathed his father in gold, where he remained to that day in the palace vaults.

"King Soteris made many of the instruments you see here for my predecessors," Master Aeneas told me, fondly resting a hand on the top of a beautiful golden globe of our world, the continents and countries and rivers and mountains drawn in silver.

The old Master was kind to me despite how I must've annoyed him.

Perhaps it was because he pitied me. His students had a glorious sort of freedom that a girl of my birth would never have without magic. If I did not marry, as Mistress Precia insisted I must, my options were sadly limited, while Mages of the fairer sex had prospects all their own and not only those acquiesced by kindly fathers or doting husbands.

Whatever his reasons, he did not mind my boundless curiosity, and even let me look through some of his books on magical history.

Being the wild, bloodthirsty child I was, I only read the bits about torture and murder and political coups that ended in more torture and murder.

And, of course, I read all about the Gate and the construction of the fortress of Asperfell.

Ever since I'd witnessed Prince Elyan's banishment, finding out more about the ring of light and the land beyond it had become somewhat of an obsession, and how could it fail to be? It was something out of a fairytale that could not possibly be true, and yet it was: a prison no one had seen, that held Mages of extraordinary power and extraordinary darkness, in a land no one had ever returned from.

I learned it had been two great Mages, Masters Viscario and Rhowyn, who had discovered the weakness in the barrier between this world and the one beyond, created the Gate, and ordered the construction of Asperfell once they were well and truly certain that no one could ever return. I was surprised to find that both men had come from humble origins, hailing from a tiny village once called Beheren when it was part of a very small kingdom beyond our southern border. When one of Tiralaen's kings decided to conquer and absorb the kingdom, the town was given the name Kithia after his beloved daughter.

Their aptitudes were exceedingly rare: one a Blood Mage, the other an Alchemist. But what was rarer still was the fact that they were brothers. For two Mages of such powerful and fearsome aptitudes to be born to the same parents made certain their infamy even before they'd even conceived of the Gate.

Though accounts of their childhood were scarce, what did remain painted them as quite remarkable, skilled and determined and together in all things. When the king of Tiralaen had need of a solution for a dark Mage who had committed atrocities—and, if one was being honest, held power to seize his place upon the throne—it was to Viscario and Rhowyn he turned, and the two Mages, young and flush with power and possibility, took up the challenge with gusto.

When I asked if I might see an image of the prison of Asperfell, Master Aeneas shook his head sadly and told me that, at the bidding of its creators, all information pertaining to Asperfell's designs or complicated spellwork had been burned before the two Mages crossed the Gate themselves. As for what became of them afterward, there was no way to know. Not even they could return, much less any messenger to share news of their fate.

"Did they build the fortress themselves, Master Viscario and Master Rhowyn?" I asked.

"Goodness, no," he chuckled. "They designed it, but the builders were mostly indentured servants. They agreed to go in exchange for their freedom once Asperfell was complete."

I frowned. "But no one can come back through the Gate. You told me that."

"Indeed, they did not," he answered. "They were set free on the other side, to make their way as they would."

How extraordinary those Mages must've been! To leave a life of the familiar, even life as a servant, for one of toil and suffering with no chance of return… it took courage such that I could not imagine. The price of their freedom had been high indeed.

I leaned forward. "Do you suppose their descendants might be there still?"

"Perhaps. I suppose we'll never know. A great pity, that."

"If I was a Mage, I don't think I should like to go through the Gate, no matter how much I'd like to see Asperfell."

"It is fortunate, then, that you are neither Mage nor criminal."

Master Aeneas told me that, as the centuries passed, the number of Mages sent through the Gate grew fewer and fewer. He believed this to be the natural progression of an increasingly civilized society, particularly in the last hundred years. King Gavreth and his forebears had been dedicated to reform and rehabilitation and used the Gate only for the most abhorrent of Mages. With my childish innocence, I argued that perhaps Mages simply feared to misbehave, given the risk of never seeing those they loved again, for surely even the most wicked of men and women loved something.

To me, this was the most horrifying consequence of banishment through the Gate; not the prison itself or its inhabitants, but the certainty that whatever your life had been before, it was gone forever. I was, after all, a child beloved and kept safely in the bosom of my family. I could not fathom a life without them.

Of the banished prince, very little was spoken except to christen him the Raven King of Asperfell, for if he lived still, he presided now over a kingdom of criminals. I imagined him sometimes, a tall, sorrowful figure high in a tower, staring out over a desolate land and longing for home.

3

One afternoon Livia and I returned to our suite from our lessons with Master Omerus to find my father and uncle deep in conversation with another man in front of the fire. He turned at the sound of our intrusion, and I saw a face that was both deeply familiar and utterly foreign to me. The young man's gray eyes met mine, and a memory stirred of a conversation I was not meant to hear on the night a prince murdered his father.

"How were your lessons, girls?" Uncle Geordan asked pleasantly, as my father moved to an ornately carved table to pour himself several fingers of brandy. The other man regarded us calmly and said nothing.

"Most instructive, uncle," Livia answered dutifully.

"And you, Briony?" He smiled at me, a conspiratorial twinkle in his eye. "Were your lessons also instructive?"

I met his gaze frankly. "Oh, yes. We learned all about Eddwyn the Conqueror and how he beheaded his enemies, flayed their skin off their faces, and displayed them in a trophy room in velvet cases."

A gale of laughter burst from my uncle as my father choked on his brandy, and I thought I saw the man with the gray eyes smile ever so slightly.

"That's enough of your cheek!" my uncle gasped merrily. "Go and see your mother now. And pray do *not* tell her anything about Eddwyn the Conqueror and his cases of flayed heads."

"Briony!" Livia hissed, as she gripped my hand and pulled me down the corridor to our mother's sitting room. "The things you say sometimes are so horrible!"

I could still hear Uncle Geordan chuckling, so I wasn't entirely sure the things I said were *that* horrible.

My mother would likely side with Livia, and so I dutifully kissed her cheek and said nothing of severed heads, flayed or otherwise. She was sitting on a lush velvet settee, flanked by her two lady's maids, Alys and Issa, working at a loom with skeins of silk. I could just make out the pattern emerging within the strands: cranes in flight.

Livia, skilled in needlework like our mother, sat at her feet, the skirts of her silk day dress spread out, and began to gossip with Alys and Issa. They spoke of much and of nothing, and I soon became bored of the conversation and longed to escape. Specifically, I longed to hear what my father and uncle were discussing with the gray-eyed man.

And so, I took advantage of their distraction and inched toward the open door. When I was sure they had forgotten all about me, I slipped through the crack and into the corridor.

Making my footfalls as silent as I could, I crept back to the great room where the men still sat beside the fire, deep in conversation. Back against the wall, I slid down until I was hunched into a ball, my arms wrapped around my knees, as though making myself as small as I could would render me invisible. I rested my cheek against my arms and listened.

"The queen has advised him against it." My uncle's voice. "I believe that is all that is holding him back."

"Where did you get this information?" My father, this time.

There was a pause. And then, "From Macon."

"You heard this from him directly?" This time it was the man with the gray eyes who spoke.

"He has a loose tongue when he drinks."

"And you believe him?"

I heard rather than saw the shrug in my uncle's voice. "He's the king's cousin. No doubt he is privy to information we are not."

"That guarantees *nothing*."

"Macon cares for little beyond the latest court gossip," my uncle snapped. "That he should take a peculiar interest in this guarantees it is no passing fancy."

My father sighed heavily. "The people will no doubt support it, at first. That is the damnable thing."

"And by the time the truth of it comes out, it will be too late," the man with the gray eyes agreed.

I heard the sound of a glass against wood, and my father's muffled curse. "I suppose he will go after the wielders of the Arcane first."

"He'll record everyone at first, just to make it seem fair. But yes—that is his intent. His brother was a Mage of the Arcane, after all," the gray-eyed man said. "But we may yet have time to sway him. What is it, Magnus?"

There was a long silence in the room. I held my breath.

"The queen is unwell."

My father's words fell like stones.

"How unwell?" my uncle asked, and his voice sounded strained.

My father's silence told me all I needed to know. The queen was dying.

"By the Gods. If she dies—"

"I'm afraid it's not a case of 'if' but 'when,'" my father corrected him. "And when it does happen, Keric will likely act on the impulses Alenda is keeping at bay."

"Then we must do our best to quash these impulses, so far as we are able," Uncle Geordan declared. "We might still wield a measure of influence. Keric is young and impressionable, to a degree."

"I think you overestimate our influence. And underestimate the citizens of Tiralaen," the man with the gray eyes said. "Since King Gavreth's death, they are understandably wary of magic. Keric's paranoia will only stoke their fear, and they will follow him blindly as a result of it."

"I fear a registry would be only the beginning," my father agreed. "A way to weed out Mages he fears, even if they have never given cause for suspicion. Even if they have just come into their powers."

"Their fellow citizens will turn on them," Uncle Geordan added. "They will do the work for him. Soon they'll report each other over the slightest perception."

"Reporting one another is the least of what an ignorant population will do," the man with the gray eyes said.

"You believe there will be violence." My uncle's words were not a question.

"Of course there will be violence," my father said. "It is only a matter of time."

Their voices fell silent, and I heard the unmistakable sound of liquid being poured, the tinkling of a crystal stopper being put back in its decanter, a log being thrust into the fire, and the hiss of young unseasoned wood. So comforting and familiar were the sounds that I did not notice the heavy footfalls approaching. Then I looked up and saw the man with the gray eyes standing over me.

He did not look angry. In fact, his expression was almost kind. He lowered himself onto his haunches and held out his hand to me. "My name is Cyprias."

"Briony," I answered, taking his proffered hand and shaking it with all the dignity my eight-year-old self could muster. "Do you work for my father?"

"Of a sort. He and I have been friends for a long time."

"Are you going to tell him I was listening?"

Cyprias smiled. "No. In fact, I am glad you were."

"You are?"

"I don't believe any of us can afford to be ignorant during these times. Knowledge is the most powerful weapon any of us can possess, and even the smallest of us can wield it. Your longing to be informed does you credit. It may even save your life someday."

I wrinkled my nose. "Knowledge is a weapon?"

Cyprias laughed. "Yes! Yes. And it is so very precious. Always seek it, and never waste it. Knowledge makes warriors of us all."

"But I'm a girl," I pointed out. "Girls aren't supposed to be warriors."

"Do you agree with that?"

"No."

'Neither do I." Cyprias smiled. "I suspect that if you put your mind to it, there is no end to what you can do."

I was in awe of these words, though I was far too young—and far too inexperienced—to understand their gravity. All I knew was that they made me feel important, though I was only a girl huddled in a corridor. The idea of wielding anything of power, even something as intangible as knowledge, gave me a thrill.

"I want you to promise me something, Briony," Cyprias said, and I nodded mutely. "Promise me that you will not reveal to another soul what you have heard us speak of here today. For your father's sake." The corner of his mouth quirked up in a sardonic smile. "And mine."

"I promise," I said solemnly.

"Very good." Cyprias's hand was heavy on my shoulder. "Be safe, young Briony. Now run along back to your mother."

"I detest needlework," I informed him.

"So do I," he told me quite seriously.

In the end, my father was right: Alenda's strength continued to wane.

The queen hailed from the lands to the south, and she was as gentle a person as I had ever met. Everything about her was soft, from her dark limpid eyes to her voice, rich and supple as the finest doeskin. But she was not strong; not in the way that she needed to be. Gradually, that fine skin grew paper-thin, those eyes sunken. She stopped laughing, and then stopped smiling.

Her illness confounded the healers who came from all over Tiralaen and beyond. Elixirs and tisanes and possets were brewed by the palace Mages and coaxed into her mouth by her worried ladies, but they did nothing at all to impede her decline.

"But she is so young," Livia said one night, as we sat with my mother on her bed, watching Alys unbraid my mother's heavy coronet. "Surely she will get better!"

"I do not believe the queen's illness is one that can be cured," my mother said sadly, cupping Livia's stricken face in her hands. "She loved her husband. And her son. I think, perhaps, she simply does not wish to live without them."

"What a horrible waste," Livia whispered.

I was not as sentimental as Livia. I thought it was a terribly selfish thing to allow oneself to die simply out of grief. Then again, I knew things that Livia—and perhaps even my mother—did not.

For a time, Keric continued to seek his mother's council at her bedside, and for a time, it seemed as though the thing that my father, uncle, and Cyprias had feared would not come to pass.

The celebration of Serus drew nearer, and despite the shorter days and flurries of dry, powdery snow that settled on the grounds of the Citadel, there was an air of cheer amongst the court. I preferred the rites of Solarium, celebrated as they were in the summer to honor the longest day and the coming of the light. But Serus, for all its solemnity, had its merits. Particularly the food, though the presents were not entirely unwelcome either.

Serus was the longest night, the welcoming of the darkness that shrouded the bitterest months when the soil grew harsh and unyielding and death was everywhere. As the day afforded little natural light, candles and tiny flames encased in glass littered the Citadel, their tiny flickering lights dancing on the gleaming white walls and floors, and fragrant evergreen boughs and bunches, hardy winter rosemary, and hellebore blossoms of white and deepest aubergine decorated doorways and beams and windows.

That year, our family attended the Serus celebrations with the rest of the court, and I watched as my father and uncle laughed and smiled with the young king. Keric had celebrated his fifteenth birthday only a few months before, but he seemed years older, and far more subdued than I remembered. He was still a handsome youth, and charming, but he smiled far less than he used to. And when he did smile, it did not quite reach his eyes. He received our gift of fine books trimmed in gold, and he smiled at Livia and me graciously, though his eyes lingered on my sister far longer than on me.

We sat at tables groaning with roasted meats, vegetables swimming in exotic sauces, fruits that burst with sweetness on the tongue, breads and cakes, and vats of wine and ale, though I took none of those. I was still far too young.

The fashions of court were on full and glorious display, and I stared, entranced, at the jewels encircling slender white throats, rich velvet brocades, impossibly cinched waistlines, and sweeping trains of silk. My own little gown was a lovely pale blue trimmed in gold, and I had a new necklace from my Uncle Geordan, filigree and clear stones. I felt quite grown up, though I knew I still looked like a child while Livia, resplendent in claret, was already garnering gazes that no doubt made my father very nervous indeed. Livia was only fourteen, but I was certain that when she came of age, she would not want for suitors.

It was splendid, all of it, and yet my eyes were increasingly drawn to the place beside King Keric, empty out of respect for the absent queen, alone and wasting in her bed. How much we all had, and yet she had lost everything that meant the most to her in all of the world.

In the end, it proved too great a loss. Less than a week after Serus, Queen Alenda died.

Nobody thought much of the Registry at first.

In fact, just as my father had suspected, most citizens of Tiralaen agreed that an official record of those who practiced magic would benefit everyone. After all, what would a loyal, upstanding subject of the crown possibly have to hide?

A year after King Gavreth's death, Mages in every household in Tiralaen were identified, and their names, ages, and aptitudes recorded. Parents were ordered to report any sign of magical talent in their children within two days or face heavy fines, or even imprisonment in the Tower. A clutch of guards was assembled solely for the purpose of patrolling the streets of Iluviel to ensure the king's edicts were followed. They knocked on doors and spoke to citizens and paid for secrets, ferreting out any whiff of magic that tried to remain hidden.

Trials to determine aptitude were no longer private affairs but were conducted at the palace in the presence of the king's Mages so that their results could be recorded properly. Mages in the Arts of the World and the Arts of Truth were largely ignored. It was those who showed proclivity for the Arcane who merited special notation on Keric's list. The young king insisted the list be public so the people might know who walked amongst them. It soon took its toll.

Arcane Mages had always been feared, though there was often little reason for it. My father told me it was because their gift was little understood and people were afraid of what they couldn't reason out. After Prince Elyan murdered his father, the people abandoned what little pretense of acceptance they'd had for wielders of the Arcane and very publicly turn against them; their gifts were openly scrutinized and judged for how they might be used against their fellow citizens rather than how they could help them.

Necromancers—needed to calm the restless dead in places of great bloodshed—found themselves being forced to prove time and again they were not amassing those same dead into an army to overthrow the king, and yet never did their neighbors believe it, nor the whispers stop. Likewise, Siphons—called upon to draw dark magic from cursed places—regularly awoke in the morning to find the doors and windows of their homes had been chained against them from the outside, out of fear they might become physically transformed in the night by the magic they drew into themselves, emerging under the full moon as ravening beasts that devoured the flesh of livestock, if not of women and children.

Who, then, could wonder that parents of young Mages of such aptitudes often panicked and tried to hide their children's gifts?

Or worse—among those families who could afford it, many parents attempted to have the children bound when the results of their Trials were not favorable. Binding, as I understood it, was extremely difficult and disastrous if gotten wrong. Several young Mages died as a result, though the kingdom did not mourn them.

Those who did not embrace the new fashion of fear—or did not do so with required zeal—also found themselves ostracized by former friends and angry neighbors. This was especially true of those immigrant families from the rich, fertile lands in the south and the blistering deserts of the east. In these places, magic was known to be celebrated and Mages held in honor. Further proof, as if any were needed, that Tiralaen was surrounded by dangerous and uncivilized kingdoms. Fearful murmurs and pointed fingers followed them in the streets, and they soon found themselves barred from shops and homes where they had previously been received.

It spread like a disease, stealing into every crevice of uncertainty and every corner of doubt, where it festered even in those with the most stalwart of constitutions, even as it unfurled its black, decaying tendrils throughout the Shining City.

Then one morning, a family from Cyr with a son who was a Battlemage woke to find a symbol painted in red upon their door: the letter M drawn twice, interlocking. No amount of scrubbing removed it entirely, and the next day, it was back again, darker this time.

The first time I saw it, I thought it was mountains and wondered why anyone would associate mountains with fear of magic. It was Master Aeneas who told me what it really was: an ancient symbol for Magefire, one of the first spells.

The symbol began appearing on other doors wherein dwelled wielders of the Arts of Might and the Arts of Truth, a warning to all that they could not be trusted, that they were to be feared and reviled as much as those whose aptitudes were the Arcane. Then it began to appear on the doorways of Animalises, of Hearth Mages, of Naturalists—Mages never before thought to be a threat to anyone. It came to be synonymous with magic, which in turn had become synonymous with fear, and within months it was everywhere.

As the streets of Iluviel began to change, the air in our suite of rooms seemed to grow thick and stale, and we moved slower and with more sober purpose. My father talked frequently in private with Lord Falstone, Cyprias, and Uncle Geordan, and I found myself frustrated by the lack of opportunity to hone my weapons, as Cyprias would've said. I sometimes caught my mother and father watching me during moments of silence, studying me with worried expressions, though what they were looking for I did not know.

I toiled away at my studies, and the world outside the Citadel grew darker and more dangerous.

The autumn arrived, crisp and golden, and a festival with it to give thanks for a bountiful harvest. Livia and I begged our parents to allow us to attend. My father was quite reluctant, and, in the end, it was Uncle Geordan who convinced him that it would lighten the family's spirits considerably to leave the walls of the palace for an afternoon. My father's face was grim as we settled into our carriage, blankets of thick wool over our laps, our hands bundled into rabbit fur muffs, and his countenance did not change as we left the gates of the Citadel, a company of our household guard at our front and rear.

We passed a lovely afternoon. There were jugglers and fire-breathers and dancers who wore brightly colored costumes and feathered masks. They contorted themselves into all manner of shapes and swung above our heads on lengths of silk, and I drank it all in, my cheeks flushed pink with excitement and the brisk autumn chill.

My father bought us meat pies and tiny spice cakes drizzled with icing and cups of hot cider, and we ate and drank as we wandered among the booths where merchants sold their wares. Livia and I had each been given coin to spend at our leisure. Livia bought a beautiful length of velvet in a deep, rich brown that she planned to ask Alys to add to the sleeves of her gold gown. I wanted to purchase a dagger with a jeweled hilt that was perfectly suited for my small hands, but my father refused, no doubt fearing my mother's retribution, and so I settled for a book, thinking perhaps Cyprias would be proud of my choice.

It seemed as though my father might finally have found some modicum of peace; his face smoothed from worry to ease as we rode toward the Citadel and he laughed heartily at my impression of the jesters who wore bells on their ankles and distorted their faces into shocking caricatures. That was, until we reached Lower Gilding. Ahead, we heard voices raised in shouting, the murmuring of a crowd. My father reached up and banged his fist twice upon the roof of the carriage, and we pulled abruptly to a stop.

"Wait here," my father instructed, and swiftly exited the carriage.

Through the window, Livia and I watched him approach the door-step of a modest stone dwelling two stories high where a group of people had gathered, including four guards in black and silver livery and a Mage wearing black robes lined with silver silk and trimmed in silver brocade.

"Make way! Make way!" my father shouted, as he pushed through onlookers gathered on the street.

The Mage, recognizing him, lifted his hand and the guards came to an abrupt halt. Between them, they held the arms of a struggling boy of perhaps thirteen with hair the color of doeskin. His mother and father were pleading with the Mage; their hands gripped the rich velvet of his sleeves desperately. At my father's approach, they fell silent, their pleading eyes turned on him.

"Magnus." The Mage gave a slight bow. He was a man of fifty I had seen about the palace, short and unassuming, with a hooked nose.

"What misconduct is this?" my father asked, and although his voice was level and calm, I could not mistake the tension in his broad shoulders. "What is this boy's crime?"

On the door of the house behind the terrified parents, I saw the ancient symbol for Magefire painted in crude strokes.

"Failure to register," the Mage replied crisply. In his hand, he held a large book bound in black leather with heavy silver clasps.

"It's a mistake," said the boy's father. "He isn't a Mage, sir. If he were, we'd have registered him straightaway."

"Silence," the Mage cut in swiftly. "First you flout the king's laws, and then you dare to lie in front of a member of his privy council!"

My father raised a gloved hand. "Enough." He looked down at the young boy, terrified, clutching his mother's hand. "Does he speak true, boy? Are you a Mage?"

"No," he whispered, but he did not meet my father's eyes. "No, sir."

"Do you know why the king's men would have cause to think you so?"

At this the boy lifted his wide, fearful eyes and shook his head, his brown curls flying about his ashen face.

My father turned to the king's Mage. "And you, Penrick. Where came by you this information?"

Penrick shifted defensively, his cruel eyes sharpening. "A reliable source, and one who does not wish to be named."

"Who has accused him?" shouted the boy's father, face twisted in fear and fury. He looked around at the crowd, grown larger since our carriage had stopped. The faces that stared back at him were sympathetic; they were undoubtedly friends, neighbors. But they were also subjects of the crown, and afraid. The father's eyes landed on a man lingering in the doorway of a house across the street; his face twisted and changed into something I did not recognize, for at my tender age I had seen little of true hatred.

"Halfreth, you bastard!" The father surged forward.

The palace guards were quick to grasp his arms and haul him back, even as he struggled mightily and shouted obscenities at the man in the doorway, who shrank back into the shadows, defiance on his sallow face. The boy's mother had begun to cry, clasping her son to her.

"Enough of this!" Penrick screeched at the boy's father. "Control yourself, sir, or it will be to the Tower with you!"

The boy's father stopped struggling, but his face still twisted with fury. "How much did they pay you, Halfreth?" he snarled. "What was the price his life? Of ours?"

The man did not reply, but stared back at his neighbor, perhaps once his friend, with a dour expression in his yellowed eyes.

Penrick made a sound of disgust. "There is only one way to settle this," he snarled. "Give me your arm, boy."

Inside the carriage, I gripped Livia's hand tightly. "What are they going to do to him?" I whispered.

The boy was pried away from his sobbing mother and brought before Penrick, his sleeve pushed up roughly to expose the skin of his arm. The boy's father moved to take his distraught wife in his embrace, and they watched helplessly as Penrick laid his hand upon the boy. For a long moment, I thought nothing at all would happen and it would be just as the boy's father said: he was no Mage at all, the accusation against him unfounded.

And then the boy's skin began to glow. Under Penrick's hand, a silvery light bloomed and the boy began to struggle, gasping, his mouth opening and closing like a fish washed ashore.

"Stop!" the boy wailed, as he tried in vain to pull free. "It hurts!"

With a snarl, Penrick threw the boy to the ground. His arm was fairly glowing now, tendrils of light swirling and eddying beneath the surface of his skin, tears of pain and terror streaming down his cheeks. It would be many years before I understood exactly what it was I had just witnessed, but I knew then that the boy and his parents had lied. He was a Mage after all, and his parents traitors to the crown.

Beside me, Livia was shaking her head. "We shouldn't watch," she said. "We shouldn't watch this."

I ignored her and pressed my face closer to the glass.

"You lied." Penrick rounded on the boy's parents. "What sort of Mage is this child? What is his aptitude?"

A look passed between father and mother, a look of fear, of desperation, of resignation, and the father's voice was barely more than a whisper as he answered: "A Blood Mage."

His wife buried her face in her hands and wept.

"Penrick," my father said in a low voice.

If the king's Mage heard my father, he gave no indication. Rather, he was staring at the boy with what could only be described as a fierce hunger, a glint of triumph in his eyes. He reached down and hauled the terrified boy to his feet. "He comes with us to the Citadel."

"And his parents?" one of the guards asked.

"Penrick," my father tried again.

"Take them to the Tower," was the Mage's reply. He did not look at the guards or the boy's parents as he said this, but was still staring at his young captive intently. "And search the house. Who knows what they might be hiding?"

As one of the guards moved to take the boy's mother, the boy himself thrust off his captor, sending Penrick tumbling backwards in surprise. He threw his hands forward with a raw, guttural scream, and flame erupted from them, spiraling viciously and without mercy toward the guard. He was untrained, but his rage and desperation made him powerful indeed. Fire engulfed the guard entirely and he staggered back, piercing screams of pain rending the air.

The boy's mother dropped to the ground and screamed, "Stop! Janus, stop!"

The boy's father rushed forward, gripping his wife's shoulders tightly and hauling her back against him as the boy, Janus, turned his fire on the other guard.

Penrick had managed to scramble back to his feet, and with a thrust of his hand, the fire that had engulfed the two guards sputtered to nothing in the span of a single heartbeat.

"That was exceedingly foolish," Penrick hissed at the young Mage. His hand cut through the air, and the boy was blown back—his body, seemingly so full of power only moments ago, falling to the ground like a rag doll. "Take him."

The guards, their fine livery thoroughly singed but otherwise apparently unharmed despite the spectacle, hefted the boy's unconscious form between them and dragged him away and out of my sight.

Tears coursed down his mother's face, her mouth open in a silent cry of anguish as her son disappeared into Penrick's carriage, but his father was like a stone. His gray face had gone slack, his eyes staring off into the distance as though his grief and fear had taken him somewhere else entirely. I'd seen little of misery in my short life, save the banishment of Prince Elyan when Queen Alenda had wept beautiful tears behind a veil. Grief of another sort radiated from the boy's parents in waves, visceral and raw.

My sister had turned her head into the velvet curtains, but I refused to do so. I bore witness as the soldiers hauled the mother and father to their feet. The mother's sobs had ceased, though silent tears still flowed freely down the crags of her worn face; they both looked as though they'd aged years in only moments. They did not protest as a guard approached with shackles and bound their hands, and they followed numbly as they were led away.

The carriage that bore their son lurched to life and I watched it disappear, carrying him away toward the Citadel to begin his new life.

The moment we returned to our suite of rooms, my mother gathered us both into her arms and held us until we squirmed and complained. No doubt she'd been well informed as to what we had encountered on our way back from the festival. When she drew away, she held us both at arm's length, staring at us as though she were memorizing our faces. Her smile was meant to be reassuring, and perhaps to Livia it was, but when she looked at me, I thought I saw sadness in her eyes.

She bid Alys fetch a Mage to heat the water in the copper basin in our washroom, and we were stripped of our clothes and scrubbed until our skin was pink and raw and smelled of lavender. Nightgowns were produced, we were bundled into them, and then we were tucked into bed, our candles blown out.

I lay awake for some time, staring at the golden stars on my ceiling and waiting to hear my father's voice outside my door.

I waited a long time.

Sleep had very nearly claimed me when I heard the distant rumble of male voices, and I sat up in bed wide awake and ready. My feet made no sound as I padded down the corridor, and I kept my body flush against the wall so that my shadow would not be seen. Then I peered around the corner into the great room and saw a figure crouched in front of the fire, pushing the glowing coals about until the wood above caught. He stood, his hands clasped behind his back, and I recognized him at once.

"Cyprias!" I whispered.

There was genuine surprise in his eyes when he turned, squinted in the darkness, and saw me. I took a certain satisfaction in it, that I had managed to catch my father's spy off guard. "Briony," he said, relaxing visibly. "Good evening."

"Good evening. Are you here to see my father?"

"I am. But he has been called away, and so here I wait."

I moved into the room. "Called where?"

"To the king, I expect. Would you care to sit?"

I adored the way he spoke to me, as though I were not a girl of nine up far past her bedtime but a companion, a friend. He gestured to the settee and I sat obediently, tucking my cold bare feet into the folds of my nightgown. He sat opposite me, a goblet of wine in one hand.

"Cyprias," I ventured, "did my father tell you what happened today? About the boy with glowing skin?"

"He did, indeed."

"Is that why he's been called to the king so late?"

"I suspect so."

"It was awful," I whispered, and despite the warmth of the fire, I shuddered. "What will become of him now?"

Cyprias drank long and deep from his cup of wine. "I am not entirely sure," he said at last. "His aptitude is particularly rare, and extremely dangerous. Keric will want him under thumb, and so here he will remain, likely to be trained by Keric's own Mages until he can be of some use to the crown."

"And if he is not?"

His answer hung between us in the silence.

"Why did they not register him, like the law says?"

"I imagine they thought they were protecting him. In truth, his fate was sealed the moment his Trial concluded."

I frowned. "What exactly is a Blood Mage?"

"Blood magic is the rarest sort of magic there is," Cyprias answered. "And so, naturally, we know very little about it. There have only been a handful of Blood Mages in all of Tiralaen's long history."

"One of the Mages who built Asperfell was a Blood Mage," I said, suddenly remembering what I had read in one of Master Aeneas's books.

"That's right." Cyprias smiled faintly at me. "Collecting knowledge, I see. Blood Mages use their power to control those with magic in their veins, and can even drain magic blood for use in spells and potions. Or so I am told."

"How awful."

"Indeed," Cyprias nodded. "I'm sure you can see why the boy would be of such value to Keric. A very skilled Blood Mage could weave a spell to eviscerate enemies, even topple armies, if he or she is strong enough. Better to make an ally of him than to have him as an enemy."

"And what if he does not wish to become an ally?"

Cyprias said gently, "He will not be given much choice."

I imagined the boy, alone and afraid somewhere in the vast Citadel, missing his parents, uncertain of his fate, all because he was born with magic in his blood, magic he did not ask for and perhaps did not want.

Cyprias drained his wineglass and stood. "The hour is late, Briony, and your father may not be back for some time. Perhaps it is time we both sought sleep."

I dutifully rose. Cyprias gave me a bow, and halfway through my own answering curtsey, I changed my mind and bowed in return, which earned me an amused smile. Then I made my way back to the corridor from whence I'd come.

At the corner, I hesitated and turned back. Cyprias had resumed his vigil by the fire, his back to me, and I thought his shoulders seemed even more hunched than they had before. "I used to want to be a Mage," I told him quietly. "Not anymore."

4

The spring I turned ten, I fell ill.

I grew tired and listless, and shuffled about like a tiny lost spirit until I finally collapsed during my lessons. I expected to be tucked into bed and poked and prodded by the palace Healer until I was forced to swallow some vile concoction, but the moment my mother and father saw me, a bundle in my uncle's arms and delirious with fever, they called for Master Aeneas instead.

I do not remember being stripped of my gown or put into bed, but I remember wailing that my room was far too hot and begging for Alys to bring me water, a cold cloth, anything to relieve the fire that burned under my skin and made me sweat and shake and cry from the pain.

Master Aeneas's hands were kind and he spoke in gentle, soothing tones to my mother and father as I writhed and twisted in sheets soaked in my own sweat.

At the height of my fever, I felt as though my body were ablaze and I screamed and screamed until I was hoarse. My mother wept at my bedside though I could not see her. A great shout went up, and I felt my body lifted and the sheets pulled from under me until the bed was stripped to nothing, and still I screamed and thrashed and choked. The room smelled of smoke.

Cold, wet cloths were placed on my naked body, removed when they grew warm, then replaced with new ones. A strong hand on my back held me upward, and the cold silver rim of a cup was placed between my lips. I drank the icy liquid greedily, half of it spilling down my chin.

My mother's haggard countenance, eyes red from weeping, hovered in the dark corners of the room like a malevolent specter, and once or twice I thought I woke to see my father kneeling at my bedside. I heard Master Aeneas's melodious voice, low and soothing, and felt his gnarled fingers touch my face. The words he was speaking were nonsense, but I was too far gone to care.

My world narrowed and grew dim, and at last I slept.

On a bright, cold morning three days after I first fell ill, my eyes opened.

The gilded stars above my bed swam into view and the tears that slid from my eyes, wetting my hair, brought them into sharp focus. I breathed in deeply once, twice, and though I felt peace and an overwhelming fatigue deep in my bones, there was something… different.

A shape at the corner of my vision coalesced into the figure of a man, and I turned my head on the pillow and saw Cyprias sitting in a chair near my bed, an open book in his lap.

"Cyprias?" I said, and my voice came out as a croak.

He looked up, and his gray eyes softened with a smile. "Well, there you are," he said, and, setting his book aside, he stood and crossed my room to the door where he spoke in low tones to someone outside. Then he closed the door softly and returned to the chair once more. "I've sent for your mother. She and your father are attending court, but asked to be notified the moment you woke."

I struggled to lift myself from my pillows. My head ached something fierce, and my mouth was as dry as though I'd stuffed it with my own bedclothes. "Water," I rasped, and Cyprias filled a cup from a pitcher on my nightstand. He held it to my lips; the cold liquid soothed my parched throat and I felt my head clear somewhat. "What happened?"

"You've been very ill, Briony. You've been asleep for days."

I sank back against the pillows, weak as a newborn kitten. "I remember such heat," I whispered. "It burned terribly. Was it a fever?"

"Of sorts. By the grace of the Old Gods, you've come back to us."

I turned my head on the pillow. "I feel strange."

"Do you?" he asked me mildly. "I imagine it is fatigue and dehydration, nothing more. Your strength will return in time."

My recovery was met with joy, but also by wariness, and my mother and father now seemed even more fraught with worry than they had before. I could not account for it. I thought they would have been pleased that I had not only emerged from my ordeal but seemed to bear no lasting harm, but their faces were tight and drawn, their eyes filled with shadows.

Alys and Issa attended me faithfully as I convalesced, plying me with broth and tea, and Livia kept me abreast of my studies, though she wisely left out any of my etiquette lessons. She brought me a handsome portfolio of thick, rich bound paper that she'd asked our father to order from town and a set of charcoal sticks in various sizes, and I thanked her profusely and spent many days scribbling and sketching things that would've made Mistress Precia faint dead away.

From time to time, Master Aeneas visited me. He sat in a chair near my bed and read from my favorite ghastly sections of his magical books until he grew tired and dozed, which I did not mind. My mother read to me often and sat for hours holding my hand while I slept, but of my father or Uncle Geordan I saw very little.

"These are difficult times, Briony," my uncle told me on one of the rare and therefore cherished occasions when he was able to visit me. "Your father has many worries."

"I could help him," I offered. "I've been collecting knowledge."

My uncle smiled, and I realized that I had not seen him do so in a very long time. "I've no doubt you have, little one," he said kindly. "But even knowledge may not be enough to set this worry right."

I was not yet fully recovered when my father announced quite unexpectedly that Livia and I were to leave the palace for our country estate in Orwynd far to the north. For how long, he did not say. I did not think he meant for us to return anytime soon.

Livia was despondent. "But why must I go?" she wailed.

We had all clustered around the fire to hear my father's news. I was tucked into the chair closest the blaze, a velvet blanket covering me from head to toe. I had only just been allowed out of my chambers the day before—in fact, I'd eaten a supper of broth and bread in my room while the rest feasted in the hall on roasted pork, bitter greens, celeriac swimming in butter, and stewed apples with sweet cream. Although I was not overly sad to have missed the bustle of court, I was severely disappointed to have missed the apples.

"Your sister needs you," our father responded.

"No, she doesn't!" Livia said in the very moment that I asserted, as indignantly as I could from my velvet cocoon, "No, I don't!"

"Enough!"

My father's voice shocked us all into silence. Not the boom of it, but the strain, and the rough edges.

He turned his back on us and rested one massive arm against the mantle above the fire. "Enough," he said, softer this time. His eyes stared into the flames. "Livia, you will go with Briony. You'll pack your things tonight and leave by coach tomorrow at dawn."

"Surely the girls are not meant to travel alone," my mother protested. "There are all manner of creatures on the roads at present."

"Of course not." My father turned to her, his eyes softening.

"Cyprias will accompany them. I have an errand for him in the north."

Cyprias! Excitement and confusion warred within me. I longed to ask my father what errand it was, but I did not think he would thank me for it. I looked to my uncle, who was unusually quiet, but he was staring at his hands and would not meet my gaze.

"We will return someday, won't we, father?" Livia asked, her voice small.

My father had turned back to the flames. "By the grace of the Old Gods," he said. "When the time is right."

He said no more that night, and Livia and I were sent to pack our things. Silent tears coursed down Livia's cheeks as gowns were bundled into trunks, which made her look even more beautiful somehow, and I hated her just a little bit because when I cried, my face grew red and my eyes swelled up and I very closely resembled a tomato.

I could hear her weeping through the wall that separated our bedrooms once we were tucked into bed and I did feel sorry, then, for I knew she was happy at the palace. If I was entirely truthful, I had become used to it myself, and though I did not thrive amongst the court the way my lovely sister did, I had come to value my lessons with Master Omerus, and my friendship with Master Aeneas, and Cyprias.

I wondered what would become of us in Orwynd. The estate had been in our family for generations, but I had never seen it. It was said to be a lonely place, isolated and surrounded by a wild wood that was haunted by all manner of eldritch creatures. There was no other home near it for miles and miles; the nearest village was half a day's ride away. We were to be quite solitary, a very different life than the one we led now. No doubt my father had chosen it for us for a reason.

The firelight danced on the stars and moons on my ceiling, and I lay awake and listened to Livia sob and wondered.

Livia had wrung herself dry by the morning, and all that remained of her impotent sorrow was her red-rimmed eyes. We huddled in our cloaks in the foggy gloom of the early morning as our trunks were hoisted onto the back of the carriage, redolent with our family's crest: a stag beneath a tree bearing golden apples.

My father and mother had come to see us off, as had our Uncle Geordan.

I'd already bid a tearful farewell to Master Aeneas earlier that morning. He had brought with him a gift: a beautiful leather-bound book of the plants and animals of northern Tiralaen so that I might better acquaint myself with the world I was to inhabit.

My mother and father held us both close, pressing kisses to our faces and promising that when the time was right, when the turmoil in Iluviel had settled, they would fetch us back. In the meantime, they promised to write us every week. As Livia threw herself into our mother's arms one last time, my father knelt at my feet so that we were eye to eye and regarded me solemnly.

"Do you remember what I told you the night King Gavreth died?"

"You told me to seek the light," I said. "Wherever I could."

"Yes, yes." He gripped my arms, pulling me close and pressing his forehead to mine. His rough beard tickled my face, but I stood still, as still as a stone, and breathed in the scent of him, his warmth. "Oh, my fierce, wild girl. You carry so much of it within you. Have courage, and do not ever give up."

They were the oddest of parting words. I'd have thought he'd have told me how much he loved me, that I shouldn't be worried, that he would see me again soon. But as he stood beside our carriage and Livia and I gripped his hands, tears streaming down our little faces, he looked into my eyes and said again, "Have courage. Both of you."

"And never give up," I said, even as the whip cracked above us and our carriage lurched forward, our parents fading into the distance behind us until I could no longer see them.

* * *

Four hours into our journey north from Iluviel, Livia fell asleep. She had been reading a book, a romance about a prince and a series of trials to win a maiden in a tower who contributed nothing to her own salvation. It fell from her hands onto the floor of the carriage, and I placed it beside her and tucked her cloak around it.

I was glad for the solitude, for I had many questions and Cyprias sat beside me, staring out the window, a wealth of knowledge at my fingertips.

"Why is my father really sending us away?" I asked him in a whisper, glancing at Livia to make sure she did not stir.

Cyprias turned slowly and fixed his gray eyes on me. "For your comfort and safety," he replied. "Do not fear, young Briony."

"I am not afraid," I informed him.

Cyprias smiled. "I would never have imagined so. But your father fears for your recovery. Orwynd is a much more pleasant place to convalesce than the Citadel."

He was not lying, but he was not telling me the whole truth. Rather it was smoke and no substance. A lovely half-truth meant to satisfy me so that I delved no further. I was not so easily mollified.

"I am nearly myself again. And Livia did not even catch my sickness, and yet she is banished with me."

"You are growing more and more clever with each passing day. But I am afraid there is no more to this than I have told you."

I fixed him with my most stubborn gaze. "What errand has my father sent you on in the north?"

I might've imagined it, but I thought a cloud passed over his face. "Not one that I may share with a child."

My embarrassment and disappointment must've showed in my face, for he touched the tip of his finger to my cheek gently. "The work I do for your father is dangerous, young Briony. I cannot in good conscious betray the trust Magnus has put in me by making his daughter a part of it."

"But I want to be a part of it!" I exploded, and on the seat across from me Livia stirred.

"Peace," Cyprias said, and the easy smile was back in his gray eyes. "I rather suspect you will whether I will it or no. But not now. Not now."

I would have to be satisfied with this, for he said no more and, by and by, the gentle rocking of the carriage and the boredom of silence lulled me into a fitful sleep. We stopped only briefly at Daharyn to change out the horses, and Cyprias pressed steaming meat pies into our hands and demanded that we eat. I thoroughly burned my mouth devouring them and begged for ever more. In the weeks since my sickness, I'd been allowed little other than broth and these pies seemed nothing short of a holiday feast. The food settled warmly in my stomach and, enveloped in my cloak, I felt cozy and satiated. I must've slept, for when I opened my eyes again, the sky outside the carriage was dark and full of stars.

We rode on through the next day and did not stop until nightfall at an inn called the Hare and Hearth just off the road. Livia and I shared a room where we ate a supper of stew and brown bread and fell asleep to the raucous sounds of men below in the tavern.

We were roused gently in the morning by the lady of the inn.

She had brought us sweet buns filled with raisins and apples and wedges of soft, white cheese and water from a clay jug. Livia used some of the water to rid the sleep from her eyes, and I copied her, blinking in the wan light of the new day and feeling even more exhausted than I had the night before. Then we were bundled back into the carriage with blankets tucked around our laps and a basket of provisions from the lady of the inn, and we set off again in the clear light of the morning. Livia read her book, and I stared out the window and watched the countryside grow increasingly wilder as we passed. I longed to speak to Cyprias again, but he had taken the air outside of the carriage and was riding alongside us on his fine black stallion.

We passed the evening at Plimpethyn next, and after a hearty supper of fish stew and brown bread, Livia fell asleep, nothing but her dark curls visible above the worn coverlet, while I snuck from our room and huddled at the top of the stairs that led to the tavern, clutching the rungs of the staircase between both hands so that I might watch the bustle below.

Cyprias kept to a table in the corner of the room, his hands clasped around a pint of ale that he barely touched, his gray eyes surveying the room with what could've easily been mistaken for detached curiosity by anyone who did not know as I did that Cyprias was quite engaged in collecting knowledge, just as he had once bade me to do. I felt certain he saw the very heart of every man and woman assembled and knew each and every one of their secrets though they'd spoken not a word to him. Whether or not it had anything to do with the duty he performed for my father in the northern lands I knew not, but twice on our journey he handed small scrolls to two of the liveried men who accompanied us and bid them ride back in the direction we'd come, no doubt to deliver news to a waiting hand in Iluviel.

Thus we journeyed on for nigh on a week before, at last, Cyprias informed my sister and me that we were but a day's ride from Orwynd. My sister was delighted for she had little enjoyed sleeping on uncomfortable beds and riding for hours upon end, so used to the comforts of the Citadel was she, but I was decidedly less enthusiastic, fearing the isolation our new home promised. I'd not minded at all the quaint, sometimes raucous inns we'd patronized, nor the simple rustic fare we'd consumed, so different it was from everything I had ever known. And I'd relished the opportunity to watch Cyprus, to talk with him, and did not want to part company just yet. Also, I must admit, I'd grown more than a little curious of what was in the messages he dashed off and sent away.

A steady rain was already falling when we set out toward our new life, and I watched it sullenly from the window of our carriage whilst chewing on a bun flavored with cinnamon, anise, and cardamom. Opposite me, Livia prattled on and on about our aunt's reputation as a highborn lady and that at least she would be able to instill in us the skills necessary to our ascension to wives of influential men in Keric's court. Eventually my eyelids drooped, my chin dropped to my chest, and I slept.

I was shaken awake by Livia, her eyes bright and her mouth pressed into a thin line. The carriage had stopped, and she was staring out the window at something in the distance. I followed the direction of her gaze and saw the place that would become my new home.

Orwynd was the ancestral seat of House Tenebrae before my father's grandfather abandoned it for the larger, more modern Crenswick Castle south of Iluviel, leaving it in the care of his sister, Kaestra, who at that time was well into her thirties and a spinster. Upon her death, the house passed to my grandfather, and then to my father, neither of whom cared for it but did not wish to see a piece of our family's history pass from our hands. When it became apparent that my father's sister, Eudora, would follow the same lonely path as Kaestra, the house became her charge, and as far as I knew, she had been there ever since.

The house itself was a massive, ancient thing. Only fine craftsmanship and very, very old magic kept it from collapsing in on itself in a twisted pile of stone and ivy.

Surrounding the crumbling manor was something far older than the house itself: the Morwood.

Tales of the Morwood were ubiquitous and each more terrifying than the last. Like most of Tiralaen's children, I had indulged myself with too many tales told too late in the evening and had screamed myself awake, shivering deliciously in the darkness as I imagined the tendrils of the Kelpie's mane still twining around my arms, pulling me down into the murky depths of its watery kingdom. I was, after all, still young and possessed of a fine and overactive imagination. My feet had scarce touched the ground when I was already off, searching for toadstool rings and eldritch mounds sure to hold the most wonderful mysteries below.

Livia, upon seeing our new home, had begun to cry again, and this was how our Aunt Eudora found us. A more formidable woman we had never seen, and her effect on us was immediate. Livia stopped crying, I let fall the moss-covered stick that I'd been using to lift up a patch of old leaves, and we stared up with wide eyes at the woman who was to be our guardian.

Aunt Eudora looked like a softer version of my father, and she'd inherited the same deep auburn hair. Piled atop her head in a mass of curls, the strands caught the sunlight and formed a halo around her face, still handsome despite her years. She took us in from head to toe with sharp, intelligent eyes.

"So, you are Sabine's children," she said at last. "Come on, then." She turned and, without sparing us a backwards glance, disappeared inside the cavernous maw of the manor's entrance.

Livia followed her straight away, but I hung back, glancing toward the carriage. The staff had already begun the task of bearing our trunks from the carriage into the house, and I wanted to say goodbye to Cyprias before he departed for the north.

I found him in conversation with the driver of the coach. He must have sensed my unease, for he excused himself from the conversation and knelt before me quite seriously, our eyes level.

"Please don't leave me here," I begged one last time, knowing it would be fruitless and hating my own helplessness. "Let me come with you—I promise I'll be helpful."

He laughed. "I have no doubt that you would be. But you know I cannot." He rested a heavy hand on my shoulder. "Think not of this as a punishment, but an opportunity. There is happiness to be found here, even if it does not seem so now."

"What will happen to you?" I said, giving voice to the fear I felt for his dangerous journey north.

"Nothing that you need fear, Briony."

"I'm not afraid."

"I do not doubt it." He chuckled. "Mind your aunt and learn all you can."

"Briony!" My sister's shrill cry pierced the air and, dismayed, I looked toward the steps where she stood, hands on hips, looking for me. "Where are you?"

Cyprias's hand came down on the top of my head, large and warm and solid, and he ruffled my curls. "It's time."

"Wait," I said, panic rising within me. "Promise me. Promise me I'll not be left alone in ignorance. Promise me you'll come and bring news."

Cyprias went down on his knees before me, the way a gentleman might to a lady although he was a spy and I was a girl of ten. He took my hands, and they were positively swallowed by his. "I will come and see you when I can," he told me. "I promise."

He stood and, with a smile, bowed to me with all the seriousness of his station, and of mine. I dipped a truly awful curtsey in return, and he smiled at me once more.

"Briony!" Livia's shout sent me scampering up the steps with my wet skirts clutched in my hands, leaving an unfortunate trail of mud. Behind me, the great doors of Orwynd shuddered and closed.

5

Ten Years Later

In the late spring afternoon, the air in the greenhouse was a heavy, oppressive fog of rosemary, mint, and loamy soil. A sketchbook rested on my knees, and I dipped the nib of my quill into the pot of ink I'd balanced on a stack of broken terra cotta. Drops spattered on the hem of my dress despite my efforts to hold my hand steady, and I sighed as I surveyed the damage. The pinpricks of black stood out in sharp contrast to the pale green fabric, a gift from my mother on my last birthday. Upon further inspection, it appeared this stain was not the first this dress had endured. There was a larger blotch nearby that might've been dirt or possibly blood, but was most definitely an unseemly brown that Aunt Eudora was sure to notice.

I had reached my majority two years before and she had no grounds now to scold me for the sorry state of my wardrobe. But to my guardian, pride was no sin, but a right and honorable state in which to keep oneself, particularly if oneself is born of a noble family such as ours. Somehow, the perpetually sorry state of my hems was an affront to the House of Tenebrae.

I chewed on my lower lip as I carefully traced the outline of the butterfly's wing. I'd left the greenhouse door open that morning and come back in the afternoon to a visitor opening and closing his beautiful wings on a large bloom of echinacea. He would be given his freedom soon enough, but in the meantime, I had decided to draw him. I would add color later; I did not have a shade in my box of paints that exactly matched the rich purple, but I could perhaps mix two or three together and come close.

In truth, I was supposed to have returned to the house hours ago. My aunt had sent me to collect lemon balm for a salve and I had never returned. I'd slipped a novel into my basket and spent the afternoon in the Morwood beside the stream with my shoes and stockings off, my gown hitched up around my knees, and my feet submerged in the glacial water.

The butterfly launched himself off of the flower and I sighed, my sketch incomplete. Perhaps he suspected my truancy. My stomach growled, and I realized I hadn't eaten since that morning.

I snapped a few hearty stems of lemon balm and thrust them into my basket before I threw the doors of the greenhouse open and freed my accidental captive. The smell of the balm was intoxicating, and I could not stop smelling my hands all the way back to the manor, where I was met by a maid servant. I narrowly managed to snatch my novel from the basket before it was borne away to the kitchens, and when I straightened myself, I was face to face with Aunt Eudora, standing at the bottom of the staircase.

Before she could scold me or profane to die of embarrassment from the stains on the hem of my gown, I gave her a bright smile. "Shall we have tea?"

Aunt Eudora loved taking tea. It had, of course, become a distraction I used often when she disapproved of me. Even now, I saw her stern countenance begin to soften.

"As it happens, I have a letter for you," she said. "From Iluviel."

A letter! It would be from mother and father, or Uncle Geordan, perhaps. My aunt positively delighted in hearing all the news from court, but she had few friends left amongst the nobility there; correspondence from my parents was, therefore, cherished. As for me, I had another source of the goings-on at the Citadel entirely, though Aunt Eudora was completely unaware of the fact and it was best she remained so.

We sat in the large parlor opposite one another, and I broke the wax seal on my letter while Aunt Eudora sipped her tea and watched me over the rim of her cup. The letter was from my Uncle Geordan. He began with the usual pleasantries, along with a few jabs at the fact that I had not outgrown my red hair, though it had become quite a bit more like my father's dark auburn over the last few seasons. Not that he would know that, of course. I'd not seen him in nigh on two years; my father I'd not seen at all. The weight of what Tiralaen had become over the past twelve years rested heavily upon his shoulders, even as he fought tirelessly to prevent further devastation, if such a thing were possible. Once a proud, prosperous people, we dwelled now in shadow and fear.

The high hopes my uncle had once had for the return of sense and tolerance to the throne had been dreams born of a vast underestimation of the creature that sat atop it. Keric was no longer a boy-king, and the thing he had become was far less than a man. My father and uncle did not advise him now so much as try to manage his more dangerous impulses as best they could. And when they could not, they struggled to live with the consequences. Keric's paranoia of magic had led to outright control of all who wielded it, and punishment for those he could not control.

Practicing magic was now forbidden to all except those who did so in direct service of the king. Women and those not native to Tiralaen were not allowed to practice it at all. The Gate had become a relic of the past; any Mage who incurred Keric's wrath was executed. Once rare and prized, magical bloodlines were snuffed out on scaffolding by a king who would see all magic removed from his kingdom.

Tiralaen was, as a result, condemned by kingdoms who were once our most loyal allies. Keric's soldiers patrolled our borders, demanding proof of any person who crossed that they were not of magical blood, nor sympathized with those who were. If a noble family was found to sympathize with Mages, their children were taken from them and brought up at court as wards of the crown, doomed to serve in Keric's bloody war as punishment for the crimes of their parents. Common families who aided those of magical blood were slaughtered.

To this end, Keric's surrogates traveled to villages throughout the kingdom and preached of the dangers of magic and the horrors that awaited us of all should Mages rise up. Stirred into a frenzy, fingers pointed, accusations flew, and bodies swung from tree branches, left to rot in the sun as a gruesome warning.

Against this, my father and uncle stood alone and in secret, and their bravery exacted a heavy toll.

"Your father is ill again," I read, dread pooling in my stomach. "Master Aeneas has had some difficulty keeping him abed, and I fear that if he continues to shirk his bed and table, he will waste away to nothing at all. With your mother gone away to visit Livia and the children across the Lucet Sea, only I am left to remind him that he is, in fact, human, and fallible."

Aunt Eudora leaned forward and plucked the letter, now dangling from my limp fingers. I took a large, scalding swallow of tea as she read my uncle's words. It burned all the way down my throat and my eyes began to water, but it was a welcome distraction.

Aunt Eudora skimmed the letter. I supposed I would have to read the rest of Uncle Geordan's news later. "No other news of Livia," she said at last. "Perhaps letters are not traveling across the sea in the commotion."

The commotion, of course, being the war. My aunt certainly had a way with words. My cup of tea finished, I took the letter and rose.

"I think I'll write back, and perhaps to Livia as well."

"Do be careful," she said, raising one perfectly groomed eyebrow pointedly.

She did not need to remind me. I always wrote as though my letters would be seen by eyes other than for whom they were intended, as did my uncle and my father.

I stopped in the kitchens, lost in a brewing storm of dark thoughts, and greeted our cook, Layn, with a kiss to her cheek, which was warm from the steam rising from the soup she was stirring in a great vat on the stove.

In addition to being our cook, Layn was also an herb woman. She had a stillroom off the kitchen where she dried bunches of herbs and flowers and plants that she used for teas and tinctures and possets. Since I'd come to Orwynd, Layn had taken it upon herself to teach me all she could about the plants that grew there, and their uses. My aunt felt it would be of little use once I was permitted to return to court and become a wife, but as I was in no particular hurry to rush toward that fate, I took great pleasure in keeping a book in which I pressed samples of the flora I collected, along with their uses and deeper meanings in ancient lore.

"You smell heavenly," she told me. "What sort of a fuss did the mistress make about that hair of yours?"

"Why?" My hand flew up to my curls, and I leaned over to inspect my reflection in the glass of one of the kitchen's many windows. There were several leaves and other bits of woodland ephemera stuck in my now disheveled coiffure, and I extracted them carefully. Aunt Eudora must've been too distracted to notice. As Layn pulled the last of the bits from the tangled strands I could not reach, I skimmed the rest of my uncle's missive.

As always, he promised he would come and visit me as soon as he was able, and assured me that he and Master Aeneas would mind my father's health such as it was. There was no mention of Cyprias at all.

Layn supplied me with two blackberry cakes to assuage my still-protesting stomach, and I devoured them ravenously on the way up to my chamber. I had a lovely little writing desk that I'd positioned in front of a large window overlooking the gardens and, beyond that, the Morwood.

I dashed off a reply to my uncle's letter. As he'd said little, there was little to say in return. I begged him to keep my father safe and to keep me abreast of any and all news that he could, and sent them all my love, as always.

Then I stared out at the vast expanse of green while I chewed the end of my quill and thought about what to say to Livia.

My sister had spent five years at Orwynd before my parents relented and allowed her to come to court at the age of nineteen. Such was the lot of little sisters that I did not realize how much I had enjoyed her company until she was no longer here, but my father forbade me from following her. I raged around Orwynd for weeks, sick with fury at her for leaving me alone and desperate with longing for her. Although there was no great affection between us, during the five years in which we were alone at Orwynd, we had become easy companions through our shared experiences. I still thought her silly, and she still disapproved of my unruly nature, but she was my sister and I was hers. It was a bond that transcended our squabbles, and I found that I missed her dearly when she left, even if she did not miss me.

Livia had dreamed of attending a season at court as a woman of marriageable age her whole life. On cold nights in Orwynd, we had shivered in our separate beds until one of us would sneak into the other's, and we would huddle under the covers listening to the wind whistle and shriek outside the windows and talk of everything and nothing the way sisters do. Livia's eyes positively shone when she described the gowns and jewels she would wear, the way she would style her hair, the slippers she would dance in all night. And, of course, the men. As the daughter of an ancient and respected family, Livia was dutifully chaste in both thought and conduct, and as such I never heard her talk about anything shocking, which was unfortunate because as a child that was *all* I wanted to talk about. But she made no secret of her desire to find herself a handsome, rich young lord, preferably titled though not necessarily depending on the size of his estates.

This was, after all, what our mother had done, and her mother before her, and it was what was expected of us. I viewed it as something that, despite having its advantages, was unpleasant and to be delayed as long as possible. It was Livia's sole ambition. She longed for children of her own and a position at court, and a husband was the means by which to do this. She had assumed that, in the usual way of things, our father would make for her a good match from the sons of the other nobles who sat on the privy council.

But the moment Livia's satin slippers had touched the marble of the ballroom upon her return to court, King Keric was besotted with her.

Anyone would assume that the potential to marry into the royal family of Tiralaen would send any family into a tizzy of delight and ambitious scheming. Instead, the mere idea of it chilled my father's bones to their very marrow.

Abandoned and seemingly forgotten at Orwynd, I had to decipher this between the lines of the letters that arrived from the capital in a near constant stream during that ill-fated season. At first, Livia enthusiastically accepted Keric's advances. Despite what she had heard about his cruelty toward magic-born, he was, after all, the king, and so very handsome and charming. He showered her and our family with gifts: jewels, fine casks of whisky and wine, and even a palfrey for Livia that glowed as white as moonlight. But my father knew what he truly was, knew that any loving father could not give his daughter to him. And so, he was in the impossible position of wanting to refuse his sovereign but being unable to do so without angering him to the point that he put himself and his family at risk.

They danced about for weeks. My father gave Livia's innocence and reluctance to leave her family as reason to slow their courtship. Keric strengthened his suit in response, and for a time, my father resigned himself to the inevitability that in order to remain in his sovereign's good graces and, in doing so, protect the kingdom as best he could, his daughter might pay the price.

But one evening after revels with the visiting court of Esanoth, Livia returned to our family's suite of rooms sobbing and disheveled, and what she told my mother and father ended all possibility of a union between the royal family and our own.

It happened that Keric had decided to assemble a small party of some twenty nobles in his private sitting room, and Livia thrilled at being invited. She sat beside the king to the envy of every other unmarried woman in the room, radiant and beautiful in silver silk with silver hairpins dotted with diamonds holding her glossy curls. Bowls of a strong, spicy punch flavored with pomegranate and cardamom were served, and Keric brought Livia's to her in a delicate crystal glass and bid her sample all manner of sweet things from the kitchens. He paid her compliments; she lowered her lashes demurely; they were the very picture of a handsome young king wooing a beautiful chaste maiden.

And then Keric stood and ordered his servants to bring out the entertainment for the evening.

The entertainment turned out to be a young girl of no more than fifteen and her brother some six years younger. They were painfully thin, their dark eyes over-large in their faces, and their faded clothing hung off of their frames. Livia's euphoria dissolved at once.

From the chaise where he lounged beside her, King Keric gave a predatory smile. "Friends, I have a rare treat for you all this evening." He gestured magnanimously to the children, his smile wide and wild. "We are in the presence of a truly extraordinary Mage."

Curious whispers broke out amongst the glittering throng.

Keric had always been charismatic. He held his audience in the palm of his hand, and he knew it. The nobility hung on his every word, leaning forward, cups forgotten, eager and breathless.

"This girl…" He paused dramatically. "Is a Necromancer."

His words were met with titters and gasps, fodder for Keric's vanity. Livia, clutching the stem of her glass tightly in her fist, looked at the faces around her and saw that while many were fascinated and eager, others were uneasy, even sympathetic.

By now, the girl had begun to cry, her brother folded into her side, clutching her hand tightly. Livia studied her intently. She did not look at all what she'd imagined a Necromancer to look like, though she supposed there was no proper way at all for any Mage to look, only storybook notions. The girl's feet were dirty and bare, and Livia could see angry red welts around her wrists where they must've bound her. She reminded Livia of a bird, a wren perhaps: small and slight, with dark, fearful eyes.

"She was arrested by my guard this morning and is sentenced to be put through the Gate for raising the dead," Keric continued, thoroughly enjoying the shock his speech elicited from his guests. He turned to the terrified girl. "Is it true?"

"She didn't mean to!" It was the little boy who answered. He detached himself from his sister's side and faced the king defiantly. "It was an accident!"

"Who was it, girl?" Keric prompted, ignoring her brother's fierce glare. "Who did you raise?"

"Our grandmother." Again the boy answered for his sister, who was struck dumb with fear.

"Silence!" Keric thundered at the boy. "And let her speak. Girl, is it true? Can you raise the dead?"

"Yes," the girl whispered. "But I didn't mean to. I couldn't control it. I'm sorry—I won't ever do it again. Ever." And she shuddered as though the very thought of using her magic caused her physical ill.

"Oh, I think you will." Keric's tone was deceptively light, a sharp contrast to the wicked gleam in his eye. "You see, before you're sent through the Gate, I want to see this magic for myself." He smiled then, a horrible smile full of malice. "And I did promise my guests entertainment."

The boy's protests were swallowed as one of Keric's guards grabbed him roughly by the arms and hauled him away from his sister, thrusting him down on the ground between her and the king. The girl threw herself at her brother, but Keric's guards were swift. They materialized beside the girl as if they were conjured from the air itself and grabbed her arms.

Too late, Livia realized why Keric had summoned the boy with his sister.

The king jerked his chin toward his guard, and his man drew his short sword and ran the boy through as if he were made of nothing at all. The girl wailed, a guttural, animal sound that echoed off of the marble walls and echoed over and over as she thrashed against her captors. Her brother's sad, broken body lay on the floor where he fell, and the ladies seated closest gathered their skirts away from the slowly widening pool of blood. Livia felt a drop of water on her hands, clutched together tightly in her lap, then another and another, and she realized she was crying.

The wails of the girl still echoing in the utterly silent room, Keric approached the boy and nudged him with his toe until he'd flipped the body over on its back. The eyes were open and staring, yet saw nothing. "Oh dear. He's dead." Keric's lip curled in distaste. Then he looked up at the girl. "Now bring him back."

"I can't!" she cried. "I don't know how! I told you it was an accident!"

Keric stalked toward her. "Rubbish. You did it before, you can do it again. Bring him back." He grabbed her by the arm and hauled her over to the body of her brother. "Bring him back. Now."

The girl, sobbing in great shaking gasps, laid her hands over her brother's bloodied, broken body and closed her eyes. The crowd had fallen silent and watched intently for signs of life from the small body. After a long moment, the girl gave a frustrated cry and her eyes snapped open. "I told you, I can't!" she wept. "Oh Gods, I can't!"

"Do it!" Keric was angry now. The fantastic spectacle he'd promised his guests was melting into chaos before his eyes, and there was a dead child lying in a pool of blood on the gilded floor. "If you don't do it, girl, he'll be gone forever!"

This seemed to steady the girl somewhat, and she moved her hands over her brother's body once more, her eyes closing. "Please," Livia heard her whisper. "Oh please."

At first it seemed as though this attempt would be identical to the first, but the girl's shaking gradually began to quell and her gasping breaths became even and steady. A calm radiated from her, and she might've been asleep she was so still. She drew a deep breath, and her eyelids fluttered and opened. Beneath her bloody hands, the chest of the boy began to rise and fall, and he choked, blood spraying from his mouth.

The crowd gasped and cried out, agog at the sight of the dead boy now breathing, coughing, and trying to lift his head. His sister was sobbing again, tears of relief streaming down her face as her hands clutched at the front of his ruined shirt. "Stay still," she begged him. "Stay still."

Livia released the breath she'd been holding and looked at the other lords and ladies around her; she saw looks of relief on their faces that must've mirrored her own. Keric was beaming triumphantly.

"There!" He clapped his hands together, his face alight. "What did I tell you? True death magic."

A few guests, unsure of what to do, began to clap awkwardly as if they had just seen a play performed; others spoke to each other in low murmurs, looking at the girl and her reborn brother with a mixture of awe and suspicion. Necromancy was a branch of Arcane magic that was not only rare in its occurrence, but rarely seen as well, and never as entertainment. Keric truly had outdone himself.

Despite the girl's protestations, the boy wouldn't settle. He struggled on the floor against her hands. The girl pleaded with him, spoke to him in soothing tones, brushed the tangle of dark hair away from his face, but he still would not settle. He began to thrash against her hold on him, a low, harsh growl growing in his throat.

"What is this?" Keric demanded. "What's wrong with him?"

"I don't know." The girl's hands were on the boy's face now, and she struggled to hold his gaze. His feral eyes darted past her and fixed themselves on the king. "Hush, dearest," she crooned to the boy. "You're back with me, I'm here. Hush now." Still, he struggled in her arms, blood smearing them both.

Keric's cousin, Macon, spoke up from where he sat on a low cushion beside a white-faced girl with a halo of golden ringlets. "You know, she did tell you that she didn't know how to do it properly."

"Make him stop," Keric ordered the girl.

"I'm trying, your highness." The girl was attempting to pin the boy's arms to his side, and he fought her, his once sweet face distorted with anger and pain. In the end, her attempts proved futile. Small as he was, he tossed his sister aside like a rag doll.

Then, with a snarl, the boy lunged at Keric.

The room plunged into chaos. Keric bellowed at his guards to seize the boy, while his sister, covered in his blood and crouched on the floor, sobbed and begged the guards not to hurt him. Glass smashed as Keric's guests abandoned their drinks and decorum and scrabbled back away from the commotion, pressing themselves against walls and attempting to shield themselves behind ornate furniture.

"Kill it!" Keric was screaming shrilly. "Kill it!"

The guards drew their swords. The girl screamed one last, terrible scream, and then there was silence. The boy's body crumpled to the floor, unmoving.

Livia staggered off of the chaise, fell to her hands and knees, and heaved the contents of her stomach onto the cold floor. The alcohol burned her throat and stung her eyes.

"Clean it up," Keric growled at his guards. His hair was disheveled, his face red and sweating, and there were drops of blood sprayed on the front of his brocade tunic. "Take the body away and burn it. And take the girl to the Tower."

From where she crouched on the floor, Livia watched the guards haul the girl to her feet. She hung between them, limp and lifeless, tears frozen on her cheeks, her eyes vacant. As the guards dragged her dead weight out of the room, Keric turned to his guests, the attempt of a smile on his face.

"Music!" He gestured to the quartet of musicians. They had abandoned their instruments in the upheaval and were huddled in a corner together. "We need music! And drinks—bring more punch!"

The corpse of the boy was rolled into a length of cloth and carried unceremoniously from the room and the blood washed away. The nobility, soothed by the removal of the carnage and the peaceful strains of the quartet, gradually floated back into the room, tittering excitedly about the scintillating and grotesque event they had just witnessed, though some still looked decidedly sickened.

Livia waited until Keric's back was turned in conversation before she staggered to her feet and slipped out of the door unnoticed. Once the door closed behind her, she broke into a run. Hairpins scattered, letting loose her dark curls, and sobs hitched in her throat. Faster she ran, ignoring the curious stares that followed her until she reached our family's suite. She ran straight into our mother's arms and the whole story poured out in excruciating detail.

My father, mother, and uncle spent the night deep in conversation while Livia was coaxed into a bath and spoon-fed a lavender posset. She passed the night plagued with dreams and woke in tears.

The king was told that Livia was unwell. She kept to her chamber for two days, and then quietly departed Iluviel in the early hours of the morning with the King of Esanoth's entourage. She shared their ship across the channel and away from her homeland. There, she would marry a man our father had chosen for her, the son of an old friend who would inherit a title and fortune. Livia would become the lady of his estate deep in the countryside and bear his children far away from Keric and the court of Iluviel. It was not, perhaps, the grand match my parents had hoped for Livia, but they knew she would be safe and well cared for.

When the king, furious at Livia's departure, confronted my father, he apologized profusely and told him Livia had disobeyed his wishes in marrying Jacan and he would've preferred she had married his illustrious majesty, of course.

With an ocean separating them, and a wedding ring firmly ensconced on my sister's finger, Keric quickly lost interest in Livia and forgot her altogether within weeks.

The girl whose life the king had destroyed for his amusement was imprisoned in the Tower. The first night she tore strips of cloth from her skirts and attempted to hang herself from the rafters, but the cloth was poor and tore under her weight. Had she been an indentured servant born without magic, particularly magic as dangerous as hers, she might've been stripped naked and left in the Tower to die. But she was a Mage, and several of the guests at the king's revels had grown uncomfortable with what they had been privy to and had begun to talk. The girl was bundled into a gray gown and thrust through the Gate before she could invite trouble, lost to Asperfell and forgotten entirely.

6

As a girl, I'd promised Cyprias I would gather knowledge, and though I was isolated at Orwynd, I'd kept that promise as best I could.

Livia and I had tutor when we'd first arrived at the manor: a kindly, round-faced man from a village four hours away by horseback, whom my father paid handsomely to ensure the continued literacy of his two daughters. I liked him very much and did not reveal that I had caught him many a time in the kitchen when Aunt Eudora was asleep, drinking spirits and playing dice with the servants. He did not mind teaching me whatever I took a fancy to, believing all knowledge was worth having as long as he was kept deep in his cups.

I was sixteen when he did not rise from his bed one morning, sending one of our maids into hysterics. His heart had given out sometime during the night and he died with a smile on his face.

Aunt Eudora declined to hire another tutor for me, and my father was far too busy at court to concern himself with it. I was, in Aunt Eudora's opinion, far too educated already in subjects irrelevant to my future as a wife, and not educated enough in overseeing a household, so for a time she attempted to take me in hand and teach me, but I was an awful student and she soon gave up. So, I became a bit of a wild thing, coming and going as I pleased, alone more often than not.

When the weather was fine, and even sometimes when it wasn't,

I traipsed about the Morwood for hours, discovering the rich worlds hidden amongst the ancient trees. I learned from Layn how to put offerings for eldritch folk in the hollows of twisted roots of trees on the longest and shortest nights, and though I never saw them, the offerings were always gone the next day and occasionally a gift was left in their place: a glossy black feather, a string of rowan berries, a smooth green rock, a bunch of periwinkles. These I kept in a trunk in my chamber, and I never showed them to Aunt Eudora.

My aunt was no fool. She worshiped the Old Gods and believed in the primordial, otherworldly presences in the Morwood. But rather than the curiosity they inspired within me, they filled her with only fear. They were said to be what remained of the creatures sent by the Old Gods long ago to punish and reward mankind in equal measure, and I supposed it was the notion of the former that rendered her quite unwilling to suffer any talk pertaining to the eldritch folk whatsoever.

It was a lesson I learned most unfortunately one afternoon shortly after Livia and I arrived at Orwynd.

I'd snuck out to explore the grounds on my own and found a small graveyard some distance from the house, containing old tombstones within a filigreed fence made of iron. The gardener kept it as neat and tidy as he could, though many of the older stones wanted for a good washing. I scrambled over the iron fence, tearing my gown in the process, and winded my way through the stones, pausing here and there to read the names of my distant ancestors and the dates of their births and deaths until, bent over the small stone of a child who had died some two hundred years ago, I saw a glimmering white shape hovering under one of the nearby trees.

Thinking it must've been a trick of the light, I scrubbed at my eyes, blinked several times, and looked again. The apparition seemed more solid now, distinctly human in shape, and it was staring right at me, staring with endlessly black, ghastly hollows where its eyes ought to have been.

I'd never known such revulsion as that which spread through me at the sight, and for a horribly long moment, I could not move at all, so stricken was I with fear.

When at last feeling returned to my limbs, I stumbled over the baby's grave in my haste to escape and fell sprawling on the grass in a heap; then I picked up my skirts and fled. I ran like a thing possessed all the way back to the house and went straight to Aunt Eudora to tell her what I'd seen.

She and Livia were sitting in the parlor taking tea, and they both looked up in surprise at my sudden, wild-eyed appearance.

"I saw a spirit in the graveyard!" I cried.

Livia's wide eyes turned to our aunt, looking for reassurance perhaps that I was mad, or dreading confirmation that I was not.

Aunt Eudora pursed her lips and set her cup down. "Nonsense, child. Your eyes are playing tricks on you."

"They're *not!*" I insisted with the passion of a child who knows herself right and feels helpless anger at an adult's pessimism. "I saw her! She was all white with horrible black holes for eyes."

Aunt Eudora's stony gaze was slowly turning into a frown. "Now see here, Briony Tenebrae. You've frightened your sister with your wild tales. There is naught in that graveyard but bones."

"But—"

"Never speak of it again, do you hear?"

She sent me to Mora to wash the filth off of my hands and face and pluck leaves and bits of grass from my hair, and she forbade me from ever speaking of phantasms again, insisting it was my overactive imagination and nothing more.

Two months later, Cyprias arrived to see to our wellbeing, and although I longed to tell him everything about what I'd seen in the graveyard right away, I feared Aunt Eudora's wrath, and so I sat as still and quivering as a rabbit in a trap through six excruciating courses of dinner until I managed to get him alone.

"Not here," Cyprias told me in a low voice, his arm at my elbow as he watched my aunt and sister disappear into the parlor. "Later."

I was perched on my bed in my nightdress many hours later, candle in hand, when a servant came to my door to fetch me. I followed him to the parlor where I found Cyprias standing before the fire, and he'd scarce closed the door before I'd burst out: "I've seen a ghost!"

Cyprias set his goblet on the mantle and turned to face me. "A ghost, you say?"

"Yes! In the graveyard. A woman—a white woman with the most terrible holes where her eyes should be!"

"A white woman," Cyprias repeated thoughtfully. "Indeed."

"I tried to tell Aunt Eudora about her, but she forbade me from speaking of such things."

"Well, you may certainly speak to me of such things."

And so we did speak of such things and many more besides until I grew drowsy and Cyprias sent me to bed before my aunt discovered us, but not before we made a pact: when he visited Orwynd to see to my sister's and my wellbeing, we would meet in secret and discuss all of the things we could not say in the presence of my aunt.

We'd kept this pact for the last ten years.

Cyprias made the journey to Orwynd at least twice a year under the guise of an interest in my progress toward becoming a lady worthy of a place at court and the arm of a suitable young man chosen for me by my father.

Whenever he graced us, Aunt Eudora would trot me out, dressed in some fine gown or other, and force me to sing and play the harp and show off my wretched embroidery, which I believe he found quite amusing though he never let my aunt see his mirth. He always assured her that the pains she'd taken with me were much appreciated by my mother and father and that I would make an excellent wife some day in the (regrettably) not-so-very-distant future.

Then we would sit down to a sumptuous feast before, *finally,*

Cyprias would give my aunt some excuse or other, and we would flee to the Morwood where he would tell me all the things that my uncle's letters could not. So fiercely did I love those brief hours when my insatiable curiosity could be satisfied that I looked forward to Cyprias's visits more than anything else in the world, and like the creature of knowledge he'd hoped I'd become, I used the time in between to keep my weapons honed. Of course, my aunt thought I was merely seeking to expand my marriage prospects by learning languages, geography, and strategy—useful skills for the wife of a royal diplomat or adviser— and it kept her satisfied and at a distance and so I did not deny it, though she did draw the line at hiring a swordsman to teach me how to properly defend myself.

"Honestly, Briony," she'd scoffed, "the very last thing my sensibilities need is you running about with a sword. And what man will want a wife with calloused fingers?"

"None whatsoever, except those I might consent to marry," I shot back, then dashed off to the kitchen before she could box my ears.

By the time my uncle's latest—and, as it turned out, last—letter arrived, I'd not seen Cyprias for nigh on eight months, and though I'd not yet begun to worry, I grew more and more anxious for news from the Citadel.

A rumor had reached us through a cousin of one of the housemaids that Keric's soldiers had raided and set fire to a village some days away from us to the east and strung up the elders for harboring Mages, and I longed to discuss with Cyprias whether he thought such bloodshed would reach us at Orwynd. But no word came from court, and the road was barren.

The weeks passed. Spring gave way to the bright fragrant days of early summer, and then one afternoon, he finally arrived.

My aunt and I were sitting together in the parlor, a soft breeze drifting in through the open windows. Layn had found a patch of wild sorrel near the orchards and I was making a study of its medicinal properties, copying what I'd found in my book of plants beside a drawing I'd made of the rich, green leaves. A novel, quite forgotten, dangled between my aunt's fingers; she'd fallen asleep sitting up some time ago.

In the distance, I heard the unmistakable sound of horse hooves, and I bolted upright, my book sliding from my knees to the floor just as my aunt sputtered awake.

"Briony!" she said sharply, but I ignored her and flew to the wide-open window, leaning so far out I nearly fell into the rambling rose bush below.

A single rider dressed in plain traveling clothes was approaching; he bore no colors or sigil, but I knew at once who he was and my heart swelled.

"Cyprias!"

My aunt stood, alarmed. "Cyprias? Here? Now?"

"He's come at last!" I gathered my skirts and fled the room, my aunt on my heels barking orders to the staff to ready his room.

I burst through the great doors of Orwynd and tumbled down the stairs, my hair flying behind me and my smile so wide my cheeks ached from it, but I did not care. Oh, how I'd missed him! I took the last few steps two at a time and rushed out to meet Cyprias as he slid down from his horse and handed the reins to our groom.

"Briony Tenebrae!" my aunt shouted after me. "I'll thank you to behave more civilly, and for goodness sake, keep your gown free of dust!"

This was a near impossible feat given the impressive cloud the horse had kicked up. Indeed, Cyprias's own traveling clothes were caked in brown. Ignoring my aunt's protestations, I took Cyprias's hands, my own swallowed entirely by his rough leather riding gloves, and beamed up at him. By my reckoning, Cyprias could not have had more than forty-five years, but he looked far older, and even more so than the last time I'd seen him.

"We expected you weeks ago!" I chided him. "I've grown positively mad waiting!"

"My deepest apologies for the delay, Mistress Briony," he said, bowing as though I were King Keric himself. I might've thought him quite serious were it not for the twinkle in his gray eyes. "It could not be helped, I'm afraid."

"Don't call me Mistress Briony. I am plain old Briony and nothing more."

"Are you indeed? Then I must apologize again for I quite mistook you for a lady of court."

"Liar. Not with this hair."

Cyprias smiled at that. "Lady Feryndel has hair very nearly the same shade."

"Yes, but not a face full of freckles to go with it," my aunt scoffed, having joined us at last. "I beg her not to cavort out of doors for the sake of her complexion, but I believe she does it just to spite me."

"Eudora." Cyprias greeted her with a bow.

"Cyprias," she answered stiffly. "Do come inside. You'll want a bath to wash all of that dust off. I've prepared your usual room, and I'll have Layn send up a tray for you."

"I thank you. I'll confess I stopped only briefly at the inn at Harlan such was my haste."

Harlan was at least two days' ride away. I glanced up, but Cyprias shook his head almost imperceptibly before I could ask.

"Come along, then." Eudora picked up her skirts and ascended the stairs. "The heat is positively exhausting."

I waited until she was well out of earshot, then asked: "What is it? What has happened?"

Cyprias pressed his lips together in a grim line, his eyes following Aunt Eudora's progress into Orwynd. "Nothing that may be discussed at the moment." He offered me his arm. "Later," he promised. "I will tell you the whole of it later."

* * *

The afternoon passed with excruciating slowness, and I cursed heartily my aunt's slavish devotion to propriety. She insisted I demonstrate for Cyprias everything I had accomplished in the months since he last visited us so he might inform my father that she was doing her level best, and so I was made to play the harp very poorly, recite a poem in ancient Ultan, and show Cyprias my recent sketches. He nodded politely and assured my aunt that she had done a marvelous job with me, which she assured him was an arduous task indeed.

That evening we dined on duck trapped only that morning, the skin perfectly crisp and the flesh meltingly tender and glistening with fat, fresh greens studded with cherries and tangy goats cheese, tiny golden potatoes, and tender, young beans I'd helped Layn pick from the trellises.

"I'm sure our country fare is quite plain compared to what you are used to in the capital," my aunt said, as though it were bread and water we feasted on. "We are, as you know, quite dependent on our own gardens and livestock here."

"You've nothing to apologize for," Cyprias told her. "Truly, I've not enjoyed such a magnificent meal in a very long time."

I loved duck, and I should've been ravenous so late was the hour, but I found myself distractedly pushing my potatoes round and round my plate, glancing up at Cyprias every now and again, waiting and wondering. At last the pudding was served, and although I loved cooked cream and the fat raspberries and drizzle of honey that accompanied it, I pushed my plate away after only a few bites.

Finally, Cyprias laid his napkin gently beside his plate and rose. "I am quite unable to eat another morsel. Please pass my compliments to your excellent cook as always."

My aunt, ever the hostess, flushed with pride. "I shall indeed. Shall we take tea in the parlor? Or port, perhaps?"

I looked up at Cyprias with alarm. I was sure that if I had to wait one moment more, I would go mad.

"In a moment, perhaps," he said. "I'd like to take the air if it is agreeable to you. I've been too long in Iluviel and miss the scent of the woods."

Aunt Eudora waved her hand at him. "Bah. Off with you, then."

He bowed courteously, then left my aunt and me alone in the dining room to stare at each other across the flickering candles. I waited until the sound of Cyprias's footfalls grew faint, then stood.

"Forgive me, aunt," I said, "but I've a headache. I'll retire to my room."

Aunt Eudora raised her eyebrows. "A headache? Shall I ask Layn to make you a posset?"

"No," I said quickly. "Rest is all I require."

"Very well, then," she acquiesced, though she did not look particularly pleased about it. "Though I dare say you'll be sorry to miss Cyprias when he returns from his walk. The Gods know how long it will be before he visits us again."

"I'm sure he will understand," I said gravely.

Escape from my room was not difficult. I'd learned various stealthy ways in and out of Orwynd over the years and employed them regularly. The moon favored me that night. Hanging low in the sky, ripe and round, it cast its pale light on my path as I hurried toward the Morwood. I found him in our usual clearing, where the massive trunks of fallen trees served us as well as thrones to kings so happy we were to be in one another's company.

"We've not long," he said. "Your aunt will be expecting me."

I snorted. "No doubt she wishes to discuss the current state of fashion at court." As if such a thing affected us so far removed from the capital! I arranged myself on a fallen trunk and set my lantern beside me. "What news? Does the rebellion yet live? How many Mages have you and my father smuggled to Sidonia?"

Cyprias lowered himself upon the large, flat stone he had sat upon so many times over the years and hunched forward, his hands lightly clasped and hanging between his knees.

"It lives," he conceded. "But our numbers dwindle with each passing day. Our allies are being unmasked one by one, and Keric's retaliation against any who would oppose him is swift and merciless."

"But my father is safe, is he not? And my uncle?"

"As safe as may be. Keric has discovered Mages are being smuggled from our lands, but not by whom. At least, not yet. Time is now our enemy, Briony. None of us can hope to remain secret forever."

I swallowed the words like stones.

Three years before, Cyprias had finally revealed to me the reason for his many excursions north on behalf of my father: he had been forging an alliance with the young queen of Sidonia beyond the Sundering.

Queen Gwynliere had ascended to the throne at only fifteen years, upon the unexpected death of her father. By the ancient traditions of Sidonia, she was expected to yield her sovereignty at once to one of her male cousins. Her hopeful kin were met with quite the nasty surprise when she not only refused to abdicate her throne to a man, but had them slaughtered in their beds for good measure. Indeed, they had quite underestimated the ruthlessness cultivated in her by her adoring father since the moment she'd been born a girl.

Queen Gwynliere's mother had been a Mage, and while she abhorred King Keric's enslavement and slaughter of all magic-born, she refused to send her army on Tiralaen soil to war over it. But through Cyprias, my father *had* convinced her to harbor Mages fleeing persecution and death.

"Does the path to Sidonia remain clear?" My voice came out a whisper, though I did not mean it to be.

To secret away the Mages born in our country, my father had found allies in the priests and priestesses of the Old Gods. Horrified at the spilling of magical blood, they harbored Mages by day within the ancient passageways and hidden rooms of their temples through-out the countryside. By night, the Mages made the long march toward Sidonia.

Cyprias bowed his head. "Keric has openly accused Queen Gwynliere of conspiring with enemies in his midst at court. She denies any involvement, of course, but I do not know how long she will continue to aid us, even in secret."

"In his midst," I echoed. "Does Keric suspect my father?"

"He suspects everyone. For long years, it has been to our benefit that the king's suspicions follow neither reason nor evidence but are fanned this way and that by his temper alone, which your father is well accustomed to avoiding. But I fear he is closing in on the truth at last, in spite of himself. The time may soon come when your father need abandon his part in our rebellion if he hopes to keep his head."

I scrambled from my trunk, tripping over my skirts, and knelt at Cyprias's feet. "You must not let him be discovered! Tell him he must cease what he is doing at once!"

"Do you imagine I could stop him, Briony?" Cyprias answered fiercely. "He risks his life so that Mages may live and it is not a conviction he takes lightly."

"But what of his family? What of me?" I winced at how childish I sounded. How I wish I could've been braver for Cyprias, and for my father! But fear for him had taken hold of me and I could not shake it away.

Cyprias looked very much as though he wanted to say something, but then, evidently changing his mind, shook his head and gripped my hands. "I will do all I can to shield him. He and your uncle both. But I am afraid there is more."

"More," I repeated numbly.

"Do you remember the boy from Lower Gilding? The Blood Mage?"

Although ten years had passed, I could still recall his face with perfect clarity. "Of course."

"He is a boy no longer. And it is because of him that Keric sends Mages through the Gate no longer." Here he paused, as if the words were painful in their utterance. "When Mages are arrested, they are executed without exception. And their blood is collected by the Blood Mage for Gods know what end."

"It is blasphemy," I whispered. "Of the highest degree. I cannot believe he would do such a thing!"

"Keric no longer cares that he blasphemes, only that he remains in power."

"But he worships the Old Gods!"

Cyprias's face twisted. "Pretense, nothing more."

"We must tell the people! They would rise up—"

"The people? They worship the new god and despise magic. They would see no blasphemy here, only salvation."

"But the noble families keep to the old ways. If they were told…"

"If they were told, the king would know at once who his betrayer is. The few who know the truth are perfect in their loyalty to Keric, save your father."

I sat back on my heels, my mind racing furiously. "There must be some way to stay the executions."

"Not without risking Keric's paranoid eyes falling upon us. And if that happens, there will be no one left to help the Mages of this kingdom. I know you are loath to hear it, but we must bide our time."

"And how many people will perish while you and my father bide your time?"

"Far less than if we raced heroically to the gallows."

He was right; I knew he was right. But still my heart ached. "Let me come back with you. Let me help you and my father. I've learned so much—I could be of use to our cause, I'm sure of it!"

"Briony—"

"I could be a spy, like you," I pressed. "I'm short and skinny—I can fit into ever so many places. Perhaps I could hide and listen for information. Or I could smuggle messages! You could teach me whatever code it is you use. Oh, please let me help you!"

"Oh, Briony," Cyprias smiled ruefully. "You are many things, but I fear a spy is not one of them."

"And why is that?"

"Because you were never meant to live in the shadows. Indeed, I do not think you could if you tried."

"But I want to help!"

"I've no doubt you will," Cyprias answered.

I carried Cyprias's words with me all the way back through the library and up the staircase to my room. Below, I heard my aunt berate him for taking so lengthy a walk, and then the parlor door closed and I could hear no more. He would be gone before the rising of the sun, back into the viper's nest to protect my father and, in so doing, all those born with magical blood. And I would be left at Orwynd to traipse about the Morwood and read inappropriate literature and be a general disappointment to my aunt.

My aunt had once feared that when I reached my majority, I would steal a suit of clothes from our stablehand and strike out into the kingdom with a borrowed sword, determined to set things right, so fiercely did I love this land and hate its king. She was right to fear it.

It was the thought of my father that stayed my hand, and my mother and uncle and sister, but not because I feared their retribution; what I feared was retribution against *them* for my transgressions. I could not bear the thought of them coming to harm because of my foolishness. But I now feared it would not be long before inaction became unbearable.

In the end, I did not have to court danger; it sought me out instead.

7

Three weeks after Cyprias departed for the capital, I was sitting on a blanket in the shade of a golden plum tree, drowsing over a tedious book of poetry, when a single rider came into view on the road and, as he drew closer, I could see he wore the colors of House Tenebrae: an envoy of my father. I stood, the stupor of the afternoon sun and swimming words falling from me.

The doors of Orwynd opened, and my aunt appeared; someone within must've seen the rider's approach. She took up her skirts and hurried down to meet him. I'd never seen her move with such swiftness, and it alarmed me. There could be only one reason for my father to send a rider in such haste. Fear for my parents, for my uncle, for Cyprias took me in hand and held me fast.

The rider drew up to the front stair, but he did not dismount. Instead, he pulled a letter from the satchel at his side and handed it to my aunt with a swift nod before turning his horse back toward the road from whence he came. He did not spare me a glance as he thundered past.

"What is it?" I rushed to my aunt. "What has happened?"

She read the short missive first, her face white and pinched, then thrust the paper at me.

Briony,

I have fallen out of favor with the king and I fear our family is in grave peril. I am sending Geordan to you in haste. Be ready. Take very little. The road to safety will be long and difficult, but you are strong and courageous, and I know we shall meet again soon. Do not be afraid.

Your loving father

This last line was dashed off in a scrawl so untidy I could barely read it. My eyes met Aunt Eudora's, and I saw my own fear reflected in them.

I have fallen out of favor with the king.

I knew very well what he meant: Keric knew. My father's secret had been betrayed.

"Come. We must get you ready," she said briskly, taking me by the arm. Then she turned to Saren. "Fetch your boy to me. I have a job for him."

This job turned out to be climbing the tallest turret of Orwynd and scaling the wall to an old perch that generations of Tenebrae children had used as a lookout over the vast Morwood and the roads beyond. I myself had attempted the climb before the groundskeeper saw the flash of my skirt and betrayed me to my aunt. I had been confined to my room for two weeks after she recovered from the shock. Saren's boy was small and quick and had spent many an afternoon hiding from his mother and shirking his chores on the lookout. Aunt Eudora charged him to alert us immediately if he saw anyone on the road and sent him scurrying up the stairs.

While Layn put together a basket of food, Aunt Eudora and I filled a satchel with my things and I exchanged my muslin and shoes for more a more serviceable gown and boots. It took me several attempts to tie the laces; my hands would not stop shaking.

As Mora finished re-pinning my hair, we heard the shrill cry of Saren's boy. "Riders on the road, Mistress!" he shouted from the turret. "Five riders and a carriage farther on!"

"What is their sigil, boy?" Aunt Eudora shouted.

There was silence, and then: "A bird! A bird and a branch of thorns!"

The raven and thorn. The king's men.

"What's happening?" I demanded.

"They're here," Aunt Eudora whispered. "I feared this day would come." Her eyes were not on me but seemed very, very far away.

"What day?" I took both of her arms in my hands now, forcing her to face me. "Tell me what's happening!"

She never got the chance. The boom of a fist striking wood sounded from below.

"Eudora Tenebrae! Open this door in the name of the king!"

Mora cried out and clasped her hand over her mouth to stifle the sound.

Aunt Eudora grasped my arm. "You need to hide. Mora, unpack Briony's things and hang them back up. Then go down to Layne to unpack anything she has prepared."

"Wait—why?" I asked my aunt. "What's happening?"

She did not answer me, but kept a vice-like grip on my arm as she pulled me down the corridor to her own bedroom. She closed and bolted the door, then crossed to the center of the room, grasped the corner of the woven rug that lay there, and pulled it back to reveal a small door in the floor.

My aunt was certainly talented at keeping secrets; I'd had no idea the door had been there.

She pulled the hatch open and gestured to me. "Come—climb down. There is not much room—you'll have to hug your knees to your chest—but you should fit."

"Why?" I did not move. The bolt hole was dark, and fear had

made me unwilling to do as I was bidden. "Tell me why! What's happening?"

"Briony Tenebrae, for once in your life, do as you're told." My aunt's voice was tight and desperate, and it jolted me into compliance. Grasping her proffered hands, I lowered myself into the hole and made myself as small as possible while she replaced the door and rug. Hugging my knees to my chest, I closed my eyes and tried desperately to slow my ragged breathing. Above me, I could hear my aunt's footsteps as she left the room, and then silence.

In his letter, my father had said he'd fallen out of favor with the king, that our family was in danger. What could the king possibly want with me? I'd not been at court for ten years; surely I posed no threat to anyone. And what had my aunt meant when she said she'd feared this day? These thoughts and many more raced through my mind as I lay in the darkness.

Far below me, I could hear the muffled sound of voices; my aunt must've admitted the soldiers. No doubt she was telling them her story about my being in the Morwood. Evidently she was not believed, for a moment later I heard the sound of heavy boots ascending the staircase to the second-floor corridor.

I heard them searching the other rooms at the far end of the hall: my room and several guest rooms that had not been used since I'd arrived. And then they were on the threshold of my aunt's bedroom. I squeezed my eyes shut and tried to smother my breath in my hair, my gown. *Please*, I thought. *Please let them not find me!*

The footsteps stopped, and there was silence.

Light blinded my eyes as the hidden door was yanked open so hard it nearly came off of its hinges. Rough hands reached down and grasped my arms, hauling me from the bolt hole, and I came face to face with a snake of a man wearing the robes of a royal Mage. His long fingers were laced elegantly together, and he was smiling at me, a horrible smile full of malice, shrewd eyes gleaming.

"Oh, look," he said. "Here is Miss Tenebrae returned from the Morwood. Clearly your aunt is not as acquainted with your whereabouts as she believes."

The Mage swept from the room, his robes billowing behind him, and the two guards who held my arms followed, dragging me between them. Determined to make their job as difficult as possible, I squirmed and kicked and shouted at them to let me go, but this only made them grasp me tighter, so hard I gasped aloud from the pain. I stumbled at the bottom of the stairs, and they hauled me upright.

Four guards stood with my aunt and the entirety of her terrified household, save Saren's son, whom I doubted the guards had bothered to look for. With luck, he was still perched atop the tower well out of sight. They stood silently, their faces white, and I could tell Layn and Mora had been crying.

"I told you I would find her." The Mage addressed my aunt, who returned his oily smirk with steely resolve.

"She is an innocent," my aunt replied. "You have no right to take her."

The Mage sneered. "Her father is a traitor, as are her mother and uncle, and you as well. You have all conspired to conceal her true nature. The king has commanded she be brought before him. This gives me *every* right."

"I already told you, I didn't know," my aunt answered. "None of us knew what she was."

What I was? I looked to my aunt in confusion, but she refused to meet my eyes.

"Every breath you breathe is a lie," the Mage hissed, his face so close to my aunt's that I saw her flinch. "And you will pay dearly for it."

"Please," my aunt whispered. I had never heard her beg. "Please don't take her."

With a wave of the Mage's hand, the two guards marched me

through the great door of Orwynd to a carriage bearing the king's colors and crest. I was unceremoniously thrust inside, and the door slammed so hard behind me that the glass rattled in the window frame. I heard the unmistakable scraping sound of a key in a lock, and then the crunch of boots as my captors left me alone.

I pressed my face to the glass, desperate for a glimpse of Aunt Eudora, of the men and women who had cared for me for so many years, but the door to the manor did not open. My mouth ran dry with fear over what was happening inside.

A face appeared at the window, a snarling, ugly face that startled me back against the velvet seat. The guard yanked a wooden panel over the glass, blanketing the carriage in darkness.

A fist pounded twice on the roof, and then, with a sickening lurch, we began to move.

The last time I'd made the journey between the Citadel and Orwynd, I'd been a child, protected and comfortable in my privilege. Now, shrouded in darkness and fear, I sat bolt upright on the velvet-lined seat, my mind racing. At first, I was certain I was to be a hostage to force my father and Uncle Geordan from hiding. After all, I'd played no active role in any rebellion or espionage, exiled as I was at Orwynd. There was no criminal allegation that could be laid upon me directly, by my father's clear design and instruction.

But Cyprias had been visiting me twice a year, whispering secrets deep into the night of the Morwood: my father's secrets, and those of the King of Tiralaen.

Had Keric somehow discovered what I knew? Was I to be made to talk?

A surge of nausea churned in my stomach and panicked heat began to radiate from deep within me, racing to the surface of my skin. What if they'd captured Cyprias, tortured him? My father wrote that he was sending my uncle to me, not his spy. Even now, he might be hanging from chains in the dungeons of the Citadel, enduring unimaginable pain, unaware of the truths that slipped through his cracked and bloodied lips.

But even as I pictured it, the chains and darkness and screams, I did not believe it, because of one sentence echoing over and over again in my mind: *You have all conspired to conceal her true nature from us.*

My true nature, concealed from the crown by those closest to me, worth sending a Mage into the wild north to retrieve me.

I was no Mage!

Magical blood ran in my family, it was true, but long ago, and my power would've manifested when I was a child.

Surely I'd gone mad. And yet... and yet. A memory stirred in my mind from long ago: my limbs on fire, tangled in sheets soaked in sweat, and words; words spoken above me, strange words and gentle hands.

Could it possibly be true?

Oh Gods, I was going to be sick. I slammed my hand against the roof of the carriage. "Stop!" I shouted. "Stop, please!"

But they did not stop, and in the suffocating darkness of the carriage, I remembered what Keric did with Mages who refused to swear fealty and use their power in his name. With all of my strength, I screamed and struck the walls and roof and kicked the doors of the carriage until I exhausted myself and collapsed into a terrified, quivering heap on the seat, unable to stop the flood of hot tears that streamed down my face and wet my hair and the velvet beneath my clenched fists.

I knew full well what Keric did to Mages. If it was true, if magic dwelled within my blood however deep, what might he do to me? What might he do to the ones I loved?

We did stop, eventually, but only for fresh horses. The wooden panel over the window opened, then the window itself, and a bundle was thrown onto the seat beside me. A chunk of bread. I tore into it hungrily as the panel slid shut again. When I asked if we might stop so that I could use the privy, I was marched into a nearby wood and endured the humiliation of squatting near a cluster of bushes, while two of Keric's guards stood nearby. We returned to the carriage and I was thrust unceremoniously inside, where I curled onto the seat, hands cradled under my head, and stared into the darkness until exhaustion overtook me and sleep claimed me. Thus I passed several days in fear, hunger, and darkness.

At long last the dirt road beneath the horses' hooves gave way to stone, and inside my stifling prison I heard the unmistakable sounds of the city. The carriage door was wrenched open, and grasping hands pulled me into the light. After days in darkness, it was blinding, and I squeezed my eyes shut against the onslaught. Two guards brought me up roughly, and I found it was difficult to stand. I was so tired.

"Take her in," a gruff voice said. "He's waiting."

"Please," I croaked, my throat dry from lack of water and use. "What's happening?"

The man on my right, stinking of ale and horse, took pity on me. "You're being brought before the king."

"Do you know where my parents are?" I begged. "Please—Magnus Tenebrae. My father is Magnus Tenebrae."

But his charity extended no further. In silence, they brought me the hidden way, the disgraceful way, through tunnels not even the servants moved through. I was grateful; I'd never cared that my hem was dirty or my hair peppered with ephemera from the Morwood, but now the sweat and filth of five days' travel soaked into my gown and hair. I no doubt looked the criminal they thought me to be, and for perhaps the first time in my life, I felt shame at my appearance.

Gradually I began to recognize my surroundings and hot tears sprang to my eyes. Two years of my childhood had been spent roaming these corridors. My stomach churned, a forge hot with indignation and helpless rage and sorrow for what was lost. There were the stairs, spiraling up into the heavens, where I'd sought refuge in Master Aeneas's room of wonders and dreamed the innocent dreams of a child whose possibilities in life, though limited, were golden. There was the passageway that led to the smaller ballrooms where Mistress Precia had taught me the court dances, where she'd boxed my ears if my boundless energy drove me to unruly antics. Where Livia had scolded me, an eternal embarrassment to her, despite our fierce affection for one another.

Where was she now? Had the soldiers come for her, too? Was she protected by the laws of her husband's family, his king?

We were now in the long corridor that led to the throne room. Mageguard stood at attention, lining our path, though they seemed to pay no notice to us as we passed. Was it simply that I had not seen them in years, or did they look even crueler now, their armor sharper, their swords curved more wickedly? Two Mageguards opened the ancient wooden doors and I saw Keric lounging on his throne, a finger on his chin and one on his temple, watching us with glittering eyes. He'd been a handsome man once, tall and proud and well made, everything a young king ought to be if Livia's fairytales were to be believed. That man was gone now, and in his place was a creature of malice and hate, as abhorrent without as he was within.

He was not alone. The Mage who had ferreted me out at Orwynd stood on one side of the throne, and two other Mages stood slightly behind him. The robes of all three were black and threaded with silver and bore the raven and thorn sigil of Keric's house.

To Keric's other side stood men I recognized as once having sat on the same counsel as my father, as well as the king's handsome, fair-haired cousin. These were men who had laughed with my father, supped with him, stood with him in defense of the kingdom and all within it. Now they stared at me, his daughter, with eyes of stone, as if they'd never known him.

I was pushed roughly to my knees before the king, and he leaned forward to study me with what almost appeared to be amusement.

"Are you sure this is her, Valens?" He looked to the Mage who had discovered me, one perfectly groomed eyebrow raised in doubt. "She doesn't look like much." His nose wrinkled. "And she's filthy."

"This is she, your majesty," Valens confirmed. "I pulled her from a hole in the floor myself."

Keric leaned forward, drumming his fingers against his leg. "I suppose she does look vaguely familiar. The same red hair as her traitor father. Not as pretty as her bitch sister, though. Eyes too big for her face." He grinned. "Maybe I'll pluck them out."

There was a titter of laughter from the men on his counsel, and Keric slumped back in his throne, apparently satisfied that I was who he thought me to be.

"Your highness," I spoke, and it took all of the willpower I possessed to keep my tone even, not to launch myself at him and scream and claw at his wretched face. "My father—"

"Is a traitor!" Keric bellowed, and I shrunk back from his sudden rage. "And you a liar!"

"I'm no liar!" The words left my lips before I could stop them, and I instantly regretted it. Oh, why had I never learned to hold my tongue?

Keric rose slowly and, eyes full of fury and hatred, descended the dais until he was directly above me. I flinched as he reached out and ran a finger softly down my cheek. I stayed as still as stone, my heart pounding so loud I could hear the blood rushing through my ears. At my jaw, Keric paused his touch as soft as a lover's caress, and then with a snarl, he wrenched his hand into my hair and yanked my head down. Tears of pain and shock sprang to my eyes as my cheek met the cold marble with a sharp crack.

"How *dare* you speak to me thus," the king hissed into my ear. He leaned hard on the arm that held me down, pushing my cheek against the floor so fiercely I feared the bones beneath the fragile skin would break.

He held me there, my head throbbing, the room utterly still and silent, and then with one final excruciating press, he released me. A sob escaped me, and I lifted my head. Some of the men looked uncomfortable, but none spoke. Only Macon Eleutheris, the king's cousin, met my gaze, and only for the briefest moment.

Keric threw himself back into his throne. Color had risen in his cheeks, and his eyes still had a wild look to them. They flickered to his Mage. "Show me."

"Of course, your majesty," Valens replied, descending the steps to where I crouched.

"No!" I screamed, as the Mage reached out and grasped my arm, hauling me to my feet. I could not fathom what it was Keric wanted Valens to show him, but the side of my face, red and angry and aching, told me it could be nothing good. "Stop it! Leave me alone!"

He wrenched my arm, bringing me closer to him despite the fact that I had begun to struggle in earnest, and shoved the sleeve of my gown up beyond my elbow. Then he laid his hand on my bare skin.

I had expected pain, but instead felt warmth as light began to bloom under Valens's hand. It twisted itself into fine, glimmering tendrils that snaked slowly across my skin and the warmth turned to heat, a glowing ember that seemed to radiate from inside of me, the silvery evidence of it visible on my arm. I gasped; I could not help it. It was beautiful and terrible, fascinating and revolting, and the warmth in my blood began to grow into a fire, fanned by Valens's hand.

"You see, your majesty!" Valens declared, holding my glimmering arm aloft. "Magnus Tenebrae lied to you! His daughter's veins hold magical blood!"

"No," I begged, trying to pull my arm free from his painful grip. The heat was beginning to become unbearable. "I'm not—I don't—"

"I knew it," Keric whispered, a triumphant smile on his face. "I knew it!"

Valens released me at last, and I stumbled back, cradling my arm. My skin was hot to the touch and the glimmering tendrils remained, moving across the surface of my skin like liquid.

"How long have you known?" Keric had risen from his throne again. "How long did you and your wretched family conceal this from me!"

"I didn't know," I whispered desperately. "Please, you must believe me—I didn't know."

"She could be powerful, your majesty." Valens's voice was thoughtful, a warning. "Even though she *is* a woman."

"Yes, yes," Keric muttered, lost in thoughts only he could decipher. "If Magnus went to such great lengths to hide her, she must be powerful indeed." Then he looked up at me as though he were seeing me for the first time. "There is no question of what needs to be done. She must die. Today."

Valens bowed so low the voluminous sleeves of his robes touched the floor. "As your majesty commands."

I began to struggle with all the strength I possessed, thinking that if I could break free, I could dash into one of the hidden passageways I'd roamed as a child. Perhaps I could find Master Aeneas. If he was still here, if he was still alive, I knew he'd help me.

But it was not to be. Valens reached out a long, bony finger and no sooner than he'd touched my forehead than the world went black.

8

I woke in near darkness with a terrible headache. Gingerly, I probed the side of my face with my fingers and winced at the tenderness there. No doubt there would be a mess of bruises.

I was lying on my side on a slab of stone, and someone had thrown a threadbare blanket over me. I sat up slowly, taking care not to jostle my head, and looked at my surroundings. The cell was crudely carved from stone and contained only a stubby candle set into an alcove in the wall and some straw scattered upon the floor. Opposite me was a wall of iron bars, thick and rusted with age. The cell across the hall from my own was empty. In fact, I could hear nothing at all, save the dripping of water somewhere far away.

I rolled up the sleeve of my gown and held my arm into the weak candlelight. There was no evidence at all of the silvery markings, and the heat had entirely gone away. I might've thought it a dream if I'd woken in bed at Orwynd and not in a prison cell awaiting my death.

I was mulling over the possibility of Valens having created the marks simply to convince Keric to execute me when I heard a voice whispering my name. I looked up to see a hooded figure standing outside of my cell. Hands came up, the hood was lowered, and the face of my beloved friend, my father's spy, was revealed.

"Cyprias!"

Ignoring the pain in my head, I rushed to the bars, gripping them in my hands so tightly my knuckles turned white. Cyprias reached out and laid his hands over mine, squeezing them tightly.

"Thank the Gods you are here," I said, my voice a whisper in the echoing gloom. "Are you here to get me out? Where is my father? Where is my Uncle Geordan? Are they with you?"

Cyprias's eyes were sorrowful and he was quiet, far too quiet, for far too long.

"Keric says I'm a Mage. Is it true?" I demanded.

"Please, Briony, be still," he begged, and there was such desolation in his voice that I fell silent obediently. "There is much you must know, and I will tell you everything, but please, you must promise me: do not judge us harshly. Know we only meant to protect you."

"I don't understand—"

"Trust me," Cyprias bid. "Trust me, and listen."

I nodded.

Then he told me of the night King Gavreth died, how my father agreed to provide his younger son with guidance and counsel even as he suspected that the elder was not entirely as guilty as everyone assumed. How he'd fought to prevent his banishment through the Gate but was overruled by a boy-king who would hear no argument against his brother's guilt.

He told me how my father's suspicions grew with each passing day at court, how he'd recruited his wife's brother and his longtime friend to help him discover the truth, how they'd spent ten years chasing whispers and shadows, grasping at mist, and hoping, as the world began to burn and crumble around them, someone knew what had really happened that terrible night.

He told me how they'd finally found the man they sought in a land across the sea, Master Aeneas's one-time apprentice, who'd fled after the king's murder for fear that Keric would discover he knew the truth.

And he told me how their plans had crumbled to dust in a devastating instant when it became apparent they'd been betrayed. The apprentice was liar, a spy for the king, and knew nothing but betrayal.

Finally, he told me the truth of my childhood illness, which was not an illness at all, and how my father had tried to protect me in the face of growing fear and violence toward the magic-born. My parents had bid Master Aeneas to bind the magic in my blood and they'd concealed me in a crumbling manor deep in the Morwood, where I lived blissfully unaware of what lay within me and the danger I posed to all of us should Keric ever discover what they had done.

I listened in silence, tears streaming down my face, as the life I knew and the people who had shaped it, so beloved to me, twisted and warped with his words, becoming strangers.

So it was true, then. I was a Mage. I'd yearned for it once, as a child. Tucked away in Master Aeneas's tower amongst his tapestries and stained glass and golden instruments, I'd yearned for it, and for the freedom it brought, and now I would've ripped it out of my own skin if I could've, if it would save my father. If it would set me free.

"Why didn't they tell me?"

"Do not hate them, Briony," Cyprias said fiercely. "They knew their pursuit of the truth carried great danger and sought to protect you from it once your magic became apparent."

"No." I shook my head. "No. They should've told me. *You* should have told me." My voice was much harsher than I'd meant it to be, but I could not bring myself to care to spare his feelings. "I'm to be executed as a Mage anyway, and my father…"

I realized then that, wallowing in my own misery, I'd entirely forgotten that he'd not yet told me where my father was.

"My father. Where is he?"

"Briony…"

"Where!"

The silence hung heavily between us, and Cyprias finally said,

"The Gods willing, a better place than this one. He was executed yesterday."

I slid slowly down the bars until I was kneeling in the dirt and straw, the fight utterly gone out of me. "And my Uncle Geordan?"

"Gone," Cyprias replied. "I know not where."

I felt Cyprias's calloused fingers against my cheek, wiping my tears, and I lifted my head. Together we knelt in filth, in darkness, on opposite sides of iron bars. "Your mother is with your sister, across the sea. They are safe. For now, at least."

I was too overcome to feel relief or comfort in this news, though I knew it was the best that could be hoped for. I tried to call my father's face to my mind, but all the memories I had of him were those of a child, faded and rosy, like the afternoon sun through the stained glass panes of Orwynd, a half-remembered dream pieced together that was both truth and untruth, and if I tried too hard to see it, it vanished into nothingness, a trick of the light. It was his words that I clung to now, when he'd crouched before me in the dust of the stable yard and bid me to have courage. I was not sure that I could. My misery was suffocating.

"I know there is nothing I can say to ease this pain." My friend's voice sounded far away. "And there will be time enough to grieve, Gods be willing, but now is not that time. Now, we must focus on your survival."

"How? I am to be executed this very day. The guards could be back any moment, and you do not have the key to this cell."

"No, I don't," Cyprias conceded. "But there may yet be a way."

His eyes gleamed in the darkness, and hope bloomed within me, the hope that was born of trust. My father had trusted Cyprias, with his secrets and with his life. I would do no less.

"Tell me."

"We're going through the Gate to Asperfell. We're going to find Prince Elyan and bring him back."

I must confess my reaction was perhaps not what he expected. I let out a short, breathless laugh and shook my head. "You cannot go through the Gate with me. To do so, you'd have to be—"

"A Mage," Cyprias finished softly.

In the darkness of my cell, light bloomed beneath his skin, chasing away the shadows and filing me with wonder. Unbidden, my own skin began to glow and light spread to every corner of my cell.

"Did my father know?"

"Of course."

"But how were you able to keep it from the king?"

"Well, I *am* a spy. Between my aptitude and the grace of your father—"

"Your aptitude! What is it?"

"Can you not guess?" He tapped a finger gently against his temple. "My power is modest, and my skill is unrefined, but that your father—and you—have remained shielded from Keric so long is a testament to the formidable might of the Arts of Truth, even if there are many who find them quaint."

"A Dreamwalker," I said.

He nodded. "Just so."

A sudden thought struck me, almost too painful to voice but I had to know. "Did you have anything to do with the binding of my magic?"

"No." Cyprias gripped my hands fiercely. "I tried to dissuade him, but he could not be swayed. Briony, you must believe he thought he was keeping you safe until such a time as the binding could be undone safely, when…"

"When Keric was no longer king," I finished softly.

Cyprias nodded. "Which will only come to pass if we are successful. Now, listen carefully. Here is what you must do."

* * *

My role in Cyprias's plan was to do what I had no choice other than to do: stay in my cell, go willingly with the guards when they came for me, ascend the scaffolding in the courtyard when the time came. It was, I supposed, exactly what would have happened if he had not come to me at all.

And so, when the guards came to me, I met them with silence and obedience. They thrust a gray gown into my cell and I nearly wept: the color of the lost. It was strangely luxurious and entirely impractical. The bodice, which I had considerable difficulty fastening, was tight and far too low, and the skirt, made of layer upon layer of gauzy material, ballooned around me as though I were bound for a ball and not my death. I splashed my face with water, unpinned my hair, and combed the tangles out.

I was ready.

When the guards came for me once more, I was sitting primly on the stone slab, my hands folded neatly in my lap: the very picture of decorum in the face of certain death.

There were two of them, large and lumbering, and they would not—or could not—meet my eyes. They led me from my dank cell through a long corridor and, at last, to the light above. I emerged into a bright summer afternoon, sweltering and oppressive, the sun obscured by clouds but no less intense.

The last time I had been in the Mage Courtyard, I'd been eight years old and hungry, about to witness a prince's banishment and, unknowingly, the downfall of Tiralaen. There had been witnesses, then. A small crowd of the rich and influential, those amongst whom I had belonged until so very recently. This time, the courtyard was utterly empty, save for three dark figures on the scaffolding: my executioners. My heart began to hammer within my chest.

"There will be guards with me," I'd said to Cyprias, when he'd told me of his plan. "Guards and executioners. Will you be able to engage them all?

He had smiled at this. "Do you doubt me?"

"No! But you are a spy, not a soldier."

His eyes went dark. "There is much you do not know about me, Briony. But in this, you've no cause to worry. I will protect you. You have my word."

Three executioners and two guards. How on earth could Cyprias manage all five?

Three of the men on the scaffolding wore long black cloaks with hoods that concealed their features. They stood over a crude wooden block, the sort with a curved bowl for the necks of the condemned. The figure closest to the block held an axe, which glinted dully in the fading light.

Beheading. Not hanging.

Why did that make my heart hammer? My throat closed tightly like a fist, and I struggled to breathe. It shouldn't matter. I'd be rescued before the sentence was carried out. And yet, any courage I'd carried with me from Cyprias's vow dissipated at the sight of the blade meant to take my life.

A hand against my back shoved me and I stumbled, then righted myself. They led me to the base of the scaffolding, and I ascended the stairs alone, my eyes darting helplessly to the many archways and corridors that surrounded us. Cyprias would have to enter the courtyard through one of them, but I saw no sign of movement, heard nothing but my own footsteps.

One of the robed figures gestured to the block, and I stared down at it. Old, dried blood stained the wood where others had laid down the last of their burdens, and my gorge rose.

Gentle hands pushed at my shoulders, and I fell to my knees before the block. "Your hands on either side of it," a voice said from inside the hood. "Grip it tightly."

My hands clutched the rough-hewn wood, and I began to tremble in panic. It had all failed, Cyprias's plan, and I was about to die on this scaffold, clutching a blood-stained block, surrounded by strangers. *Will it hurt?* I prayed the executioner would strike true.

"Briony Tenebrae, Mage, daughter of the traitor to his majesty, you have been condemned to die," one of the men in the hoods behind me intoned, and his voice sounded strangely familiar. "May the Old Gods have mercy upon you."

This was it, then. My blood would mingle with those who had died before me and that would be the legacy of my short life. The wood felt smooth against my neck as I laid my head down, my hair cascading over the block. The executioner brushed the strands away from my neck, and I shivered.

I felt rather than saw the executioner take his place behind me, and I closed my eyes so that I would not see the instrument of my demise. My hands clutched the block.

The axe arched high into the air. *Father*, I thought, *I'm coming.*

And the axe swung away from me. Steel connected with the soft flesh of man, and one of the robed figures behind me cried out and crumpled onto the scaffolding.

The executioner pushed his hood back, and I looked up from the block in astonishment to see Cyprias. His face was fearsome; I had never seen it's like. My chest swelled and fierce joy surged through me. He reached beneath his robe and drew his hidden sword.

The third executioner had also thrown back his hood, and his hands began to move in a peculiar pattern, one I'd seen long ago but quite forgotten. I'd not seen him in ten years, and he'd grown far older and more feeble than I could've imagined—but I would've recognized his kind eyes anywhere.

It was Master Aeneas.

The air around us began to shimmer, and I felt the most peculiar sensation deep inside my skin, within my very blood. It was not entirely unpleasant, though I hardly had time to ponder it, for there was a sudden commotion at the foot of the scaffolding.

The two guards drew their blades and rushed up the steps, and I scrambled away from the block in time to see Cyprias fling out his hand toward them. Fire, bright, brilliant fire, erupted between him and the guards, engulfing them, and they were blown backwards by the force of it.

They staggered to their feet again, bellowing in pain, skin hideously blackened and bleeding, and my stomach heaved at the smell of burnt flesh. Cyprias charged forward with his sword, and within seconds, their cries of pain I were silenced.

"That was magic!" I exclaimed.

"Yes."

"Do it again!"

"Now is perhaps not the best of times." He gave me a brief smile, then turned to Master Aeneas. The ring of silver had expanded between his hands, and I could see the land beyond this one: a barren moor, a gray sky, and the towers of the great fortress of Asperfell.

For the first time since I'd read my father's letter, I felt hope rise within me. I could not yet fathom how we would achieve our impossible task, but it was with love and trust that I would journey beyond the Gate with these two men at my side.

"Just... a few moments more," Master Aeneas croaked. "The two of you must cross first. I'll follow."

Cyprias held out his hand, and I moved to take it.

The heavy sound of metal boots then filled the courtyard. Men in black armor were spilling in like a flood, their tunics bearing the sigil of the raven and thorn: Keric's Mageguard.

The hope that had blossomed within me was extinguished like a candle. The Gate was opening too slowly. The Mageguard was too powerful.

My dear friend's eyes met mine, and I saw a grim determination within their gray depths that I understood all at once.

"No—"

"It must be this way!"

"I can't go without you!"

Cyprias took my shoulders in both hands, his gaze fierce. "I am unimportant. It is Prince Elyan upon whom all of our lives depend. If he lives, he is at Asperfell, and you must bring him back!"

"How?" I shook my head wildly. "I can't!"

"You *can*," Cyprias said. "And you must—for all of us. It is the only way to bring down Keric!"

The first of the Mageguard charged up the steps, fire erupting from his outstretched arms like the wings of a giant bird. Cyprias turned from me and leapt toward the flames, meeting our enemy, halting their charge.

"Briony!" Master Aeneas shouted. "It's almost done! Be ready to cross!"

I had no weapon, knew no magic. There was nothing I could do to help Cyprias fight. But neither could I just leave him to die. I could only stand there, staring, as he hacked down the first of the Mageguard.

As if sensing my eyes upon him, Cyprias turned to me. He thrust out his hand and a force like a thrown hammer collided with my chest, tossing me backwards. Thus I fell sprawling through the Gate and landed on my hands and knees in the dirt on the other side.

I whirled around, and through the pulsing ring of light, I saw Cyprias's white face staring back at me. Behind him, Master Aeneas had fallen to his knees, blood spreading and staining his white robes, a black sword protruding through his stomach. Immediately, the Gate began to shrink away.

Cyprias raised his sword. "Find him! Bring him back!"

And then the Gate was only a pinprick of light, and I watched with desperate horror as it vanished entirely.

9

I sat on the hard ground in a heap of gray skirts and watched the place where the Gate had been only seconds before, as though at any moment I might see lines of silver split the air and reveal Cyprias's face beckoning me back. As the moments passed, my folly began to fade and I was left with growing despair. The Gate would not open again. No one was coming for me.

And I would not be going back.

I was alone in a world not my own, banished and tasked with the impossible; the weight of it all was staggering. As my grief and hopelessness swelled, a keening wail split the gray stillness around me, and I realized the sound had come from my own lips. I had never felt such pain; I had never imagined I could. Unseen hands held fast my heart and pressed until my chest was aflame and my cries became great, racking sobs that forced me to the ground where I buried my fingers in the harsh earth.

The urge to stay curled on the ground and close my eyes against the desolation and dread that threatened to consume me was powerful indeed, so powerful that I very nearly surrendered. It was the promise I'd made to my father the last time I'd seen him that was my mercy; I'd promised to be courageous, to never give up, and so I did not.

My palms flat against the ground, I drew a shuddering breath and pushed myself up onto my knees; it was one of the hardest things I had ever done. Then I squared my shoulders and turned to face my fate.

The fortress of Asperfell stood alone in a vast moor of nothing but scrub and stone, its many turrets and towers rising high into the gloom of the fading day. There appeared to be little order about it, with some spires decidedly circular in design and others made of sharp, square angles, placed here and there with little care for the overall aesthetic, as if they'd been afterthoughts. And perhaps they had been: the whims of Mages left to languish for five hundred years with wild imaginations and magic to equal them.

They gray stone of its walls had become weathered and worn with time, though it looked to be far better preserved than any ancient keep I'd seen in the Tiralaen countryside half as old. Magic, I supposed. Although splendor was not likely to have been a factor in its design, built as it was to hold Mages of the most dangerous nature, there was a terrible beauty to it nonetheless, a desolate grandeur. There were a great many more windows than I would've expected in a castle so old, their elegant, diamond-patterned lattices worn black with age, and the crenellations atop the turrets were finely carved. Ivy, though it may not have been ivy in this world beyond our own, climbed one tower with abandon.

It was, without doubt, the strangest, most fascinating thing I had ever seen.

Still, for all its melancholy beauty and the quiet strength of its walls, there was something deeply unsettling about Asperfell, a wrongness to it that slid across my skin and stole inside of me like a phantom.

I shivered and looked away, taking in the bleak landscape that surrounded the prison.

The moor was vast, the shrubs and plants that grew there were unfamiliar, and surrounding it all was a forest that was even more wild and savage than the Morwood, its trees ancient and towering, and such darkness within, rich and green and teeming with secrets. Between forest and prison stood an unbroken ring of statues taller than any I'd ever seen, at least twice the height of a man. They stood sentinel, some hundred yards or more between each one.

They looked to be knights clad in armor, and every single one was down on one knee with both hands grasping the pommel of an enormous sword. Their heads were bowed, but despite this I could tell they bore no features; their faces were smooth and revealed nothing. The helms they wore were similarly austere, with a simple pointed crest and cheek plates. I wondered: were they guarding the prison, or the forest?

I stood, wiping my throbbing hands clean of dirt and bits of gorse on the skirts of my gray gown, and approached the one nearest to me curiously.

The statue immediately sprang to life as though he were made of flesh and blood and not of stone. He rose to his impressive full height and, with surprising speed, swung his sword in an arc above his head, the blade crashing into the ground mere inches from where I stood.

In sheer terror, I stumbled backwards and landed in an undignified heap on my backside. The statue lifted its sword again, and I scrambled to my feet and ran. Looking over my shoulder, it was apparent that the statue no longer deemed me at risk of escaping into the trees. It lifted its sword and, moving slowly, returned to its original crouched position, both hands grasping the hilt of the sword, and bowed its head once more. Clearly the statues were there to keep those sentenced to Asperfell from escaping into the forest beyond.

It appeared I had two choices available to me: stay out on the moor in the growing darkness or present myself at the keep. Thunder had begun to rumble in the distance, and the clouds overhead had darkened menacingly. I cast a glance toward the forest beyond the statues. Even if I could get past the statues, there was no way of knowing what other terrors lay amongst the trees.

I gathered the voluminous skirts of my gray gown and began the long walk across the moor to Asperfell.

In the distance, thunder rumbled again, closer now, and the first drops of rain began to fall.

By the time I'd come close enough to the fortress to see within its many windows, I was thoroughly drenched. Through the dripping tangle of my hair, I looked up at the faces behind the panes of glass, dozens of them, staring down at me with slack jaws and wide eyes. It was then I remembered no Mage had crossed the Gate to Asperfell in nigh on three years.

The enormous, rough-hewn door of the keep opened with a deep groan, and a face peered out at me. It was not an attractive one: broad and bulbous with a nose that appeared to have broken several times. Eyes narrowed, the man looked me up and down.

"We saw you arrive," the man said gruffly. "Hurry up and get in."

I clamored up the stairs with some difficulty, given the sorry state of the stone and my sodden skirts. As I slipped through the narrow opening, he grunted and pulled the door shut behind me. We stood in a vestibule lit only by torches set in alcoves carved into the stone walls, a rustic cry from the glass spheres of the Citadel. A long corridor lay ahead, and though I could make out little of what lay beyond, the distant sound of voices filled me with dread.

"Welcome to Asperfell," the man grunted, and I could not tell if he meant this sincerely or as a means of mocking me.

I fixed my eyes upon the man's broad back as he led me down the corridor, which eventually opened into a cavernous courtyard surrounded on all sides by colonnades punctuated here and there by arched passageways and doors that led to where I knew not. The vaulting rose high into the heavens, and I had mere seconds to gape at the myriad of staircases and corridors that made absolutely no discernible structural sense before I was quite overcome by the clamor around me.

There were people everywhere, and I shrank away from their desperate eyes and voices. I stared at them quite unabashedly for they were nothing at all like I had imagined they would be after so many afternoons in Master Aeneas's tower letting my considerable imagination run wild.

Clanking chains and terrible moans and blades slick with blood; viciously barred yellow teeth; rags hanging from emancipated frames; the rising dead, clothed in billowing smoke; these were my imaginings. Here were no such horrors. Instead, these were robust, keen-eyed men and women who, although shabby, could easily be mistaken for the everyday denizens of Iluviel. Surely these could not be the most fearsome Mages in all of Tiralaen?

Their voices were raised in a high-pitched racket of impetuosity as they showered me with questions, and I nearly slammed my hands over my ears. How demanding they were, and so great in number!

"What news? What news from Tiralaen?"

"Does my manor still stand? Who lives there now?"

"My son! Have you seen my son? Does he yet live?"

"I can't," I stammered. "I don't—"

The man in front of me let out a dreadfully loud grunt and swatted at them with a burly arm. "Get back the lot of you! The Master and the Steward want to see her first!"

At the mention of this Master and his Steward, the crowd retreated slightly, and though their voices followed me through the colonnade, they surged not upon me again. Whomever I was about to meet must've been very powerful indeed to hold such sway. The man led me into the courtyard, and I gaped in awe as we reached a wooden door set within an archway beautifully carved with insects and other tiny creatures. I had little time to admire them before the man opened the door and gestured within.

I crossed the threshold into a large room with tall ceilings and rich wooden beams. The same alcoves I'd seen in the vestibule lined the walls, filled with merry flames that threw long shadows across the floor, where a worn rug that might've once been handsome lay on the uneven stones. There was little furniture to be seen: a long table upon which sat only a single candelabra, a stack of scrolls in varying states of decay tied with frayed ribbons, and a pair of high-backed chairs in front of a fireplace with a handsome stone mantle carved like the archway. In the flickering light of the fire, the tiny creatures seemed impossibly lifelike; perhaps in my wearied state I simply imagined it, but I could've sworn I saw the wings of a dragonfly flutter delicately and then lay still.

I longed to stand before the flames and let their warmth wash over me while I examined each and every wing and carapace, but my attention was instantly drawn to the woman standing before me, a woman as hard and unyielding as the prison itself.

She was very tall, and her brown hair, just beginning to gray, was parted down the middle, pulled back severely, and pinned at the nape of her neck. Her bony face was long, and her gown covered her from chin to toe. The puffs at the shoulders and tapered sleeves of her gown had long gone out of fashion, and I wondered how long she had been here. Around her waist she wore a large circlet of ancient keys.

"Welcome," she said, and her voice was every bit as steely as I imagined it would be. "My name is Philomena, and I am the Steward of Asperfell. This is Dagen." She gestured to the large man who had brought me in. He had moved from my side to hers and was watching me now with guarded interest.

"I'm Briony," I said, and my voice was very small. I cleared my throat. "Briony Tenebrae."

"I have summoned Master Tiberius," Philomena continued, as though I ought to know who that was. "He should be here shortly."

"She doesn't look dangerous, does she." Dagen was still studying me intently.

"Looks can be deceiving." Philomena gave me a wintry smile. "Pray, what was your crime, child, to earn banishment to such a place?"

The inside of the prison was no better for warmth than the soaked moors from whence I had just come, and I had begun to shiver with cold. My voice trembled as I answered her. "Nothing, truly."

Philomena raised one eyebrow and her smile grew sharp. "No one is sent to Asperfell for nothing. Come now—what have you done?"

"Master's here," Dagen mumbled to her suddenly, and I followed his gaze to the narrow passageway at the other side of the room. My eyes met those of a man with white hair and a close-trimmed beard, wearing robes of deepest blue. Unlike Philomena's sharp edges and frosty countenance or Dagen's blunt features and unnerving gaze, this man had pleasant, warm eyes that put me at ease for the first time since I'd fallen through the Gate.

"Well now," he said pleasantly, as he crossed the threshold into the courtyard. "We haven't had a new arrival in years."

"This one claims she has done nothing to merit the privilege." Philomena looked back at me.

"It's true," I told them. "I've committed no crime."

"What is your name, child?" Master Tiberius asked, and whether or not he thought me mad for this insistence, his tone was gentle.

"Briony Tenebrae," I replied. "Please, you must believe me. I've done nothing."

"Is that so? Then why are you here?"

I chose my words carefully. "I was sent by a Master of the Citadel to find Prince Elyan and return him back through the Gate. Is he still alive? Is he here?"

I heard Mistress Philomena snort derisively. Surely to her I sounded mad.

"He is," Master Tiberius said slowly. "Child, surely you must understand—"

My relief at discovering that the prince was still alive and within reach was palpable, and I could not help the exhausted sigh that escaped me. "Oh, thank the Gods. Please, I must see him. It is a matter of urgency."

Master Tiberius's expression was patient and thoughtful. "I will fetch him for you, I give you my word," he began. "But first, you must answer the same questions as every other person who has passed through the Gate. Tell me: what is your aptitude?"

If they had not thought me mad before, they certainly would now. My throat was dry, and I swallowed; the words stuck there stubbornly, and I struggled to free them. "I have none," I managed. Then, louder: "Or if I do, I know it not."

"That cannot be." Mistress Philomena frowned and glanced swiftly at the Master of Asperfell. "Surely she lies. A Mage of her age with no aptitude?"

Master Tiberius was frowning as well, though there was no menace in it. "What is your age, Mistress Briony?"

"Please, call me Briony. And I've twenty years."

"You see?" Mistress Philomena said. "Far too old to have never undergone her Trial."

"I do not know my aptitude," I told the Master of Asperfell. "I did not even know I was a Mage until today. I might never have known if the king's Mage had not laid hands on me."

"It's not possible." Mistress Philomena was staring at me as though I were something detestable and not to be trusted. "She is a liar—she must be."

"I'm no liar," I said, finding my voice at last. "I did not even suspect until I was arrested. And I did not know for certain until a man put hands on me and there were silver marks." I held up my arm, though the whorls that had marked me as a Mage had long since faded.

"I must speak with the prince. I need to explain—I was sent to find him."

Mistress Philomena turned her incredulous gaze on the Master of Asperfell. "You cannot believe this, surely."

Master Tiberius studied me with a quiet intensity, his white eyebrows drawn together. "You were bound," he said at last. "As a child."

"Yes. How did you know?"

"A vile practice, binding. And one that I had quite hoped was stamped out, but it seems not."

"They're not vile, my parents," I said softly. "They were trying to protect me."

"I would hear your story, child," Master Tiberius said. "But first, I will fetch Prince Elyan—I have a feeling he would hear it as well."

He disappeared back through the archway into the darkened passage beyond, and I was left with Philomena for company. I was cold and tired and hungry, and although Mistress Philomena seemed decidedly less hostile now that her suspicions about me appeared to be unfounded, she was still a harsh, unyielding presence in a harsh, cold room. The fire in the grate beckoned, but I did not dare cross the formidable Steward to reach it.

"Do you really know no magic at all?" she asked me suddenly.

"None."

"This place will not care, nor will the people in it," she answered, and for a moment I thought I saw her expression soften. "I fear you will not survive."

"Perhaps she is stronger than she looks," Dagan said quietly. I had forgotten him entirely. I turned grateful eyes upon him now.

"What are *your* aptitudes?" I asked.

"I'm an Animalis," Dagan answered.

Mistress Philomena said nothing.

There was the sound of footsteps in the arched passageway, and we all turned as one.

Master Tiberius had returned, and he was not alone. A tall figure followed him in the shadows of the passage, ducking through the archway. Though he was a man grown now, nearing thirty, I could still see the whisper of the boy he'd been all those years ago, a thin figure standing alone on a platform, all sharp angles and black curls, eyes full of anger. I had not forgotten those extraordinary eyes. They fixed me now with a fierce, slightly mad look, and I instinctively took a step back, and then another.

"Who are you?" he demanded, striding into the room. He had been tall as a youth; he positively towered over me now, and I had to tilt my head all the way back to look at him.

"Briony," I answered. "Briony Tenebrae."

"Tenebrae," he repeated. "I know that name." And then it came to him, and he pointed a finger at me. "Magnus. Magnus Tenebrae."

"He was my father," I replied, horrified to find that my father's name threatened to wring tears from me.

"Was?" The prince frowned. "He is dead, then?"

I swallowed, fighting against the onslaught. "Just yesterday."

Prince Elyan smiled grimly. "I'm glad to hear it. He lasted far longer than I had expected he would."

My immediate, visceral horror at his words must've shown on my face, for he added, "Do not mistake me, Briony Tenebrae. Magnus was a good man. I would not have expected my brother to allow him to live long."

The cruelty of his demeanor and his careless words emboldened me far more than I thought possible. "It is not your brother's fault, but yours," I spat. "He would never have sat on the throne if not for you."

Prince Elyan's eyes widened slightly at my outburst, then narrowed again. "And yet you are sinless, Tiberius tells me. How does a person who has committed no crime get sentenced to go through the Gate? If it is so, you must be extremely dangerous." His voice was deep and melodious, and, in another time and place, I might've thrilled to hear it. Now it filled me with nothing but disdain.

"I did nothing," I told him.

"Extremely dangerous it is, then." Prince Elyan's tone was icy. "Though you don't look like much. What sort of Mage are you?"

There was nothing for it. "I don't know."

"What do you mean you don't know?"

"I don't know what sort of Mage I am," I repeated, and heat suffused my cheeks. It was absurd to feel guilty when I'd only just discovered I had magical blood mere hours earlier, but there it was, and a sudden wave of anger at my parents engulfed me. If only they had not hidden it from me, if only they had not bound my magic, I might not have been here in this wretched place with this wretched man.

"Mistress Briony was until now unaware of her magic," Master Tiberius spoke at last, his voice a kindness after Prince Elyan's harsh barrage. "She was bound when she was a child."

This stunned the prince into silence, and he stared at me as though I were a thing not of this world. To him, a skilled Mage since his youth, perhaps I was. I straightened and jutted out my chin, a habit my mother had chastised me for endlessly, believing it made me look impertinent.

"Bound," Elyan said at last. "By whom?"

"Master Aeneas. At the Citadel."

Prince Elyan snorted. "That old fool. I'm amazed he knew how to do it so thoroughly."

"Master Aeneas was my friend."

"It was no friend who ordered you bound."

"My parents told him to do it," I answered. "Surely you do not mean to suggest they are my enemies as well?"

"Why?" Incredulity and derision warred in the prince's voice. "By the Gods, why would they ask him to bind you?"

"I expect they thought I would be safe if nobody knew the truth, what with your brother's crusade against magic."

The prince's lip curled with disdain. "Then they are fools, for they left you entirely unable to defend yourself. Perhaps you would not have ended up here if they would've taken better care."

I could suffer it no longer. I straightened and, instead of jutting my chin and showing my impertinence, I fixed my eyes on his. "How *dare* you insult them so! They put themselves in terrible danger to help you. And they paid dearly for it."

"Help me?" The prince looked well and truly surprised. "How?"

"By uncovering the truth," I replied. "That you weren't the one who killed your father."

The ghost of a wintry smile appeared on the prince's face. "Oh, is that the truth, now?"

This gave me pause. I had not known what to expect from a man who had been wrongfully imprisoned these twelve years. Cyprias had quite convinced me of his innocence, yet the man before me did nothing to convince me. A wary suspicion began to grow. Could Cyprias, could my *father* have been wrong?

"They believe it," I said at last. "As do many others. Whether you are deserving of it is yet to be determined."

Elyan's eyes narrowed, and as he opened his mouth to respond, Master Tiberius laid one hand on his arm, and one on mine. "Briony," he said. "I am certain you could use a cup of wine and a seat by the fire." He smiled. "And I think it's time for you to tell us your remarkable story from the start."

10

Master Tiberius had a work room in the southeast tower of Asperfell, though how he knew one tower from another in the confusion of stairs and corridors was quite beyond me. He held a bright flame aloft in his hand and I followed him through labyrinthine corridors of gray stone, Prince Elyan behind me. The air inside grew colder the farther we went, and I shivered in my impractical gown with its ridiculous skirts of tulle and wished for a cloak. On we marched until we reached a heavy wooden door that Master Tiberius opened with a wrought-iron key.

The room was dominated by a table, enormous in size and made of rough-hewn wood. Nearly every inch was covered. There were glass flagons and phials, most filled with liquids of varying colors, some filled with mist and smoke, and one filled with what looked like tiny pinpricks of light. A short crate held small jars with labels bearing spidery cursive that was so faded I could not make out what they held. Heavy books formed piles beside rolls of parchment, quills, and tiny stoppered bottles of ink. Plants overgrew chipped pots, their green vines, tendrils, and leaves spilling onto the table and beyond. Amid an odd assortment of crystals and stones, there were, I shuddered to see, what looked to be human bones.

The room was lit by an enormous fire at one end, where two moth-eaten velvet chairs stood, and it was there Master Tiberius led me. I sunk into the cushions, savoring the warmth from the blaze, while Prince Elyan lowered himself into the other chair and fixed me again with a disapproving stare. Master Tiberius plucked a dusty green bottle from among a shelf covered in cobwebs and placed it on a low table beside my chair, along with three musty goblets.

"Now, then," Master Tiberius said. "From the beginning, if you would."

For the briefest moment, I hesitated and thought of Cyprias, and of the many hours I'd spent in his counsel. He'd taken me for a wretched spy despite my longing to join his ranks, so enamored was I of the shadowy world he inhabited. I was too curious, too opinionated, too given to speaking when it suited me and not when it suited the intricate rules of the society into which I was born. I was, therefore, quite desperate to prove him wrong and not carelessly reveal all.

But I was utterly alone in this place, and were I to survive even the night I needed allies. Cyprias would've approved, I was certain.

And so I told them everything, uninterrupted, until I reached the far north, Queen Gwynliere, and the Mages that my father and Cyprias had smuggled into her protection.

"And how are you so deeply acquainted with all the intricacies of your father's plots?" Prince Elyan demanded. He'd been watching me with what could only be described as distrust if not outright disdain.

I lifted my chin proudly. "I purposed to join him."

"I had not hoped to hear an end to Keric's reign of terror," Master Tiberius said with a frown. "But it is far worse than I'd imagined. And what of the Mages the king apprehends? You are the first prisoner sent through the Gate in years. Perhaps you can enlighten us as to why."

I stared down at the red liquid in my glass, dust floating on the surface.

"He kills them," I said softly. "And takes their blood."

"How?" Elyan said sharply. "How does he take their blood?"

I was taken aback by the intensity of his expression, the demand in his voice. "A Blood Mage, I believe," I managed to answer. "There was a boy when I was just a child. He was taken to the Citadel and no one knows what became of him, but he was a Blood Mage. I think perhaps Keric is using him."

Elyan swore while Master Tiberius inhaled sharply, clutching his goblet with white fingers.

"If Keric no longer uses the Gate, how is it that you came to be with us, Mistress Briony?" Master Tiberius asked.

Elyan, long finished with his wine, listened to this part of my tale with the empty glass dangling from his long fingers, watching me. I am certain he was seeking for any loose threads in my story he could grasp and untangle, so evident was his distrust of my character. However, he held his tongue until near the end.

When I told them how my father had been betrayed, thus destroying any chance of the truth coming to light, Prince Elyan made a sound of disgust and reached for the bottle of wine. "Who else knew of this man whom Cyprias found, other than Magnus?"

"My uncle, Geordan," I said. "But he would never betray my father. Never."

Prince Elyan's laugh was low and mocking. "You would be surprised to find what family is capable of."

"Where is your Uncle Geordan now?" Master Tiberius asked.

"I don't know," I said. It was not the most convincing argument against my uncle's guilt. "He disappeared when they seized my father. Likely in hiding."

"And your mother?"

"In Cyr with my sister, Livia," I answered. "My father sent her away some weeks ago. I can only imagine he had some idea of the danger to come."

"So, of the three people in Tiralaen who know the truth and are yet living, two have disappeared, and the other is you." Elyan reclined back in the chair, his angry gaze fixed on the liquid in his glass. He took a long swallow. "And how exactly did they mean for you to help me? Even if you were the most powerful Mage in Tiralaen, nobody has ever escaped this place. Did your tutors teach you nothing?"

"Of course they did." I glared at him. "But surely—"

"Surely nothing. I've been trapped here for twelve years. Master Tiberius has been here near on forty. We are both Mages of considerable skill. If neither of us has managed it, or the many who came before us, rest assured it cannot be done."

I looked over at Master Tiberius, who said nothing. I'd thought him to be about sixty when I'd first seen him, but his eyes gave me pause. They were ancient eyes, and they gave nothing away. He was staring into the fire, lost in his thoughts. I had certainly given him much to think on.

"I don't know how I'm meant to help you," I conceded. "But surely I have to try, or they died for nothing."

"It is a noble cause," Master Tiberius said gently, looking from the fire to me. "But not one to be accomplished tonight."

"But I have questions—"

Master Tiberius held up his hands. "Questions I promise to answer, but not tonight. You look utterly exhausted and the hour grows late."

"I am tired," I admitted.

"Elyan will show you to your chamber," Master Tiberius said. I noticed he did not use Elyan's title but spoke to him as an equal. Perhaps in this place he was. "Tomorrow we shall speak further."

I followed Prince Elyan from Master Tiberius's workroom back the way we'd come. The number of prisoners in the courtyard had dwindled with the lateness of the hour, but there were a few here and there, waiting, it seemed, for me. They looked up hopefully when we entered, but upon seeing my escort, they fell back and cast their eyes downward in deference. I was grateful for it, for it gave me a chance to better see the extraordinary room.

From each of its four corners, grand staircases of worn, weathered stone rose into the four wings of the prison, and from the landing above that surrounded the courtyard, they branched off again and again in a dizzying array of columns and arches, exquisitely carved. Beyond them, so many passageways and spiral staircases ascended so far into the heavens that I could not possibly count them all.

The colonnade held several other doors similar to the one Dagan had taken me through when first I'd arrived, as well as corridors lined with alcoves of flame that led to I knew not where; no doubt I would discover it for myself if I were ever afforded the chance.

What fascinated me the most about the courtyard was the set of identical wide staircases at the north and south that descended to a pair of enormous doors fortified by metal filigree of extraordinary complexity, riddled, no doubt, with spells beyond my comprehension. Standing at attention before each door, their faces solemn and in shadow, were two Mages. What was it they guarded, I wondered, for surely that was their purpose.

"What's down there?" I called to Prince Elyan's back, growing farther and farther away the longer I stopped to linger.

He ignored me entirely.

I glared at his back, his increasingly lengthening strides making it difficult to keep up with him, and was on the verge of opening my mouth and saying something I likely would've regretted when I saw something so astonishing that I stopped, little noticing or caring that Prince Elyan continued on without me. Before the western wall of the courtyard was a stone dais upon which grew a single tree unlike any tree I'd ever seen.

The bark was smooth and black as night, and it bore no leaves at all, only gnarled branches that curled into the air like smoke as they rose from its twisted trunk into a glorious canopy, grotesque and beautiful in equal measure. Rather than soil below, the roots of the tree disappeared into fine, white sand.

"How extraordinary!" I breathed. "What sort of a tree is this?"

"A black oak," he answered me curtly. "The symbol of Asperfell."

"Does it ever grow leaves?" I had seen plenty of oaks, filberts, and willows on the grounds of Orwynd with branches as twisted, but they'd only ever shown their shape during the winter months when all their leaves were shed.

"No," he said, then abruptly turned and walked away.

I had to run to keep apace of his long strides. "Might we slow down?" I asked his back irritably. "There's so much to see!"

"And you've your whole life to see it," he answered without looking back.

We climbed an enormous staircase at the northwest corner of the courtyard and then up several sets of crumbling spiral stairs to a quiet corridor with a large cathedral window at the end. The prince used a large rusted key to open a door, then pressed it into my palm as he ducked through the doorway. I imagined with his height he was used to doing so in a castle so old.

Light bloomed in the prince's hand and he held a flame aloft to light the chamber. The room was a comfortable size, and I was pleased to see that it had a window. There was a trunk at the foot of a bed with a moldering canopy that I feared would crush me in my sleep, and the bedding was a once-rich gold that was woefully faded. I wondered if anything had taken up residence in its moth-ridden folds. Everything was so old and decaying I felt as though I'd stepped back in time a hundred years or more.

The prince leaned against the doorframe, flame in hand, and I felt his disapproving eyes on my back as I walked gingerly into the room. Someone had left a plate covered with a cloth on the trunk at the foot of the bed. I lifted it to find a wedge of cheese, a portion of dark brown bread, and a chunk of apple.

"A palace it is not," said Elyan. "I believe the last resident was a lady of some infamy. Killed all three of her husbands. It's not been occupied for some time and your arrival took us quite by surprise, but the menders should be able to help you with the linens tomorrow. I bid you goodnight, Mistress Briony."

I turned, confused. "Wait—I don't understand. This is a bedroom, not a cell."

"Perceptive, aren't you?"

"Where are the locks? The bars?" I held up the key he'd given me. "This is a prison. Surely we can't all come and go as we please."

"Not all of us, no," Elyan agreed, a mocking smile tugging at the corners of his mouth. "We only lock up the dangerous ones."

"And you aren't a dangerous one?"

"Verily I am," he agreed. "Which is why you can sleep soundly. No harm will come to you, for there are none here who would much desire to cross me."

He turned to leave.

Bitter, gnawing cold had been seeping into my bones since we'd left Master Tiberius's workroom, and now, standing in the bleak room that was to be my mine for the rest of my life, I found that I was unable to control the shaking in my limbs. My teeth clenched, and I moved toward the fireplace opposite the bed.

I had experience lighting my own fires—there were mornings at Orwynd when our small staff could not get to my room to light them before I was awake, and rather than shiver, I taught myself how to stack kindling and strike the long matches and coax the small flame into a roaring fire. I searched around the dirty hearth, but I could find no matches.

Or wood, for that matter.

"Your highness!" I called after him. I realized abruptly as he turned and raised an eyebrow at me that it was the first time I'd addressed him thus. I flushed. "Where can I find wood?"

He frowned at me. "Wood? Whatever for?"

I gestured with one hand to the empty grate. "I'm freezing. I want to light a fire."

"Why would you need wood to light a fire?" Then, as realization dawned, his expression became incredulous. "By the Gods," he muttered. "You cannot conjure Magefire."

I bristled as he swept back into the room, eyebrows drawn together in obvious frustration at me. He thrust his hand out toward my empty grate. At once a merry little blaze erupted, and I felt its heat drench me like the summer sun.

"Amazing," I breathed, as the warmth suffused my cheeks.

"Yes," Elyan agreed. "It is amazing. A Mage who cannot do even the simplest magic."

I glared at him, but he ignored me and stalked to the door. "It'll burn forever," he called over his shoulder. "Just don't put your hand in it."

"I'm not going to put my hand in it!" I shouted after him, but he shut the door behind him and I was left alone.

I sank to the floor and tore ravenously into the modest supper left for me until every last crumb was gone. The cheese was sharp and salty, the bread warm and soft, and the apple burst with sweetness across my tongue. I'd supped with royalty and nobility, eaten course upon course of the richest, most succulent dishes teeming with butter, swimming in sauces, and dusted with spices from the farthest exotic lands, and yet none of it had ever tasted as good as this simplest of fare, so hard-won after days that had seemed destined to break me.

The excitement of the past few hours had, it seemed, held the most fragile and untried of my emotions at bay. No longer. The courage and desperation and anger that had sustained me throughout my ordeal slunk back into the dark corners where they waited to be of use once more, and I was left with fear, and with sorrow.

I'd spoken with bravado in the courtyard upon my arrival, and again in Master Tiberius's workroom, but in truth, Elyan's pessimism, born of fact and of experience, had quite humbled me. Doubt began to seep into the marrow of my bones, a gnawing, persistent invader, troublesome and obstructive and entirely unwelcome. It would not do to assume failure before I had even begun. This, and the thought of Prince Elyan's arrogance and unkindness, bolstered me enough to wage a furious campaign against my own weakness.

I dragged myself up off of the floor, wincing at the sudden pain in my limbs, and stumbled over to the bed. A plain cotton nightgown had been folded and placed near the pillows, and I shook it out, fearing the worst. It was simple and plain, but quite serviceable.

The covers smelled of mold, but I found nothing lurking inside of them, and so, once dressed, I fell onto the mattress and pulled the covers over me, coughing at the cloud of dust that rose up as I did so. Cocooned in filth, staring at the light from the fire dancing on the stone walls, my eyes grew heavy and closed.

The pounding of someone's fist against the door of my room woke me the next morning.

I had burrowed into my dirty covers like a mouse in a nest of scraps, the warmth from the Magefire sufficient but not enough to entirely chase away the ache deep in my limbs. As I freed my head from the tangle of sheets and my own hair, I remembered exactly where I was.

I was a prisoner in the great fortress of Asperfell, beyond the Gate. The grief and despair I felt in that moment were so strong that I very nearly pulled the covers back over my head and sobbed with abandon.

Unfortunately, whoever it was at my door refused to be ignored and the pounding continued, louder than before. "Yes?" I called out hoarsely. "Hello?"

A gruff voice answered: "Food."

I contemplated not opening the door and staying safely ensconced inside my tiny, dirty haven, but the twisting in my stomach reminded me that my meal the night before had been scant, nor had I eaten well for days before it. The broad, scarred face of Dagan the Animalis met me as I pulled the door open, and he abruptly shoved an earthenware bowl into my hands. I looked down at the congealed beige mass at the bottom of the bowl and forced a smile I hoped did not resemble a grimace. Wordlessly, Dagan handed me a scratched spoon with a bent handle.

"Thank you."

He grunted in response and turned to leave.

"Wait—" I reached out and touched his sleeve. "Do you know where I can find water? Soap?" I glanced behind me at what I highly suspected were droppings from some creature or another in the corner of my room. "A broom?"

He stared at me as though I had just asked him for diamonds, silks, and the finest wines. My cheeks burned as I realized that, like Prince Elyan, he expected me to be able to conjure water or banish dirt. The enormity of what it would be like to live out the rest of my days in this place without at least a basic grasp of magic was staggering, and I suddenly felt very small and very, very alone.

Without bothering to answer, Dagan left me standing in my doorway, clutching my bowl of gruel.

I was pleasantly surprised to find it far more than tolerable, and I savored it standing next to my window. Below was the most enormous garden I had ever seen, and I supposed it would have to be, to feed all of Asperfell. It was orderly and precise, nothing at all like the wild tangle of Orwynd's small plot, with sections separated by low stone walls and sturdy fences. Rows and rows of trellises, surely fortified by magic, hung heavy with the weight of their summer burden, and two women in drab gowns and kerchiefs on their heads moved around them plucking vegetables and placing them in large woven baskets. Other Mages, men and women both, knelt between rows, plucking weeds and slicing through thick stems and stalks with small curved knives. A short distance away, men in shirtsleeves held their hands out over the soil, and I watched in fascination as the earth gently turned over and over, revealing stones which they levitated away as if they were mere feathers.

Near the garden was a small orchard, and though I saw no ladders, a large crate stood full to bursting with ripe red apples; another extraordinary act of magic, I suspected.

Beyond all of this, the tombstones of a vast graveyard jutted like crooked, rotten teeth in the dim light of the morning; a single plot such as might be found in the Tiralaen countryside behind a church could never have held them they were so many. Where the back wall of the cemetery might have been, instead lurked the massive, hulking forms of the Sentinels. The porridge I'd eaten hardened in my stomach, and I turned away.

Unsure what to do with the empty bowl, I opened the door of my chamber, and a broom fell inside; evidently it had been left for me there. On the floor at my feet lay a bowl of water covered with a cloth. I looked up and down the corridors, hoping to see who had left me these gifts, but I saw no one. I carried the broom and water into my room, leaving my empty porridge bowl in their place.

I took in after the dust at once, collecting three piles of dirt, dead leaves, and hair that I pitched out of the grimy window. Then I took after the bedsheets, holding them up and beating them with the broom. It would have to do until I could wash them. Hoping perhaps to find an extra blanket, I opened the heavy lid of the trunk at the foot of the bed. There were no blankets, but I did find three gowns that must've belonged to the previous occupant: a simple, serviceable muslin, a deep teal taffeta, and the other a wine-red velvet. To my chagrin, they were terribly fragile and so desperately out of fashion that they must've been a hundred years old or more and I could not hope to wear them without the help of a seamstress.

Beneath their delicate folds, there was a small mirror and a chipped comb, and a painting of a snub-faced dog wearing a ruff. I took the mirror and comb from the trunk, but left the gowns, smoothing them over the odd portrait.

I cleaned myself as best I could with the water and cloth, donned once more my gray gown, and was brushing my hair with the comb when there was a knock on my door.

"It's Philomena," said a crisp voice, and I abandoned my tangled hair.

She gave me a frosty gaze as she looked me up and down, and I lifted a hand to my hair, wondering if I should've finished it after all.

"Come with me," she said. "You've a long day ahead of you."

//

Mistress Philomena's strides were brisk and purposeful, like her manner, and, quite unlike Prince Elyan, she seemed to take great pleasure in pointing out for me that which she believed I should know about the place that was now my home. By the wan light of the morning, I could better see the ancient gray stone that surrounded me, and I marveled at the unexpected beauty of the gently curving archways and the windows—oh, the windows! They were indeed made up of smaller panes in a charming diamond pattern, though I could discern nothing of what bound them.

"There are two hundred and thirteen prisoners who reside within Asperfell's walls," Mistress Philomena told me as we walked. "But there are no staff. We do the work ourselves, even the most highborn among us. It is our burden and our survival."

I had difficulty imagining Prince Elyan pulling turnips in the garden or cleaning the latrine.

"We do try to assign work that closely aligns with aptitude of the Mage in question, but as you have none..." Mistress Philomena turned and faced me. "Surely you possess other skills that may be put to use here."

"I can read and write in three languages," I offered. "And I can draw reasonably well."

Mistress Philomena dismissed this with a wave of her hand. "I mean any *useful* skills!"

My embroidery was abominable, but I could darn, provided she did not expect the stitches to be even. Back at Orwynd, I'd created more chaos in the kitchen than Layn could handle and was often banished. But I was good with plants and herblore, and I told her this.

"The garden it is, then, I suppose." She seemed resigned and I had the distinct feeling she thought me quite a disappointment. Then she turned abruptly, and I pulled a face at her retreating back before I gathered my skirts and hurried after her.

"This is the courtyard," Mistress Philomena told me as we descended the grand staircase. "You'll have seen it last night, of course, but it is quite different by daylight. All four wings of Asperfell are accessible from here, as well as the floors below, though I hope you'll never have cause to set foot down in that cursed place. The southwest tower has sustained heavy damage and should be avoided as well."

I heard this last bit as though from very far away, so captivated was I by what lay before me.

Excitement had risen in me since we'd left my chamber, and my desire to see Asperfell in the daylight had become quite insatiable. Now, I drank it all in and let it wash over me, the realization of a childhood wonder, even though the Briony of then would've been sorely disappointed at how perfectly ordinary it all seemed. Asperfell's prisoners walked to and fro, alone, in pairs, in groups, nary a chain or manacle in sight, and they laughed and conversed together as though they were attending court at the Citadel and not wasting away in isolation.

A group of finely dressed ladies sat on a circle of stone benches beside the dais of the black oak, with yards of cloth spread out on their laps and pooling on the floor around them. While they talked in high, bright voices, they moved their hands nimbly over the bleached fabric, though I saw no needles and thread. They reminded me much of Queen Alenda's chamber ladies, though they were older, closer to an age with my mother.

"What are they doing?"

"Mending. Lady Orial manages all those adept at the craft. As you can imagine, with cloth nigh on five hundred years old, it requires particular care and skill to maintain it."

"And him?" I pointed to a rakish, dark-haired man in a leather apron carrying a bowl of what looked to be sand. He noticed my attention and gave me an ungentlemanly wink.

"Quite a few windows have been damaged by Gnashers," Mistress Philomena replied. "Layth is constantly busy restoring them."

"Ah," I said. Then, "What are Gnashers?"

Gnashers, as it turned out, were rodent-like creatures native to this world who delighted in gouging holes in the windows with their horns until they were able to wriggle inside and plunder the kitchens' storerooms.

"They are, unfortunately, immune to the influence of our Animalises," Mistress Philomena said. "If you happen upon one in your chamber, toss it in your Magefire—that usually does the trick."

By daylight, I could better see the two sets of descending staircases at the north and south ends of the courtyard. Just as with so many of the doors in Asperfell's courtyard, these also boasted archways of stone, beautifully carved. But unlike the others, which were decorated with plants and other living things, these bore images of unimaginable pain and suffering: human bodies in chains, contorted and writhing, their eyes bulging and their mouths slack in silent screams.

Standing before each door was a Mage holding a fearsome blade, and I started in shock at seeing Asperfell's prisoners so armed.

Mistress Philomena followed my wide-eyed gaze. "Those are the lower levels. Where prisoners who are a danger to others are kept. We are grateful for the bravery of the men and women whose job it is to see that they never set foot in the light."

"So, these are the dangerous ones of which Prince Elyan spoke last night!"

"You seem the curious sort," Mistress Philomena tutted. "I would advise against any curiosity of the lower levels."

Which is exactly what she should not have said to me had she actually expected me to avoid them.

As we passed the north staircase, the heavy door that led below groaned open just enough for a man to slip through, a man with close-cropped golden hair and bright blue eyes, before closing again with a boom that reverberated throughout the courtyard. He paused to speak to the Mage standing at attention there, then ascended the stairs into the courtyard two at a time. I watched as he strode to the colonnade and disappeared.

"That is Thaniel," she answered my unspoken question. "If there is a warden of Asperfell, it is certainly he."

I gaped after him. "Did he volunteer for his post? Or did his aptitude make his appointment a necessity despite his inclinations?"

"He volunteered," she answered shortly.

She did not speak to me again as we crossed the courtyard and traversed a series of twisted passageways leading downward. At the end of an impossibly long corridor lay a door that opened into the cavernous kitchens of Asperfell. At one end of the room was the most enormous hearth I had ever seen, and over it five fine black cauldrons bubbled with I knew not what. A girl only a few years older than myself was stirring one pot while several other men and women chopped vegetables and herbs at a massive, rough wooden table. From a room beyond, I could hear a low-pitched female voice barking orders and the clanging of pots and pans, the hissing of steam.

"Junta runs the kitchens," Mistress Philomena told me. "Willow there is her primary assistant, absent minded girl that she is."

I glanced over at the girl holding the wooden ladle as she yelped and promptly dropped it.

"Idiot girl," Mistress Philomena snorted. "There are nigh on thirty Mages who toil away here in the kitchens."

"So many!"

Mistress Philomena's eyebrows rose. "We are many mouths to feed, Mistress Briony."

I shot Willow a sympathetic look as we passed, and she blushed and turned back to the pot she was stirring.

We left the kitchens and stepped down into a darkened room that I realized right away was a vegetable storeroom. Ropes of garlic hung from hooks along with bunches of herbs drying upside down. There were untold bins overflowing with turnips and potatoes and carrots, sacks of grain and oats and flour, and bottles of spices. The room was massive and stacked from floor to ceiling, and from where I stood, I could see several doors that likely led to even more rooms filled with provisions. But where on earth had it all come from? I did not remember seeing fields of grains when I'd looked out my window that morning. I desperately wanted to ask Mistress Philomena, but she was already leading me up a set of unsteady wooden steps to another door.

The door opened up into the garden and I shaded my eyes as we emerged into the sunlight. Two prisoners were working nearby, and they both looked up when Mistress Philomena led me out. One was a hulking man with a bulbous nose and dark, beady eyes. He was holding a crude hoe crusted with soil and lifted it onto his shoulder, watching us closely as we neared. The other was a woman who looked to be near thirty. Her long hair was a plain, unfortunate shade of brown, but she was wry and strong, and her face was kind. She smiled at us and straightened from where she knelt among the rows.

"This is Briony Tenebrae," Mistress Philomena said. "She has no magical skills whatsoever but is evidently good with plants. Please see that she makes herself useful."

She departed without another word, leaving me standing near a bush of rosemary.

"Hello, Briony." The woman came forward and grasped my hand with both of hers. "My name is Yralis, and this is Grenn."

Grenn said nothing and immediately went back to tilling the ground. He was strong; *very* strong. His blows split the earth like a knife through warm butter. I wondered what sort of a Mage he was.

"Battlemage." Yralis must've noticed me staring. "He has a black thumb, I'm afraid, but he's very strong, as you can see."

"What sort of Mage are you?" I was not sure if this was appropriate to ask, but I could not help myself; the curiosity was overwhelming.

"I'm an Elemental, like Mistress Philomena." She grinned. "Although I'm water, and she's earth and stone."

"Can you command the water, then?"

"Yes, of course," she said, as though it should've been obvious. "I speak to the water that is already in the soil, tell it what to do to help the plants."

As I watched, she rested her hand at the base of one of the plants— a beet by the look of the root rising above the soil—and instantly droplets of water rose to the surface of the soil, came together to form rivulets that trickled up and over her hand, cutting through the dirt there to reveal clean flesh below. I gasped in awe, and Yralis turned her head with a smile.

I longed to ask her what it was that she had done to end up here in this place, but I couldn't bring myself to do it. It was easy to forget as I watched Yralis tend the plants with tender hands that she might be capable of cruelty or violence.

As I could not call water, nor did I have the strength of the silent, burly Grenn, Yralis put me to work pulling weeds and snipping the flowers off the ends of thyme, basil, and oregano plants. After she finished with the beets, she called me to help her sow rows of potatoes.

"I don't understand," I told her, as I pushed dirt atop the potato cuttings. "How came you by the seeds for all of this? And where did the grain in the storeroom come from?"

The original seeds for every vegetable and fruit in the garden and every tree in the orchard had come with the builders of Asperfell, Yralis told me as we worked. They had been carefully planted and harvested, their seeds multiplied by Mages, until the gardens could produce food for a thousand prisoners or more at need. There were no wheat fields; the bags of oats and grains in the storeroom were replicates of the bags brought by the original settlers. They were heirloom varieties that didn't even exist anymore in the world on the other side of the Gate, Yralis said. There were also a paddock and small barn that housed a great flock of chickens, several goats, and two mournful-looking cows who stared at me with limpid eyes, all of whom were what Yralis called Renovas: animals reborn from their original incarnations again and again and again throughout the centuries. Natural reproduction did not occur among the animals, as they were all female.

No wonder the cows looked rather dour.

In all the afternoons I'd sat in Master Aeneas's tower reading about Asperfell, I'd never imagined how the people there must've survived for so many years cut off entirely from our world. Without magic, it would simply not have been possible.

Some distance from the vegetable garden was a smaller plot that Yralis told me was the Healer's garden, which, naturally, I insisted upon seeing. Oh, but Layn would've swooned at the sight of it! I recognized a few of the things that grew in neatly ordered rows: borage, pennyroyal, mandrake, juniper, fennel, garlic, and even tall stalks of purple foxglove blooms. And here and there were also plants I did not recognize, not even from the books Layn had kept in the stillroom at Orwynd.

"I have some training in herblore," I told Yralis as I leaned over to inhale the heady fragrance of lemon balm. "Our cook at Orwynd taught me, but our garden was not as fine as this, and I don't recognize all of the plants."

"Oh, some are native to this land," Yralis told me. "This is called Lydus after the Mage who first discovered its medicinal purposes." She caressed the sharp, purple leaves of a vicious-looking bush. "And this one is Solbery," she said of clusters of bright orange berries hanging low on pale green vines. "I'm rubbish with what they all mean, though. The healers might be able to tell you that, if you truly wish to know."

As I inspected the Solbery plant, a sudden thought struck me. "If you've discovered plants in this world that can heal, what about food? Is anything on the moor edible?"

"A few," she answered. "And mostly tubers. They're all right, I suppose, though I don't much care for the texture."

Mistress Philomena returned for me when the sun was high in the sky and I was well and truly filthy. She looked with disdain at my dirt-covered hands, likely knowing that I would not be able to banish it magically without aid, and snorted.

"Come with me," she said. "The Master wants to see you."

"Wait," I said helplessly, holding up my hands.

A wave of her hand, and the dirt fell from mine.

"We shall have to see about a pair of gloves for you, I think," Yralis said, and she gave me a smile in farewell as I tromped unhappily after Mistress Philomena.

Master Tiberius looked up from the book he'd been writing in and smiled at my entrance. "Mistress Briony. You survived your first night."

By the Old Gods, I loved this room, and felt so very much at home within it. Although it was nothing to the golden splendor of Master Aeneas's tower and there was no stained glass to be seen, it was warm and welcoming and full to bursting with the most fascinating things. It would be all too easy to linger for hours inspecting the contents of each shelf and cabinet that lined the walls, and the thought cheered me somewhat. "Please call me Briony. And yes, I survived. But I imagine I would've been rather cold were it not for Prince Elyan. I couldn't even light my own fire."

Master Tiberius chuckled, closing his book and setting it beside him. "I believe his highness did mention something about you asking for wood."

"His highness," I muttered under my breath. "Yes, he does believe himself very high."

Master Tiberius regarded me with a merry, conspiratorial gaze and I pressed my lips into a thin line. It would hardly do for me to openly criticize Prince Elyan, and only one day after I'd arrived.

"Please," I said. "If I am to live out my life here, I must at least be able to light my own fires and conjure my own water."

"If you are to live out your life here, you will need quite a bit more than the ability to keep your chamber warm." Master Tiberius's tone was kind, but I understood the gravity of his words well enough.

I would need to defend myself.

"You require a teacher," he said, putting voice to my thoughts, and relief surged within me until he spoke again: "I will speak to his highness about tutoring you a few hours each day."

"No!" The word came out more forcefully than I meant it to, and I cringed. "I mean, is there anyone else? I would hate to inconvenience his highness."

Master Tiberius gave me an odd look at that. "My dear, this is a prison, not a university."

"Please," I pressed, "could you not teach me?"

"I've taught very few students, let alone one so… inexperienced."

"But surely the concept is the same."

"Elyan is a highly skilled Mage, and young enough to remember far more from his years as a student than I," Master Tiberius answered, folding his hands together in front of him. "He can be ill-tempered at times, but I assure you there is no one better."

"He does not care for me," I said miserably. "And I believe he would consider it an impertinence."

Master Tiberius laughed. "Elyan finds a great many things an impertinence. But I believe you may be right."

"Please," I said again, sensing a chink in his armor. "Won't you teach me?"

He stroked his beard thoughtfully. "I suppose I could tutor you a bit each day, provided you are willing to work hard. You have the advantage of age, which means your body will likely tire less easily from the strain of magic than if you were a child, but it is by no means an easy thing."

"I'll work hard," I promised.

He sighed, and when he smiled at me, I knew I'd won him over. "All right, all right! I will teach you as best I am able."

"Oh, thank you!" I sat down on the bench beside him, my grin so wide my cheeks ached. "I meant it—you will never know a more dedicated pupil than I."

"We will begin tomorrow," he said. "After you've fulfilled your chores for Mistress Philomena. She can become terribly cantankerous if any of us neglect our duties."

To save Philomena the trouble of coming back to fetch me, he offered to walk me back to my little room. I was grateful, for I had questions that had been clamoring in my mind since I'd arrived, and I took the opportunity to ask them as we traversed the dimly lit, winding passageways of Asperfell.

"I was ill when I was a child. My parents sent for Master Aeneas, and I suppose that might've been when he bound me."

"I would imagine it must've been."

"But why was I ill? Does it happen to all Mages?"

"It does happen from time to time. Usually because the Mage in question is older than usual when his or her power manifests." Confusion must've shown on my face, for he went on: "We are born with magic in our blood, and in most cases, when we reach an age in which we are strong enough physically to begin wielding it, the magic manifests in some way or another. Sometimes, as in your case, there is a delay, and the magic grows until it can no longer be contained. An unfortunate anomaly, I'm afraid."

"Master Tiberius," I said. "You've known Elyan—that is, the prince, since he arrived, have you not?"

He nodded. "I have. Certainly the most famous internee at Asperfell. In my time, anyway."

"Do you believe him guilty? My father is—*was*—assured of his innocence, but his behavior, the things he says, his manners…"

"When he first arrived, Prince Elyan was only a boy on the cusp of manhood," Master Tiberius answered thoughtfully, and I could tell he was choosing his words very carefully, though out of care for my sensibilities or the prince's reputation, I did not know. "He was bitter, vengeful, and entirely certain of his own guilt. It took me nigh on a year to pry the truth from him."

"The truth?" My heart raced.

"It is a funny thing, the truth, is it not? Twist it and bend it and it still retains some semblance of its former self, though it may deceive and mislead. The truth is, Elyan believes he is guilty, though whether he is, whether he *truly* is, cannot be so easily determined."

Master Tiberius paused beneath one of Asperfell's many windows and together we looked down at the moor and the Sentinels far in the distance.

"Did he mean to kill his father?" he said. "No, I do not believe it. But kill him he did. And the guilt has altered him irrevocably."

I thought of the austere young man with his dark curls and extra-ordinary eyes standing tall on the scaffolding, and then of the man he had become: cruel and thoughtless and cynical.

"Would he make a good king?" I asked.

"What makes a good king?" Master Tiberius said with a gentle shrug. "He has been molded since birth to possess all of the trappings of the glory of his blood. He is intelligent and cunning and courageous, and when he wants to be, charming enough to sway men's hearts. But does this a good king make, or merely an efficient one?"

These were all traits that Elyan's father, Gavreth, had possessed, and he was thought to be one of the greatest kings Tiralaen had ever known. But it was more than that. Gavreth had been fair and generous, equitable and kind. His people and his lands had prospered, and certainly, I thought, some of it was to do with his royal lineage and the privileges bestowed on him therefore. But not all of it could be learned; it was a part of the man himself.

I asked Master Tiberius: "Is Elyan a good man?"

"I expect you will come to know him in time," he told me by way of an answer. "As I am sure you have ascertained, he is very hard to figure out when he wants to be. But he has been my friend these twelve years, and a steadfast one. And my friendship is not given lightly. It is earned."

It was not the answer I was hoping to hear, but it did give me much to think on. And at that moment, I hoped very much that I, like Prince Elyan, would earn the regard of the Master of Asperfell.

Mistress Philomena was waiting for me at the bottom of the staircase leading to my chamber, her mouth pressed into a hard line.

"Best to go with her," Master Tiberius warned with a grin. "I was not exaggerating when I said she can be quite cantankerous."

I dipped an awkward curtsey, unsure which rules of my former life were still to be followed at Asperfell and which had been forgotten entirely. Master Tiberius smiled, waving a hand at me before he turned and ambled away.

"Will he be teaching you magic, then?" she asked, looking down at me through shrewd eyes.

"Yes," I said. "Yes, he will."

"Good. I don't know how long I can be bothered to walk you to and fro all over this place as though I have nothing better to do."

She turned and, without another word, marched up the staircase, leaving me struck utterly dumb until I gathered my skirts and hurried after.

12

There was a translucent figure hovering just outside of my chamber door. Human-shaped, a man perhaps, though I could make out no details. He might've worn a ragged cloak, or it might've been a trick of the milky light filtering through his ephemeral substance from the window at the end of the corridor. Certainly, dark stains stood out against the pearly white of his torso. At the sight of it, I stopped abruptly.

"What is that?" I gasped.

Mistress Philomena shook off my hand; I had clutched her sleeve tightly in my shaking fingers. "It's only an umbra. Don't tell me you've never seen one of them."

The figure turned at our voices, and I had the horrible sensation of being plunged into cold water as the black, fathomless holes where I supposed his eyes were to bore into mine. At the ghastly sight, a memory stirred in my mind of eyes very much like them in a graveyard long ago.

"What are they?"

"Dead Mages." Mistress Philomena's tone was brisk and matter of fact. "Or the shade of their magic, as it were. When we die, our magic does not. It turns into them. Most fade away to the land beyond, but there are others who stay because they can't find rest for some sad reason or another. They may linger a day, or a thousand years, but never forever. They all disappear eventually."

"Can anyone see them?"

"Only magic-born."

So that was why Aunt Eudora had been so adamant to silence me about the woman in the graveyard all those years ago! This was both terrifying and deliciously fascinating and I longed to know more, but Philomena did not seem interested in discussing it further. Instead, she turned to what she likely believed was a much more pressing matter.

"You're filthy. You'll be needing a bath after all that work in the muck."

I feared she meant to dump a bucket of water on me and call it sufficient, but she led me instead to a room in which several large copper basins of varying sizes stood, all filled with water. I'd never seen such a room. In the Citadel, our suite had its own washroom with a single tub, though we did not all share the same water; it was drained and refilled by Elemental Mages, heated to absolute perfection, and perfumed with all manner of oils and salts. At Orwynd we'd had no magic, and so the basin was brought to my room whenever I wished to bathe, and the water heated in cauldrons over a fire.

Philomena placed her palm against the side of the largest basin, and within a few seconds, tendrils of steam began to rise from the surface.

"You'll want to wash quickly," she informed me, as she scooped a handful of soap shavings from a barrel and pressed them into my hand. "I'll put a basic locking charm on the door, but others will be wanting the water, and they won't wait to barge in if you take too long."

My voice rose to a squeak: "You mean, someone might come in?"

The withering look that Mistress Philomena gave me indicated the answer was obvious. "We share washrooms, even the highest born among us. Asperfell is no place for delicate sensibilities."

Then she promptly left me standing beside the steaming basin of water. I wondered how much time I had.

I shed my filthy gray dress quickly and debated using one of the other basins to wash it, but I had brought nothing else to wear, and so I set it on a nearby chair with a grimace. Sliding into the water, I found it wonderfully warm and I nearly sobbed aloud with the sheer joy of it. Heeding Mistress Philomena's warning, I washed myself quickly with the soap shavings, dismayed as the water turned from clear to murky brown. I tipped my head back and awkwardly scrubbed my long, unruly curls as best I could. I was squeezing the excess water out of the ends when I heard the latch of the door rattle.

"I'll only be a moment!" I shouted.

Still dripping, I rose and reached for my gown. It was a struggle to pull the fabric onto my wet skin, but I managed it.

I opened the door to a short, thick woman who more closely resembled a toad than a person. Her hair may have once been brown, but the little of it that I could see beneath a dirty blue cap was streaked with gray. "I hate to interrupt yer highness at yer bath," she mocked, then turned her bulbous head and spit squarely on the ground. "But you've been in long enough, missy!"

"I'm sorry," I said, and I clutched my gown to my chest, awkwardly inching my way along the wall until I was clear of the doorway. "I didn't think I took very long—"

"Ages!" the woman declared, and it appeared she was missing several of her teeth. "I take my bath at sundown sharp, without fail. You'd do best to remember that. You ain't in Tiralaen anymore."

"Of course I know that," I bristled, clutching the bodice of my gown tight.

"Oh, aye, have we a lady, then?" The woman threw back her head and cackled. "Listen to that accent!"

She proceeded to gleefully mock me for several excruciating seconds while I stood dripping on the stone floors, and fearing the magic I knew she possessed, I was forced to endure it. I fixed my gaze on the uneven stone behind her head until she grew tired of me and moved into the washroom. I sighed and, clutching my bodice, padded back to my room.

The umbra with the ghastly stains was still standing outside my door, and for a moment I considered finding a hidden corner to sleep in rather than risk coming anywhere near it. But I was desperately cold, and so I steeled myself and approached.

The umbra did not move as I approached with furtive, careful steps until I drew close enough to lay my hand against the handle of my door. I breathed a sigh of relief. "There, now. That wasn't so hard."

The umbra turned, and despite the fact that he had no gaze to speak of, I sensed that he was looking right at me. My courage failed me, and I opened my chamber door quickly and slid inside, grateful for the wall between the ghastly figure and myself. I did not know if he stayed through the night, but he was gone in the morning.

My next days at Asperfell passed in much the same fashion. I rose with the dawn to a bowl of porridge left outside my door and pinned my hair up as best I could before Mistress Philomena arrived to walk me to the gardens.

I stayed by Yralis's side and learned what was planted and where, and how to care for the fruits and vegetables that fed Asperfell's residents. On any given day, there were a dozen Mages or more moving about the rows of vegetables and trellises.

I also spent a great deal of time in the herb garden caring for the plants and learning all I could about those foreign to me. The Healer who ran the stillroom was an eager and kindly teacher. She was of an age with Master Tiberius, perhaps older, and she wore her white hair in a neat plait down her back. When first we met under the watchful and no doubt disapproving eye of Mistress Philomena, she'd examined me thoroughly before she found my knowledge sufficient and my intent pure enough to be allowed to tend the garden, and supplied me with several books written over the years detailing the garden's contents and the medicinal purpose of each plant, along with detailed instructions for the brewing of cures and tinctures and potions. Many required the aptitude of a Healer or an Alchemist, so they were quite wasted on me, but I thoroughly enjoyed the learning of them regardless.

As for Mistress Philomena herself, there was little doubt she despised having to lead me about to and fro. I tried asking her to draw me a map so she did not have to go through the trouble of escorting me, but she scoffed at the idea. I suspected it was not merely my sense of direction that she feared would fail me. There was some danger here that her presence could allay and mine could not.

We always took the long route from my chamber to the storeroom, through a maze of passages, and encountered almost no one save a few umbras. They unnerved me but, true to Mistress Philomena's word, they were not harmful—simply a nuisance one learned to ignore, in so far as I could ignore the shades of dead Mages. What no one could understand was why they sought me out.

On my third night at Asperfell, I settled into the warm water to wash off the filth from the day and saw one sitting on the edge of the copper tub. I yelped, sloshing water all over the floor as I lunged backwards. This one was unmistakably female, with very, very long hair that curled like smoke and looked as though it were dripping. She had the same dreadful black hollows where her eyes ought to be, just like the others, and I thought I saw the small shapes of her hands folded in her lap.

I watched her warily, waiting for some sign as to her intentions, but after several long moments in which she simply sat, her fathomless gaze fixed on me, I decided she was no more harmful than the rest. I finished the rest of my bath under that gaze, and despite the warmth of the water, I could not help shivering.

The umbra with the bloody stains had taken up permanent residence outside of my chamber door. Sometimes he patrolled the corridor in a steady, footless march, and sometimes he simply stood at attention, but he was always there. I had to admit I found it somewhat reassuring.

Although Mistress Philomena told me that he could neither hear nor understand me, I had taken to speaking to him when I left my chamber in the morning and returned in the evening. The first time, it had been a simple hello followed by my name.

The second time another hello and a request for *his* name. The dark hollows of his eyes bore into mine, but if he answered my question, I could not understand him.

Every afternoon after toiling away in the dirt, Mistress Philomena walked me to Master Tiberius's chamber where I tried and failed to learn magic.

There were, regrettably, no books I could read on the theories and fundamentals of spellcasting in the library of Asperfell. Most of the books had been written by prisoners over the years, prisoners who already knew how to do enough magic to wield it against others. The books in the library that did traffic in magic were far too advanced for someone such as me to comprehend, let alone use.

Most of what was written in the copious scrolls, manuscripts, and tomes bound in what I highly suspected was *not* leather was, in fact, quite mundane: records, diagrams, and memoirs of the many Mages who had resided in the prison over the last five hundred years. Evidently there had been a number of self-proclaimed writers, and as a result there were several novels and books of poetry. All of these were available to anyone who wanted to read them, which I did alone in my bedchamber. This was the only recreation I was allowed in those early days; knowing no magic, I had been repeatedly cautioned not to walk the grounds alone, and no one came to escort me anywhere but to my duties and my lessons.

Master Tiberius kept a ledger that detailed which prisoner took what and when it was owed back, which I supposed was for his own benefit because the books were spelled to return to the workroom when the reader's time with them had run out. The biographies and histories varied in their fascination depending on who had authored them and when, and some of the poetry was quite good. My favorite was a book of love verses by an unknown hand, penned some hundred years before. It evoked tears that left me thoroughly wrung out and spent, my heart both sore and hopeful.

It was the job of five of Asperfell's oldest Mages to restore and preserve these accounts, a great feat given the age and fragility of the parchment and ink, as well as of the Mages themselves. By the light of Magefire, they copied and transcribed and translated and maintained the history of Asperfell and those within its walls. Occasionally, a finely dressed man with silver hair and sharp, hawk-like features popped in now and again, and from what I could discern, he did little more than stand about looking important and give the elderly Mages instructions that, from what I could tell, they ignored the moment he departed.

Master Tiberius furnished me with parchment and quill, and I took diligent notes as he attempted to explain the essence of magic, what it was, what it could do. The last I understood well enough, but I was even more confused by the nature of magic at the end of his lecture than I was before we began.

"But what *is* it?" I asked helplessly.

He blinked and looked slightly taken aback, as though no one had ever asked him this before. Perhaps no one had. "Why, it's power, my dear. It's energy. It's a living thing that surrounds us all, but only we—Mages, that is—can feel it, can command it. Bend it to our will."

"Why?"

"Because it exists within us," he explained. "In our very blood."

I found this terribly confusing. "So, because it is inside of us, we can feel it… elsewhere?"

"Yes. No." He scratched his beard and sighed. "I did warn you that I've not taught students in many, many years. Magic finds its like in us, in Mages. And that is why we can command it, because it will respond to us."

"Like asking a question of it?"

"A bit," he said thoughtfully. "But you do not ask, you command. Your intent, and the strength of that intent, are what bends the magic to your will."

The very first task he set me to was to light a candle.

He placed it before me near the end of the lesson, my head swimming with instructions that had seemed so clear while he explained them and now jumbled together such that I could not pull them apart.

I sat in front of the little candle, my hands flat on the table on either side of it, and willed it to light. But no matter how hard I tried, I simply could not do it. Master Tiberius suggested I imagine it as an unspoken conversation with an invisible participant, and so I did, stating my desire, then commanding, then begging. And still the wick remained pristine. The hours passed, and Master Tiberius left me to my one-sided colloquy, sweating from the effort, my eyes beginning to tear, until Mistress Philomena came to collect me.

Master Tiberius smiled kindly as I collected my parchment, quills, and ink bottles and assured me that it sometimes took time, but I remembered all too well the children at the Citadel rushing in and out of their lessons with Master Aeneas and how, at so tender an age, they were able to perform spells far more complicated than lighting a fire.

On the second day, when I was still unable to call flame to wick, Master Tiberius frowned and wondered if the fact that I had been bound had any bearing at all on my complete inability to produce magic whatsoever. He took my arm, passing his hand over the flesh and bringing the tendrils of light once more to the surface of my skin,

a testament to the fact that there was magic inside me, magic I could
not control or command.

I did not think I could possibly feel lower until the third day of
my lessons when I looked up from my still-unlit candle to see Prince
Elyan in the doorway of Master Tiberius's workroom. I had not seen
him since my first night at Asperfell, and that suited me just fine.
Just the thought of his haughty, disapproving expression when he'd
discovered I could not do magic made me hot with shame and anger.
The idea of him bearing witness to my failure was excruciating.

"And how is your young pupil today?" He folded his arms and
leaned his tall frame against the doorway. "Already conjuring shields,
are we?"

"Oh yes," I said through gritted teeth, as I stared so hard at the
candlewick I thought my eyes would burst. *Light!* I begged. *Please, light!*

Master Tiberius came to my rescue. "I believe Briony's troubles
may stem from her binding. We cannot know how extensive was the
spellwork without speaking to the Mage in question."

"Aeneas was a fool," Prince Elyan snorted. "I cannot imagine the
spellwork would be very strong."

"Do not speak ill of him." Frustration at my inability to light the
candle exacerbated my irritation at the prince's rudeness. "He was my
friend."

"Still a fool," Elyan said. "The only thing keeping you from lighting
that candle is you."

I glared venomously at him. "I am *not* keeping myself from lighting
it. I'm trying as hard as I can to command it."

"You're not commanding, you're asking." I could feel him behind
me, looming. "Do not ask. Magic is a slippery thing and will evade you
if it can."

"I don't understand." I tore my gaze away from the irksome candle
and looked over my shoulder. "How?"

"Magic is within your blood, and because it resides in you,

wherever else it resides in the world, you can exert power over it," Elyan replied, echoing what Master Tiberius had said during my first lesson. His gaze flickered from me to the candle and within that split second, the wick burst into flame. "When I give it a command, I am exerting my power over it; I am exerting my will. My will must be stronger than the magic or it will resist me."

He blinked, and the flame went out. A curl of smoke rose from the blackened wick, and I watched it rise to the ceiling and bloom into tendrils against the arched stone.

"Because the same power flows through your veins, you have power over it, if you are strong enough; if your *will* is strong enough. If your command is weak—if *you* are weak, it will resist you."

I balled my hands into fists on the worktable and stared at the candle once more. *Light,* I willed it. Nothing happened.

"You doubt yourself. You must be certain." Elyan swooped down, and I gasped in shock as he grabbed my hands in his and pushed them flat against the wood once more. He splayed his hands atop mine, holding me fast, though I jabbed my shoulders into his chest. "And do not *clench*, Briony! It is not anger, it is control. Now, try again."

"I don't know *how!*" I fairly shouted at him. I tried to pull my hands free, but his were much larger and he kept them pinned. He was too warm, too close, and frustration rose within me like a wave.

"You doubt yourself because you've been left to believe your whole life that you have no magic, but you do. You know you do." He was speaking very quickly, his deep voice somewhere near my ear. "You've seen the marks—the light. You've felt the pain. That you're here is testament enough. Now, command it."

The desperation and despair swelled in me and I felt a heat surge beneath my skin that I had felt only once before: as a child of ten, writhing in the dark, with the soft words of magic spoken above me. The memory caused a surge of panic and I struggled in his grip, but he held me and did not let go.

The heat spread to the very tips of my fingers and then began to ebb, leaving behind a feeling of fullness, and a warm tingling that was not unpleasant, only unfamiliar. My hands flattened fully under Elyan's as my gaze fell once more on the candle before me. It was as if I could see exactly what I wanted the magic to do, to *be*. I had only to command it.

Light.

The wick flared to life, a merry beacon of validity at long last, and I let out a shuddering breath.

Master Tiberius gave a joyful shout, clapping his hands together, and Elyan's hands squeezed mine. Then he lifted them away and stepped back while I stared into the tiny, dancing flame. The warm tingling was beginning to dissipate, and I felt a profound sense of pride and relief.

"I did it!"

"Yes, you lit a candle flame. A monumental achievement." Elyan's sardonic tone was back, but it was softened with amusement.

"Excellent, excellent!" Master Tiberius extinguished the candle with a wave. "Now, light it again."

This took several attempts though, thankfully, it was nowhere near as difficult—or as physically trying—as lighting the candle in the first place. This time, when I felt the heaviness of the magic within me, I did not panic but embraced it, a glowing ember at the heart of me, a gentle warmth and welcome friend.

And thus, my first successful lesson passed. I must've lit the candle flame thirty times before Mistress Philomena came for me, each time quicker than the last. I was still laughably slow for a Mage grown, but I grew quicker each time, and for that I felt a sense of accomplishment.

By the end of my lesson I felt as though I'd been thoroughly wrung out. Master Tiberius handed me a foul-smelling concoction in a goblet. I took an experimental swallow and nearly spat it back out again all over the worktable. "Oh, that is *vile!*"

"It certainly is," Master Tiberius said with a chuckle. "But in these early weeks it will help revive you until your strength grows. And we will keep to simple spells until then."

I sighed, then pinched my nose and drank down the revolting liquid. While I gagged and spluttered, Master Tiberius busied himself with a pile of scrolls. "What is your aptitude, if I may ask? Not Hearth Mage, to be certain," I said, wincing at the lingering taste on my tongue.

Since my first night at Asperfell when I'd asked Mistress Philomena what her aptitude was and was rewarded by silence and eyes of stone, I had avoided asking the same question of my fellow prisoners. I was desperate to know, of course, but I understood so little of the rules that governed this new world I'd been thrust into and I did not know if my curiosity would be welcome or tedious.

"It is nothing so rare as Elyan's gift, I'm afraid. I am a perfectly ordinary Elemental. Fire, as it were."

He lifted one hand and Magefire blossomed in his palm; simple magic, really, until the merry little flame began to dissipate into hundreds, then thousands of little flames that rose up from his hand and flew about the room, whirling and spinning, forming patterns, dancing. I could not help gasping delightedly. As they winked out, one by one, I turned to look at Master Tiberius in wonder.

"Not ordinary," I breathed. "Not ordinary at all."

13

Prince Elyan had spoken of magic as a living thing, capable of obeying or disobeying commands, and to my dismay, I found this to be entirely true. Extinguishing the candle flame turned out to be far more of a challenge than lighting it.

"You've given the magic an outlet," Master Tiberius explained kindly from across the worktable. "And once given, it is very difficult to take it back. Magic longs to be put to use. You are commanding it to cease doing the very thing it wants to do."

By the end of the afternoon, I could make the flame flicker slightly, and by the end of the next, I'd managed to put it out completely. For the briefest of moments, I wished Elyan were there if only so I could see his insufferable face fall ever so slightly when I managed it.

Every now and again he darkened the doorway of Master Tiberius's workroom while I was practicing. Although the frustration and anger that flared up within me could at times lend me focus, resulting in success, I was always left flustered and ill-humored afterward.

"He teaches the way he was taught," Master Tiberius told me one afternoon, after Prince Elyan had stalked off. "After his Trial, he was under the care of some of the most talented Mages on the continent."

"You knew them?" I looked up, surprised. The fatigue I always experienced after the end of a particularly grueling lesson was beginning to set in.

"Oh, yes, once upon a time. I have no idea what has befallen them now. I have not been in Tiralaen for many years, after all."

"What does he do all day?" I wondered out loud. "I never see him about, and Mistress Philomena did say we all have to work."

"Indeed, we all contribute in our way," he answered. "Prince Elyan is no different. Though what he mends, he caused himself."

"What do you mean? What did he cause?"

"Never you mind what he caused." Master Tiberius shook his head, looking as though he very much regretted the direction our conversation had taken.

I wheedled and cajoled and pleaded, but he would say no more of it. I could not ask Elyan, of course, and so I was left to wonder what he caused and what he spent his days mending until one afternoon I decided to stretch my legs after being hunched over in a bed of turnips for well on an hour and discovered something very strange indeed.

"Stay close so that Grenn and I can see you, just in case there's trouble," Yralis told me as I arched my back in the late autumn sun.

"I'll be fine, I promise."

I'd not walked long at all before I saw him.

In truth, I very nearly did not recognize him; his shirtsleeves were rolled up, his hair was a tousled mess, and there was a sheen of sweat on his brow. He was crouched at the foundation of the great fortress, looking up at a fearsome crack that split the gray stone of Asperfell some ten feet high or more. His gaze traveled the length of the crack, narrowed and scrutinizing, and what he saw did not look as though it pleased him. His long fingers reached out and probed the jagged edges of the split stone gingerly. Then he laid his palm flat against the surface of the wall, and the glow of his magic rose to the surface of his skin, answering his unspoken call.

My understanding of magic was severely limited, but surely it was Mistress Philomena's task to repair the crumbling stone of Asperfell, herself an Earth Mage? How was it even possible that Elyan, a Siphon, was able to do it at all? Yet as I watched, the edges of the crack pulsed with borrowed magic, *Elyan's* magic, and like lovers reuniting after a long absence, hesitantly, gently, they began to knit themselves together. It was excruciatingly slow. I must've stood watching him for a quarter of an hour until Elyan's hand slid from the stone and he went down onto one knee, gasping.

I knew I risked his anger by revealing myself, but he looked alarmingly pale and he'd begun to shake almost imperceptibly, and so I dashed forward and called: "Are you all right?"

He whipped around, and I expected he meant to fix me with a murderous glare. But whatever he'd done with his magic and the crack in the stone of Asperfell must've rendered him unable to do me even the smallest discourtesy because he sagged to the ground in defeat with his eyes closed, a look of utter exhaustion on his face.

"What are you doing here?" he asked me, when I crouched down in the dirt beside him. "Aren't you supposed to be in a lesson?"

"Not at the moment. Would you like me to send for the Master?"

He waved me away and drew himself back up to his knees. "I'm fine. Again, what are you doing here?"

"You certainly do not *sound* fine," I told him. "And I was just in the garden and wanted to stretch my legs. How was I to know you'd be here doing… what was it you were doing, exactly?"

Evidently he'd regained enough of his strength to scowl at me, for he did, voraciously. "Never you mind."

"You know, it is growing increasingly tiresome being told to 'never you mind' whenever I ask a question."

"Shocking though it may be for you to believe, there are things here you simply are not ready to know." Elyan rose onto his knees again, with a concerted effort I could tell he struggled to hide from me.

"You're not an Elemental Mage," I pointed out. "How did you do whatever it is you won't tell me you're doing?"

He regarded me with wary eyes under the disheveled curls that spilled over his forehead. "The damage was done by magic," he said at last. "And it can only be undone by the same."

I did not understand what he meant, but he had at least answered, and so I offered him my hand. To my surprise, he took it and rose smoothly to his feet.

"You really ought to see the Master," I told him, my reward a stony glare before he stalked past me and disappeared from sight.

The longer I lived within the ancient walls of Asperfell, the stranger I found it.

The fortress was a vast sprawl of endless staircases and corridors and passageways and rooms, and they did not always stay as they were. A staircase that led in one direction one day might lead somewhere else entirely the next. Rooms vanished and then reappeared again. Windows changed with the passage of time, and furniture rearranged itself. Without Mistress Philomena to lead me about, I feared I would be swallowed up by Asperfell entirely, lost in a forgotten place.

Cracks like the one I'd seen Elyan repairing were within as well as without, and I felt a strange sense of unease whenever I was near them, a stirring of magic such that I was certain they had not been caused by the passage of time alone. Although the fortress was strong, immovable and stalwart and unchanging even as the centuries passed and its denizens lived and died within its walls, the unnatural cracks had weakened it, and allowed the world outside to burrow within.

Ivy and other tangled vines studded with thorns and tiny white flowers stubbornly climbed the façade and, if left unchecked, made their way inside wherever they found a crevice. Feeding on magic as if it were water, they grew quite unruly until they had overtaken several rooms in the abandoned southwest tower. As beautiful as they were twining around the frames of old windows with cracked and venerable glass, I learned they were deadly in equal measure when Master Tiberius was called one afternoon to free an old and ailing man who had allowed the vines to permeate the walls of his chamber. Whether this was because he could not fight them back or because he simply did not wish to, no one would ever know: by the time Master Tiberius reached him, the vines had grown up around the canopy of his bed, snaked across the mattress of feathers, and wrapped themselves around his ankles, his arms, his throat. He died surrounded by white flowers.

"It's gotten worse in recent years," Master Tiberius told me. "Too many cracks, too many loose stones. And they grow back as quickly as they are eradicated."

"Why does no one help Prince Elyan fix the walls?" I asked. "Surely Mistress Philomena would help, if she knew it risked the destruction of this place?"

Master Tiberius smiled at me sadly. "She certainly would, but the burden is not hers to bear, and so she cannot."

"But the vines are killing people!" I objected, aghast. "If Elyan is the only one who can stop it, why doesn't he do more?"

"He does, Mistress Briony," Master Tiberius said, and his voice was like steel. He was so often jovial that I forgot how fierce he could be, how severe. "Elyan does more for Asperfell than you could possibly know."

"I thought you said what he mends, he caused himself."

"Yes," he admitted reluctantly. "Yes, I did say that, but it is far more complicated than you know."

"Then explain it to me. Please. I want to understand."

But he did not.

Despite the damage caused to the walls of the dead man's chamber by the invasive vines, the room was quite large and, therefore, was set upon immediately by other prisoners wishing to claim it. Possession of rooms and property within Asperfell was decided not by birth and gold as it was in Tiralaen, as much as the noble-born longed for it. Claims were made and challenged, and the winner was usually the Mage with the strongest and most dangerous skill. For this reason, I imagined Elyan's room to be a palace; I could not imagine any Mage wishing to confront a man who could drain their magic and use it against them.

Even if I had possessed magic enough to make a bid for the dead man's chamber myself, I had little interest in it save the furniture. My little desk was quite rickety and tilted slightly to one side; the one in the newly vacant room looked to be made of sturdier stuff, and I was sorry not to have been able to claim it for my own.

Every piece of furniture at Asperfell was ancient, and it was only by very clever magic that any of it still survived. Several hundred years ago, one of Tiralaen's kings, a Mage in his own right, took upon himself the reformation of the prisons within the city of Iluviel, and extended his generosity to Asperfell as well. Unfortunately, no monarch since had taken up the cause, and as a result, residents of the prison were forever condemned to exist in the past while the world marched on without them.

I was not often left alone as I had no means of defending myself from my fellow prisoners should the need arise, but gradually I came to know the men and women who surrounded me.

The squat woman who resembled a toad and tormented me endlessly whenever I attempted to use the washroom was called Walfrey, and she was a Hearth Mage. She was also notorious for having poisoned an entire tavern full of bannermen from a rival house, and thus was not allowed anywhere near the kitchens. They'd not died as she'd intended, but, as Master Tiberius so delicately put it, they shat endlessly for a month afterward.

Her constant companions were two men whose appearance was

even stranger than hers, if such a thing were possible. One was very, very tall, as tall as Prince Elyan, and slender. His pale skin stretched thinly over his bones and his eyes were sunken deep into his face, giving him a most unsettling appearance. He never spoke, which I learned later was the result of his tongue having been cut from his mouth before he was sent through the Gate. The other man was bullish and brawny with coarse black hair, a fearsome beard to match, and beady black eyes. He smiled at me often, though his smiles were not friendly. Their names were Samuel and Dox.

"Highway robbery," Elyan told me, when I asked what the two had done to warrant their life in Asperfell. "Did you never hear of them? Perhaps you didn't—it was a dozen years ago at least. Amassed quite a bit of my father's wealth, actually, before they were caught."

"Highway robbery doesn't sound too particularly dreadful," I said cautiously. I'd learned in my short time at Asperfell that nothing was ever as it seemed.

"There was also murder," he admitted. "Quite a lot of murder, actually."

Of course there was.

On the floor below mine, there was a man who very seldom left his room and cried often. His crime was also murder, and the guilt he bore was so overwhelming it had quite overtaken him, a vast difference from the oft-laughing Dox. The first time I saw him, Mistress Philomena was escorting me to the gardens when we passed a closed door through which floated the sound of weeping. Against Mistress Philomena's vigorous protestations, I nudged the door open and peered inside.

The man inside was a broken, pitiful thing. His shaggy hair was unkempt and framed a face drawn and red from weeping. His shirt, covered in stains and ragged in places, hung off his sickly frame, yet he seemed entirely unbothered by it. He was hunched in a chair in front of his fireplace, staring into the flames, and did not move at all at the sound of the creaking door. His shoulders trembled, and he sagged forward and buried his face into his hands, crying afresh.

I felt a hand on my shoulder. "He cries all day and night, that one," Mistress Philomena said. "Best not to trouble yourself over it."

The man's name was Sebben, and he'd killed his wife and children. They were starving, scraping a living off of rocks and the poorest of soil, and their meager crop had been destroyed by fierce storms that swamped their fields. His children's empty bellies twisted in pain and they cried and grew pale while his wife wasted away before his eyes. He was a Dreamwalker, a Mage, and could do nothing but watch them suffer until it destroyed him.

He crept into their dreams one night, soothing them, giving them lovely thoughts and pleasant memories, and then he set fire to their cottage with Magefire and prepared to burn with them. Only he didn't burn. When the smoke overcame him, and the flames licked his hands and face like a dog come from hell, he panicked and blundered from the house into the snow.

His wife and children, deep in dreams of his making, did not stir. The flames consumed them until the cottage was reduced to ash, and Sebben was sent through the Gate, though it might've been kinder to kill him.

A particularly amorous couple shared the chamber next to Sebben, and the sound of their passion mingled quite unfortunately with the sound of his sobbing, producing a cacophony that made me blush and despair in equal measure whenever I happened to be nearby.

On the floor above me, in one of the largest and finest of Asperfell's rooms, resided Lord and Lady Ashwinder.

They had not arrived at the prison together, but quickly found one another through a mutual longing for the halcyon days of their time at court, and the spectacle was both to be pitied and laughed at. She was already nobility when she arrived: Lady Elsemore, a title gained through marriage and five years spent in the bed of a rich old man dying of leprosy. She'd been stripped of the title when she was sent through the Gate for treason, and upon her arrival styled herself Lady Ashwinder. When Hilbren Scith arrived two years later, she married him and bestowed upon him the title of lord with a borrowed blade and bloated ceremony.

Thus, as Lord and Lady Ashwinder they paraded about in whatever finery and ornaments they could produce, and they mingled with other likeminded prisoners: former persons of great wealth or influence who saw no difference between Tiralaen and Asperfell. Their clothes may have been several centuries out of fashion and their country estates reduced to chambers filled with cobwebs and candles and vines, but proud they remained, and so they formed an elite society.

They took as their symbol a large insect called a papilem that had infested Asperfell long ago, a moth-like creature with three pairs of impossibly soft wings that did not so much flutter as undulate, making their progress in the air a slow but achingly lovely affair. I suppose they thought it far more refined than the gigantic and, quite frankly, terrifying beetles that scurried about Asperfell in shocking numbers. Master Tiberius claimed their iridescent carapaces made spectacular paint when ground and mixed with various oils.

Sometimes their society held balls in a large dusty room in Asperfell's southeast wing. These balls were astoundingly well attended, though I could not say whether this was because my fellow prisoners were positively starving for entertainment or because they were truly spectacular. I did not know; I'd never been invited to one. They called these gatherings the Melancholy Revels.

"I daresay you'll receive an invitation to one of their gatherings before too long," Master Tiberius told me one afternoon, as I sat at the table in the workroom examining an ancient, crumbling parchment that depicted the interior of Asperfell. Unfortunately, it was two hundred years old and in the years since a great many things had been changed, the natural result of men and women with extraordinary power and a great deal of time on their hands.

"Why so?"

"You are the first Mage to come to Asperfell in nigh on three years, my dear, which makes you a curiosity. And if that were not enough, you have no aptitude, which is a true oddity."

"So I am something for them to laugh at," I sighed.

"Perhaps," Master Tiberius conceded, "although it may be kinder to say you are a worthy conversation piece. But you are also of noble blood, and they value the company of their own."

"How perfectly ridiculous," I scoffed, "to prize such things here!"

"Ridiculous to you, perhaps. But do remember some of these Mages have dwelled here for decades, and they wish it to resemble their past life as closely as they are able."

This I found abhorrent. "And so the world continues as it ever has, even beyond the Gate."

"Indeed," Master Tiberius agreed. "To them, their position is as vital as the air they breathe, and wherever they go, they will claw and scrape and climb over whomever they must to ascend to the top and stay there."

"Then why on earth would they want to see me? Surely they know I care little for such things."

Master Tiberius smiled, then. "Why would anyone invite a stranger into their midst? To know them better." He paused. "And determine whether they are friend... or foe."

I had not been at Asperfell long by my reckoning before I saw my first fight. Indeed, Master Tiberius told me he was shocked it had taken that long, but then I did not go anywhere without escort, and they were usually formidable enough that the other prisoners demurred in their presence.

Mistress Philomena and I were on our way from the gardens to my lessons one handsome, golden afternoon when we heard a great commotion from above. With a swift glance in my direction that clearly indicated I was to follow, Mistress Philomena took her skirts in hands and hurried up the twisted steps.

A large crowd had already gathered in the courtyard, shouting and jeering at something beyond them, and I stood on my tiptoes so that I might see what it was they found so entertaining.

"There's Prince Elyan." Mistress Philomena pointed across the crowd. "Stay by his side until I return with the Master."

She left me then.

Above the crowd I saw Elyan's dark, curly head easily, and I pushed my way through to his side. His attention, and that of those around him, was on two men facing one another under the black oak tree.

One was of middle years, with rotting teeth bared in a grimace and a face covered in ugly purple scars. The other was closer to my own age, with golden hair and beard cropped short and fierce blue eyes that seemed familiar. Behind him, it seemed, was the reason for the altercation: a young woman. She lay on the ground some distance from the golden-haired man, covering her head with her arms and screaming, begging for them to stop.

Both men held weapons: the elder a rusted longsword and the younger a massive, brilliant blade, the like of which I'd never seen. The surface of the metal looked as though it were alive, swirling like water over stones.

"What's happened?" I gasped.

Elyan looked down at me and frowned. "No idea. Burtroch's an arse, though, so it probably has something to do with that."

"Which one is Burtroch?"

"The ugly one."

"Move!" the scarred man bellowed. "I need her!"

The golden-haired man did not seem the least bit affected. "I told you, mate," he replied calmly, "that's not going to happen."

"Move, or you die."

"I'm not moving."

Burtroch lunged for the golden-haired man, who evaded him easily. Their blades came together, and the force of the blow, the force of the magic that resided in both blades, caused them to stagger back from each other. A snarl from Burtroch and a cocksure, breathless laugh from his golden opponent, and blade met blade again. The sound of the blows rang throughout the courtyard, mingling with the gasps and exclamations of the gathered crowd.

"Shouldn't someone stop them?" I shouted to Elyan over the commotion.

"Why bother? They'll sort it out well enough between themselves."

It was not the two men that worried me.

The young woman was still crouched on the stone floor, rocking back and forth, hands pressed over her ears. I did not know if she was trying to shield herself from the harsh sound of the swords or something inside her own head. But I did know that if she did not move, she was likely to be a casualty despite the golden-haired man's evident protection.

Luckily the crowd's attention was on the two swordsmen before them and not a woman in a tattered gray dress, and so I darted through them unmolested, pushing and shoving my way toward the young woman. I thought I heard Elyan shout something behind me, but I ignored him and pressed on.

I dropped to my knees beside the crying woman and gripped her by the arms as Livia had done to me so many times when, as a child, a bout of crying grew beyond my control and I needed a good shaking to calm down. She flinched at the touch and pulled away from me, staring at me with enormous dark eyes through a tangled curtain of equally dark hair.

"I'm not going to hurt you," I told her, trying to sound as soothing as I could. "But you have to move."

I succeeded in pulling her backwards a few feet before we collapsed, and she refused to move any farther. She weighed almost nothing, and so I clutched her against my side as if she were a sack of grain and scrambled backwards until I was certain that we were out of harm's way.

"You're all right," I told her, hoping I sounded far more confident than I felt. "It will be all right."

In the end, Burtroch's size and strength were no match for the golden-haired man's blade. A weapon forged and wielded by an Alchemist, surely. A surge of power snaked from hilt to point, and with a surge of blinding light, the golden-haired man's sword shattered Burtroch's blade into glittering dust, sending him sprawling back against the stone wall with a sickening crunch.

There was, to my horror, a smattering of applause from the crowd, grown larger since my arrival, and I saw scraps of paper being exchanged. A thin old man with ebony skin and a shock of white hair pressed two fingers to the unconscious Burtroch's throat. At the announcement he was still alive, simultaneous groans and cheers went up, and more scraps of paper passed hands.

"Get him to the sick room!" the golden-haired man shouted, and two men hefted Burtroch between them and dragged his dead weight away. Then the victor turned, searching for the young woman who had evidently been the cause of the altercation.

"I told you to hide," he admonished gently as he approached, and he stretched his hand down. The girl's tiny hand was enveloped in his, and he pulled her to her feet.

"I'm sorry," she replied, her voice soft and delicately accented.

The golden-haired man's bright blue eyes moved past her and fixed on me, still sprawled out awkwardly on the ground. He offered his hand, and I took it gratefully.

He was still holding the magnificent blade that had shattered Burtroch's sword and I could not help but admire it. It seemed to glow from within, smoldering like an ember.

"Thank you," he said. Then, taking in my gray gown: "You're the new one, yes?"

I nodded. "My name is Briony."

"I'm Thaniel, and this is Phyra." The young woman had shrunk close to him, her fingers combing through the ends of her dark hair. She stared at me with wide eyes and said nothing.

Recognition took hold of me at last. "I've seen you before," I told him, smiling. "Coming from the lower levels!"

"I imagine you did," Thaniel replied. "I'm the warden of those parts." For all the grimness of the task, I detected a hint of pride in the way he said this.

"Is that not terribly dangerous?"

Thaniel shrugged and slid his magnificent blade into the scabbard hanging at his left side. "It is indeed. But it suits me just fine."

Elyan's scathing voice came from behind me. "What did Burtroch do this time?"

"Killed Torum," Thaniel replied. "Tried to use this one to raise him." He jerked his head at the silent Phyra.

"Torum's dead?" Elyan whistled.

"What do you mean raise?" I blurted out, entirely unable to help myself. "That is, I mean to say... are you saying you're a..."

"Necromancer, yes," Elyan finished for me, the irritation obvious in his voice. "Briony is somewhat new to our world."

"So I've heard." Thaniel eyed me curiously. "They say you were bound as a child. Is it true?"

I nodded. Then, not wanting him to press further into the circumstances of my magic, I looked down at his magnificent sword. "I've never seen its like," I said. "It's beautiful."

"Thaniel is an Alchemist," Elyan told me.

"Not easy to find materials in this place." Thaniel drew the sword again with an easy smile. "But I managed it."

I watched the mercurial surface churn with brilliant colors, living magic trapped in steel.

"Does it have a name?" I asked. "My uncle used to tell me all the best swords have names."

Thaniel grinned. "Your uncle was a wise man. This blade's name is Maelstrom."

I thought this a proper name, and said so. Then Elyan and Thaniel fell into easy conversation about Torum, Burtroch, and who had benefitted most from the wagers placed on the fight.

While they talked, I looked over at Phyra curiously. I'd always imagined Necromancers to look as chilling as their aptitudes, and although she was a slight thing, and lovely, she did not disappoint in that regard. There was something decidedly unsettling about the silent, wide-eyed girl with her anxious fingers and long, tangled black hair. I wondered what she had done to warrant her imprisonment.

As if she'd sensed my thoughts, Phyra tilted her head, her dark eyes meeting mine, and then she turned and walked toward the black oak. I followed, watching in silence as she climbed up on the ledge of the dais and, holding her arms out for balance, began to traverse the perimeter slowly, one bare foot before the other. She was taller than I was, and willowy, her limbs long and graceful, and her skin was the soft brown of the eastern lands. The gown she wore, like the clothing of most of the prisoners of Asperfell, was ancient, and although she'd cinched the kirtle tightly, it still slipped down off of her shoulders and billowed behind her as she walked.

"Thank you for what you did before," she said, looking down at me. "I was not myself."

"I'm just glad you're all right."

She nodded. "People die in Asperfell all the time. Burtroch is not the first to ask me to raise the dead, and he won't be the last."

"We should go," said Thaniel, taking Phyra's hand in his.

"Phyra doesn't use her gift," Elyan explained, as we watched them walk away toward the southwest stair. "She made a vow long ago, and in all the years she's been here, I've never known her to break it." His face darkened. "Of course, that doesn't mean others do not try to persuade her."

"She has a strong protector. Do you know him well?"

"Thaniel fought the good fight against my brother before he came to Asperfell. Much like your father, I suppose." Elyan drifted into his own thoughts for a few moments, then looked down at me pointedly. "He also had notions of liberating me when he arrived. He eventually gave up, as will you."

I could well enough imagine Thaniel cutting a swath through Keric's soldiers. He wielded Maelstrom as though it were an extension of his very self, and the look in his eyes when Burtroch fell was far from contrite. If he'd been born in a different time, into a different world, he might have been a member of the king's Mageguard, might have been their captain. His defense and gentle treatment of Phyra reminded me very much of the knights in Livia's courtly romances, and I wondered at the nature of their relationship.

"How on earth did Phyra end up here?" I asked. "She doesn't seem as though she could hurt anyone."

"As your very presence suggests, not all prisoners of Asperfell are guilty," Elyan replied. "Phyra is here because my brother is villainous filth and for no other reason. You are, I'm sure, familiar with Keric's proclivity for using cruelty to amuse himself?"

I nodded. Aside from the vivid letters I'd received from Uncle Geordan and Livia, I remembered all too well the feeling of cold marble against my cheek, Keric's hand pushing my face against the floor...

"Phyra's parents were indentured servants to a merchant family in the capital. Although it was clear to them that their daughter was magical, they rightly feared to subject her to one of my brother's public Trials. Thus, the child had no idea of her power when she discovered the body of her beloved grandmother, whose heart had given out. She raised the old woman entirely by accident."

"How awful," I murmured.

"It did not take long for word to reach my brother, and before she was sent through the Gate for practicing magic, he brought her to the Citadel to entertain his guests." The word *entertain* spilled from his mouth like a poison, as if it were foul even to speak the word.

A sick feeling had begun to creep over me as he spoke, a fist in my stomach that forced its way to my throat, catching my breath and rendering me lightheaded. I could not believe it was possible, but I had heard this story before. I knew its wretched ending.

"What do you mean entertain?" My voice sounded dull and far away against the roaring in my ears.

Elyan looked down at me. "He killed her brother in front of her, then demanded she bring him back from the dead," he said at last. "Inexperienced as she was, he rose incorrectly, and had to be killed a second time."

I was right; I *had* heard this story before. It was the reason my sister was not now the Queen of Tiralaen, the reason she escaped the Citadel to marry a man she'd never met in a faraway land. Phyra and I had only met that day, but our lives had been connected by a shameful, heartbreaking thread since a king tried to win the heart of my sister, and, in a single night, destroyed it instead.

14

I tried to talk to Phyra after that day in the courtyard, but I never could seem to find her. Elyan told me she had cultivated quite a talent for hiding, and I did not blame her for this. In fact, sometimes I wished I possessed her canny knack for it. I had begun to notice Grenn staring at me as I worked in the garden with an expression I did not care for.

That look made me long for the day Master Tiberius would decide I had advanced enough with my magic to learn defensive spell work, but I was still learning rudimentary commands such as banishing and mending. The first I practiced on my little room, and after several failed attempts, including one that actually resulted in the amount of dirt *doubling*, I managed to banish the dirt I'd tracked in on my muddy boots from the garden. Unfortunately, my command was weak, and my intent not fully realized, and so instead of *to the outside* as I'd intended, the pile of dirt actually ended up on the bed of the prisoner in the room directly below mine.

The second I tried on the muslin gown I'd found in the trunk below my bed. This took considerably longer, and I nearly lit the fabric on fire trying to fortify the seams, but in the end I managed to repair it, and I nearly wept with relief as I shed the gray gown at last. I would've burned it for all I cared for it, but I was not entirely convinced my magical handiwork would hold and so I folded the gown carefully and placed it in the trunk.

It was in an effort to avoid Grenn and his gaze that I found myself skulking in a kitchen storeroom, taking far too long to deposit the baskets of turnip greens I'd been charged with delivering.

That was how I met The Cat.

There was a shelf in the storeroom that held several small stoppered bottles with labels too faded to read. If the bottles had belonged to Master Tiberius, I would've avoided them entirely as any one of them could've resulted in a minor explosion if opened. Because they were kept with Asperfell's provisions, I doubted they were more than spices and I decided to pass the time by making an exploration of them. I had just pried the stopper out of the first bottle and held it to my nose when there was a crash behind me, followed by the violent scuffling of feet and a screech so high pitched and terrible that I dropped the bottle.

Whatever had caused the commotion had disappeared behind a cluster of barrels, and I was left with a slowly spreading puddle of deep, ochre liquid on the stone floor.

"Oh no, no, no," I gasped, and fell to my knees beside the mess, wrinkling my nose as a sharp, acrid smell filled the air. I desperately tried to use my new banishment spell to send the liquid from floor to bottle. *Into the bottle, into the bottle, into the bottle.* But the liquid remained stubbornly put. There was nothing for it; I would have to tell Mistress Philomena.

As I stood, steeling myself for what was sure to be a spectacular lecture, I saw a pair of yellow eyes gleaming in the darkness. They grew closer and closer and gradually a sleek black cat emerged, carrying the limp body of a rather large Gnasher. It was unmistakably, most certainly, a cat, though I could not account for its presence here at all. How had a cat managed to get through the Gate?

"Hello," I breathed.

The cat stared at me and cocked its head to one side.

"My, you are beautiful." I crouched down, holding my hand out. The cat set down his prize and crept closer to me, his enormous eyes never leaving mine.

"I never expected to see a cat here," I told him, and when I finally sat on the floor, my skirts spread around me, the cat rubbed his whiskered cheek against my proffered hand. "What is your name, I wonder? How did you get here?"

The cat, purring loudly, wound around me with his tail held high. I smoothed my hand down his sleek fur and scratched under his chin as I cooed over him and told him how beautiful he was, and how clever to have caught such a large creature for his supper. I was so absorbed in the simple pleasure of the cat's presence that I did not notice Mistress Philomena until I glanced up and saw her standing in the doorway, her arms folded, her face like thunder.

"Look at this mess!" She stormed into the room, gesturing to the awful-smelling puddle I'd entirely forgotten.

Irritated by the sudden interruption, the cat bounded away from me, took up his prize again, and slunk off into the darkness behind the barrels. I stared after him longingly, wishing I could do the same because Mistress Philomena looked ready to thrash me soundly for the mess I'd made.

"I'm sorry I'm late!" I wailed, barging into the workroom quite out of breath from dashing down the hallway. "Did you know there's a cat here?"

Master Tiberius was nowhere to be seen. It was Elyan, slouched in a chair with his feet on the worktable and a book in his hands, who looked up at me and said, "Yes, of course there is."

I plopped down in the chair opposite him, slightly deflated. "You already knew?"

"Of course I knew," he snorted. "The Cat has been here for centuries."

"Truly?" I said. "Centuries? No cat is that old. How is it possible?"

Elyan looked over the top of his book at me and I swear the disgust in his face could've curdled milk.

"Oh," I said. "It's a magic cat."

"Very literally," he replied. "Someone smuggled it in and here it has remained, imbued with magic and everlasting."

"When? *How?*"

"In his pocket," said a voice from the doorway, and I turned to see that Master Tiberius had joined us. "Hundreds of years ago. I forget the man's name now..." He scratched his beard, then shrugged. "No matter. He was obsessed with brewing a cure against aging."

At this, Elyan rolled his eyes. "Bloody Alchemists."

"He never did figure out how to make it work on himself, but The Cat has been with us ever since."

"And what is his name?"

"The Cat."

"Yes, the cat," I answered. "What is his name?"

Master Tiberius chuckled. "No, that's it—his name is The Cat."

"That's it?" I frowned.

"I'm afraid so."

"That isn't terribly creative, is it?"

"But he *is* one of a kind, is he not?" Master Tiberius said, and I could not help but smile. Of all the wondrous things I had beheld since coming to Asperfell, an immortal cat should not have been anywhere near as fascinating as I found it. Perhaps it was the fierce joy of seeing something so tangible from the world I thought I had lost forever. Or the thought that whoever smuggled The Cat into Asperfell with him must've carried some affection for the creature to bring him to this dreadful place.

"He's lovely," I said. "And clever. Will he live forever, then?"

"Oh, I imagine not," Master Tiberius chuckled. "And I'll be quite sorry when he does die. He's a remarkable creature. None of us but the most powerful can cheat death, Briony. No Mage in living memory has ever done it."

I had no time to ponder this as Master Tiberius set me promptly to my lesson.

Because I never imagined I'd do magic, it was still a thrill every time I felt that warm thrum of power in my veins, still an elated surprise when I could feel the magic obeying my command, an unadulterated joy watching the result of it. Even something so simple as banishing still took my breath away. No doubt I seemed woefully simple to Master Tiberius and Prince Elyan, even someone to pity, but I didn't care. I was a Mage, and I could remove dirt from a floor without a broom. In my eyes, it was truly remarkable.

Today I was tasked with moving objects toward my person. This, Master Tiberius told me, was the final lesson I had to learn before he could begin to teach me to conjure shields. And shields were a first step toward being able to move about unescorted amongst my fellow prisoners.

Being able to walk the length of a corridor alone would be utter bliss. I smothered a laugh with the back of my hand as Master Tiberius placed a small, golden apple on the worktable some feet away from me.

I managed, after two exhausting hours, to roll the apple slightly to one side, and I slumped back on the bench happy and sweating and shaking. The familiar feeling of exhaustion that came with using magic for long periods of time washed over me, and Master Tiberius placed a goblet of cool water on the table beside me.

Elyan did not look up from his book the entire lesson.

A short while later, Mistress Philomena rapped on the door to the workshop, bowed stiffly to Master Tiberius, and handed him a letter sealed with wax of the deepest aubergine.

"She wants to meet her," Philomena said, jerking her chin in my direction as Master Tiberius broke the seal and read the contents of the letter, a smile twitching on his lips.

"Indeed," Master Tiberius replied, and handed the letter to me.

It was written in an ornate script with ink the same color as the wax seal and decorated with all manner of birds, flowers, and insects. It read:

> *My dear Master,*
>
> *Will you kindly inform Briony Tenebrae that her presence is required in my chambers this afternoon? I wish to inspect her.*
>
> *Your servant,*
> *Marcellena Lessops, Countess of Bayl*

"Is it from the Countess?" Elyan asked. "What's the old bat want?"

"To inspect me." I frowned, reading the letter again. "What on earth does that mean? Who is the Countess?"

Elyan raised one eyebrow at Master Tiberius. "Should we tell her now, or let it be a surprise?"

"A surprise, I think," Master Tiberius replied. "It must be seen to be believed."

"Oh, you two!" Mistress Philomena evidently did not find them the least bit amusing. "A little respect, if you please."

"Frankly, I am surprised she waited this long." Elyan rose and flicked an enormous beetle off of his leg that had escaped the rusted lantern Master Tiberius had stuffed it in earlier. "She hardly waited an hour after I arrived before she demanded my presence."

"Yes, but you're a prince." I reminded him. "And I am—"

"Late," Mistress Philomena interrupted. "And the Countess does not abide lateness."

"I'll take her," Elyan volunteered. "I owe the old bat a visit."

"Oh, stuff and nonsense," Master Tiberius snorted with a merry smile. "You just want to see what our dear Briony makes of our resident diviner."

This and Elyan's wide grin made me exceedingly nervous as we ascended one of the turrets of Asperfell to the very peak.

Elyan rapped on the door and a resonant voice intoned, "Enter!"

"After you." Elyan's shoulders shook with barely repressed laughter, and I glared at him as I opened the door and slipped inside.

The circular room was positively enormous and littered with candles flickering brightly despite the sunlight that poured through the ornate windows, the finest I'd seen in the entire prison. In fact, everywhere I looked there were riches however faded, from the chandelier above me to the rug at my feet.

And at the center of it all stood an enormous, gilded chair holding the oldest woman I had ever seen. She was gnarled and bent, clutching a cane in hands like claws, and her hair was a tangle of cobwebs, white as bone and piled atop her head, the ghost of a fine lady's coiffure now ravaged with time. Her black gown, square-necked and trimmed with gold, was nearly of an age with those that resided in my trunk, and her neck, ears, and fingers were adorned with jewels. She watched us with rheumy eyes and thin lips surrounded by wrinkles earned, no doubt, from pursing tightly in disapproval.

"I have heard whispers in the stars of late, whispers in the dark," the old woman said by way of greeting, her voice a low rustle, like a dusting of leaves in autumn. "The dead keep the secrets of the living."

She looked at me then, and when her cloudy eyes met mine, I saw that they were the most peculiar shade of violet. Her piercing gaze and strange words unnerved me, and I longed to look elsewhere, anywhere, even at the infuriating man I felt certain was smirking at my discomfiture behind me, but I found I could not.

"You are Briony Tenebrae," she said at last.

"I am."

"A Mage, and not a Mage." She gripped the top of her cane and leaned slightly forward in her throne. "I saw you arrive." Then her head dipped low and she muttered something unintelligible.

When she looked up again, her gaze was fixed beyond me, and Elyan stepped forward to take her proffered hand, which he bent and kissed as though she were the heroine of one of Livia's tiresome romances.

"My raven and thorn," she said with a faint smile, as she lifted the hand he'd kissed and patted his cheek with it.

"How fare you, Countess?" Elyan asked. "You look ravishing, as always."

"Bah," the Countess waved this away. "I have not been radiant since your father was in swaddling clothes. Where is the Master? I have not seen him in an age."

"Burdened with a tedious task these past weeks, I'm afraid," Elyan replied, his gaze sliding to me. "He sends his regards."

"It is unconscionable of him!"

"I agree, and he ought to be punished forthwith."

"Punished," the Countess whispered, her head drooping again. "Punished, punished. The dead keep the secrets of the living."

I glanced questioningly at Elyan. It was clear her behavior was in no way strange to him; he had evidently seen it before. I remembered that in the workroom he'd called her an "old bat" and wondered just how many times he had made the climb to her tower.

"My dear Countess," Elyan said, his voice light, a golden counterpart to the shadows the Countess seemed to have fallen into. "You sent for Briony. Did you not intend to inspect her?"

"I did?" The Countess raised her head once again. "Yes, yes. Come here, child."

She beckoned me with one hand, and stepping closer, I found myself once more the subject of her scrutinizing eyes.

"Too short," she said at last. "Chin too pointed, hair like dirt and blood. Hair with leaves in it."

My hand flew to my hair, but I found nothing but my own curls. There had been leaves in my hair back at Orwynd, many times. Was she seeing my past, then, or my future? I thought of the leaves on the trees in the graveyard, ready to return their borrowed color to the summer and turn their natural brown.

"I've heard whispers, Briony Tenebrae," the Countess said. "Whispers of evil that festers even as it lies and lies. A Mage and not a Mage. You are learning?"

"Yes, your ladyship," I answered.

"Her Trial." The Countess ignored me and addressed Elyan. "Will she undergo her Trial soon?"

"Soon enough." Elyan said with a shrug. "She still wants for much improvement."

The Countess nodded. "I must be told. I must be told when she completes her Trial."

"Why?" I asked.

The Countess fixed me with her strange violet eyes. "Whispers in the stars. Whispers in the dark," she muttered. "I cannot understand them."

"Your ladyship?" I asked, quite confused as to what this had to do with my Trial and her particular interest in it.

She leaned forward, the jewels in her rings glinting dully in the candlelight as she clutched her cane. "Do you believe in fate?"

Taken aback, I stammered: "I've not considered it, your ladyship."

"Consider it."

It was not a request.

"I suppose I'd prefer to be responsible for my own life, such as it is," I answered carefully. "Rather than it be decided for me."

"You are destined, I have seen it," the Countess said, and despite the rasp of her aged voice, there was determination in her words.

"Destined for what?"

Unfortunately, what little strength she'd summoned failed her then, and she slumped back in her chair, muttering nonsense, lost in dust and velvet.

"Your ladyship?"

"We've exhausted you, I'm afraid," Elyan said. "And taken up too much of your valuable time. I'll bring Miss Tenebrae another afternoon, shall I?"

The Countess nodded heavily, and I took this as a sign of our dismissal.

I lowered myself in the most graceful curtesy I could muster, which was not very graceful at all. "It was an honor to meet you."

The Countess ignored this. "Whispers in the stars. Whispers in the dark."

Elyan gave a short bow, and then I followed him out of the door, the Countess still rambling behind us.

"Is she mad?" I asked Elyan, as we descended the narrow staircase from the Countess's turret.

"She's a Scriviner," Elyan said with a shrug, as if this explained away what I had just seen and heard. Perhaps to him, it did.

"I don't understand," I reminded him. "What is a Scriviner?"

"By the Gods," Elyan swore. "A Scriviner divines magical signs, or tries to, as it were. It is perhaps the most imprecise branch of magic of them all."

I considered this. "She sees the future?"

"Yes," Elyan said. "And no. She sees magic as it has been and as it is, and tries to divine the future from it. Sometimes it's complete nonsense, and sometimes it's useful. One thing it never is, is certain."

"She said she saw my coming," I pointed out.

Elyan snorted. "Her window faces the Gate. She probably saw you arrive like everyone else."

"Oh," I said. Then, "Did *you* see me arrive?"

The corner of his mouth lifted. "Yes."

"And you saw me with the Sentinel…"

His smile grew. "Yes."

My cheeks flamed, and I quickly diverted. "She also said that I was destined."

"Ah, but as you said, you do not believe in destiny."

"Have any of her predictions ever been correct?"

"A great many, in fact, which is how she ended up here. You see, Scrivening is not only an obscure and unreliable branch of magic, but its use in certain cases is against royal law."

"What cases?"

"Cases where you poison your lover's rivals because you saw in a vision that may or may not have been true that it would help him overthrow the king," Elyan replied drily.

"Goodness," I said faintly. I thought back to the woman I'd just met, holding court over a dark and empty room, a sad, threadbare echo of the once formidable and influential figure she must've been.

"The funny thing about Scriveners," Elyan continued, "is that the stronger they become, the less able they are to determine if what they see and hear is real or not, and then every wandering thought or wish or fear that pops into their head becomes a prediction."

"So she isn't *exactly* mad, then."

"Her age and her magic and this wretched place have muddled her senses," Elyan said. "But in her mind, she is the same wealthy, powerful woman who once very nearly toppled a dynasty. She expects her predictions to hold sway over us all, even if they are nothing more than fears and half-remembered dreams."

15

Though I was still gaining my footing in the strange place I now called home, I thought daily of the task that Cyprias had set me to when he and Master Aeneas had sacrificed themselves to send me here. Prince Elyan was clearly uninterested in aiding in his own escape attempt, so futile he thought the effort, and although Master Tiberius was certainly kinder in the telling of it, he made it abundantly clear that my focus should remain firmly on the acquisition of magical skill.

So I kept my research on Asperfell and any potential ways to free Elyan to myself.

At first, I devoted hours every evening to reading through everything I could find about Asperfell, its grounds, and the moors that surrounded it, making careful notes on parchment of anything that might prove useful in an escape attempt. Eventually I discovered I could fill only a single page, as there was little useful information to be had.

"What of the two men who discovered the Gate?" I asked Master Tiberius one day, as I sat surrounded by what had appeared at first to be lovely sketches of the flora and fauna of Tiralaen, but upon closer inspection turned out to be filthy poetry hidden within the graceful lines of petals and vines. The verses were quite clever, actually, despite their debauched subject, and I managed to get through a few lines before Master Tiberius figured out exactly what it was I had unearthed and plucked them away.

"Those are *certainly* not meant to be read by a lady of quality," he said hurriedly, stuffing them inside a book on one of his shelves.

I agreed, but noted nonetheless which book he'd buried them in.

"And as for the founders, well…" He sat down on the bench closest to me. "I cannot recall reading anything about them in that lot." He gestured to the small library. "Quite odd."

"I learned a bit about them in Iluviel when I was at the Citadel," I told him, remembering Master Aeneas's wonderful tower room. "But I can't remember any of it now."

In fact, I could not even remember the names of the two men who had first crossed the Gate and built the fortress that was now my home. Even if I could, Master Tiberius was right; there was simply no record of any of it. Likely Asperfell's earliest documents, despite whatever magical preservation had been bestowed upon them, had simply been lost to the ravages of time.

"Perhaps there really does exist a way to escape the prison and the builders did not want anyone to know about it," I said, my imagination quite taking over me, "so they destroyed the evidence!"

"Anything is possible, my dear," Master Tiberius answered kindly. "But it is highly unlikely."

Several prisoners over the years had attempted this feat before me, and unlike the builders of Asperfell, copious records existed of their failures. Every hundred years or so, it seemed, a Siphon would whip his fellow Mages into a frenzy and they would try to summon the Gate from this side, believing that if enough of them lent their power to the endeavor, it would succeed. Each attempt had proven a failure, and in each case the Siphon had lost his or her life, unable to contain so much magic within them.

Studying the Sentinels had turned out to be every bit as fruitless. The magic that had made them and held them fast to their task was strong and quite unbreakable. The scrolls I read were littered with the names of Mages who had died trying to run off into the wild forests that surrounded Asperfell.

"What good would it have done?" I asked. "What lies beyond us?"

"No one knows, as no one has ever managed to make it without being decapitated," Master Tiberius said with a shrug. "No one from Asperfell has ever learned what lies in the forest, or beyond it."

I huffed. "Well, that is disappointing. For all we know, there could be a hundred Gates, a *thousand* Gates just beyond those trees waiting to whisk us away home."

One afternoon while I helped Master Tiberius sort through a crate of dusty bottles and jars, I asked him if Elyan, for all his scoffing, had ever attempted to escape from Asperfell himself. "He is adamant it cannot be done," I said, pulling the stopper out of a green glass jug with some difficulty. A plume of white smoke curled up from the mouth of the jug, filling the workroom with an intoxicating floral aroma. "But has he even tried?"

Master Tiberius took the bottle and fanned away the white smoke, then peered down into the glass. "Ah! I've been looking for this!" He smiled up at me. "Essence of Amova. Excellent for restorative possets."

On a small bit of parchment, I wrote *Essence of Amova* in neat script, then handed it to Master Tiberius. With a brush of his fingers, he affixed it to the bottle with magic, secured the stopper, and set it aside. Willow had just that morning found the crate tucked in the back of one of the cupboards in the kitchen, and because the labels had quite worn away with the years, she had assumed it to be filled with forgotten bottles of extracts and vinegars. When she drew the stopper from one to smell its contents, she was rendered quite unconscious by the fumes from a potion meant to bring a dreamless sleep and was found by Mistress Philomena, snoring, two hours later. The box had been delivered to Master Tiberius immediately.

"Honestly, I thought it had been lost to time," Master Tiberius said. "Isn't it marvelous to discover something you had thought you'd never see again?"

I did not see how he had managed to misplace an entire box of potions, but the Master of Asperfell was given to bouts of whimsy from time to time. Indeed, it was one of my favorite things about him.

"You still haven't answered my question," I pointed out.

"Have I not?" Master Tiberius said innocently. He reached into the crate and drew out a tall, thin bottle of clear glass filled with what appeared to be sand. He handed the bottle to me, and I tipped it up into the light, marveling at the veins of gold that ran throughout the grains. "Sand from the deserts of Tolus," he said, gesturing to the bottle. "I, for one, have not found them to be the least bit useful, but it is popular among Mages of the air and wind."

I wrote labels for Tolus Desert Sand, Extract of Siliph, Powdered Rot, Ganwyn Horns, Bitter Tala Root, the venom of two different poisonous serpents, the sleeping potion that the unfortunate Willow had succumbed to, and, for some reason, fermented horse urine. I nearly gagged when I undid the stopper on that particular bottle and handed it quickly to Master Tiberius, my eyes watering. When we were finished, we arranged the bottles on one of the shelves of the workroom, with the exception of the Extract of Siliph, which Master Tiberius told me was highly dangerous before locking it away, though he did not tell me why.

Attempting an escape in the fashion of those who had come before me seemed futile, and so I abandoned my research in favor of something that seemed even less attainable, but the only option available to me: undergoing my Trial and emerging in command of a rare and powerful magical aptitude.

Within each of us was a singular gift, our very identity as a Mage, really. And if I were to have even the slightest chance of liberating Elyan from Asperfell, whatever aptitude it was that lay dormant within me must be up to the task.

"Do I have any choice in what sort of aptitude I'll have?" I asked Master Tiberius hopefully, as he set a star-shaped flower with five pure white petals on the worktable before me later.

"I'm afraid not," he told me. "Your levitation wants work."

He was not wrong.

I had managed after several long weeks to summon objects to my person from a short distance away; it was harder to push them away again. Eventually I was able to move an apple from one side of the table to the other, and Master Tiberius set me to moving other objects in his workroom, calling them to me and sending them away again. Unfortunately, I was like a newborn foal at the task, all enthusiasm and untried strength and completely lacking in coordination, and frequently sent things careening in one direction when they should've gone in another. Instead of summoning one book from a shelf, I sent ten of them flying to the rafters. Instead of moving a chair away from myself by mere inches, I splintered it spectacularly against the far wall. (I then spent the remainder of that lesson practicing my mending spells.)

I frowned at the flower. "What if I dislike what I turn out to be? Can I not change my aptitude?"

"No Mage has ever changed their aptitude," Master Tiberius said, and though his voice was kind, I sensed his impatience with me. "So it is perhaps for the best that you think not of it. And besides, all aptitudes are unique and useful in their own way. I highly doubt you would find yourself disliking any of them."

"What if I *do* dislike my aptitude," I continued stubbornly. "What if I dislike it so much I refuse to use it."

Master Tiberius's smile was wistful, almost sad. "You are thinking, perhaps, of Phyra."

I did not deny it. Beautiful, haunted, desolate Phyra. Elyan had told me that since she'd arrived at Asperfell, she performed basic spell work only; she'd not used her power over the dead at all. The trauma of losing her brother in such a dreadful way had closed her off from it completely.

Slowly I sent the flower away from me and watched it float as if carried on unseen hands, a thing of softness and beauty, utterly out of place.

"Had Phyra not been born into indentured servitude, her fate—and her relationship with her magic—would've been very, very different," Master Tiberius said. "She would've grown to embrace her abilities, not fear them."

"What if I'm a Necromancer, too?" The confession of my secret fear escaped me in a rush, and the flower plummeted to the table. "Or a Siphon? What if I'm a Blood Mage?"

"Then you will be a Blood Mage, though the prospect is unlikely," Master Tiberius told me. "A true rarity. The last time I met one was as a child in Beheren, I believe, and did you not say Keric had procured himself a young Blood Mage some years ago? For two to appear in a single generation is almost unheard of. But nothing to be feared."

"What good could possible come from such evil magic?"

Master Tiberius raised his eyebrows at me. "Is it the magic that is evil, or is it the intent of the Mage? Even magics considered light can be used for ill, and there are many ways that the Arcane aptitudes have helped humanity through the years."

I turned my attention back to the white flower before me.

But I noticed he did not answer my question. Not really.

That night I received an invitation to the Melancholy Revels.

"What on earth should I wear?" I asked Mistress Philomena, as I read the summons she'd handed me after my lesson, a gaudy, maudlin thing, ornate swirls of ink on ancient parchment that felt as though it would crumble in my hands.

Mistress Philomena let out a strangled sound of disbelief. "You don't intend to *go*, do you?"

"Of course I intend to go." I'd been mad with curiosity about the society and their strange gatherings since first I'd been told of them. I was not about to pass up the chance to see one with my own eyes, whatever Mistress Philomena thought.

She sniffed. "Well, *I'll* not take you. You'll have to find someone else."

This proved somewhat problematic as Master Tiberius declined to accompany me and I could not bear to ask Elyan. The almost-certain prospect of his mocking laughter at my invitation was not worth his protection, and so I asked Thaniel instead. I found him in the kitchens helping Willow with an enormous copper pot that had been spelled long ago never to empty. Willow used it to brew stock rich with vegetable leavings and the occasional chicken carcass if one could be spared. She usually kept it properly watered, but the day before she'd served broth with dinner and then fallen asleep at the hearth and forgotten all about the pot, which continued to bubble and seethe merrily on the fire until the morning. The result was a blackened, congealed mess at the bottom that clung stubbornly to the metal and caused the intricate spell work to go quite awry.

"An evening with that lot sounds positively ghastly," he said, "but if you're really so curious, I'll take you. However, mind you, I've only attended the Revels once, and their lot do not much care for me."

"Why not?"

"I am not of noble blood. But my knights and I protect them from those below, and so they accept me, however grudgingly."

"Why have you not attended the Revels more than once?" I asked. "Are they really that terrible?"

"Oh, certainly they are," he said, and hesitated. "But in truth, I had an unfortunate... *altercation* with another guest they hold in higher esteem than I."

"You must promise me not to get yourself turned out." I poked him in the chest. "What will become of me then?"

Thaniel let out a bark of laughter. "I rather suspect you'd have no trouble holding your own. But I promise to behave. Though, mind you, it may kill me to do it. Now when we arrive, try not to stare. It's all a bit strange."

He could not possibly have described the scene for me in any way that would've prepared me fully. Crossing the threshold into the hall was like stepping backwards in time to my childhood in the Citadel: chandeliers dripping with crystals and dotted with tiny flames illuminated a vast chamber with soaring ceilings; windows with heavy velvet drapes in much better condition than I'd seen anywhere else in the prison lined one entire wall of the room, and beneath them were handsomely carved benches dressed with velvet pillows where Mages sat with crystal goblets in their hands.

Cheerful music filled the air, courtesy of a group of Mages with strings and drums and flutes who played songs I'd never heard before. And at the center of it all, they danced, the most noble denizens of Asperfell, under a canopy of papilem.

The society had donned their finest for the occasion, though their fashions would be considered laughably old and quaint in present day Iluviel, better suited for a masquerade or a pantomime than a gathering such as this. I usually paid little interest to such things, but even I could see their skirts were far too voluminous, their necklines far too low, and their sleeves too long, though I'd no doubt Mistress Orial had done her best to keep their silks and taffeta in a reasonable state.

Without maids to help them, their coiffures were modest, and only some of them wore jewels. Still, they carried themselves with all the grace and decorum of what they believed themselves to be rather than what they had become.

The moment we entered, Thaniel grasped two glasses full of a clear, bubbling liquid off of a worn silver tray and passed one to me.

"Laetha," he explained, as I took a sip.

"Oh!" I gasped, and my face seized in a grimace. "That burns!"

Thaniel smiled apologetically. "First time, I take it? I should've warned you properly."

"Why would you *drink* this?"

"To get drunk," he answered. "And because we have an enchanted bottle of it." He gestured to a solitary, dusty green bottle sitting on a table laid with rich, sumptuous silks. "Never empties."

My eyes went wide. "How did they get it? I thought Mistress Philomena kept all of those under lock and key!"

"Walfrey. She nicked it from the kitchens years ago. Guards it with her life."

This did not surprise me in the slightest. Walfrey was sitting at a low table with Samuel and Dox, her glass empty and her cheeks ruddy. She'd pinned a cloud in her hair, and a short, ruffled veil fell into her eyes. Rather than giving her the mysterious air that no doubt she sought, it made her look instead as though she were going to a dockside festival. The look on her face when she clapped eyes on me could best be described as disgusted, and I quickly looked away. Judging by the way she and her companions were eschewed by the rest of the company, she was likely only gifted an invitation because of the Laetha.

"Mistress Briony!" said elegant voice, and I turned toward it.

"Ah!" Thaniel whispered near my ear. "Here is our hostess!"

Lady Ashwinder appeared to be on the younger side of fifty, of an age with my mother. She clearly spent little time out of doors; her skin was still milky white and smooth, and the delicate hands that grasped her fan did not look at all roughened by use. She wore a gown of midnight blue silk with a neckline that left little of her ample cleavage to the imagination, and between her breasts an enormous sapphire hung from a silver lariat. She studied me with catlike eyes, the same blue as the gem. Even though she had aged past her prime, she was still a breathtakingly beautiful woman. Her husband was decidedly less so, though he carried himself with all the grace and dignity of a man who believed himself worthy. Lord Ashwinder was tall and narrow, with steel gray hair and a long, pointed face that ended in a neatly trimmed goatee. He wore a long coat of silver brocade and a heavy chain of silver links.

Behind Lord and Lady Ashwinder, a small crowd of Mages had gathered, and they all stared at me with unabashed curiosity. I suddenly felt small and awkward in my gray gown, my red hair, and my unfortunate freckles.

"Welcome to the Melancholy Revels," Lady Ashwinder said, and bowed her head, a reminder of her station, and of mine.

At that moment I wished I'd heeded my Aunt Eudora's advice and practiced my curtesy during my isolation at Orwynd; the look on Lady Ashwinder's face as I struggled to dip gracefully while not tangling myself in my skirts could only be described as pitying.

"We know so little of you, my dear," she said as I rose. "And we would very much like to know you better. Who are your people? Were your family at court?"

"They were, your ladyship," I answered. "My father served on King Gavreth's privy council, and that of his son."

"Is that so?" Lady Ashwinder's countenance changed entirely then and she gave me a wide, dazzling smile. "You were raised at court, then?"

"For two years only, your ladyship, when I was very young. I spent most of my life at my family's ancestral home in the north."

Lady Ashwinder's smile faltered. "The north?"

"How far north?" her husband asked, narrowing his eyes.

"Orwynd, your lordship," I answered.

Lord Ashwinder's brow creased, and the Mages gathered behind him began to frown and whisper amongst themselves. "Orwynd, you say? I've never heard of it."

"It's quite a long way from Iluviel. Only two weeks' ride from the Sundering."

"Is it at all near Hirrus?" a Mage standing beside Lord Ashwinder asked me. He was a handsome man, gray only just beginning to appear in his thick, dark hair, and he wore a vest with a nauseating pattern of flowers woven from golden thread. "I used to have several estates near there. Lovely country."

I took a certain sort of pleasure in his use of the past tense. His vest really was quite odious. "I'm afraid not," I told him. "Farther north, on the border of the Morwood."

"A wild, savage country, that!" The man looked around at the Mages beside him. "It is said all manner of vile spirits and creatures call the Morwood home, and that many who enter its depths never emerge again." He turned back to me, his eyes alight. "I hope you took care never to enter that ghastly forest, Mistress Briony."

"On the contrary," I answered blithely. "I walked in the Morwood nearly every day."

Excited gasps and flustered tittering broke out among the Mages around us, and a smile played on the lips of the dark-haired man. "Your family should've kept you at court, I think."

"I would argue there are far worse creatures at court," I answered. "Lord..."

"Frobern," he answered, expression darkening. "Lord Frobern."

"Ah, so *you* are Lord Frobern!" I exclaimed. "I've heard your name before, actually, from Yralis."

Lord Frobern stared at me blankly. "Who?"

"Yralis," I repeated, my heart sinking ever so slightly. "She works in the garden with me."

"You work in the *garden*?" a dainty woman near Lady Ashwinder's age with chestnut curls piled atop her head squeaked. I recognized her at once: she was the head of the circle of ladies who mended linen in the courtyard. "How odd!"

I looked over at her in confusion. "Why should that be odd?"

"It's filthy in the garden! And to be so exposed to the elements, my dear, it will positively ruin your complexion!"

I thought I heard Thaniel muffle a snort of laughter behind me. Clearly, he had already deduced that I cared little for these things.

"I hear you've been to see the Countess," Lady Ashwinder said, and I was grateful for the shift in the conversation. "How did you find her?"

I hesitated. "I found her fascinating, and I liked her very much," I said at last. "Though she did find my stature wanting."

"Ah," Lady Ashwinder said, and I sensed she found my answer disappointing. "And did she make any interesting predictions?"

I thought about what the Countess had said about whispers in the dark and the dead keeping the secrets of the living. "Not predictions, exactly," I said. "Ramblings, perhaps. Very little of it made sense."

Lady Ashwinder seemed very interested that. "Is that so?"

"It is likely due to her aptitude, and not her health," Lord Ashwinder reminded his wife.

"And is she in good health?" Lady Ashwinder asked me. "I've not seen her in a very long time; she very rarely leaves her chamber."

"She appeared to be, my lady, though she is very old. Prince Elyan told me her age, her aptitude, and Asperfell itself have done her little favors."

"Prince Elyan was with you?" Lady Ashwinder's tone suddenly became sharp, and she exchanged a brief look with her husband. "What did he and the Countess discuss?"

I'd no great care for Elyan despite my hopeless task, and yet when she said this, I gave pause. "We were not in her presence long," I answered slowly. "She only wanted to inspect me."

"Did the prince speak with her alone? Perhaps after you left?"

"If he did, I know it not. He walked with me back down into the prison."

"And you're sure that is the whole of it?" Her eyes bore into mine, and for a moment I was taken aback by the intensity I saw in their depths.

"Yes," I answered.

This seemed to satisfy her. She drew back from me slightly, her gaze sliding to the door. "Did you happen to see his highness on your way here this evening, pray tell? I had rather hoped he would join us."

Lord Frobern snorted derisively. "Prince Elyan *never* attends the Revels, your ladyship."

"True." She tilted her head slightly in acknowledgement. "But I had rather thought he would tonight. He seemed to take a great interest in my inviting Mistress Briony."

I could only assume this was because he wished to see me make an absolute fool of myself and then ridicule me mercilessly about it afterward.

A red-faced, portly man with mutton chops and a wine-red waistcoat spoke up at Lord Frobern's side. "The prince is assisting with the incident in the South Wing."

Lord Frobern could not possibly have looked more disdainful if he tried. "Of course he is. Where there is menial work to be done, Prince Elyan will undoubtedly be there."

"What happened in the South Wing?" I asked.

"Some fool or another managed to cause an explosion that brought down an archway," said the man in the wine-red waistcoat.

"Was anyone hurt?" I gasped.

He waved a bloated hand dismissively, his jowls quivering with the sudden movement. "A few poor souls, but no one of importance."

"No one of importance," I echoed. "You mean, only common folk. The tending of the ill and injured is never menial, no matter what their blood."

"I think what Brethwain means to say is that the common folk of Asperfell have their own to see to their needs," Lady Ashwinder cut in with a smile that was clearly meant to mollify me. "It is not necessary for someone of our station, let alone a member of the royal family, to tend their injured."

"It is ever the duty of those with power to help those without," I replied, fighting to keep my tone civil. "Prince Elyan is among the most powerful Mages in Asperfell—surely if anyone should help, it is him."

Brethwain studied me with narrowed eyes. "You know, you sounded rather like Prince Elyan yourself just now."

He could not possibly have insulted me more. "How so, sir?" I demanded.

Before Brethwain could answer, Lady Ashwinder drew her fan and fluttered it with a high, tinkling laugh. "Now, now, Brethwain, let us not scare Mistress Briony away on her first visit to the Revels. I'm sure any one of us would take offense at being compared to his highness."

This gave me pause. "You do not care for him?"

"Of course I do," she said, and I knew at once she was lying. Cyprias had taught me far too well the signs, and I saw them now in her face. Her lip was curled, rendering her smile contemptuous, and her eyes were sharp and guarded. In her hands, the fan snapped shut, and she turned it over and over again. "I am a great admirer of his highness and I find his notions of helping the common folk quaint. We should all be led by his example."

I glanced around me. Although their finery had faded with their imprisonment, they still clung to it so desperately that I very much doubted they were led by any example other than their own self-importance.

"And what is it you do that helps the common folk?" I asked Lady Ashwinder.

"I say, helping the common folk is a worthy cause when occasion calls for it," Lord Frobern chimed in. "Lady Ashwinder herself invited the prince here tonight personally. It is an unforgivable slight."

A slight that I very much doubted Prince Elyan gave a whit about.

Mistress Orial frowned. "I did hear that several of the injuries were severe," she said hesitantly.

"There, you see?" I turned to Lord Frobern once more. "If that is true, then surely you can have no objection to Elyan choosing to aid the common folk rather than attend your gathering tonight."

Lord Frobern's lips curled in distaste. "He shuns the company of his own entirely in favor of the common folk. It is an embarrassment."

I met his gaze squarely. "I truly cannot imagine why anyone would choose to shun your company, Lord Frobern."

"Mistress Briony, what a wit you are," Lady Ashwinder said with a frosty smile, and I did not believe for a moment she thought me thus; impertinent, perhaps. Dreadfully gauche more likely.

I felt a hand on my arm then, and realized Thaniel still stood behind me. He'd been silent throughout my exchange with Lady Ashwinder and her companions, but now he bowed to them and said, "We thank you for welcoming us to the Revels, your ladyship."

"Ah, Thaniel! I'd quite forgotten you there." Lady Ashwinder's gaze fell on my companion. "I do hope your presence here tonight does not leave us unprotected from those below."

"Not at all, your ladyship," Thaniel replied easily. "My men and women are well trained."

Lady Ashwinder smiled, every bit the charming hostess she had been when we'd first arrived. "Then we shall all enjoy ourselves without worry. Pray, do the same."

I sank into another pathetic curtesy and watched as Lord Ashwinder led his lady away to join the dance beneath the papilems.

"Well," Thaniel said. "I'd say you certainly made an impression."

"Not a good one, I fear." If Mistress Precia could've seen me just now, she would've died of embarrassment.

Thaniel squeezed my hand and I smiled up at him, grateful I had at least one true friend amongst the gathering.

"What is the reason for her interest in the Countess and Prince Elyan?" I asked.

"Noticed that, did you? I'm sure you also noticed that Lord and Lady Ashwinder, as well as many of their guests, do not much care for Prince Elyan."

"I am not entirely sure I blame them."

Thaniel let out a bark of laughter. "His highness is not the easiest man to get along with, I grant you, but their objection is to his rule rather than the sharpness of his tongue."

"His rule?"

"Impending rule, I should say."

"Of Tiralaen?" How had they possibly found out about the impossible task Cyprias had set me to?

"Of Asperfell," Thaniel corrected. "After Master Tiberius is gone."

This sent a fissure of alarm through me. "He is not ill, is he?"

"No," Thaniel assured me quickly. "A few years ago, his strength began to wane and we feared it might come to that, but he actually seems to have improved greatly in the last several weeks." He gave me a smile. "Perhaps because of his invigorating new role as your teacher."

"So Elyan will replace him?"

Thaniel shrugged. "It is all but certain. Elyan is of royal blood and he is the most powerful Mage among us. Indeed, Master Tiberius has anticipated Elyan succeeding him since his arrival and has been preparing him for it for years."

"Other than his horrid personality, why would Lord and Lady Ashwinder object if Master Tiberius himself approves of his successor?"

"Look around you." Thaniel gestured with his glass of Laetha. "These are people whose greatest fear is change. Lord and Lady Ashwinder and their society worked hard to claw their way to the top of this place, and they do not trust Elyan to leave them to their own devices, as Master Tiberius has always done."

"Why?" I asked. "What would be so very different about Elyan presiding over Asperfell?"

"In the time before King Keric's rule, there were far fewer Mages at Asperfell than there are now, and a great deal more of them were of noble blood. I assume you know all about the coup to wrest the throne from King Gavreth in the early days of his rule in favor of a distant cousin?"

I vaguely recalled reading about it in one of the many books in Orwynd's library when my jolly tutor had still been alive. I nodded.

"Well, most of this lot ended up in Asperfell because they supported the would-be usurper, so naturally they have little love for Elyan, who is as much a champion of the common people as his father—perhaps even more so as he lives side by side with them here, rather than in a palace in the Shining City."

"What is it they fear Prince Elyan will do to their little society?"

"Have you ever been to the library off of the Master's workroom? The Mage who fancies himself in charge is half as talented as the men he oversees, but he was a minor lord with a vast estate. Thus, they do the labor while he…" Thaniel shrugged. "He does whatever it is he does."

"There is one such person in the garden as well," I told Thaniel. "She used to design decorative gardens on grand estates but knows nothing of vegetables. My friend, Yralis, would be much better suited for the task."

"Quite so. They fear his highness may turn this place quite upside-down."

"Is that why Lord and Lady Ashwinder care about the Countess speaking to Prince Elyan?"

Thaniel glanced sidelong at me. "Yes and no. She may be old and insane, but she is still vastly influential here at Asperfell."

"I thought she plotted against Elyan's father?"

"His grandfather, actually. She has since seen the error of her ways and supports his highness unfailingly. This Lord and Lady Ashwinder cannot abide."

"They seemed quite keen on her health," I mused.

"The Countess is both old and wealthy, and the health of the old and wealthy is always of great concern to the lesser nobility. Should the Countess's health fail at last, they fear that wealth will go to Prince Elyan, and from his hands to the less fortunate… and less deserving."

"Wealth?" I snorted. "Jewels and gowns and furniture in a *prison*? It's absurd!"

Thaniel shrugged. "Look around you. Even here, it takes a great deal of wealth and leisure to host revels such as these. It's what they live for, and absurd or not, they treasure it more than you can imagine. Personally, I am quite ready to see a change."

"Unfortunately, I am forced to agree with you."

"Why should that be unfortunate?"

"Because in agreeing with you, I am also agreeing with Prince Elyan, which is problematic as I absolutely loathe him."

"Do you? I hadn't noticed." He drained the last of the Laetha in his cup. "Come, we should enjoy ourselves while we have the chance. After that outburst, you're unlikely to be invited back again."

And so we did just that. In truth, it would have required little more than standing still in one place and watching the spectacle around us, so strange it was. As I was not keen to expose myself to further ridicule, I steered Thaniel well enough away from the dance floor. Across the room, my gaze was drawn toward a small crowd laughing uproariously at a table tucked away in a corner. It seemed a card game was being played there, something lively and full of mirth. A great shout went up and two of the Mages threw down their cards and stood, revealing the dealer.

Though it was nothing to the sharp beauty of Elyan's angular features, his was a wonderfully handsome face framed with disheveled brown hair that fell devilishly into eyes alight with mischief. His cheeks were ruddy with drink, his smile full and lively, and, had he a crown of laurel leaves, he might've been at home in a fresco at the Citadel celebrating the Old Gods.

"Who is that?" I asked.

"Arlo Bryn," he answered darkly, and steered me abruptly away to a small table on the other side of the room. Several papilems had taken refuge below the vase of flowers, and I moved one carefully aside so I could set my glass down.

Thaniel was a superb companion. He named all assembled for me and told me as much as he could about their gifts and crimes. It did not seem as though the society favored Asperfell's more notorious residents; the murderous trio of Walfrey, Samuel, and Dox were easily the most gruesomely accomplished of those gathered. Most had committed their crimes in the name of politics, being enemies of Elyan's father or his father before him. Their membership to the society, their presence at the Melancholy Revels, was clearly a longing for the halcyon days of their power and influence and luxury, and they made do with what they had, even if what they had was ancient finery that had long since gone out of fashion.

We also talked quite extensively about the lower levels of the prison as my curiosity was insatiable and I'd been waiting for ages to ask him all I could.

"First, there are those who can be and are confined to cells," Thaniel told me. "They are let out occasionally with supervision, of course, and receive all they need to survive. We try not to resort to chaining them, but sometimes it's necessary to keep them within. Of course, many have gone quite mad, so they hardly notice."

"The man you were fighting in the courtyard," I remembered suddenly. "Burtroch. Is he in one such cell?"

Thaniel pressed his lips together. "For now. He committed murder, after all, though he claims it was accidental. Master Tiberius may let him come back up one day, if he believes he can be trusted."

"And what about those whom you cannot keep confined to a cell?"

"They are the reason for my knights. Those who are strong enough, or canny enough, or possess the right sort of magic and knowledge, escape frequently. None have ever breached the doors to the upper floors in my time as warden, but I gather it happened occasionally in Asperfell's history."

"What do they do, then, if they can't breach the doors?"

Thaniel shrugged. "Torment one another until my knights apprehend them and seal them in their cells once more, or kill them in the attempt."

I shuddered. "I am never going below."

"I should hope not."

"Although I *am* curious as to what else is down there," I admitted. "While I was looking through old maps of the prison in the library, I saw a series of tunnels down there. Are they all cells?"

"No, some are old storage rooms that are no longer in use, and others lead to nowhere at all."

"Have you explored them all?"

He swallowed deeply from his cup of Laetha. "No. None of us have. Several of them are caved in, and then there's the black wall."

"Black wall?" I leaned forward in my chair. "What black wall?"

"I've never actually seen it. But there are stories of a tunnel so ancient and so far below the prison that only a handful of people have ever seen it, and not all returned to speak of it. At the end of the tunnel there is said to be a massive wall, a black wall, and a spirit waits to terrorize anyone who goes near it."

"A spirit?" I frowned. "What sort of spirit?"

"I have no idea. I doubt there is any spirit at all, but I am not keen to find out and risk being lost down there forever."

Thaniel waited until I finished my Laetha before plucking the glass from my hand and departing for the enchanted bottle, leaving me alone to watch Lord and Lady Ashwinder and their guests turn about to the music of some sort of stringed instrument, a pipe, and a drum whilst a cloud of papilem hovered above them. So engrossed was I by the sight of it that I did not realize someone had approached my table until the handsome card dealer lowered himself into Thaniel's vacant chair and I found myself face to face with his smiling brown eyes.

"Good evening. Briony Tenebrae, is it?" His voice, like his face, was warm and pleasant.

"And you're Arlo Bryn."

"So, you have been warned about me, I see!" He seemed delighted about the very prospect. "I daresay all of it is true, of course."

"I've heard nothing of you other than your name," I said, and took a certain satisfaction in watching his smile fade ever so slightly.

"Ah, well, I have heard a great deal about you. An innocent prisoner, and a Mage who did not know she was a Mage besides. You—" his broad smile was back— "are the most interesting thing to happen to Asperfell in a very long time."

"I am far from interesting, I assure you."

Thaniel had returned with our glasses, and Arlo Bryn did not give him back his seat. Rather, Thaniel had to drag one from another table, glaring at the usurper as he did so, and I gave him a sympathetic look when he handed my glass to me. It was full to the brim, and I paled. My stomach was already churning unpleasantly.

"Thaniel." Arlo greeted him with a well placed whack to his back. "How are you these days? I haven't seen you since that fight with Burtroch some weeks back—splendid show, by the way. Are you sure I cannot purchase that blade off you?"

"Quite sure," Thaniel huffed. "The price, were I willing to sell, would be far beyond your limited means."

Arlo slapped his hand over his heart and feigned a look of the acutest injury. "You wound me! I've done quite well for myself here."

"Gambling," Thaniel said scornfully, and I wondered that he took such offense at swindling money when most of Asperfell's residents were imprisoned for much greater transgressions.

Arlo shrugged, and his damnable smile widened. "We live in a prison, Thaniel! What other means have I?"

Sensing the tension, I said to Arlo quickly: "What sort of game is it you play?"

He looked over at me. "Flisket, Mistress Briony. The finest game there is."

"I've never heard of it."

"That is because it hasn't been played in Tiralaen for nigh on fifty years," Arlo replied. "It's fallen quite out of favor with the nobility there, but here in Asperfell it thrives."

"And you with it." Thaniel took a long swallow of Laetha.

"Indeed," Arlo agreed, then turned back to me. "You've yet to undergo your Trial, I'm told."

It was very odd to think so much of my life was open to my fellow prisoners. "Any advice before I do?"

"Don't choose the flowers," he laughed, though I was not privy to the joke. Then he leaned forward. "A Mage grown and no aptitude. Have you any idea at all what it might be?"

I could not say that I did, and I told him this.

"Never mind all that," he waved. "Aptitude matters naught. Although I suppose some may be considered more valuable than others." He glanced sidelong at Thaniel, and a look passed between them that I could not understand. Then he smiled and was himself again. "If I had to guess, I'd say… Battlemage."

Thaniel choked into his Laetha.

I frowned. "Why so?"

Arlo shrugged with a grin. "Why not? Can you imagine how entertaining that would be? And you've the hair for it. Isn't there some dreadful verse about redheads and fiery temperaments?"

If there were, I'd never heard of it.

"Don't you have somewhere to be, Bryn?" Thaniel asked Arlo pointedly. Evidently, he'd reached the end of his patience with his usurper.

Arlo rose from his chair and, ignoring Thaniel entirely, bowed to me. "Perhaps you will allow me to teach you the intricacies of Flisket someday, Miss Tenebrae."

"Perhaps," I answered.

"Until then." He lifted my hand for a kiss, his eyes twinkling.

"He's got a nerve," Thaniel nigh on spat, as Arlo departed our table and rejoined his game.

I said hesitantly, "He does seem quite charming."

"Oh yes, he's charming," Thaniel snorted. "And he's the reason I was kicked out of the Revels the last time."

My eyes went wide. "He's the man you fought with?"

Thaniel nodded, his eyes traveling over the couples gathered below the canopy of papilem. "Believe me when I say he richly deserved it. He is a man entirely without honor."

"What was the quarrel between you?"

Thaniel took a long swallow of Laetha—how he managed to do so without wincing and gagging was beyond me—and leaned back in his chair. "Arlo Bryn and I have a history that stretches back further than Asperfell. That was not the first fight we've been in, nor do I imagine it will be the last."

My eyes widened in surprise. "You knew one another before?"

"Oh, yes. Yes, we did. I don't suppose you'd like to hear the story?" The smile tugging at the corner of his mouth told me he knew very well I did.

"Oh, go on," I begged. "Don't keep me waiting."

And so, he began. Thaniel was the youngest of three children, raised in a small hamlet an hour's ride by horseback from Iluviel proper. His family was not poor, but neither were they wealthy. His father was a blacksmith, his mother a Mage—a Naturalist, and she served as the village's herbalist. Neither of Thaniel's older brothers were born with magic in their blood, but from the moment he'd laid hands on bars of unrefined iron and the metal surged beneath his skin, his parents had known that Thaniel was destined to shape the elements to his will.

Proven an Alchemist by his Trial, he eagerly began to help his father in his smithy, creating weapons both terrible in their might and beautiful in their craftsmanship, sumptuous and rich and coveted. It was not long before the crown recognized his talents and arrived one day to conscript him into the young king's service. They'd made a splendid procession in their black and silver livery, banners flying high in the crisp autumn wind, and they took him away on a gray palfrey as he looked back at his parents, his father standing proud and strong in his leather apron, his mother with flowers and herbs woven in her hair, tears of sorrow and joy coursing down her face.

He had been employed as an apprentice Alchemist at the Citadel for two months when word reached him that something terrible had happened in the village of his birth. He shirked his master, stole a horse from the stables, and rode like a madman to his family's cottage, his father's forge.

The flames that had consumed the forge and cottage had long since died, leaving nothing but a smoldering ruin and the burned-out husks of the house. A dirty-faced boy with hair the color and look of straw told him, stammering, that it was his mother who had drawn the ire of the Citadel.

Where his mother's skills as a Naturalist, as a healer and herb-woman, had once been revered in the hamlet and beyond, in the years since the registry her every waking moment had come under intense scrutiny. When the use of magic by any other than the king's men was outlawed, she ceased practicing out in the open but, to her husband's dismay, continued to help the poor wretched women who came to her seeking remedies to quicken their wombs or to purge children from them, to bring down a fever, to cure a winter cough. She could not abandon them; they had no one else. In the end it was a midwife, a loyal citizen of the crown, who turned her in after a woman heavy with child had shunned her services in favor of Thaniel's mother, her touch gentler and her price attainable.

Thaniel never returned to his master at the Citadel. Instead, he joined the rebellion against Keric and fashioned explosives for the resistance. It was Thaniel who crafted the bomb that killed Arlo's wife three months later, though the target had been five members of the king's reviled Mageguard and not the convoy of prisoners they escorted. But she was dead all the same, and it was his creation that had killed her.

Arlo himself had triggered the bomb, not knowing it was there, when he charged straight into the heart of the convoy on a great black courser, racing toward his wife in a desperate and doomed attempt to rescue her. The metal shoe of his horse sparked the fine silver powder, and an eruption of blue flame separated him from his wife forever.

Thaniel was arrested in the commotion that followed, and Arlo as well. Five days later, they were sent through the Gate one after the other, already bitter enemies even before setting foot in Asperfell.

"It was his interference that doomed us all. His reckless, mad, stupid plan to rescue his wife from five Mageguard. It never would have worked. They would have killed him on the spot, and likely her as well, had the flames not…" He trailed off, and his eyes grew dark. "Besides, Niven wasn't the only innocent we lost that day."

Then, as if to shake off the shadows that had gathered around him, Thaniel suddenly rose and held out his hand to me. Uncertain what words might suffice in that moment, I silently took his hand and allowed him to lead me to the dance floor. Any concern I might embarrass myself had been rendered petty and inconsequential by the weight of his confession.

We danced like a pair of fools, Thaniel and I, under the canopy of papilem in the company of the society in all of their ancient finery. We drank more Laetha after, or rather Thaniel drank more Laetha while I politely sipped mine, and then we were treated to a performance: a dramatic reading of an original poem by Lady Ashwinder herself. As she bowed dramatically to rapturous applause, I stifled a yawn with my hand and asked Thaniel if he might walk me back to my chamber.

I remembered the way well enough, but unfortunately Asperfell was in a mood to play tricks that evening. As we ascended the stairs that should have led to my chamber, I realized we were in quite another place entirely. "Blasted stairs!" I cursed.

Thaniel, who had been walking on unsteady legs since we'd left the Melancholy Revels, squinted into the gloom. "Where exactly are we?"

There was a large bank of windows to the right of me with a large, finely carved bench below them, and I looked out the dirty glass. "The western hall, I think. I'm not sure. My chamber is in the northwest tower."

Thaniel sighed, looking very much as though he'd rather lie down upon the bench and sleep than help me negotiate the way back to my chamber. "All right, back down we go."

We made our way back to the courtyard, where Thaniel lowered himself down on the ledge below the black oak while I examined the other staircases, looking for some indication that one of them led to the north hall. I had to shake my companion awake once I'd made my decision, and he followed me, grumbling and scrubbing his hands over his face, banishing the still-clinging ghosts of sleep.

Unfortunately, the staircase I'd chosen did not lead to my chamber, but rather spat us out in a dimly lit hallway hung with decaying drapes of gold velvet, with naught but a single door at its end. My hand hovered on the latch, and I glanced behind my shoulder at Thaniel.

"Worth a shot," he said with a shrug, and I began to lift the latch. *Not that way.*

Startled, I jerked my hand away from the door. "Did you hear that?" I hissed at Thaniel.

"Hear what?"

"That voice," I said. "It said: *Not that way.*"

Thaniel raised one eyebrow. "And you are inclined to believe it?"

"You really didn't hear anything?" I looked about the corridor, but saw nothing but shadows and old velvet. I must've sounded mad. Perhaps I was.

"Right," Thaniel nodded, and his hand was on the latch. "Let me."

Not that way, the voice said once more. *That way! The stairs–take the stairs!*

"Stop!" I gasped, and Thaniel started at my outburst.

"Gods, what is it?"

To the left of the door, shrouded in darkness and half hidden behind gold drapery, was a staircase, crumbling and ancient, that led down to I knew not where. But the voice did.

"There," I said, pointing. "We need to go down there."

Thaniel shrugged. "Suit yourself," he said, and Magefire rose in his hand, a torch against the dark. I followed him down the narrow, crumbling stairs.

We emerged in a familiar hall. "The northeast tower!" I exclaimed. "That's Sebben's chamber. Mine is only one floor above."

"What do you know?" Thaniel whistled. "Your voice was right after all."

I glanced back at the stairs. Deep within the shadows, I thought I saw something move, something gleaming in the dark, but before I could investigate further, it vanished.

"Yes," I said softly. "I suppose it was."

16

The strange voice in the darkness so occupied my thoughts that I had quite forgotten what transpired at the Melancholy Revels until the next morning. As I knelt between rows of cabbages with Yralis, I heard voices close by and lifted my eyes to see several finely dressed men and women entering the garden, taking great care to avoid any smattering of mud and casting the most disdainful of looks at those occupied with the laborious task of cultivating the food that they would no doubt complain about heartily that very evening.

Pushing a thick lock of hair out of my sweaty face, I was chagrined to see that one of the men was Lord Frobern himself and, on his arm, Lady Antonia wearing an entirely impractical gown of pale celadon trimmed in ivory. Behind them were two other women I thought I recognized from the Revels, though I'd not paid much attention to them as all they'd done was hover and gasp and giggle behind hands that had never seen a day's work. At the rear of the company was a man whose tunic was quite stretched over his rotund belly.

I ducked my head, hoping fervently that he'd not seen me, but my damnable red hair must've given me away. A pair of boots stopped near the patch of cabbages and a voice drawled: "I say, is that Mistress Briony?"

I sighed, then lifted my head. "It is," I said with false brightness. "Good morning, Lord Frobern."

"My goodness, Mistress Briony!" Lady Antonia gasped, her hand over her heart in what I very much suspected was mock concern for my welfare. "They are quite overworking you! And in the dirt. Your hands will feel like a laborers' before long."

"Lord Frobern," I said, ignoring her entirely. "This is Yralis."

"Charmed, I'm sure," he answered without sparing her so much as a glance, which was perhaps fortunate as she was staring at him with all the open-mouthed grace of a fish. "By the Gods, Mistress Briony, I thought you were in jest last night when you said you worked in the gardens."

Glaring into the sunlight, I gestured to the cabbages around me. "As you see, I was quite in earnest."

"Why do you not ask Lady Dorcas to share her duties?" Mistress Antonia suggested, waving a delicate hand below her wrinkled nose. "This is not work for a woman of quality."

"I've no objection to this work."

Lord Frobern stared the length of his nose at me. "Which says far more about you than it does about the work."

I sat back on my knees and met his gaze squarely. "Well, that is excellent. I should hate to be thought too high to pick the very food I eat." My eyes slid to Mistress Antonia. "Do you not agree, Mistress?"

Her smile was as cold and bright as the gems she wore. "Oh, indeed, Mistress Briony. One without even the slightest skill with magic would be far better suited to harvesting—what are those, cabbages?—than attempting and failing to be one of us."

I should have ignored her and turned back to the thick, pale green stem in my hand. Indeed, it would've been in my best interest to do so. But instead I answered: "I would rather be a cabbage in this garden than one of you, Mistress Antonia, for at least I would provide a useful service to someone."

"You disgrace your station."

"We are in *prison*," I reminded her. "I'd say we've already disgraced ourselves quite spectacularly."

Mistress Antonia pressed her lips together. "I grow weary of the sun," she told her companions. "And the stench. Let us back inside."

"Indeed," Lord Frobern agreed.

Yralis watched them walk back toward the prison, then turned her wide eyes upon me. "I've never seen Lord Frobern in the gardens before," she said. "How extraordinary!"

"I may've upset his delicate sensibilities last night at the Melancholy Revels. Likely he thought to retaliate by ridiculing me in front of my betters."

Yralis's eyes went wide. "You attended the Revels last night? Oh, Briony, you must tell me everything!"

"It is a ridiculous gathering of ridiculous people clinging to ridiculous sentiments that are entirely unimportant." I dug my trowel viciously in the dirt, punctuating each word with a spray of soil and clumps of roots. "Honestly, I'd have thought being exiled to this place would've cured them of their own self-importance, but clearly they are more tenacious than I gave them credit for. Or stupid. I cannot decide which. Honestly, who cares for such frivolities in a *prison*?"

"I do," Yralis said, and I looked up from the mess I'd made. "I would love to attend the Revels."

The hurt on her face was plain as day, and I was its cause. Dropping my trowel, I grasped her hand in mine. "I spoke thoughtlessly just now. I'm sorry. I'll tell you whatever you want to know."

"It's all right," she answered, though I could tell she was still smarting from my callousness. "I'm sure it really was as ridiculous as you say, only I would like to see it for myself at least once."

It shamed me to hear her say it; I'd blithely mocked my own privilege only moments before with the confidence of one who had never lived without it.

"I'll take you, then," I promised fervently. "The next time I am invited, I will take you as my guest and you can see it all for yourself."

Which did not seem likely after how I'd just behaved toward Lord Frobern, but I did not tell her that.

I filled the rest of the morning with as many details as I could about the Revels, though I remembered far more about the papilem and the horrid Laetha than the gowns and jewels that interested Yralis. It happened that her mother had been a seamstress and, before the young Yralis had left home to apprentice with an Elemental Mage after her Trial, she'd spent many an afternoon admiring the gowns her mother created for ladies of wealth, gowns that cost more than their family made in a year.

When at last the passage of the sun heralded Mistress Philomena's imminent arrival to escort me to my lesson, Yralis bade me take a pair of baskets back inside and return them to their proper place before she arrived.

"And take a wet cloth to that face of yours," she advised me with a smile. "I dare say you'll not want the Mistress to see you in such a state."

Smiling at her gratefully, I seized the two tightly woven baskets at her feet and dashed down the path back toward Asperfell. In the cool darkness of the storeroom, I searched the neatly ordered shelves and found similar baskets on a shelf far out of my reach.

I could hardly be trusted to perform levitation magic that did not send every single basket and box flying off the shelves into a disheveled heap, and so I dragged a crate over to stand on. As I stepped up, the heel of my boot lodged itself firmly in the hem of my skirt, and my heart leapt from my chest as I pitched backwards, a scream lodged in my throat and my limbs flailing.

Large, sturdy hands grasped my waist, halting my undignified plunge to the ground, and I twisted around to see Grenn's pockmarked face staring back at me, his beetle-black eyes boring into mine.

"Grenn," I stammered, and the scream trapped within me escaped as a breath of relief. "Thank you."

He lowered my body slowly to the ground, but his grip about my waist did not slacken and a feeling of unease bloomed within me. I attempted to disengage myself from his grip, but found myself trapped between him and the shelves at my back.

I swallowed. "Please let me pass. I must see the Master."

"You could've fallen," Grenn said. He lifted one hand from my waist and brought it to my face, trailing one dirty finger down my cheek, to my neck, to the swell of my breast above the neckline of my gown.

I went utterly still. No man had ever touched me thus, so intimately and without invitation. It was so grotesque a violation that it left me utterly without breath, without speech, without even thought; a void, a nothingness.

Shame came then, and revulsion, spreading through me like ink spilled upon parchment, blotting out everything beneath, leaving a stain that could never be scrubbed away. And mingled with the shame, anger: such breathless anger the likes of which I had never felt.

"Take your hands from me," I demanded, my voice low and shaking with fury. "How dare you touch me thus."

Grenn's eyes flickered from the path his finger had traced upon my skin and met mine. "You should be grateful," he intoned. "I saved your pretty neck."

Fury, white-hot and consuming, gave me the courage I required.

With both hands flat against his chest, I shoved violently at Grenn, and though he seemed more stone than man, as unmovable as the Sentinels that surrounded the moor, surprise was my ally. He stumbled backwards, and I was able to wriggle beneath the arm he'd braced against the shelves.

If he called out to me, I did not hear him; I took my skirts in my hands and ran from the storeroom in the direction of the kitchens, where I knew other Mages would be milling about in droves. Willow stood at the great table, her hands outstretched and her fingers moving in a brisk, repetitive pattern. Below, three knives danced to her command, chopping mounds of pungent herbs. The familiar scents of thyme, marjoram, savory, and sage filled my nostrils.

Willow's head snapped up when I drew near and her hands stopped abruptly, sending the knives clattering in an undignified heap atop the piles of herbs.

"Mistress Briony!" she squeaked. "You startled me!"

"I'm sorry," I told her. "Truly. Do you mind if I stay here with you a while until Mistress Philomena comes to collect me?"

Willow nodded silently, her eyes wide with curiosity; no doubt I looked a fright. Indeed, now that I was well away from Grenn, the heat that had suffused my body had quite evaporated, leaving me cold and quite shaken.

I slid onto a bench while Willow fetched a shallow bowl from a shelf nearby and then dipped a ladle into one of the steaming cauldrons hanging over the fire. "Broth," she told me, as I lifted the bowl with both hands and inhaled the fragrant steam. "I thought perhaps you needed it." She flushed to the roots of her mousy brown hair. "I mean no offense, Mistress Briony."

"And you gave none, Willow. Thank you for the broth."

Willow gave me a shy smile. Then she resumed her place before the piles of herbs and, closing her eyes, began to move her hands back and forth in the same pattern as before. The knives were slow to respond, but gradually they rose and fell and rose again, faster and faster until, under Willow's skilled ministrations, they resumed their chopping.

I did not know whether it was the broth or the soothing motion of Willow's hands, but my racing heart began to slow. Yet I could not banish entirely the knot of worry and confusion that twisted uncomfortably within me at the memory of Grenn's fingers and the foul-smelling bulk of him. That men took liberties with women was, as my Aunt Eudora used to say, a regrettable certainty.

But that I should feel shame for the treatment I'd received at the hands of a brute was unexpected and most distressing. Had not the fault been his and his alone? I had hardly encouraged him. Indeed, before that afternoon, I had done my utmost to avoid him, compelled by misgivings that, after what had just transpired, had been entirely justified. And yet, shame remained, though it was like no shame I'd ever known. A child I'd been before, for shame had been simple, and now it was not.

I'd finished my broth and Willow was starting in on her third bundle of herbs when Mistress Philomena found me, her lips pursed in disapproval; I'd forgotten all about my face.

"I do believe I am wanted," I said, and pushed my empty bowl back across the table with a grimace.

"Here." Willow handed me a cloth. "Best hurry."

After scrubbing my face so vigorously my cheeks hurt, I followed Mistress Philomena silently to Master Tiberius's workroom, lost in a stew of my own thoughts; indeed I was so preoccupied that I nearly forgot to tell him about the strange voice in the darkness until he asked me how I found my first visit to the Melancholy Revels.

"Oh!" I exclaimed suddenly. "Yes, the Revels. Ghastly. But afterward, when the staircases changed and I couldn't find my way back to my chamber, I heard a voice in the darkness that guided me!"

Master Tiberius raised one eyebrow. "I am curious as to why you found the Revels ghastly, but we'll come back to that. Was the voice human?"

"I believe so, though it sounded strange—not at all like any voice I've ever heard. And I think it was male, though I cannot be sure."

"And you saw no one?"

"No," I said, and hesitated as I remembered movement in the shadows, the gleam of eyes. "I thought I might've seen something move in the darkness, but if anything was there, it did not stay for long."

"And have you ever heard this voice before?"

I shook my head. "Never."

He studied me shrewdly. "It could be any number of things," he said at last. "None of which we are likely to discover until you undergo your Trial. It may be that your aptitude is beginning to emerge."

I felt a thrill at these words, and it was exceedingly difficult to focus on the rest of my lesson; indeed, I made a number of unfortunate errors, one of which caused a number of dusty glass flagons to fly off a shelf near the door to the library. As if the sound itself had not been dreadful enough (and earned a round of hearty condemnations from the scholars within), the smoke that arose from the contents of one of the bottles was possessed of an unholy stench that caused our noses and eyes to run.

Despite such accidents, I continued to advance in my study of magic at a rapid pace. In mere months, I had already learned what children took years to master due to the greater reserve that came with advanced years. There were still days when I had to force Master Tiberius's putrid tonic down my throat and walk on shaky legs back to my chamber, but they grew fewer and far between.

Magefire was especially difficult for me, and when I failed to progress to his liking, Prince Elyan decided to increase my motivation by extinguishing the fire in my grate and refusing to light it again.

The first night, I stayed awake shivering, curled into a tiny ball in my covers and cursing Elyan with every fiber of my unbearably cold being. The second night, I attempted to use on my blankets the same warming spell I'd learned to heat the water in the copper tubs in the washroom. Unfortunately, the warmth I felt beneath my palm turned out to be me burning a hole straight through the fabric. It smoked something terrible, and so I had to open the window to air it out, letting *in* the frigid autumn air. Thus, I spent another night in cold that made my limbs ache.

The next day, I was exhausted and sour and determined to prove Elyan quite wrong. In Master Tiberius's workroom, Elyan extinguished the Magefire in the grate and prowled like a large cat behind me, arms crossed, while I struggled and failed to bring it to life again.

"Hurry it up, will you?" he sighed. "I'm freezing."

"You are welcome to light it yourself," I answered through gritted teeth. My own hands were positively shaking with cold.

"If I do, you'll never learn."

I was not entirely sure I would learn with or without his help. I'd thought, foolishly, creating flame from nothing at all would be no more difficult than lighting a candle wick. I was quite mistaken.

Again and again, I thrust my hand toward the empty grate.

Elyan sighed heavily behind me. "Alas, another long, frigid night awaits."

Already so cold that my limbs had stiffened and my nose ran, something inside me snapped in that moment, and I whirled around furiously. "If I knew how to conjure Magefire, rest assured I would use it on you!"

"It is lucky for me, then, that you are completely inept."

"I'm not," I said through clenched teeth.

"You are."

"I'm not!" I shouted, with an emphatic gesture in his direction, which sent flames erupting from my outstretched fingers. He shouted in surprise and threw himself to the ground in time for my disastrous first conjuring of Magefire to fly past him. Instead, it hit the far wall of the workroom where it scorched the stone and set fire to several nearby shelves.

"Coleum's balls!" Elyan roared, pushing himself back up and fixing me with a murderous glare. Master Tiberius quickly rushed to inspect the damage I'd unwittingly inflicted.

"I'm sorry!" I wailed.

"You'll be the death of us all," Elyan snarled.

"As if you never made mistakes when you were a student."

"Not mistakes that nearly killed my teachers!"

"It's not your fault, Briony," Master Tiberius told me as kindly as he could, with Elyan still fuming and ready to condemn me to a cell where they kept the dangerous ones. "Your advanced age gives you power, but your lack of knowledge and practice denies you control. It will improve with time."

I slumped into one of the chairs in front of the empty grate miserably. "I'm exceedingly sorry I almost lit you on fire, but please light the Magefire in my grate again. I can't spend another night in the cold."

"I told you, you'll never learn if I continue to do it for you."

"Magic cast under duress is unpredictable and dangerous," Master Tiberius warned Elyan. "I'll not have her setting fire to her room."

A bargain was struck in which Elyan agreed to light the fire in my grate when night fell so that I did not freeze to death in my bed but come morning he would extinguish it once more so I could practice.

I stood wrapped in a blanket and scowling at him the first morning he came to plunge my chamber into ice, and nearly sobbed with relief when he appeared later that evening. In between, I'd manage to conjure Magefire several times, just not where I intended to, and my grate remained empty, though the stones around it were scorched with my failed attempts.

The next day, wrapped in my blanket, I watched Elyan disappear down the corridor and promised myself he would have no further reason to return. So, I sat cross-legged before the empty grate until I finally felt the blessed warmth of the flames bathe my face and then I rose, let fall the blanket around my shoulders, and dashed from my room in search of my tormenter.

He was in Master Tiberius's workroom reading a book, and when

I burst through the door, he looked up only briefly before returning to his manuscript. "Yes, what is it?"

"I did it!"

"Did what?"

"Lit my own Magefire!"

"Congratulations." He did not look up.

"You are positively odious," I told him. "Aren't you at least going to feign happiness for me?"

"I don't have to feign anything for you," he replied. "I'm a prince."

I very much considered grabbing a nearby jug and shattering it over his head.

At last, on a frigid morning four months after my arrival at Asperfell, Master Tiberius decided I was ready to undergo the Trial to determine my aptitude.

Elyan disagreed, of course, but that may have been because I'd been practicing my levitation on a large stoppered bottle weighed down with sand and, in an effort to propel it higher, sent it smashing into the ceiling right above where Elyan happened to be sitting, showering him with glass shards and filling his hair with sand.

"You cannot truly believe she is ready," Elyan protested, gingerly picking slivers of glass off of his shoulders. "Look at this mess."

Master Tiberius frowned at the worktable, then whisked the sand away with a wave of his hand. "Her magic needs focus," he argued. "Her spells often backfire, I believe, because there is simply too much power behind them. Control will come with training, yes, but determining her aptitude will allow her to funnel her power into the gift she was born into and weaken the impulse of her magic to overcompensate."

If Elyan disagreed with Master Tiberius, he did not say so.

The day of my Trial dawned, and I was so mad with anticipation that I felt as though I might jump out of my skin. Tradition, though whose I could not say, dictated that the ceremony must begin at sundown, and though I begged Master Tiberius to let me do it earlier, he adamantly refused and sent me off to work in the garden with Yralis and Grenn.

Yralis did her best to keep me occupied training vining plants onto trellises and constructing slings of cloth to cradle the fruit already growing. We tied each end of an improvised sling to the sturdy wooden trellises, leaving enough room for the squashes to grow full and robust without resting on the ground. They would be harvested soon and placed in the cellars to dry.

I glanced across the garden to where Grenn was standing, leaning his bulk against the hoe he was using to split the earth and extract the roots of the summer vegetables long gone to seed. His beady eyes met mine and an uneasy feeling settled in my stomach at his expression. I spent the rest of my afternoon with my back to him, trying to keep my hands busy.

At last Yralis sent me back to my chambers to scrub the filth of the day off of my skin and out of my hair, and to dress for the evening.

I had planned on wearing one of the gowns I'd found in the trunk at the foot of my bed and, possessing little faith in my own mending abilities, I'd asked Mistress Orial to assist me in making it presentable.

"Oh, dear," she'd said, genuine distress on her face when I'd held out the teal fabric for her inspection. "I would help you, I would, but…"

"But?"

She glanced swiftly at Lady Antonia, who was hovering nearby, her eyes narrowed. "It's just that I am very busy at the moment," Mistress Orial finished unhappily, and cast her gaze downward.

I stole a glance at Lady Antonia and, as expected, her painted lips were twisted in a triumphant smile. Evidently, she'd not forgotten that day in the garden.

And so, without Mistress Orial's help, I attempted to strengthen the seams with a binding spell of my own and prayed they held and the fragile fabric did not fall to pieces in front of Prince Elyan and Master Tiberius. I did not think I would ever outlive the shame.

I had just finished spreading the gown out on my bed when there was a knock on the door and I opened it to find Philomena standing there looking quite awkward.

"Good evening," she said crisply. "The Master bid me see if you needed anything."

Unaccustomed to her concern for my comfort, it took me a moment to answer. "I'm fine, thank you. Although, I wouldn't mind a second look at my seams."

"Where did you find this?" she asked, as we stood beside the bed together and looked down at the taffeta. "It looks ancient."

"I think it *is* ancient."

"Why did you not have Mistress Orial and her ladies mend it?"

My cheeks flushed. "It is possible I insulted Lady Antonia in the garden some weeks ago," I admitted.

"You may have, or you did?"

"I most certainly did."

Mistress Philomena snorted derisively. "Lady Antonia thinks very highly of herself. I imagine it did not take much." She pursed her lips as she poked and prodded the stitches I'd done, turned the fabric over and over in her hands, tugged here and there, and pronounced it serviceable. I breathed a sigh of relief.

I thought she intended to leave me to my preparations, but instead she hesitated in the doorway, her hand splayed against the wood, and turned back to me.

"A Trial is a momentous occasion in a young Mage's life," she said. "We've never had one here before, as you can imagine. But all of us, myself included, remember what it is to go through it." Her eyes lingered on the gown, my long, unruly hair. "I remember my mother bought my dress from Shefelt. Crimson, it was. The finest fabric my family had ever seen."

I looked up at her stern countenance, her gray hair, and tried to imagine a girl in her place, a girl in a red dress. I thought perhaps I could. "I'm sure it was beautiful."

Her eyes saw beyond me, her smile wistful. "It was. And my hair—" she brought her hand up, touched the severe bun she always wore atop her head, not a hair out of place. "She spent an age at the glass with a hot iron and ribbons. I did not recognize myself when she was through."

Had I come of age as a Mage in a world in which Keric was not king, I could imagine that my mother would've been meticulous in choosing my gown, that my uncle would've presented me with some lovely trinket or another, that perhaps Livia and I would've set aside our squabbling and she might've helped me with my hair.

"Never mind all that." Philomena collected herself, any trace of gentleness gone. "Come. I'll help you with that hair."

Her hands were steady and sure as she brushed my hair and arranged it with pins she pulled from a pocket on her dress, and afterward she helped me into the gown and tightened the lacing down the back. I'd never cared for fine clothes when I'd had them, a source of endless frustration to my mother and sister, but now, running my fingers over the fragile fabric, I found myself excited to wear it.

"The color suits you," she said, as I stood before her nervously smoothing my skirts with both hands. "Come now, best not to be late."

When at last we arrived at Master Tiberius's workroom, the sight that greeted me took my breath away.

The table had been swept clean of its usual bric-a-brac. In a row beginning with flowers and ending with a goblet of blood stood the items that would reveal my aptitude, the magic I had been born to wield. My eyes feasted on each item, recognizing them for what they were, what they were meant to be, and I felt a fissure of excitement run through me: a pot of tiny white flowers, a Gnasher in a cage, a sheaf of wheat, a pile of earth, a bowl of water, a candle, a single leaf, a golden feather, a rod of iron, a long-handled knife, a bleached white bone, a crystal full of swirling gray smoke, and the goblet of blood.

Master Tiberius stood at one end of the table, Prince Elyan at the other, their faces solemn in the flickering light of the many candles lit for the occasion. Elyan was dressed all in black shot through with silver, and I realized he was wearing the colors of his house, the colors of Tiralaen. He looked every inch a king, and I suddenly felt nervous in my borrowed finery.

Philomena nodded briefly to them, and then departed silently.

"You look lovely, my dear," Master Tiberius said by way of greeting, and I flushed with pleasure. I'd not often been called lovely, and might normally have been inclined to laugh heartily at his words, but that night, in my teal gown, I was pleased.

"She'll do," Elyan put in drily.

"I don't know what to do," I confessed, drawing nearer to the table, the skirts of my gown rustling softly. I counted only thirteen relics in total. "Is this all? Are there not more branches of magic?"

"There are others," Master Tiberius agreed. "Like our dear Countess the Scriviner. But they are somewhat difficult to test. If you do not feel your magic call to one of these relics, we will consider them."

I nodded. "All right, then. What shall I do?"

"Stand before each relic," Master Tiberius instructed, "and reach out with your magic. Like calls to like. If the relic represents your aptitude, you will feel a pull, a connection. And you will be able to manipulate the relic as a result."

It sounded easy enough, but then, so had every lesson in magic I'd had at Asperfell, and none of it had been at all.

"I'm nervous."

"Do not be," Master Tiberius said gently. "All will be well."

I moved to the worktable, directly in front of the pot of flowers. The relic of a Naturalist. I stared down at the while petals, then stretched my hand over them, feeling for any trace of magical connection. I felt nothing at all.

"Ought I to feel something?" I asked, looking up at the Master. "Am I doing it incorrectly?"

"Not at all. This just means your talents do not lie in nature. Not at all surprising." He gestured to the cage. "Continue."

Nothing happened when I stood in front of the Gnasher, though it did hiss and snap at me horribly, nor the sheaf of wheat. The pile of dirt provoked nothing, as did the bowl of water, the candle, the leaf, and the rod of iron. So, too, the feather. They were nothing but objects to me; my magic did not stir.

There were only a few relics left: the knife, the bone, the smoke in the crystal, and the goblet of blood. I lingered over the knife, hoping I would feel a pull to the steel, but it lay immobile and silent, and whatever confidence I had felt in my new-old gown and beautiful hair began to ebb.

The bone, I feared. I could not help but think of Phyra as I looked down at it. It was an awesome power, to be sure, to raise the dead. But it was not one I wanted for myself. My relief was palpable when I felt no magical connection to the bone and left it where it lay.

The crystal was, I knew, the relic for a Siphon, Price Elyan's aptitude, one of the rarest branches of magic. Inside the clear facets, a dark gray plume of smoke swirled.

"Try to pull the magic from the crystal," Prince Elyan told me quietly, when I glanced up at him. I tried to no avail. I could feel no pull between the smoke and my own magic, and it stayed firmly ensconced within the crystal, indifferent to my command. I was clearly no Siphon.

There was only one relic left: the goblet of blood. The relic of a Blood Mage. It was this aptitude I feared the most; yet I could not deny its power, and power was what I sought. I stared down at the pool of red so dark it was nearly black, and willed something, anything to happen. But just as with all of the other relics, I felt nothing at all.

"Not a Blood Mage, then," Master Tiberius said in the growing silence, and I was grateful that his tone was brisk and purposeful, not sympathetic. He clearly had not given up on me despite the fact that I was very close to giving up on myself. I refused to imagine what Prince Elyan was thinking. No doubt it would've shamed me to tears. "Perhaps a Scrivener, then. Or a Truth-Teller."

"Wouldn't she have felt a pull to the water, then?" There was skepticism in Elyan's voice. "You did place it in a bowl, after all, and not a goblet."

I glanced at Master Tiberius, who was rubbing his beard, a thoughtful expression on his face. "Yes, yes. But it is worth another try."

Although I did not relish eventually appearing quite mad the way the Countess did, the ability to divine the future could prove useful in trying to find a way to escape Asperfell and return Elyan to Tiralaen. I was led back to the bowl of water and told to place my hands on either side of the vessel and look deep within the water. In the flat surface I saw my face, but nothing more. I reached out with my magic, seeking something, any sort of connection at all to what lay beyond the reflection of myself. There was nothing. My spirits sunk even farther.

Determining whether or not I was a Truth-Teller involved seating me before Prince Elyan, our chairs drawn so close together that our knees touched, and listening to him tell me a story. He spoke in low, even tones about finding a raven with a broken wing when he was eight years old and his brother six. Keric had wanted to bring the bird back to one of the Citadel's many healers, but Elyan, knowing the bird would not survive the painful journey, took the tiny neck in his fingers and snapped it quickly; a clean death. They'd buried the broken body, and Keric had cried the entire way back to the palace.

"Is it a truth?" Elyan asked me, his eyes fixed intently on mine.

I reached out with my magic. I thought I felt something, a stirring, but whether or not Elyan's story was true, I could not tell.

"I don't know," I said at last, my shoulders sagging. "I feel magic, but I think it's just you—your magic, nothing more."

"Try again." Elyan leaned forward, his elbows against his considerably longer legs. Our faces were only inches apart.

"Nothing." I shook my head. "I don't feel anything. True, false, it could be either."

Elyan leaned back in his chair, and I felt acutely the emptiness that lay between us now. "It was a false story, as it were," he said. "It was Keric who snapped the bird's neck, and me who cried all the way home."

Master Tiberius pulled one of the benches out from under the worktable and lowered himself upon it.

"I failed," I said gloomily.

"Not necessarily." Master Tiberius looked over at me. "Perhaps you are simply not ready, or your magic is not strong enough to find its like in a relic."

"There are other branches of magic we have not considered." Elyan thrummed his fingers on his thighs. "Archaic ones certainly, and perhaps not very powerful, but it may be worth seeking them out."

Not very powerful. My hopes at once turned to ash in my mouth.

"I'm going to be like The Cat, aren't I? Something for this place to wonder at. A Mage who has no aptitude and whose spells consist of lighting candles and moving piles of dirt."

"Don't forget smashing little glass bottles." Elyan's tone was wry.

"Oh yes." I attempted to laugh, and it came out as an unladylike snort instead. "I'll need that one to keep folk away who've come to gawk at my complete ineptitude."

"You're not completely inept."

"That is perhaps the nicest thing you have ever said to me."

"Rest assured, it will not happen again."

"The Cat," Master Tiberius said slowly, and Elyan and I looked over at him. He was staring into the shadows, a strange expression on his face, as though he were slowly reasoning something out. "The Cat," he said again, and looked up at me abruptly. "We must find The Cat."

Elyan and I followed Master Tiberius wordlessly with identical expressions of surprise on our faces as he threw open the door of his workroom and charged down the corridor toward the kitchens.

"Why do we need The Cat?" I asked Elyan, as I struggled with the long skirts of my gown on one of the tightly coiled spiral staircases. "I thought I already tried the relic for an Animalis."

"No idea. He's known for the odd tangent every now and then, but this is especially strange."

The Cat was not in the kitchens that evening. Willow, who was cleaning up after the evening meal, told us she'd not seen him for an hour at least. He'd gone off chasing something.

"Check the storage rooms, perhaps the garden," she told us. "Good luck to you. That damnable animal never comes when called."

Master Tiberius's eyes gleamed. "He may yet. Briony, you'll return to your room while Elyan and I continue our search. When we find The Cat, we'll bring him to you."

"I still don't understand what all of this is about," I said, as they deposited me like a sack of grain at my chamber door. Elyan, I noticed, gave my umbra guard a wide berth and a wary eye.

My courage bolstered by the presence of my guard, I decided to make sure The Cat had not decided to hide in the washroom before I settled in my chamber to await the return of Master Tiberius and Prince Elyan. The washroom was, unfortunately, empty. I even lifted my gown up and got down on my hands and bare knees to check under each of the tubs and in the corners behind the barrels that held the soap shavings. I found only a rather large spider enjoying a meal of I knew not what, and I left him to it. Dusting myself off and fluffing my voluminous skirts, I left the washroom and ran headlong into the immovable bulk of a man.

The impact of my body against his knocked my breath from me, and I fell back against the door.

It was Grenn.

17

Grenn stared down at me, his broad, blunt features drawn in anger and something else, something wild and desperate and terrifying. A visceral fear chilled me to the bone, an earthly fear more tangible than umbras or spells or Sentinels had ever been. I could scarce breathe.

I gathered my courage. "Grenn," I said, my voice low and steady. "Please move out of my way."

He said nothing, but brought his arm up, his large, beefy arm, and placed his hand firmly beside my head. I ducked under and broke into a run toward my chamber, the long skirts of my gown tangling with my legs. I had always been fast, skinny as I was and much practiced in the art of escaping my tutors, but for all Grenn's bulk, he was my equal. Within a dozen steps, I felt his hand grasping at my waist, twisting my body, slamming my back into the stone wall.

The air went out of my lungs entirely and my mouth opened in a silent cry of pain as he pressed his body against mine.

Wildly I tried to cast a shield, but the command would not come; in fact, nothing came at all. In my panic, my magic had utterly, completely deserted me.

I fought him with everything that I was, kicking and shrieking and clawing at his face. I could feel the evidence of his desire against my middle through the poor cloth of his trousers, and my gorge rose. I knew well enough what it was; I'd plied the truth from the maid-servants at Orwynd long ago, but I never could've imagined that this was how I would discover it for myself, pinned against a wall in terror by a man three times my size. One of Grenn's bulbous hands groped at my breasts, kneading my flesh so hard that tears sprang to my eyes, and finding my voice at last, I screamed in pain and impotent rage.

Grenn tried to muffle my cries with his hand, and seizing the opportunity, I bit him, hanging on until I tasted the copper of his blood in my mouth. He released me then, staggering back with an angry bellow.

"Help!" I screamed as I ran, my chamber door in sight. "Elyan! Master Tiberius!"

He had caught up with me, and when I wrenched my hand from his grasp, the effort sent me sprawling on the hard stone. I might've cursed him as he bore down on me, his face twisted in rage and pain, if I'd not glimpsed behind him a pearly glow, the only other living—or not, as it were—person who might be able to help me in the absence of all others.

Deep within me my magic stirred, and I welcomed it. I felt the command surging through my veins, through every inch of my being, and I knew it as surely as I knew myself. Like called to like, Master Tiberius had said, and in that desperate moment, I knew.

"Defend me!" My voice, rich and strong and sonorous, rang throughout the corridor as if it belonged to someone else entirely, someone powerful. "Defend me now!"

My guard, my faithful sentry, seemed somehow more substantial, more defined by my words. I thought I could finally see the outlines of his face: a proud face, well made and strong, and from his glimmering cape he pulled a ghostly sword.

Grenn, drawn by my gaze, my command, turned too late. My guard bore down on him with a terrible vengeance, and though I'd not thought a shade could inflict bodily harm on a living person, somehow the impact of his charge sent Grenn sprawling on the ground. I hastily scrabbled to my feet. In the corridor beyond, I heard footfalls and Elyan's voice shouting my name.

"Elyan!" I screamed, as my guard hovered above Grenn, the point of his ghostly sword pointed at his breast. I knew not if it could pierce him, though neither did Grenn, and his fear and uncertainty bought me time—time enough for Elyan and Master Tiberius to find us, our hideous tableau.

"Briony," Master Tiberius breathed. "What have you done?"

It was with difficulty that I found my voice now that the urgency, the fear for my life, had left me. "Stand down," I said to my guard, reaching out with my magic. "Leave him be."

The ghostly sword was withdrawn, and Master Tiberius dispatched of Grenn with ease, rendering the odious man unconscious and a threat to no one. I was dimly aware of Elyan above me, his hands grasping my own, his eyes searching me for blood or bruises.

"I'm all right," I said, my hands closing tightly around his. "I'm all right."

I looked to my guard, withdrawn now, and I felt a rush such that I had never felt in my life. He had been a man once, and I knew nothing about him other than that he had saved my life and I would owe him for the remainder of my days. I didn't even know his name.

"We set off to find The Cat, and yet you proved what I suspected all along without him," said Master Tiberius. "I'm sorry it came to this, but my dear, *this* was your Trial."

"I don't understand."

"Orare," Master Tiberius said. "You are an Orare."

"A what?" I'd never heard the word, knew not what it meant.

"A speaker. You can speak to magic," Elyan told me.

To speak; this was my aptitude? I was torn between laughing and crying. I'd done it, I'd managed not to fail my Trial, only to discover that my power was no power at all.

"When you said you heard a voice in the darkness that guided you in the right direction, when you thought you saw something move in the darkness, I wondered if it might've been The Cat speaking to you. I suspected your talents might lie in communication, but I needed to be sure." Master Tiberius gave me a look that may have been pride in me or triumph in his own brilliant deduction. Perhaps something of both. "An umbra is difficult to command. It is an impressive feat indeed, my dear."

"I can speak to umbras? Is that the extent of it?"

"Not umbras," Master Tiberius corrected. "*Magic*. There are a great number of things both naturally and unnaturally imbued with magic. If there is a way to communicate with them, an Orare will find it." He laughed suddenly. "*That's* why they've all been following you! The umbras!"

"Of course," Elyan said. "You've talked to them before, haven't you? You didn't realize it at the time, but they probably felt the pull of your magic."

Master Tiberius was positively beaming, and there was even a faint smile on Elyan's face. I forced myself to look happy, to conceal the disappointment in my gift.

"This is splendid," I said. "Truly! I'm so glad I didn't fail after all."

"Oh, we would've discovered where your talents lay eventually," Master Tiberius chuckled. "But I am very glad it did not take us until the sun came up."

The hour was, in fact, very late, but I found that I was wide awake, my heart still racing in the aftermath of Grenn's assault and the discovery of my aptitude. Pride warred with dissatisfaction and frustration to produce a peculiar sort of giddy madness in me.

Somewhat reluctantly, Master Tiberius bid me goodnight so as to return to his workroom and sweep away the relics of my Trial, promising to tell me as much as he knew about my aptitude tomorrow.

Elyan took responsibility for Grenn's sprawling body, levitating it and escorting it down the corridor, looking quite as lost in his own thoughts as I was.

I nearly called out to both of them to stay. What had transpired that night transcended every moment I'd spent in the workroom lighting candles and banishing books. I was frightened and thrilled and knew not where to settle myself between the two. I watched them disappear and, save for my savior, I was alone.

My hand on the knob of my chamber door, I turned and looked at my soldier. I did not feel the same riotous power flowing through my voice this time as when I'd commanded him to take arms in defense of me. It was a far subtler connection between us, but I felt it nonetheless. And I knew he understood me as I said, softly and solemnly, "Thank you."

The gown I had worked so hard to restore had torn in several places during Grenn's attack. I fingered the sleeve with dismay where it was coming loose from the bodice. And I was quite certain that if Mistress Philomena could see my hair now, she would despair at the ruination of her hard work.

I had scarce begun to pull the pins from the curls that *were* still in place when there was a soft knock at my door. I opened it to find Prince Elyan holding a dusty bottle and two small glasses.

"There's usually a celebration of some sort after a Trial," he said by way of explanation. "Not often with alcohol, mind you, as the Mage is usually a youth, but... I thought it was appropriate in this case."

He offered me the glasses and I took them by their stems, stepping back to allow him room to pass. He sat on the trunk at the foot of my bed, his long legs stretched out in front of him, and pulled the cork from the bottle, then filled the two glasses with deep red liquid.

"To you," he said simply, and touched his glass briefly against mine before he drank. I took a small sip, letting the bright flavors of the claret spill across my tongue. It was delicious.

We drained our glasses in companionable silence. Elyan refilled them, stuck the stopper back in the neck of the bottle, and looked over at me. "You are disappointed."

"A bit," I confessed, and felt mingling shame and guilt as I did so. I was a Mage. I could command magic; my aptitude should've been of little concern to me. But I could not deny the bitterness of discovering that my power was of little consequence to the daunting task I'd been given. The weight of the day had settled on me, and the wine had already begun to loosen my tongue. I longed to unburden myself, but this man with his sharp tongue, a perfect companion to the planes and angles of his haughty face, was a cypher; one moment I was sure I'd seen every facet of him, and the next I'd discovered a new one.

"Why?" he asked, no trace of mockery in his voice.

"Master Aeneas died holding the Gate open so I might pass through," I said. "I know you hold him in little esteem, but it was by his sacrifice that I survived. He and Cyprias gave their lives so I might return you to Tiralaen."

"They meant a great deal to you."

"I only knew Master Aeneas fleetingly, when I was a child. But he was exceedingly kind to me. And Cyprias… Yes, he meant a great deal to me."

A frown creased Elyan's forehead. "Your father's spy?"

"He was so much more than just my father's spy," I said. "He was my friend. Even when I was a child and a bother to everyone else, he treated me with kindness and respect far beyond what my station afforded. And he believed in me so fiercely." I smiled, remembering the day he'd found me hiding in the shadows, far more interested in court politics than in needlework. "He once told me knowledge was a weapon that anyone could wield, that I could be a warrior in my own way, child though I was, and a girl child at that."

"Just so," Elyan said softly, and I thought, perhaps, he did understand. "Whatever their intentions, the old man had to have known it was a fool's errand even if your spy did not. They never should've yoked you with such a task."

"There was no other way. If you do not return, Keric will destroy Tiralaen and everyone in it, whether they be Mage or otherwise." I sighed heavily. "I had hoped I possessed a stronger gift, one that could help you escape this place so that Cyprias did not die in vain. Nor my father, nor Master Aeneas. But my gift is nothing but my voice, and I have no idea how it might help you. I may as well have failed today."

He reached out and touched my jaw lightly with the tip of his finger, raising my face so our eyes met. "There is power in a voice such that you cannot imagine," he said softly. "Do not doubt it."

His fingers fell away, and he turned back to the fire. The skin where he had touched me felt so peculiar, and to distract myself I took a too-large swallow of wine, savoring the burn it left in my throat as I drank it down. Already I could feel my head beginning to swim.

"There is something I must know," I said. He tilted his head at me, an indication to continue. "Master Tiberius told me you did not mean to kill your father, but you said you deserved to be here. I have to know. My father died believing you innocent."

He said nothing, and I was afraid I'd broken the fragile connection that seemed to have grown between us. He stared into the Magefire, the light throwing his face occasionally into shadow, until at last, he spoke. "Do you know how my father died?"

"Magic," I said, and only now did I realize how inadequate that answer was.

"Blood magic."

"But you're not—"

"A Blood Mage, I know."

And then I understood. "Master Tiberius said he met a Blood Mage when he was a child. Are they one in the same?"

Elyan nodded. "I suspect so, yes, and Keric found him and somehow convinced him to weave a spell into my father's blood. When I found my father that night, he was near death and so I did the one thing an arrogant, power-drunk boy could be counted on to do: I tried to save him myself, use my gift to heal him."

In the firelight his face had become so bitter, so twisted, that I drew back from him a little, though I doubted he noticed. He was lost in the recollection of a memory so painful, so full of horror, that I may as well have not been there at all.

"Only it didn't heal him." His voice was devastatingly quiet. "The spell was woven so tightly that when I pulled the magic from his blood, his life came with it."

My hand crossed the space between us and I gripped one of his. He blinked as if coming out of a trance, and I felt his fingers curl around mine.

"He died in my arms." Elyan's rich, deep voice cracked. Something inside me shifted in that moment and I saw him not anew, but with far greater understanding.

"It wasn't your fault," I whispered. "You tried to save him."

"I shouldn't have tried at all." The self-loathing in his voice was palpable. "I should've called for a Healer, should've sent for a Master. In my conceit I thought my gift could save him, but my gift is a curse, Briony—meant only to harm."

"That's not true," I said, remembering what Master Tiberius had told me. "The magic isn't itself evil, only the intent of the Mage. And you were trying to save his life, not take it."

"I was arrogant," he replied, and tossed back the dregs in his glass with contempt. "And in my hubris, I took a man's life. So, you see, your father was entirely wrong about me. I did kill my father."

"No." I shook my head. I was gripping his hand so tightly my knuckles had gone white. "A Blood Mage killed your father. You tried to save him. My father and many more besides have died because they believe you innocent, and you are."

He gave a short, bitter laugh. "My intention may not have been to kill my father, but I am far from innocent. You forget I have lived these twelve years imprisoned. Do not for a moment make the mistake of believing I did not dirty my hands to survive when the occasion called for it."

"I did not imagine otherwise," I said, and I fervently hoped my shaking voice did not betray the fact that, at times, I did worry very much about the things he had done as he came of age in this place. "But you did survive. And my father did not die so that you could wallow in self-pity." I nearly laughed at the indignant expression on his face, but his silence gave me courage to press on. "It doesn't matter that no one has ever escaped this place before. It only matters that no one has done it yet. I do not intend to simply give up."

Those extraordinary eyes met mine, and I thought I saw a glimmer of hope in them. "You confound me," he said at last, and his gaze became shuttered once more. "I do not deserve your help, and even if you could somehow restore me to Tiralaen, they would never accept me as their king."

"You cannot know that."

He was silent for a very long time. Then he squeezed my hand briefly before he let go to take up the wine bottle. "You should get some rest."

He watched as I drained the last of my wine, then he plucked the glass from my fingers and stood. He left me sitting on my trunk, staring into the Magefire.

"Elyan?"

He turned in my doorway, an eyebrow raised in question.

"Thank you."

A swift nod, and he was gone.

18

I no longer required Philomena to walk beside me to and from the gardens or Master Tiberius's workroom. There always seemed to be an umbra hovering nearby, and I discovered it was not so much that my fellow prisoners were afraid of them; they were afraid of what they thought I could make them do.

The tale of Grenn and my soldier had spread like wildfire throughout the prison. The umbras that had for so long been a source of discontent among my fellow incarcerated were now feared and avoided, just as I was. I did not mind: I finally had the freedom to go about as I pleased, and I found this suited me very much. No doubt this suited Philomena; no longer was I her burden.

I did not encourage their fear, except in the case of Walfrey. She was terrified of the long-haired umbra who occasionally visited the washroom, and I used this to my full advantage, warning her that if she dared to barge in on me while I was in the bath ever again, I would make sure the woman haunted her every step. She had no idea, of course, that I could do no such thing—or if I could, I had not learned the way of it yet—but her bulbous eyes filled with wary fear, and, grumbling under her breath, she left me alone. I did feel guilty somewhat for my treatment of her, but she had tormented me so that the feeling quickly faded, helped as much by my ever-growing ease with the intricacies of Asperfell and not necessarily my own conscious.

As for Grenn, he no longer worked in the gardens. In fact, he did not dwell above ground at all. A tall, lanky man named Jessop with stringy hair the color of straw had replaced him, and although he was not as strong as his predecessor and took twice as long to do the same tasks, I was grateful he kept to himself and did not bother me. Yralis, if she minded, said nothing at all. In fact, from time to time I saw her glancing curiously at our new companion, and I wondered if she'd finally come to her senses regarding Lord Frobern.

The autumn had finally given way fully to winter, and she and I scrambled to pick the last of the late harvest apples from the orchard even as the trees shed their golden leaves. These would be pressed into cider and set away in one of the cellars off the storeroom for next season. The last of the winter squashes, grown round and heavy on their vines, were cut and dried, and we tended carefully the beets, parsnips, rutabagas, carrots, and greens still clinging to life despite the frigid nights.

It was after we'd handed the last of our baskets, heavy with our labor, to Jessop and sat on a carpet of leaves in the orchard eating apples when Yralis told me something truly wonderful and entirely unexpected.

By her reckoning, Serus would soon be upon us, and it would be celebrated by all. "There's been a Serus celebration here every year as far back as anyone can remember," she said. "Although it is probably very different than the fine parties you're used to."

"I've not been to a Serus feast since I was a child. What is it like here?"

"Well, it's always outside, in the grove near the garden. The food is all right. We usually kill and roast chickens—that's the best bit— and there's bread, of course, and whatever we have most of at the end of the harvest. There will be ale and wine, and the last few years we've had music and dancing. Oh, and there's almost always a fight or two."

"That sounds wonderful."

Yralis wanted to know what Serus had been like at the Citadel, and so I told her as much as I could remember. She listened with wide eyes as I described the fine clothes and jewels, the glorious music, the intricate dancing, and the mouthwatering delicacies of the nobility, which I remembered best of all being a child at the time, and a constantly hungry one at that.

I spent hours sitting outside my chamber door talking to my soldier and, gradually, I learned how to listen. Because they had no corporeal bodies with which to make sound, the speech of umbras was heard in the mind, and a great many times, images accompanied their sparse, garbled words. It was as if they'd quite forgotten language entirely, so long had they gone without its use. The oldest umbras, those who hardly resembled men and women anymore, were the most difficult to understand. Even those who had died in more recent times still required time and patience.

What did seem to help, provided they could remember them after so many years, was their names. It was as if in hearing them, they were brought back to themselves. My soldier's name, I discovered after several attempts to decipher the hoarse whisper in my mind, was Logas, and I used it as often as I could, a reminder to us both that he had been a man once, a Mage, even if all he was now was the shadow of his magic.

I still attended my lessons every day, for even though my aptitude was now revealed, my basic magic was still wanting finesse. Believing that if I had been more adept at casting shields Grenn would not have been able to harm me, Elyan insisted I practice them constantly.

The trouble was, when I was safely ensconced in the workroom with its wonderful bric-a-brac and merry little fire, it was simple to conjure a shield as I naturally felt myself in no danger whatsoever.

"You have to be able to conjure it in the heat of the moment, when your very life may depend upon it," Elyan said, and dragged me down into one of the lower passageways where he proceeded to terrify me to death by wrapping himself in shadows and jumping out at me as though he were Grenn come to finish the job.

The first time he did it, I screamed and slapped him across the face, the thought of using my magic an afterthought to my hand. I stared at him, my mouth hanging open in shock, while pink rose to the surface of his pale skin and his jaw clenched with barely suppressed rage.

His eyes met mine, chips of glittering ice. "Let's try that again, shall we?"

The second time he did it, I threw my hands out in front of me and, instead of a shield, conjured an enormous gust of Magefire. Elyan yelped and jumped back, his own quickly conjured shield the only thing that kept the fire from singing off his eyebrows.

"By the Gods, Briony!" he roared, as he slapped his hands against a few errant licks of flame that still clung to his shirt. "How are you still such an utter disaster?"

"I'm sorry!" I covered my mouth with my hand, hysterical laughter threatening to bubble up from within me. "I'm so sorry!"

His eyes went wide with indignant shock. "Are you *laughing*? You find this funny?"

"No. I absolutely do not find this funny." And at that, my laughter escaped in a torrent.

After that, he made me practice for two long hours, long after I'd successfully conjured a shield against him several times in a row without fail. Scowling, he sent me off to seek a cup of water from the kitchens and a breath of fresh air, and I was glad to be rid of him.

I took my cup out to the gardens and sat on a weathered stone bench. Although the air was brisk and carried the promise of a night of frost, my skin was hot and my limbs tired and shaking from spellcasting and I welcomed the chill against my cheeks.

I was quite near the edge of the graveyard, and as I looked out on what I could see of it, partially obscured by the afternoon mist, I thought I saw movement in the branches of one of the many trees that dotted the melancholy landscape. I watched the tree a moment longer and then saw it again—movement, and a flash of black. Thinking it must've been The Cat, and eager to see him again, I abandoned the bench and set off toward the tree, squinting up into the thick canopy of brown leaves not yet shed.

"Hello!" I called, shading my eyes against the dappled sunlight. "I know you're up there!"

There was a rustle, and a slender hand emerged to seek purchase on a sturdy branch, followed by the wide eyes of Phyra. Evidently, I had discovered one of her many hiding spots.

"Oh!" I said in surprise. "I'm sorry—I thought you were The Cat."

She said nothing but continued to stare down at me through her curtain of tangled black hair.

"You're awfully high up," I said. "Not many lower branches. How did you get up there?"

"I gave her a lift." A male voice came from around the other side of the tree, and I realized Thaniel was lying in the shade with his back against the trunk. He craned his neck until he could see me and smiled. "Mistress Briony."

I smiled warmly at him in greeting, then: "What are you doing up there, Phyra?"

"Watching."

"Watching what?"

She pointed a small, slender finger and I followed its direction. The graveyard. Among the tombstones I saw a glimmer of white, nearly translucent in the daylight.

An umbra.

"She's looking for something," Phyra told me.

"What is she looking for?"

The umbra was moving slowly between the stones, pausing here and there as though she were reading the names and dates of those who rested below.

Phyra tilted her head. "Don't know. Can't ask her."

"But she's dead," I pointed out. "You're a Necromancer."

Phyra lay herself down on the branch fully, stretched out as though she were about to sleep, her cheek cradled by the smooth bark. "I command bones and flesh," she said. "She has none; she is the shade of what was once her magic. I cannot speak to magic. But you can."

"What?"

"Orare," she whispered. "From the old tongue, *orator*. Speaker."

I shivered. "I suppose I could try."

Both Thaniel and Phyra were watching me silently, expectantly, and so I gave them what I hoped was a confident smile and stalked out from under the shade of the tree toward the graveyard.

Ancient magic and the drudgery of unlucky prisoners kept the graveyard from becoming overrun with weeds and grasses native to the moor, but the care of the graves themselves, and the dead within them, fell to the strangest pair of Mages I had ever encountered. They were Necromancers, both of them.

The woman's name was Nollie. She was short both in stature and in her manner of speaking, her cheeks ruddy and her curls often escaping the confines of the caps she wore. As quick to laugh as she was to scowl, Nollie had a thunderously loud voice, and there were many days in the garden when I could hear her bellowing at Perkin for some unfortunate mistake or another.

Perkin was, unfortunately, quite mad. He was an ancient fellow, stooped and wizened and nearly toothless, and despite the chill in the air he wore little more than a sack that hung from his torso and left bare his bowed, skeletal legs. He did not so much walk as prance, and he cackled with glee as he went about his work, though his work was as poorly done as the state of him. The first time Yralis introduced me to the pair of them, Nollie was standing over a grave in which a single rotted foot protruded from the freshly disturbed earth, her hands planted firmly on her wide hips, while Perkin was engaged in the act of escaping the result of his errant magic.

In truth, he hadn't meant to do it, at least not that time. He suffered a hopeless pull to the dead, and while working in the graveyard soothed his madness, there were times when he quite forgot himself and accidentally bid the dead to rise. This usually consisted of an arm or a leg, sometimes a torso, and only once or twice a whole body, though given the sorry state of the remains, I am not sure whether they could be considered bodies at all.

Nollie's gifts in the art of Necromancy had less to do with raising the dead than laying them to rest should they find themselves awakened. It happened that Asperfell's graveyard was positively crawling with remnants of magic that still held sway, and according to Yralis, it was not uncommon for some long-dead Mage (or part of him) to appear above ground, particularly when Perkin was feeling frolicsome.

That afternoon, both Necromancers were crouched near a large gravestone that had split quite unfortunately down the middle, and evidently how this had been done was the topic of a terse discussion between them. Perkin was accusing Nollie of pulling too many weeds, while she accused him of raising too many fingers. I cleared my throat awkwardly several feet away.

"Hang it all," Nollie exclaimed, shading her eyes against the afternoon sun. "What is it you want, then, mistress?"

"That umbra." I pointed into the distance at the pearly shape moving slowly about. "What can you tell me about it?"

"About *her*," Perkin corrected without looking up. "That one's a lady."

"She's been here for ages," said Nollie. "Long before we two. 'Sides that…" She shrugged. "I haven't the slightest."

I tried not to allow my disappointment to show. "Phyra thinks she's seeking something."

"Oh, *aye*, is the little miss about, then?" She squinted into the direction from whence I'd come. "Stranger than him if you ask me, and he's—well, look at him."

Perkin was, at that moment, tickling the fingers of a hand poking up above the ground with a long stalk of grass and cackling gleefully as they twitched.

"Perkin!" Nollie barked. "Stop tormenting the poor soul and get off with you!"

He gave the protruding appendage one last tap and darted off amongst the stones, holding the ragged edges of his—well, it was, quite frankly, little more than a sack—in his fists so high that I caught a quite unfortunate view of his sagging backside.

Averting my eyes from the sight, I looked down at the grave at my feet. "Is the whole… person awake, then, down there?"

"Oh, no. Just the bits you see, I suspect. That I can take care of, but I am afraid I cannot help you with the likes of her, unless of course you know where her body is."

I shook my head and, while Nollie began the gruesome task of coaxing the fingertips back beneath the earth where they belonged, I struck out across the graveyard. The umbra was hunched over a weathered stone and lifted her head at my approach. I was not sure I would ever get used to the chill I felt every time I saw the black, fathomless holes that were their eyes, the feeling of melancholy, of hopelessness. I hoped fervently that, were umbras capable of understanding the emotions of the living, she did not see my revulsion.

Reaching out, I felt a glimmer of the same connection I'd had with my soldier. It was weaker, difficult to grasp, but it was there, like a string pulled taught between us.

"Hello," I said, and I felt the vibration of the string within my voice.

I could not tell if she understood me. She simply stood there, and I felt no response at the other end of the string.

"My name is Briony," I tried again. "What's yours?"

The silence stretched on between us, and still I could detect nothing to suggest she could understand me at all. Eventually she turned and glided away. Not wanting to face Thaniel and Phyra with nothing to report, I followed her as she weaved between the gravestones toward a copse of white-barked trees. Several stones were clustered there, small stones that bore only initials; no dates. I had seen enough stones of the same kind in the graveyards of Iluviel to know what they were: the graves of children. The umbra touched the tips of her ghostly fingers to a small stone that bore the initials *A.L.*

I knelt in the dirt by the stone and looked up at the umbra. She said nothing at all or, if she did, I could not understand her. Then she turned and glided away and did not look back at me.

Later, in Master Tiberius's workroom, I told him about the umbra and the grove of tiny stones in the graveyard, and what I suspected they were.

"Have there been children in this prison?" I asked. I was supposed to be practicing conjuring shields around other people and objects beyond myself, but I found I could not concentrate.

If Master Tiberius was frustrated at my lack of focus, he very kindly did not show it. "There are a great many ways known to Mages to prevent that sort of thing. But yes, despite all that, there have been children here."

"The umbra touched a stone in the grove with the initials *A.L.* What do you suppose she wants?"

Master Tiberius frowned. "I suppose it could be any number of things. Perhaps you've mistaken a child for a woman and it is, in fact, her grave."

His words made a certain sort of sense, but I knew my instincts about the umbra had not been mistaken; she was a woman, and the grave was not hers. "Philomena told me umbras linger because they want something. I think it has something to do with *A.L.*, whoever that is."

"I cannot say whether or not it will help you, but you are welcome to look over the prisoner archives," Master Tiberius offered. "Though I will warn you, some were more meticulously kept than others."

He disappeared into the library off the workroom and I heard him conversing softly with one of the scholars within. After a moment, he emerged with a book of staggering size. He deposited it into my waiting arms and I nearly dropped it.

"Are these all the prisoner archives?" I asked, clutching it to my chest.

"No, no," he said cheerfully. "This is only the first fifty years' worth, give or take. I warn you, the going will not be easy. Some of the former Masters had atrocious handwriting."

"Wonderful."

I took the book back to my chamber with me when my lesson concluded and laid it on the desk below the window where I could see the graveyard in the distance. The umbra was still hovering under the copse of white trees beside *A.L.*'s tiny, forlorn stone. Seeing this steeled my resolve, and I opened the enormous tome, dry and dusty with age and disuse, and began to scan the names of the very first prisoners of Asperfell.

It was fascinating work; beside the name of each Mage, their aptitude was listed, followed by the date of their passage through the Gate and their crime. These ranged from ordinary theft to crimes of passion to offenses so grotesque and fantastical that I had difficulty believing they were true. One man had walked through his neighbor's dreams and convinced him to throw himself off of the top of the highest building in Iluviel so that he could buy his land at a greatly reduced price. Another had boiled an entire family alive using only the water in their own bodies because they would not consent to his marrying one of the daughters, which, in light of the suitor's reaction, seemed perfectly reasonable. For all of the many hideous murders, there was an equal number of crimes against the crown that had not come to violence but were considered every bit as dangerous. I suspect this standard varied from generation to generation, depending who was sitting on the throne at the time.

It took me well into the night to reach the end of the book, and I had not managed to find a single instance of a child born with the initials of *A.L.*, though I had found three other children born in the prison within the first fifty years. I was not discouraged. The stone in the grove had not looked so very old; perhaps I was looking too far back for my mystery child.

Instead of working in the garden with Yralis, I spent the following day and the one after cloistered in Master Tiberius's workroom, poring over the rest of the archives. When I finished with each book, I lugged it back into the library where the scholars grumbled and shuffled about, irked that their work had been interrupted by someone as insignificant as myself and for something so mundane as prisoner records, and begrudgingly handed me the next.

I began my task with vigor, but by the end of the second day with over half of Asperfell's long history behind me, I began to despair that I would ever find *A.L.*

"Why the dedication to this particular crusade?" Elyan asked. "You have a great many spells that need a great deal of work, you know."

"Because she needs help." I said, looking up from the spidery text. The script was near-impossible to read, and my eyes had begun to water. "And I'm the only one who can help her. After all, you were the one who told me that a voice has power."

"Well now, that doesn't sound like me at all."

With an exasperated sigh, I pushed the book across the table at him. "You know, you could help me. I don't see you engaged in any other pressing matters."

He made a great show of sliding his feet across the table and righting himself in his chair. It was a wonder and a great sorrow to me that he did not fall out of it. His eyes narrowed as he scanned the page. "Why did no one think to keep the birth records separate from the prisoner arrivals?"

Elyan complained heartily, but in the end, he grudgingly helped me sort through the archives for evidence of *A.L.* I was grateful for it, for the names had begun to swim together unpleasantly, and each line required several goings over to make absolutely sure that my spent eyes had not deceived me. By then, I'd become accustomed to the different handwritings of the Masters who served Asperfell, but I particularly liked the neat, delicate script of Master Torin some two hundred years ago. He liked to add flourishes to certain letters, and one of these was "L." I was nearing the last page of records in his pleasing script when I saw the unmistakable sign of his fancy, and my mind raced as I read the name of a child born in the depths of winter: Aldoc Lirr.

"I found him!"

No aptitude was listed, for at the time no one could've known if he'd have inherited his mother's proclivity for magic.

"And his mother?" Master Tiberius asked. "Your umbra?"

I looked back down at the birth notice. "Vala Lirr." I turned the page back and found the date of Vala Lirr's arrival. "She was with child when she arrived."

"How old was the boy when he died?" Elyan put in. "He could've lived to be a hundred for all you know, and not died in childhood. See if there is a death notice for him close to his birth notice."

I flipped through the pages, no longer in Master Torin's

handwriting, but in a much bolder, larger stroke, until I found what I sought: the date of death for Aldoc Lirr.

"Only five," I whispered. "So young."

"Well that's it then. Mystery solved," Elyan said.

Something did not feel right. I remembered what Mistress Philomena told me about umbras. "She couldn't have just wanted me to find his birth record," I said. "Umbras hang on because they want something denied them in life."

Elyan shrugged. "Well, are you an Orare or aren't you? Ask her."

19

Unfortunately, it was not as simple as all that; the umbra of Vala Lirr did not seem to want to give up her secrets. Or perhaps—and this, I suspected, was much more likely—I was simply terrible at speaking to magic.

Nevertheless, I visited the graveyard every day and followed her as she floated aimlessly among the tombstones, stopping always at her own, and then Aldoc Lirr's tiny stone under the copse of trees.

Nollie and Perkin took an interest in my task at first, but as the days passed with little to show for my efforts, they gradually left me be.

There were, Nollie argued, other umbras that prowled the graveyard, less ancient and, therefore, likely capable of speech if it was practice I sought. In fact, I had been deliberately avoiding one such umbra that had taken quite a keen interest in my comings and goings. After Grenn's attack, I suspected that, shade or no shade, umbras were capable of exerting physical strength against flesh and blood Mages, though the extent of which I was yet to determine, and this particular umbra looked far from docile. The shape of him was far more distinguishable than most of the other umbras in the prison, so his death had been recent, and the myriad of fearsome scars that ran the length of his arms and marred what little I could see of his face beyond the endless black hollows of his eyes left little to the imagination regarding what sort of man he had been in life. I gave him a wide berth whenever I visited Vala Lirr's umbra.

Sometimes, when Vala looked down at me, I thought I heard whispering, dry and thin like the wind rushing through reeds, but I was not certain whether or not it was her speech or merely my desperate imagination. I could discern no meaning from it either way.

In the end, it was Phyra who came to my rescue, and to Vala's, one afternoon when the sun had nearly set and the cold had become unbearable. I was crouched at the foot of *A.L.*'s grave, rubbing my hands and blowing what little heat I could into them when a voice spoke up behind me.

"You're here again."

Despite the sweetness of Phyra's lilting voice, I'd not heard her approach and I whirled around in surprise. She was standing a few feet away, watching me curiously. "There is nothing worse than the grave of a child."

Undoubtedly, she was remembering her brother, his life taken so callously by Keric. "You must miss him," I ventured, hoping my concern and my kindness were not ill received.

Phyra gave me a wistful smile. "Yes. Every day."

"I wonder…" I began. "I know you won't raise the dead, I know that, but in the tree, you said you could command bones and flesh."

Her shoulders tensed, and she did not look at me. "In some ways, yes."

"Is there anything at all you can tell me about his bones?"

We crouched together in silence at the foot of *A.L.'s* grave, her eyes on the stone and mine on her, and I waited and hoped while my cheeks froze with the cold.

Finally, she said, very softly: "I cannot."

"Oh," I said. "No matter, I—"

"You misunderstand." Phyra turned and looked at me with wide eyes. "There are no bones here. Only a stone. Nothing but a stone."

All at once I understood. "That's what she's looking for."

"You cannot help yourself, can you?" Elyan rubbed at his temples. "You do realize you don't have to help *everyone* you come across?"

"And *you* don't have to be so sarcastic and awful all the time, yet here we are." Even he couldn't dampen my spirits at having finally figured out why it was the umbra of Vala Lirr haunted a child's grave.

From the window of Master Tiberius's workroom, Elyan had seen Phyra and me sprinting from the graveyard and thought perhaps we were in danger. He'd met us in the courtyard, and when I told him, breathlessly, what we'd discovered, he said merely: "Oh." And then: "What?"

"It must be here in the prison," I said. "Since no one can leave, it must be here."

"It's a five-hundred-year-old prison," Elyan reminded me. "There are likely many bodies here that never made it into the graveyard. In fact, there's one down the hole of one of the latrines if you really care to know."

"Truly?"

"Truly," he answered. "And I am sure there are many more we do not know about. How do you expect to find this one?"

"Simple. I'm going to ask."

I began with my soldier. He listened, hovering silently outside of my door, as I told him about the little boy and the quest to find his body. When I finished, he shook his head slowly. It was a disappointment, but one I had expected; Elyan had not been wrong to scoff at the sheer magnitude of the task I'd set myself to.

There were two umbras who could usually be found in the tunnels to the storerooms, and I had no trouble locating them. Whenever I was near, they seemed to gravitate toward me whether I wanted them to or not. I asked them both just as I had my soldier, and they shook their heads and lifted their hands in apology.

I fared no better with the umbra in the washroom who sometimes perched on the windowsill or the side of a tub and watched me bathe. I was beginning to understand that the more human-like their shape, the more recently they had died. This umbra was the most human of them all. I could make out delicate features in the ever-shifting mist of her face, and while I talked to her, she toyed with the ends of her long hair with ghostly fingers.

It was there that Mistress Philomena found me one night, sitting on the windowsill of the washroom with my knees drawn up under my chin, the umbra staring back at me silently. I'd questioned her about Vala Lirr's child, but all she'd said in response was: *Where is she?* I could not tell if she meant Vala, or herself, or someone else entirely, but she would say nothing more.

"Walfrey is quite put out, you know." Mistress Philomena hugged a bundle of linen to her chest and fixed me with disapproving eyes. "She's waiting in the corridor."

"Oh, I know. I'll be only a moment longer."

"I knew her, you know," she said, nodding to the umbra, and my eyes widened in surprise. "She was a prisoner here nearly fifteen years ago."

"Truly?"

"Oh, yes." Mistress Philomena drew closer, and her severe gaze softened as she took in the pitiful sight of the long tangle of hair that always looked dripping wet. "Her name was Mirael. She was the ward of a powerful, rich family once. He was a member of the king's council, I believe, and his wife was the daughter of the king's cousin."

"What happened to her?"

Mistress Philomena shifted the linen bundle in her arms and lowered herself onto the window seat beside me. "She fell pregnant.

With her master's child. His wife went into a jealous rage when she found out and pushed Mirael down the stairs."

My heart seized. "Did she lose the baby?"

"She did. Which is, of course, what the wife intended. What she failed to plan on was Mirael's rage. She took a meat clever from the kitchens and hacked the wife to death in her sleep."

"By the Gods," I whispered.

"Indeed."

Mirael's umbra had taken up the ends of her hair again, and as I watched the wisps of her fingers play with the dripping ends, a thought sad beyond all imagining struck me. *Where is she?*

"The child she lost—was it a girl?" I asked.

Mistress Philomena looked sharply at me. "Yes. Yes, it was."

"How did she die?" I asked Mistress Philomena at length. "Once she arrived at Asperfell."

Mistress Philomena nodded at the copper tub upon which Mirael's umbra sat. "She drowned. In that tub. She was bathing, and a man broke through her locking spell. She'd spurned his advances several times, and he grew angry."

I imagined a strong hand atop her head, pushing her beneath the surface of the steaming water, holding on until her flailing limbs grew still. I thought of Grenn and the feeling of his hands around my neck. I might've ended up the same as poor Mirael, or worse, had Logas not answered to my desperate command.

"He regretted it immediately," Mistress Philomena said. "Pulled her out, tried to revive her, but she was gone. I found her there," she said, pointing, "on the floor. But I was far too late to save her."

"What happened to the man?"

"He did not live long. He was cast below, as all are who commit such violence within these walls, and perished two years later, a fate he well deserved. Much good it did her."

The guilt that had crept into Mistress Philomena's voice suggested she held herself far more responsible than she ought to have for Mirael's death.

"It was hardly your fault," I told her.

She did not look at me; her wistful gaze was fixed on the umbra before us. "It is my task to look after the men and women of Asperfell, criminals or no. I knew Mirael was troubled by the man in question, but I did not realize the extent of it until it was far too late; I should have."

"A heavy burden," I said. Her dark hair, pulled neatly away from her face as always, gleamed with strands of silver. "How long have you been Asperfell's steward?"

"Nearly twenty years, by my reckoning. I arrived when I was near your age, and it was five years at least before I took up Mistress Salfre's mantle. She chose me herself, you know. There were others, Hearth Mages that may have seemed a more obvious choice, but Salfre wanted someone sturdy. Someone like herself." Mistress Philomena was nothing if not sturdy. "She said it would make it easier, this sort of thing." She nodded to Mirael's umbra, who fixed her with the dreadful dark holes that served as her eyes in death.

"And does it?"

"No." She rose from the window seat. "It does not." She turned and made to leave the washroom.

There was something I had been desperate to know since I'd arrived, and I thought, perhaps, since she'd been so forthcoming with me about Mirael, she might answer now. "Mistress?"

She stopped, turned, and I quailed to see the severity that had returned to her face. "Yes?"

I forced myself to meet her eyes, to hold her gaze. "How was it you came to be here?"

"You wish to know my crime," she said flatly, and I allowed silence to be my answer. "I'll not speak of it. Though if you truly care to know, I imagine it is in the prisoner archives."

I lingered after she left, even though I heard Walfrey snarling insults outside the door. Mirael's umbra watched me silently from her perch on the copper tub, drops of shadow falling from the ends of her hair like water, but she did not speak again.

In desperation of having gotten nowhere with the umbras, I decided to try my hand at asking The Cat.

He was dreadfully hard to find; I looked behind every box and barrel in the storerooms and kitchens, under every copper tub in the washroom, in every alcove and hidey-hole I'd ever found him in, and finally discovered him when I returned to my chamber, curled up on my bed fast asleep. He regarded me with one eye half open, as though he were thoroughly perturbed with me and not the other way around.

"Hello, there," I said, as I sat down beside him, careful to avoid his tail. "I've been looking for you everywhere, did you know?"

The Cat regarded me with an expression that told me that he did not care a whit.

"All right," I said, reaching out to scratch the place behind his ears I knew he liked. "Let's give this a try, shall we?"

The Cat's magic was very different than the magic of the umbras. While the umbras were, in a sense, pure magic, the Cat was imbued with it. It was a part of him, as my magic was a part of me, though not of his blood. I could sense it in him, and I felt a stirring in response to my call, but the connection between us was muddy, murky, and difficult to grasp.

He sat on my bed, his head cocked to one side and his eyes narrowed to slits, and flicked his tail as I spoke. And when I finally threw my hands up in defeat, he fell promptly asleep.

"I am *hopeless*." I buried my face in my arms atop Master Tiberius's worktable in defeat the next day. "I've spoken to countless umbras. I even tried speaking to The Cat. Nothing."

Master Tiberius looked up from the scroll he was scratching away on. "I am not at all surprised to hear you had little luck with him. Magic he may be, but he is first and foremost a cat, and I imagine he simply does not care."

"But what of the umbras? I know *they* understand me, but none of them knows anything of use."

"You're only speaking to the umbras of the light." Master Tiberius rubbed his beard thoughtfully.

"What do you mean, of the light?" I mumbled, lifting my head only slightly so I could see him out of one eye.

There are a great many umbras that prowl Asperfell indeed, but they rarely keep to the light." He gestured expansively at the floor. "There is a whole world beneath our feet better suited for the miserable and lingering."

"But you told me I was never allowed to set foot down there on pain of death." I frowned. "As in, my death down there would be exceedingly painful."

"And I meant every word. But if Thaniel and his knights agreed to accompany you, I dare say you will be safe enough."

"I don't reckon I need to tell you how dangerous it is down there," Thaniel said grimly, when I made my request later that afternoon.

"I'll have you."

"You'll need more than just me," he answered. "I'll see if I can persuade Jovan and Accalia to accompany us."

Jovan and Accalia turned out to be a pair of Battlemages. I'd never seen a more formidable woman than Accalia; she towered over me, a pair of wickedly curved blades crossed her back, and she had the most shocking markings on her face below her eyes: lines of intricate script in a language I did not know. Jovan was a short, barrel-chested man with a clean-shaven head and the burliest arms

I had ever seen; that the sleeves of his shirt even fit him was a miracle in itself.

He smiled at me gamely when Thaniel introduced us; Accalia regarded me with indifference, and I do not believe she found me quite as fascinating as I found her.

"How far down do you think we'll have to go?" Jovan asked, shifting the axe in his hands. The peculiar gleam of the metal looked very much like Maelstrom and I had no doubt the same magic had forged both.

"I wish I knew," I answered.

"There is no scarcity of umbras in the depths," Thaniel offered. "And after centuries with no one to talk to, no doubt they will be tripping over their own ethereal bootlaces to meet the famous Mistress Briony."

"Well, I, for one, am in," said Jovan resolutely. "I enjoy a bit of adventure now and again, especially for a cause such as this."

Accalia was not so easily convinced. "It is a great risk for little to no reward."

"Do you doubt your skills as a warrior, Accalia?" Jovan asked. "We could always find someone more... competent."

This seemed to have the desired effect, for Accalia's entire countenance changed. She drew herself up to her full height so she could stare down the length of her nose at her fellow knight. "I am twice the warrior you are, Jovan, and do not soon forget it."

Thaniel rubbed his palms together. "That's it, then," he said to me.

"Not exactly," I admitted. "I thought perhaps Phyra might join us."

Jovan snorted. "That's more of a lost cause than Accalia, here."

"It was she who could sense the lack of a body in Aldoc Lirr's grave," I reminded him. "We may need her to discover its resting place, should any of the umbras be... forthcoming."

"I'll ask her, if you wish," Thaniel said. "But do not be disappointed if she is not keen to journey below."

He must've asked her that very night, for she stole barefoot into the Healer's garden the following morning wrapped in a thick woolen shawl, her hair spilling in black tangles down her back, and sat down on one of the stone benches, her feet dangling into a patch of chamomile.

"Hello," I said, sitting back on my haunches and setting my spade aside. "You got my message."

She nodded. "Thaniel told me of your need."

"You wouldn't have to bring anyone back from the dead," I rushed to assure her. "I want only to find the body, if it is even there at all."

Phyra tilted her head and regarded me with her dark, unfathomable eyes. "I want to help you," she said at last. "But I require your word that, even if one of us should fall, you accept that I will not bargain with Death."

Her words gave me pause. "Bargain? What do you mean?"

"You know little of Necromancy, I think."

I answered frankly, "In truth I know nothing."

She drew her knees up to her chest and wrapped her arms about them, all the while watching me thoughtfully. "Necromancers cannot resurrect anyone they choose from the land beyond, lest Death should lose his dominion over humanity. Just cause must be pleaded, and accepted."

"By Death?"

"By his envoy," Phyra replied. "In his stead."

"What does he look like?" I leaned forward eagerly, my hands planted in a patch of thyme. "This envoy of Death?"

"I have only raised the dead twice, and so very long ago. I cannot remember the face of his envoy."

I did not believe her, but neither did I wish to press her; Phyra revealed nothing she did not wish to. "Does your magic work the other way?" I asked her. "Can you also take life?"

She did not answer me, but slid off the bench and knelt beside a Borage bush, only a few stubborn blossoms remaining in defiance of the chill in the air. With the tip of one finger, she touched one of the pale purple stars, and I watched, fascinated and horrified in equal measure, as it slowly began to shrivel as though time passed for it all at once.

"It isn't permanent," she told me softly. "The blossom will return to its natural order soon enough. I merely accelerate for a time its natural decomposition and eventual death."

I swallowed hard. "And... can you do this with people?"

Her eyes met mine, and I saw within them a desolate landscape that stretched on and on toward nothing but shadows and sorrow.

"I do not know," she said at last. "I have never tried."

Phyra was gentle and sweet. She had ever been kind to me, and I knew most intimately how she had suffered at Keric's hands, and how it must've harmed, perhaps irreparably, her relationship with her magic.

"I will not ask you to do anything you do not wish to do."

"You are a strange sort, Briony Tenebrae." The bright winter wind carried her words to me with the scent of fennel and sage. She said nothing more, but rose from the ground, pulling her shawl tightly around her, and walked out of the garden.

I set my hands to work that I might channel the wild imaginings of my mind into proper work, and thus I forgot about the Borage blossom entirely until, taking up my basket full of herbs harvested for the stillroom, I glimpsed it upon my passing.

As Phyra had promised, her magic was not permanent; the blossom stood just as it had before she'd touched it, strong and vibrant and, if such a thing were possible, even more beautiful for having tasted the bitterness of death and survived it.

* * *

My escort properly settled, we met in front of the north door that led to the lower levels later that afternoon. As relieved as I was to see that Jovan and Accalia had not decided our excursion too dangerous after all, I was overjoyed to see Phyra standing quietly beside Thaniel, dressed entirely in black, a somber reminder of the reason for our gathering.

Thaniel pushed the door open, and we slipped inside, one by one, and then he closed it again, shutting out the light, shutting us in with the dark.

For one terrifying moment, I thought I'd lost my sight entirely so little could I see around me. Phyra's hand was clutched in mine, a comfort and a reassurance that I was not alone. As my eyes began to adjust, I could see the distant glow of Magefire in the corridor beyond, but unlike the strong and steady blaze in the alcoves of the floors above, these were feeble and gave us little to no light with which to see our path ahead.

I could not yet control my Magefire well enough to hold it in my hand without setting something nearby me on fire, but Phyra could, and she held hers aloft as we passed through another archway and down a long, wide staircase into an echoing vestibule.

"Right," Thaniel said, turning to survey our small, impossibly strange band. "I'll take the lead. Phyra, stay close to Briony. Jovan and Accalia, you'll bring up the rear." He fixed me with a pointed look. "At the first sign of anything untoward, get behind me and stay there. No heroics."

I could not pretend I did not take his meaning.

Thaniel led us down a corridor toward where I imagined the cells were located. In the distance, I could hear low moaning, and, farther still, muffled screams. Soon we passed thick wooden doors on our right and left. Each possessed two metal windows that could be slid open and closed, one at eye level and the other where wood met stone below, where I imagined the prisoners received their food.

This was the Asperfell of my imagination as a child in Master Aeneas's tower: tormented souls dwelling in darkness and agony, begging for release, or death, or both.

There was movement in the shadows, and as I peered into the gloom, I thought I saw a body lying on the stones, its limbs undulating ever so strangely. I opened my mouth to tell Thaniel but realized what I saw was not a body at all. It was a head only, and what I'd mistaken for limbs were, in fact, three Gnashers gnawing on the stump of the man's neck.

"Oh Gods!" I reeled back, my hand groping for the wall as I fought the urge to spill the contents of my stomach all over the stones at my feet.

Thaniel lifted his hand and our procession halted. "See who it is," he ordered.

Jovan lifted his axe and moved past the rest of us. At his approach, the Gnashers lifted their heads and screamed at him, their voices shrill and grating, echoing off of the walls in a hideous cacophony.

"Get on, you bastards!" Jovan swung at them with his axe and they skittered off into the darkness, gnashing their teeth and shrieking. He nudged the head with one foot, and it rolled over, baring a sightless face to the light of the Magefire in an alcove above. The man's eyes, nose, and lips had been chewed away, leaving nothing but bloody holes and a ghastly grimace.

"Vicus," Jovan announced.

"The spine?" It was Accalia who wanted to know.

"Not here."

"Wasn't Pryor, then."

I glanced behind me at the white-haired warrior, aghast. "What does that mean? His *spine*?"

"Pryor likes to remove men's heads *and* their spinal columns,"

Accalia answered. "This wasn't his work."

"Try to find the body," Thaniel told Jovan. "If I were a gambling man, I'd say Ajax is behind this."

"We can't keep him in a cell," Jovan said warily. "We've tried everything and yet he escapes again and again."

Thaniel sighed and ran one hand through his close-cropped hair. "I am aware. This is the third man he has killed this month. Something must be done."

I had listened to their exchange with horrified fascination, and now I could not prevent the question from bubbling up from within me. "Who is Ajax and why can you not keep him in a cell?"

Accalia regarded me frostily and said nothing.

"An Elemental. A devastatingly good one, in fact. And utterly insane," Thaniel answered me grimly. "He is forever coming up with new and exciting ways to escape his captivity and wreak havoc on others imprisoned down here with him."

"How can he be stopped?" I asked Thaniel, aghast. "There must be some way to hold him?"

"If there is, we have not discovered it," Accalia told me with icy disdain. "You are welcome to try for yourself if you please."

"No, thank you," I answered tartly. "I will leave that in your very capable hands."

"We go on," Thaniel said, ending the debate.

And so, we proceeded down the corridor past Vicus's head, the Gnashers watching us from the shadows, awaiting the return to their meal.

At first, the rooms we passed were mostly quiet, and I did not know if that was because they were empty or their inhabitants asleep. As we descended farther, voices began to speak to us through the doors, desperate, pleading voices.

"Let me out!" one begged. "Please! I'll not do it again, I promise! Please let me out!"

"Have pity!" another cried, followed by the sound of his fists against the wood of the door. "Have pity—I've not seen the sun!"

From behind one door came bouts of hysterical laughter, followed by loud, racking sobs. Phyra shrank close to Thaniel, staring at the doors and listening to the sounds of their ill-starred inhabitants with growing unease.

As we rounded a corner, leaving the corridor of cells and horrible, wrenching cries behind, the walls seemed to close in around us, suffocating us with stale air and darkness that was far too still and silent. In the distance, I thought I could make out a strange glow that I knew at once was not Magefire; it was white, spherical in shape, and seemed to hover some feet above the floor. Seeing it, Thaniel stopped and threw out his hand, a signal to the rest of us to go no farther.

"Is it Ceris?" Accalia asked in a low voice.

Thaniel frowned into the dark. "It may be, but proceed carefully nonetheless."

I did not know what or who Ceris was, but I felt Accalia draw close to my back and was grateful for her presence, even if I found her quite disdainful. She certainly intimidated me; I hoped fervently whatever lay beyond would be similarly deterred.

We proceeded down the corridor slowly and very close to one another. In the distance, the sphere of light pulsed, grew brighter, then split and was two spheres.

"Thaniel," Accalia warned.

"I see it," Thaniel answered flatly. "How in Coleum's name did one of them manage to get in here?"

"I beg your pardon," I interjected. "But what got in here exactly?"

Thaniel had no time to explain, for at that moment, whatever it was at the end of the tunnel let out a horrible bellow, low and gravelly, and the sound made the very hair on my head stand on end. Then came the sound of heavy feet—or were they paws?—on the stone at our feet. The two spheres became eyes and they were racing toward us. Phyra grasped my arm with far more strength than I would've thought she possessed and pulled me against the wall. Accalia and Thaniel stepped forward, their blades drawn.

My vision was filled with gleaming black fur, long, gnashing teeth, and hideous glowing eyes. Phyra and I gripped one another in terror as the beast, towering over us, taller than any horse, descended upon us. A scream tore itself free from my throat. Oh Gods, what a wretched way to end. I prayed it would be quick. I knew it would not be painless.

The moment I made my plea to the Old Gods, the beast burst asunder; black and silver dust fell like rain over us all, disappearing into nothing the moment it touched our heads and shoulders. I lifted one hand in awe, hoping to catch some, but all that met my hand was a sigh, a breath, and nothing at all.

Accalia and Thaniel looked at one another, their faces slack with shock.

"She's gotten strong," Thaniel said.

"Indeed."

A voice, a female voice, rough, heavily accented, and full of cackling mirth, spoke in the darkness. "Did you enjoy my newest trick?"

Thaniel and Accalia sheathed their weapons, something I found highly irregular in light of what had just occurred. The woman at the end of the tunnel must've been no stranger. Phyra and I followed them as they approached, and as Magefire bloomed in their hands, I saw a short, gangling woman sitting on an overturned wooden crate, grinning at us as if we'd all just had a great bit of fun. She was far younger than I would've imagined; her brown hair had not yet turned to gray. But her blue eyes bulged strangely, and one corner of her mouth turned down ever so slightly, rendering her appearance youthful in a manner that was deeply disturbing. Her clothing had been reduced to rags, whether by time or by her own hands I did not know.

"Hello, Thaniel."

"Ceris. You've grown strong."

She smiled sweetly.

"You've never even seen a Phaelor, have you?" Accalia demanded. "How did you manage to conjure the illusion of one?"

Ceris gave her a wide smile; several of her teeth were missing. "Selwyn," she answered. "He fought one on the moors once. Told me every detail. Hope I got it right."

"I dare say that you did," Thaniel answered drily. "And it was... exhilarating to witness, but how did you manage to get out of your cell?"

"Ajax."

Accalia cursed quite shockingly.

"How did *he* get out of his cell?" Thaniel asked.

She shrugged indifferently. "Someone let him out."

"Who?"

"Couldn't say."

With alarming speed, Accalia closed the space between them and brought the blade of her dagger against Ceris's throat. "Couldn't say, or won't say?"

Ceris's already bulbous eyes strained in their sockets and her mouth gaped open like a fish. "Couldn't!" she gasped. "Couldn't!"

For a very long moment, there was stillness and silence among us as Accalia kept the edge of the blade against Ceris's throat, her narrowed eyes searching for any trace of deception. Then, seemingly satisfied, she withdrew the dagger and stepped back. "However you got out, it's time to go back in."

"Don't put me back in there," Ceris said, her tone suddenly petulant and sullen. "It's dark and boring."

Thaniel shrugged. "Well, you did kill several people. However..." He paused. "If you aid us, I may let you tarry a bit longer."

"Aid you? Aid you how?"

I stepped forward. "We seek umbras. Have you seen any?"

Ceres's eyes took me in, from the hem of my skirt to my wild red curls. "Why?" she asked. "What does a girl like you want with the likes of them?"

"I'm an Orare," I explained. "I can speak to them. I seek their counsel on a very important matter."

"A very important matter," Ceris sang back at me, a mockery of my words. "What is it, then? What is so important?"

"A child."

I had not expected her to be affected in the slightest by this pronouncement, but the mirth fell from her face and she regarded me with somber curiosity. "There is a child in Asperfell?"

"No. Thank the Gods," I answered. "It is the child's body we seek. His mother died a hundred years ago and has remained an umbra for want of him. Will you help us find him?"

Ceris's gaze slid from me to Thaniel. "You'll let me stay out of my cell while we search?"

"As long as you stay with us at all times," he warned, brandishing Maelstrom so that she could have no doubt as to his meaning.

"Come on, then," She jerked her head toward the passageway to our left. "I thought I saw one of them down there earlier."

The passage was, unfortunately, devoid of any umbras, as was the one we tried after, and the one after that. Still, I was quite determined and declared my wish to carry on despite Accalia's protestations that we were wasting our time.

But as we descended farther and farther, I began to worry I was putting them all in danger for naught. I was near to telling Thaniel to turn back when at last we saw a pearly glow in an abandoned cell, its door standing open, revealing only straw in a heap just big enough for a man to lay upon.

"Let me go to it alone," I whispered in the dark.

"Absolutely not," Thaniel said.

"It won't hurt me. And you might give it cause to flee."

"I made a promise to the Master that I would return you to the surface alive and whole, and I do not intend to invite his wrath should I break that promise. I'll follow."

"Very well," I grumbled.

Thaniel held his handful of Magefire aloft as I walked toward the iridescent glow, a man as best I could discern, though little was left of him. This umbra was quite old; older than Vala Lirr. How long had he been here?

I summoned my magic, felt it wrap itself around my throat, seep into my voice, flooding it with the power I needed to be understood. "Hello," I said softly. "My name is Briony. I'm an Orare."

The umbra did not answer me, but I knew through the magic that connected us that he had heard my words.

"We are looking for the body of a boy," I went on. "About five years old. He died near a hundred years ago. Can you help us?"

The umbra's dark, vast eyes bore into mine, and then he turned and glided away from us down the tunnel.

"Come on," I said breathlessly to the others. "We have to follow him."

Thaniel sheathed his sword, which I realized he'd drawn when I'd approached the umbra, and my entourage followed me after the swiftly disappearing figure.

"It's going too fast!" Ceris wailed from somewhere behind me. "Tell it to slow down!"

Indeed, she was right; I'd never seen an umbra move so fast. My heart leapt with hope that this meant he knew where the boy was, or, at the very least, knew something that could help us. We rounded a corner into another corridor where there were no cells at all, only barren rooms that may have once been used for storage, or even bathing, but were now forgotten. It was into one of these rooms that the umbra disappeared, and we followed close behind.

There was another umbra in the room. This one sat alone in a darkened corner, the ghostly shape of her legs drawn up under her chin. The black pits of her eyes stared beyond us, beyond even the walls of the room, until the other umbra approached her, and she looked up at him. It looked as though they were speaking to each other, but despite how desperately I tried, I could not understand them. At length the first umbra drew back, and the other rose from the floor in a cloud of long, tattered skirts.

"Please," I said. "We mean you no harm. There is one of you in the graveyard, a woman who was named Vala Lirr. The body of her little boy is missing. Do you know where he is?"

The umbras looked at one another, and then they glided past me through the open doorway of the room.

"Wait!" I cried. "Please, wait!"

But they were in earnest and did not heed me. They floated together even farther down the corridor, turned, and then turned again, and I feared that if they went much deeper, we would not be able to find our way out. I remembered, suddenly, the story Thaniel had told me of the black wall and the ghost that tormented those who came upon it, and I hoped fervently we were nowhere close to such horror.

Finally, they stopped.

"What's there?" Ceris stood on her tiptoes beside Accalia, craning to see where the umbras had led us. Accalia growled in response and brandished her dagger; a warning to stay back.

I could see nothing around us but stone walls and stone floor and endless darkness. The alcoves of Magefire had ended long ago, and the only light in the tunnel came from Phyra's hands.

"I don't see anything," I said.

The umbras did not move, but stared at me silently. I cursed myself for not being strong enough to hear what they were so clearly trying to tell me. "I can't hear you," I said. "I'm so sorry—I can't hear you."

But it did not matter in the end, because with me stood a girl who could command flesh and bone, who lived every day of her life with one foot in the land of the living and the other in the land of the dead, whether she willed it or no.

Phyra moved past me and knelt on the ground below the umbras.

Light. She needed light. Lifting my palm, I prayed to the Old Gods and whomever else might've been listening, and was rewarded with a small plume of fire in my outstretched hand. I channeled my magic forth, and to my delight, the Mageflame grew in perfect union with my intention, chasing away the shadows.

"Here," she said at last, running her hands over a large stone block in the floor. "I feel him here." She looked up at me, the ghost of a smile on her lips. "He feels like her."

Thaniel knelt beside Phyra and ran his fingers along the seams of the great stone block. "Hold this," Thaniel said to me, unbuckling his sheath and passing Maelstrom into my hands. "Accalia, help me with the stone."

Then, with magic and muscle, he and Accalia began to heave the great stone upward. It gave way easily, revealing the dark earth beneath, and together they looked up at Phyra questioningly.

"Dig," she said.

I fell to my knees beside what I knew now to be the tomb of Vala Lirr's child and began to dig alongside them, unwilling to be parted from my task and made a spectator. Dirt caked beneath my nails and my fingertips protested mightily as I scratched and tore at the unyielding earth.

Before long, in a shallow grave only inches deep, my hand brushed against cloth. I jerked back as though I'd been burnt, my breath coming in short, fast gasps. Thaniel's eyes met mine grimly, and then he slowly removed the last of the dirt covering the body of Aldoc Lirr.

He was nothing but bones now, heartbreakingly small bones, with wisps of reddish hair still clinging to his skull. I feared that if we moved him, he would turn to dust before my eyes, but Thaniel was careful, gentle, and with great care he laid the unbearably small skull on the stones beside its sad little grave. Phyra dropped to her knees beside me, staring at it with haunted eyes.

"By the Gods," Accalia whispered. Beside her, Ceris stared at the bones of Aldoc Lirr in dumbstruck silence.

I looked up at the two umbras, standing silent and watchful. "What happened to him?"

The female umbra, the one we'd found in the empty washroom, leaned down and touched a finger to my cheek. It was softer than the wind, softer than a breath, but in that instant, I watched as a man carried a limp body past the door where she'd sat curled in a corner one hundred years before. Although already an umbra, she was curious, and she'd followed him from a distance as he stalked down the corridors like a caged animal, muttering under his breath, until he found a stone in the floor that was easy to pull up and large enough to hide the body of a child. He dug into the earth furiously, bothering only to dig as far down as he needed for the stone to lay flat again. He wiped his hands on his filthy tunic, still muttering to himself, and then he left him there, alone under earth and rock.

The umbra had tried to pass the story along, telling every shade and spirit she encountered, but there was no Orare at Asperfell to listen to their words.

As soon as she'd bid me see it, the memory dissipated, and I was left in darkness, tears streaming down my face as she drew back, her hands falling limply to her sides, lost in the mist of her.

I turned to Phyra. "She saw a man carry him here and bury him and leave him."

"The man killed him," Phyra said, and I realized she'd placed a hand on the tiny skull. Her eyes were glazed and unfocused, and I knew that half of herself dwelled with death and half with us. "The man didn't mean to kill him, but he meant to hurt him, and he was too strong, and he killed him."

"He must've buried him to keep his secret," I said. "And his mother never knew."

We stared silently at the pitiful remains of Aldoc Lirr, and I let my tears run freely down my cheeks, my jaw, dripping onto the stones below. He'd been so young, known so little of life, and what he'd known of it was this place, this wretched place. What lovely days I'd spent as a child of his age, days filled with the late afternoon sun and the sound of laughter. He'd known only stone.

Beside me, Phyra whispered: "He doesn't belong here."

"No," I said. "No, he doesn't."

Thaniel carried Aldoc Lirr's bones up from the depths of Asperfell wrapped in my cloak and into the light of the courtyard, where we were met with the sight of Elyan arguing with Master Tiberius, gesturing sharply with his hands, a thunderous look on his face. At the sight of our bedraggled party, they stopped immediately. What very much looked like relief—but could not possibly have been—flooded into Elyan's face, followed swiftly by anger, and he stalked toward us, Master Tiberius on his heels.

"Of all the ridiculous, idiotic things to do—" He stopped abruptly, his eyes falling on the bundle in Thaniel's arms.

"Oh," Master Tiberius said softly. "Oh my."

"You found him." Elyan's eyes flickered to mine, and though there was still anger there, there was also surprise, and not the unpleasant sort. He looked as though he had no idea what to make of me in that moment, and I found that I rather liked it.

"Yes, we found him. Would someone please fetch Mistress Philomena? I have a favor to ask of her."

Although Aldoc Lirr already had a grave of his own, we decided to intern his body with his mother's so they would never be parted again. She stood a way off, watching as Mistress Philomena lifted the earth out of Vala's grave and Elyan and Thaniel scrambled down into the hole. The body of Vala Lirr had been placed on its side in death, with her head pillowed on her hands, as though she were merely sleeping. Elyan placed a velvet satchel containing the remains of her son in the crook of her arm.

"She's holding him at last," Phyra said.

Once Thaniel and Elyan had climbed back out of the pit, Mistress Philomena settled the earth back around the bodies.

"What are their names?" she asked me, crouching down beside the headstone, so weathered with age that little remained of the original inscription.

I told her, and with her earth magic she carved them anew, together, as they were in death.

"Look." Phyra pointed.

Vala Lirr's shade was beginning to grow fainter, the edges of her ghostly form dissolving into mist and then into nothing.

"She has nothing to linger for," Master Tiberius said, smiling proudly at me. "You've done it, dear girl."

I approached her. She was fading fast; soon she'd be translucent, and then there would be nothing at all where she stood.

"Goodbye," I said, reaching out with my magic one last time.

The umbra of Vala Lirr opened her mouth, and this time I understood the words that poured forth.

Whispers in the dark, she said. *The dead keep the secrets of the living.*

I could see through her now; she was little more than a shimmer in the air.

"Wait!" I reached out desperately, as though I could anchor her to this world, but my hand passed through nothing but air. "What does that mean?"

If freedom is what you desire, seek the first.

And then, like a sigh on the wind, she was gone.

20

Darkness had fallen by the time we returned to the prison, and I was bone weary and shivering.

The last words of Vala Lirr's umbra were going round and round furiously inside my head, clamoring for attention, desperate for meaning. I could not account for it at all other than I'd heard some of it before, though it had been just as mystifying then as it was now. I realized all at once that Elyan had been with me when I'd first met the Countess.

The moment we entered the courtyard, I grabbed him by the sleeve and pulled him urgently toward one of the columns, difficult given his considerable height. He gaped at me indignantly, and before he could launch into what would no doubt be a tirade about *how dare I pull the sleeve of the heir to the throne of Tiralaen,* I cut him off.

"She spoke to me," I said in a rush. "She spoke to me before she vanished, and she said the very same thing the Countess said to me!"

He raised one eyebrow. "The imminent downfall of Asperfell?"

"The whispers! 'Whispers in the dark,' and, 'The dead keep the secrets of the living.' Just like the Countess! How could she have possibly known?"

"We live in a prison in another world inhabited by Mages," he reminded me drily. "Strange things are not entirely outside of the realm of possibility here."

"And that isn't all," I pressed on. "She also said, 'Seek the first.' Who is the first?"

"I have no idea," he answered, though he looked as though he was not at all pleased to admit it. "It could be anyone. It could be nothing at all."

"It's not nothing," I said firmly. "She said, 'if freedom is what you seek.' Freedom! A way out of Asperfell!"

Elyan groaned. "Gods save me from more of your scheming."

"I have to find this *first* she spoke of, whoever that is."

"And how exactly do you plan on doing that?"

I'd already thought that bit out. "I need to see the Countess again."

"There is every possibility she'll not remember she even made your acquaintance the first time, much less what she said all those weeks ago."

"I know. But I have to try. Perhaps if it's important enough for an umbra to know as well, it's important enough for her to remember."

He sighed, resigned. "As there appears to be little chance of talking you out of it, I'll take you to see her after the Serus feast tomorrow, if you wish it."

"Why not before? We could go now."

He scowled. "Because there is something I must see to tonight."

"Surely nothing as important as this!"

"That is a matter of opinion."

"Precisely! And in my opinion—wait, where are you going?"

He did not look back at me, the loathsome man. Yet, as I watched him walk away, I was surprised to find that I wished he would stay, if only because my excitement was ebbing, leaving in its place a wretched feeling of helplessness that was slowly festering into anger. I'd never minded my own company before, but I found it insufferable just then.

I had helped one umbra today. But what of the others? By my reckoning, there were no less than two dozen that lurked within Asperfell's walls, each of them with their own terrible, desolate reasons for lingering beyond death. To help each and every one might take years, time that Tiralaen did not have. To forsake them was a torment.

As I crossed the courtyard, I glimpsed Accalia's tall, white head emerging from the north door. She lifted a hand to Thaniel, a gesture of request, and I stopped abruptly, wondering what her trouble might've been. Had Ccris not gone quietly to her cell? Had Jovan encountered some difficulty apprehending Ajax? I thought perhaps I would ask, but before I could, Thaniel followed her back through the door and they disappeared entirely from my view.

A letter was waiting for me when I returned to my chamber, crumbling parchment decorated with black ink and bearing the mark of the papilem: an invitation to the Melancholy Revels. No doubt the society was interested in my escapades below ground. As late as the hour was, I was restless and heartbroken and made up my mind immediately to lose myself as best I could in an idle hour or two; the Revels would have to do.

I'd not yet managed to repair the tears in the teal gown from Grenn's assault, and so I lifted the lid of the trunk at the foot of my bed and pulled out the gown of wine-red velvet.

"Steady, now," I told myself out loud as I spread it out on my bed. *Sewing magic, then.* After a large number of minutes and a small number of mistakes, the gown was at last suitable to wear among company, or at least as suitable as I could hope to make it. I possessed no jewelry, nor the power of illusion to create any, and so I would have to attend the Revels woefully unadorned.

I unpinned the curls at the nape of my neck so they fell riotously down my back and walked to the south wing alone. It was Arlo Bryn who greeted me with a glass of Laetha when I arrived, and I took it with trembling fingers and drank long and deep. It burned all the way down, and I welcomed it.

"I am all astonishment," Arlo said, as we stood together watching Lord and Lady Ashwinder locked in one another's arms. "And so new to your aptitude."

To receive praise for begging ghosts to help me discover the ancient bones of a dead child was far too sorrowful a thing to converse upon, and so I only nodded, my gaze fixed firmly on the brush of Lady Ashwinder's skirt.

"And yet you are dissatisfied, I think," he said, glancing sidelong at me with a knowing gaze. "If you want my opinion, talking to dead Mages sounds dreadful, but it could have its uses, I suppose."

I hated him a bit in that moment.

"Oh, don't look at me like that," he scowled, such that a face like his could ever really scowl. "Think of it! They go everywhere, know everything—imagine the leverage you'd have over a place like this if you knew everyone's deepest secrets."

"Leverage," I said slowly. It was exactly the sort of thing for which a prisoner of Asperfell could be expected to use a gift like mine, and yet I was sick with fury at the thought of the umbras being wielded for such selfish and callous reasons. "You really are despicable."

"You've only just now noticed?"

Weary as I was with my own company, I was not so desperate that I wanted to suffer his, and so I summoned every ounce of the lady that Mistress Precia and Mistress Eudora believed I was, and said: "Do enjoy your evening." Then I left him there, staring after me with a bemused expression on his face.

I was afforded a place of honor by Lord and Lady Ashwinder and showered with questions, so many questions, and little or none to do with Vala Lirr and her son. Instead, they had everything to do with my harrowing time below, the desperate cries of the prisoners there, the blood and bones and death. They begged me to describe it all in excruciating detail, gasping in feigned shock and gruesome delight, exclaiming, "No! Stop! I couldn't possibly hear any more!" then begging to hear more in the same breath.

They drank up my words like the Laetha in their cups, leaning in close until I smelled their sickly sweet perfume and ancient taffeta. My head grew heavy and thick with voices such that I could not distinguish one from another, and still they chortled and screamed and droned on around me.

"Mistress Briony, are you all right?" Lady Ashwinder laid her delicate hand over mine, the very picture of concern.

"I cannot stay," I said suddenly, pushing my glass at her.

I rose unsteadily to my feet. The Laetha churned in my stomach as I made for the door swiftly. Oh, why had I come? I'd have been better served to seek Elyan out and endure the sharp lashing of his tongue than spend a moment in such appalling company.

Voices followed me, begging me to stay for one more drink, one more dance, one more story, but I ignored them and lurched into the night-darkened corridor, leaving Arlo Bryn and the society behind me. There was a window not far away. I rushed to it, unlocked it with magic, and, bracing my hands on the crumbling sill, leaned as far out as I dared into the black night. I drew in great gasps of icy winter air until my lips grew numb and my head was clear and the terrible roiling in my stomach had stilled.

I made my way back to my chamber on shaking legs. In the courtyard, a small group of men had gathered beneath the black oak, passing a bottle between them. It was clear to me by the sound of their raucous laughter and slurred speech that they were deep in their cups, and I passed them swiftly, enduring with clenched teeth and fists their hungry eyes upon me, their brazen shouts, invitations to stay, to show them what I was hiding underneath my gown.

Then, of the corner of my eye, I saw an umbra hovering near one of the columns of the colonnade, watching me. The men must've seen it, too, because their voices fell silent and remained so until I was out of sight. What a strange thing it was to command so much fear from a talent I'd only just begun to know. I was grateful for it.

I should've gone to my chamber. I'd meant to, certainly, but I could not stop thinking about the Countess.

Making my way to her tower would require me to go back through the courtyard and I was bound to run into someone along the way. There was the umbra I'd passed, but I was not entirely confident I could bid her to protect me should the worst occur, or that there was anything she could do to protect me at all. I'd stopped my soldier before he'd been able to use his ghostly sword on Grenn; perhaps it would've merely passed through him.

Still, I could not rid myself of the feeling that I had to speak to the Countess. And so, I slowly turned and walked back down the long staircase.

The drunken Mages who had called to me before eyed me suspiciously when I passed them once more, but if they were thinking anything untoward, they did not say it, particularly when I approached the umbra standing beside the column.

"I need protection," I told her. "Will you walk with me?"

The hazy outline of the umbra shimmered in the air as she dipped her head in acknowledgement.

She followed me like a shadow back through the courtyard and through the colonnade toward the Countess's turret, hovering just behind my shoulder so that I could see her pearly glow at the edge of my vision.

At the top of the stairs, I approached the Countess's door and rapped softly, hoping she was still awake and I was not rousing an ancient woman from slumber. She might've been old, but she was still a far more advanced Mage than I and no doubt knew all manner of spells to punish my thoughtlessness. I waited, not realizing that I was holding my breath until I heard a voice rasp from inside: "Enter."

I sighed with relief.

Inside, the air was thick and musty, and I wondered how long it had been since anyone had beaten the dust from the curtains and rugs or opened one of the windows. Magefire burned in the grate, but unlike the last time I'd visited, only a single candle was lit. It sat on a small table beside the countess's chair next to an untouched goblet of wine. A papilem perched on the edge of the jeweled cup, folding and unfolding its gossamer wings slowly. The Countess watched me with rheumy eyes as I approached, and I sank into the best curtsey I could manage before she batted a gnarled hand, startling the papilem into lazy flight.

"Briony Tenebrae," the Countess rasped. "Good evening."

"Good evening. I'm sorry to disturb you so late."

She leaned forward clutching her cane, rings sparkling on her knobby fingers. "'Tis the eve of Serus. I keep the long vigils of the Old Gods, girl. I'll not sleep until sunrise."

I rather thought that was exceedingly unlikely given her advanced age; indeed, she looked as though she were nodding off even as she spoke.

"Would you mind if I sit, then?" I asked. "I've something I'd like to ask you."

The Countess grunted and waved her hand in acquiescence.

The chair I chose looked the least unsound of those at the Countess's table, yet I still feared it might fall to pieces as I gingerly lowered myself down upon it. I folded my hands in my lap.

"Countess," I began, "do you remember what you told me when last I saw you?"

"Why?" the Countess answered archly. "Do you?"

My confidence wavered, but I continued nonetheless. "You spoke of whispers in the dark. Of the dead who keep the secrets of the living."

"Yes," she whispered. "They were restless before, and now…" Her eyes met mine with a sudden bright intensity that sent a shiver through me. "Orare," she said, and I nodded. "Ah!" The ghost of a smile passed over her wrinkled face. "Someone has come to hear them at last."

"Who?" I leaned forward in the rickety chair. "Do you mean the umbras?"

The Countess shook her head and batted my question away as though it were smoke on the air. "They've been waiting for you. Waiting and whispering. Have you heard them?"

"That's why I've come," I told her. "An umbra spoke to me today, and she used your words. She also spoke of *the first*. Do you know who or what that is?"

The Countess stared at me in silence for so long that the papilem drifting above her head floated down and landed softly atop her tangled gray curls. "No," she murmured at last. "No, no, no." Her head drooped as she trailed off, in thought or exhaustion or age I could not tell, and the papilem rose into the air once more.

"I see," I said softly. It had been in vain, then, my coming. "I'll not disturb you further."

I made to rise, but the Countess slapped her bony hand flat on the table with a smack. "Beware, child," she rasped. Her voice was harsh and pitched lower than her murmurings had been, and I felt a change in the air around us, a prickling that made the hairs rise on the back of my neck unpleasantly. "He knows you are here."

"Who?"

"There is darkness ahead, and menace." Her eyes smoldered then with an intensity I did not think she had left in her. "Seek the light. Wherever you can."

My father's words.

"What did you say?" I whispered.

But the Countess had succumbed to the cobwebs of her mind and her head drooped until her chin was buried in the stiff black crinoline of her gown. For a moment I feared that she had died, but I saw her chest rise and fall gently and heard her muffled snores.

I took my leave, closing her door gently so as not to wake her.

The umbra was waiting for me outside the Countess's door when I emerged, and she became my shadow once more as I made my way back to the courtyard. The men who'd been drinking and caterwauling had long since gone, and I paused beneath the black oak tree where they had sat and looked up into its twisted branches. The courtyard was utterly silent, and yet I thought I heard whispering. The sound was soft at first, a single voice, and then it began to grow until hundreds of voices were shouting, a cacophony of pleading and urgency and anger—and it grew and grew until I could stomach it no longer.

I slammed my hands over my ears and shook my head, desperate to be rid of the sound. "Stop!" I shouted, and the whispers abruptly ceased, all save one.

The dead keep the secrets of the living, it said.

And then silence.

I dreamed I stood before the black oak of Asperfell, alone in a desolate wasteland of snow. Unable to move, I watched in horror as blood welled up from the tree's roots, a violent stain against the pure white, and it moved slowly across the snow until everything was bathed in red. I opened my mouth to scream, but no sound came, and the blood continued to spread until it swallowed me whole.

I woke to the pale light of a winter morning filtering through my window and a dusting of snow on the panes. It seemed my dream of snow had been a herald of what was to come. Remembering the slow spread of the hideous red stain at the roots of the tree, I shuddered.

A steaming cup of cider heady with spices sat on the tray beside my morning porridge; I sipped it at my desk and watched the flurries outside gust and settle. Though I'd cherished the summer more as a child, Serus had become my favorite day of the year in Orwynd. The smell of pine boughs and spices, the twinkling of candlelight, the sound of voices raised in song, merry despite the bitter chill; I'd loved it all, except, perhaps, the new gown I was bundled into every year, the stays pulled so tightly that I always felt sick after gorging myself at the feast.

No doubt at that moment Livia and my mother were festooning Livia's home with greenery and preparing for the evening's celebrations. Was my Aunt Eudora doing the same at Orwynd? Was she still its mistress? It was more likely the soldiers had locked her away in some northern prison, and my breath hitched at the thought of it. It was best, perhaps, to keep myself busy, and today was certainly a day to keep busy; we had our own evening celebration to prepare for.

I had decided to try my hand at mending and changing the gown I'd arrived in into something less dreary. The rips in the skirts had been simple enough to mend, but it had taken me the better part of a week to successfully change the color of the fabric from gray to ivory. Still, I was proud of my work, and I thought it suited me.

"Happy Serus!" I greeted Yralis in the main storeroom, where she and Willow were heaving baskets of parsnips onto a small cart. We were having unprecedented luck with the parsnips that winter—to the point where if I ever saw or smelled or tasted another parsnip, it would be far too soon—but Willow had promised that for the holiday she would baste them in honey and spices and roast them until they were golden and sweet.

"And to you, Briony," Yralis said, as she kissed my cheek. "You look lovely!"

"Have you seen the snow? How in the world will we manage?"

In all of Asperfell's long history, the Serus feast had always taken place outside in the grove beside the garden and orchard, though I could not fathom how we would not all freeze to death, our plates covered in snow and our cups turned to ice.

Yralis grinned. "Come and see."

One of the hand-hewn wooden tables from the kitchens had been brought out into the grove, and as I watched in awestruck silence, Master Tiberius and Mistress Philomena lifted their hands and it began to grow and stretch, becoming long enough to accommodate us all. All around the table stood cauldrons of Magefire to warm us and, above it all, a woven canopy of curly willow branches, impenetrable by the snow. It was beautiful magic, a sight to behold.

"Wait 'til you see it at nightfall all lit up," Yralis said, as we walked arm in arm back to the storeroom.

Yralis and I worked the day through, stopping only to eat a hurried meal of bread fresh from the ovens and cheese while sitting on two overturned barrels in the main storeroom. At last, the sun began to set, and we clasped our hands together and laughed in giddy anticipation like two schoolgirls—until Mistress Philomena barked at us to stop as it was time to begin the festivities and we were, apparently, embarrassing ourselves.

They were arriving from every corner of the prison in all of the finery they could muster, from the highest born to the lowest, who had perhaps never attended a Serus feast before their incarceration. These were a bucolic sort, their clothing made over with magic, adorned with ornaments of flowers and foliage and feathers, if anything at all. Elyan had once told me that the prison held criminals and not men and women, and I had seen much in my few months at Asperfell to know this was true, but tonight they came to the table as men and women with flowers woven in their hair.

What might come later once they had bellies full of food and cups full of wine remained to be seen. Yralis had warned me there was usually at least one fight, which I did not find the least bit surprising.

"Mistress Briony!"

I turned to see Lady Ashwinder, redolent in deep crimson, her pale curls pinned back with silver combs studded with rubies. She, evidently, did not care to emulate the rustic nature of the evening's festivities.

I suddenly felt quite plain beside her in my ivory gown and wreath of hellebore. "Your ladyship," I said, and curtseyed.

"My, but you do look a vision tonight," she told me when I straightened. "How quaint, like a pastoral brought to life."

I very much doubted she meant this as a compliment.

"Tell me," Lady Ashwinder said, tucking my hand into the crook of her elbow, "is it true you saw the Countess after you left us last night?"

Word indeed traveled quickly in Asperfell.

"It is," I answered slowly. "Why do you ask?"

Lady Ashwinder's smile was beautiful and decidedly predatory. "I was merely curious. Of what did you speak?"

"Serus," I answered, which was the truth, even if it was only a very small part of it. "She explained the keeping of the long vigil to me."

Lady Ashwinder's smile faltered somewhat; she had clearly expected a different answer. "You left us quite suddenly last night. I thought perhaps you had important business to discuss."

"Not at all, your ladyship. I merely needed some air and thought a walk would do me good."

Lady Ashwinder turned then and, taking both of my hands, looked down at me with what I imagined she thought to be sincerity but better resembled simpering. "I trust you, Mistress Briony. And I do believe that you trust me."

"Oh, yes. Verily, I do."

"I am so glad to hear it!" She smiled. I was being well and truly cosseted. "And because I trust you, I would tell you anything that I felt was beneficial for you to know. Anything at all. You have my word." She paused, for dramatic effect, I was certain. "And I trust I may have yours?"

"My what?"

"Silly dear!" She squeezed my captive arm. "Your word. That you will be forthcoming with me in all things."

I knew I must choose my words very, very carefully. Words, after all, possessed a power that in many ways quite eclipsed magic entirely. "I am forthcoming with all peoples," I told her slowly. "When it is right for me to do so."

Her fingernails dug painfully into my arm, and I nearly gasped aloud. "I wish you to be always forthcoming with me, Mistress Briony." Her voice held no trace of its earlier sweetness; it was as sharp as a blade and as deadly. "In *all* things. May I have your word?"

Before that moment, I had always measured my response to others by my perceived intelligence over their perceived lack thereof, and reacted accordingly, usually with disastrous results. Now, a different sort of estimation quite overcame me and I saw Lady Ashwinder and myself not by our rank or by our wit, but by our magic. Her skills as an illusionist rendered her gown rich and vibrant, her hair lustrous, her skin undimmed by the passing of the years. But she could do little more than create fanciful lies. I could speak to that which was within us, and though I was new to my power, I felt pride in that power swell in my chest. And buoyed by that extraordinary feeling, I wrenched my arm from her grasp easily; for all Mistress Ashwinder's stature, she had not the strength acquired by spending one's youth galivanting about the Morwood for ten years.

"No," I told her. "No, you may not."

"I see." She drew back from me, her white face glittering with hatred, and in that moment I knew I had truly made an enemy of her. "I bid you a pleasant Serus, Mistress Briony."

As I watched her pale blonde head disappear into the crowd to rejoin her husband, Lord Frobern, and Lady Antonia, I hoped I had not miscalculated horribly and felt fear begin to unfurl deep within me. Ridicule hardly concerned me, and I certainly did not mind being excluded from her Revels or "my own kind." Indeed, I'd discovered well enough that my own kind, as they had been before the Gate, were loathsome creatures. If these were her means of revenge, they were trifles to me.

But I had learned well enough from Cyprias that there were many ways an enemy might punish one for one's transgressions. Subtle and unexpected ways, if the enemy were patient and clever enough. What kind of enemy would Lady Ashwinder be?

Alone and shaken, I looked around me, hoping to see a friendly face, or at least a familiar one.

I found Elyan easily. He was wearing his customary black, a silver circlet atop his dark curls; a poor crown for a banished king. His eyes met mine, and I made my way to his side through the press of bodies. He looked distinctly out of place, his haughty, angular face solemn where all around us there were boisterous laughter and flushed smiles.

"Happy Serus, your highness," I greeted him, stifling the absurd urge to curtesy as I might've done as if we were back in Iluviel in the throne room of our youth. His eyes had fallen on my hellebore wreath, and I reached up to touch the flowers, suddenly conscious of what he saw.

"Good evening," he replied. "What is *that*?"

"Hellebore," I said defensively. "A winter rose. Honestly, did your extravagant education not include herblore?"

"Herbs, yes. Flowers, no."

"It's highly poisonous," I told him, and his wary glance flickered once more over the blooms in my hair. "Oh, don't worry. You'd have to eat quite a lot for it to do any real damage. It's used primarily as a purgative."

"Sometimes you are exceedingly strange," he said, but he held out his arm nonetheless. "Shall we?"

I slipped my hand in the crook of his elbow, and we made our way through the crowd. "And where did you come by your knowledge of herblore, pray? I doubt your education was as extensive as mine."

"I'm sure it wasn't," I said, remembering the jolly tutor I'd had at Orwynd. "I spent most days out of doors running wild in the forest and sketching in the greenhouse when I lived in the north. I used to bring all manner of plants home with me. One of our kitchen maids, Layn, was an herbwoman and she taught me as much as she could. And whatever she couldn't teach me, I learned in the library."

"I would venture to say you had an unconventional upbringing."

I smiled at the thought. "Yes, though not as unconventional as yours."

"Fair enough. Now, what is this about sketching?"

"Never you mind," I told him, smiling slyly.

Above the great table, the willow canopy twinkled with a thousand tiny fairy lights that took my breath; Yralis had been right. It truly was magnificent. I stared at it in unabashed wonder, not caring who saw me or might've thought me simple. Magic was still so new to me that all of it was a marvel, no matter how small.

Beyond, in the orchard grove, candles had been lit, placed in glass, and hung from the gnarled branches of the apple trees around the altar of Sator. At her feet, offerings had been laid by those who still believed their prayers reached the goddess even in this forsaken place.

Mistress Philomena supervised the procession of food from the kitchen to the table by way of levitation: platters of roast chicken surrounded by potatoes glistening with fat; tureens of parsnips, beets, and carrots; bitter greens studded with tiny onions; and loaves of bread fresh from the hearth. These were my burden, wrapped in cloth to keep them warm, and I clutched them to my chest, afraid that if I attempted to levitate them, they'd end up in the dirt at my feet.

I managed to claim a place on the bench between Yralis and Dagan, who told me he liked my flowers and then proceeded to say nothing else to me throughout the course of the meal. Elyan sat opposite me, with Thaniel beside him. Phyra, he told me, never attended the Serus celebrations. There were far too many people, and she abhorred crowds.

Farther down the table I saw Walfrey, Samuel, and Dox. I gave Walfrey a jaunty wave, and she scowled at me in return. A shout of boisterous laughter drew my attention to Arlo Bryn, who was holding court with his usual clutch of card players, and I craned my neck so that I might see them. To my dismay, Arlo Bryn took this as a sign of interest in him and not mere curiosity, and he winked at me over the rim of his glass. My cheeks reddened, and I looked swiftly down at my empty plate.

Master Tiberius, resplendent in robes of deep blue, rose from his seat at the head of the table, and we fell silent. A few of the twinkling lights from the canopy drifted down and danced about his head.

"Friends," he said, spreading his arms wide. "We have survived another year in this place of exile and of penance. I give thanks for this, and for the magic that flows through our blood. On this ancient celebration of the longest night, we welcome the darkness of the days to come, and await the return of the light. May the blessings of the Old Gods be upon us." He bowed his head and we followed suit, remaining silent and still until at last the Master of Asperfell swept his robes back and resumed his seat.

A great clamor arose as we all reached for the dishes before us at the same time, knocking our elbows into one another as we heaped our plates full to bursting. Hunger had made me slovenly, and I tore into the buttery flesh of a chicken leg with abandon. So as not to further offend the sovereign seated across from me, I stifled my groan of pleasure. It was simple fare but delicious, and after months of stews and roots prepared every way imaginable, it was a splendid departure.

Conversation flowed with the wine, and my cheeks reddened. I drained my cup and Thaniel poured me another, and then another. Two of the prisoners played passable fiddle and another the drums, and as the food disappeared and wine cups were refilled, they struck up a merry tune. A pair of Mages began the dance, and others joined in until the grove was full of them.

True to Yralis's word, a brawl erupted between two Mages who tried to duel each other with spells but were so intoxicated they were able to do little more than throw off a few harmless sparks until they abandoned all pretense and began pummeling each other with their fists. They were separated eventually and doused soundly with water, but not before Arlo Bryn took full advantage of the situation by taking bets on the outcome of their tussle. I was too short and too far away from the fight to see who won, but Arlo looked quite pleased with himself afterward, so he must've correctly predicted the winner.

Master Tiberius marched the two offenders back inside Asperfell to sleep off their inebriation, and the musicians struck up a new song. Within moments, the grove was filled again with the sounds of laughter and the stomping of feet and clapping of hands.

It could not have been further from the Serus feasts I'd known my entire life. It was loud and raucous and coarse and unrefined; it was utterly wonderful.

I took up my cup and sought out a better view of the dancers. I looked for Lord and Lady Ashwinder among them, remembering how much they enjoyed the pastime, but I did not see them anywhere. However, I did glimpse Yralis and Jessop clasped in one another's arms and a delighted smile spread across my face. I was glad that, if only for one night, my friend had found some modicum of happiness. As they twirled past me, she grinned and waved.

"And how do you find your first Serus at Asperfell?"

I turned my head and found Elyan beside me, watching the swarm of dancers. His silver circlet was slightly askew, and I thought I saw a hint of pink in the sharp angles of his face. I wondered how much he'd had to drink.

"I find it quite marvelous indeed," I told him with a smile that I hoped did not betray my own slightly unsteady state. "Very unlike the ones I remember as a child at the Citadel."

"I always hated Serus at the palace," Elyan said with a scowl. "Far too much bowing and scraping and simpering."

"But the food was always wonderful. And the dancing."

"The dancing was certainly better than the flailing about done by this rabble."

"At least they *are* dancing," I said, poking him in the arm. "At Serus your father always danced with his *rabble*."

Elyan glanced sidelong at me. "Regrettably, I believe you're right. I might dance," he said slowly, "if you danced with me."

If he told me then and there that he thought me a Mage of spectacular talent the likes of which he'd never seen, I could not have been more surprised. "I will," I said, and I was surprised again.

He held his hand out to me and I took it. Then we joined the dance as the fiddlers struck up another tune.

"You know," I said, reaching for his shoulder, "you're quite tall."

"Well, you are positively diminutive," he replied, his hand sliding deftly around my waist.

I did not know the steps of the dance; it required quite a bit more stamping and contact between partners than Mistress Precia ever would've allowed. Still, it was not at all difficult to pick it up. Elyan was a strong partner and knew every step. The vast difference in our height made it difficult at first to find our footing, but once we did, we drew apart and came together again with ease and a modicum of grace, mostly his.

I danced with far too much exuberance to be called graceful, but

Elyan did not seem to mind. I laughed out loud as the energy of the dance grew and shifted. Our steps became faster, wilder, and my hair whipped about my face as we turned and twirled, and then he smiled.

I'd seen him smile before, but never like this; never in such a way that he was as utterly transformed as he was now, open and warm and guileless. It was a crooked smile, a sweet smile, and it took my breath away completely. Elyan was a beautiful man always; when he smiled, he was devastating. Transfixed, I quite forgot myself and stumbled as the dance moved on without me.

Elyan's hand was strong and sure around my own, and he pulled me against him, an anchor in the churning sea around us, a light in the darkness. In the shelter of his arms I stood with my face upturned, bathed in the light of the stars, and met his extraordinary eyes with my own. His smile softened, then, and became something else entirely.

I don't know how long we would've stood there while the dance went on without us; perhaps forever. But over his shoulder and far in the distance, I saw something that made my blood run cold. High in one of the four towers of the great fortress, billows of smoke rose into the night sky.

"Elyan," I gasped.

He turned just in time to see angry tendrils of flame burst free from one of the windows.

"The Countess's tower," he said, and then he was gone.

21

I stood, frozen in fear and shock, watching Elyan's dark head disappear into the crowd. Then I gathered my skirts and sprinted after him.

At the edge of the crowd, Mistress Philomena stood beside Dagan and Willow, sipping neatly from her cup and watching the festivities with what very much appeared to be disapproval. I did not have time to wonder about it.

"Find the Master!" I gripped her sleeve in my hand. "The Countess's tower!"

"What in the world—" she spluttered after me, but I was already too far away to hear the rest.

I ran as though the fire itself were at my heels in pursuit of me. My lungs burned with the effort of it, and I very nearly tripped over my feet and my wretched skirts and sent myself sprawling more than once. I plunged into the tower and up the spiral stairway. The smell of smoke, acrid in my nose, became stronger with each step until I reached the top.

"Briony!"

Wheezing and out of breath, I nearly sobbed in relief to see Master Tiberius hurrying toward me in the corridor. "Where is Elyan?" he shouted at me over the roaring of the flames.

There was nowhere he could be but within, and it was with a heart full of fear and my stomach in my throat that I rushed into the Countess's chamber with Master Tiberius fast on my heels.

In the center of the room, Elyan stood with his arms outstretched, bathed in light, and I realized all at once that it was coming from his very skin, from deep within him. The light pulsed, grew brighter, and I saw his face contort with the effort of it.

So *this* was what it was to siphon magic.

He pulled it from the very air around us, calling to it, commanding it, drawing it into himself. Against such an onslaught, the Magefire—for undoubtedly it was Magefire and not some normal blaze—began to grow feeble. Even the smoke began to dissipate into wisps that rose and thinned and disappeared until, at last, the flames were no more.

Elyan, bright and shining and gasping aloud with the pain of so much magic inside himself, thrust one hand out toward the window and let fly everything he'd taken. Like lightning and flames in one, the magic erupted into the night sky, dappled with so many stars, until it was entirely spent.

Elyan fell to his knees, then pitched forward onto his hands, and heedless of whatever danger there may still have been, I ran to him. His shoulders rose and fell as he struggled for air. I reached out and placed my hand on the pale skin at the nape of his neck, then jerked it back again; he was burning.

"Don't touch me," he ground out raggedly. "Not when I'm like this. I could hurt you."

He still shone bright with magic, just as my skin had the day Keric's Mage had plied the secrets of my body with his hands. I did not touch him again, but neither did I leave him.

"The Countess," he rasped. "Is she—"

"Gone," came Master Tiberius's voice, deep and low and heavy with sorrow.

He was standing before the smoldering ruin where the Countess's chair used to stand, now reduced to nothing but ash and herself with it. The Magefire had done its work quickly and without mercy.

"No," I whispered, and a fist clenched around my heart. "Oh, no…"

There was a stifled cry in the doorway. Mistress Philomena stood there with her hands pressed against her mouth, staring at the scene before her in horror. She must've followed the Master after I'd bid her find him. Little good it had done us.

"Tiberius," she gasped. I'd never heard her use the Master's name so informally before. "What *happened?*"

Tears glistened in the eyes of the Master of Asperfell. "Mistress, return to the gathering, quickly now, and tell them it was an accident and nothing more. Ply them with wine, ply them with music. Distract them but tell them nothing. Go—quickly now."

Mistress Philomena gathered herself and, with a brisk if somewhat shaky nod, hurried away.

"This was no accident," Elyan said. He had recovered enough to sit back on his heels, though his chest still rose and fell unevenly. Tendrils of light chased one another under the surface of his skin, but they had grown fainter.

"No," Master Tiberius agreed. "No, it was not."

"Magefire cannot grow that rapidly without great power behind it. The Countess could not possibly have done it herself."

"You do not mean someone did this on purpose," I broke in, aghast.

Elyan's gaze was grim. "That is exactly what I mean."

"I cannot believe it, but you may be right," Master Tiberius admitted. "But we must keep it to ourselves."

"She had enemies," Elyan mused darkly, "but none I thought powerful enough for this kind of magic."

Their voices became a drone in my head as I looked around me at the blackened walls and the flakes of ash floating everywhere. They landed on my hair, my dress, my hands, but I did not brush them away. A horrible thought had taken root in my mind, a thought I could not chase away. It was far too great a coincidence that I'd seen her, spoken with her only the night before—about Vala Lirr's umbra, about the first—and now she was dead.

"You need Lyphril," Master Tiberius told Elyan, who had risen unsteadily to his feet.

"Bah." Elyan waved him away. "I need a stiff drink."

"You need *rest*," Master Tiberius said firmly. "I imagine that is quite a bit more magic than you've siphoned in a very long time."

"Powerful magic, at that."

Elyan did not return to the Serus feast, nor did I. After leaving the Countess's ruined chamber, I followed Master Tiberius to his workroom where I sat in front of the fire, lost in the deep quagmire of my thoughts, while he busied himself mixing a tincture from the various phials and dusty bottles on his shelves.

"He says he doesn't need it, but he does," Master Tiberius said, handing me a small, stoppered bottle of green liquid flecked with gold. "Take it to him and make him drink it. *All* of it."

"I don't know where to find him," I said, realizing despite the months I'd been at Asperfell, I did not actually know where Elyan's chamber was.

Master Tiberius scrawled hasty directions on a scrap of parchment and thrust it at me.

"What will you do?" I asked him.

"Word of the Countess's death will have spread. I must return to her chamber before the vultures descend. Perhaps there remains a clue to this whole ghastly mess."

I followed Master Tiberius's map to Prince Elyan's chamber, my limbs heavy with sorrow and fatigue. Drawn by the sounds of laughter and music, I looked out a nearby window at the grove below. Although there were fewer of them now, the Mages of Asperfell still danced beneath a canopy of willow and light.

How perfectly lovely it must've been to either not know of the events of the evening, or to not care. I could not pretend I wished myself ignorant of it, but I envied them, drunk on wine and revelry. In this place, this wretched, wretched place, there was so little joy to be found that I was breathless with anger at having been robbed of it.

I found Elyan's chamber with little trouble and knocked softly on the door.

"Who is it?"

I cleared my throat. "It's Briony. Master Tiberius sent me."

There was a long stretch of silence. Then: "Yes, well, I suppose you'd better come in."

His chamber made mine look positively minute and was richly appointed, as befitted his station. I supposed he'd had plenty of time and opportunity to amass it all. The bed, twice the size of my own, was draped in rich brocade and tied back with ropes of gold trimmed with tassels. In one corner stood a table set with four chairs that bore a decanter and several finely fashioned silver goblets. There was a desk piled high with books and scrolls, a collection of quills made of feathers from birds I did not recognize, and pots of ink in every color. A large piece of parchment was held down at each corner at the center of the desk, and although I was not close enough to examine the details, it looked to be a sketch of the west tower of Asperfell. Ornate rugs covered the cold floor, and everywhere candles set into sconces dripped wax and flickered in the draft.

Elyan lay abed and did not rise to greet me. With some difficulty, I maneuvered a chair fashioned of dark wood near to him, dropped myself into it, and held out the tiny bottle.

"Sent you with Lyphril, did he?" Elyan grimaced as he took it from me and held it up to the light. The tiny flecks of gold glimmered with borrowed radiance. "Gruesome stuff."

He pulled the stopper from the bottle and downed the contents in one quick swallow.

"What does it do?" I asked, as he handed the bottle to me and sank back against the pillows.

"It is meant to restore my strength after I siphon too much magic. At least I had somewhere to expel it this time. It's worse when I can't get rid of it right away."

He did not seem to want to speak of it further, and I did not wish to press him. He closed his eyes and scrubbed his hands over his face, mussing his dark curls.

"Elyan," I ventured softly. "The Countess... It's my fault she's dead."

His eyes opened, and he regarded me witheringly. "Have you been holding back on me all this time? Truly I had no idea you were capable of such feats of magical prowess."

"I don't mean the Magefire."

"Then what *do* you mean?" He had drawn himself up onto one elbow and was staring at me intently.

I swallowed hard. "I went to see her last night."

"You *what*?"

"I went to see her last night, after the Melancholy Revels."

Elyan sat up fully in the bed and fixed me with an incredulous expression. "You went to the Melancholy Revels alone?"

I bristled at his condescension. "I was perfectly safe."

"As safe as one can be amongst criminals!"

"I am *always* amongst criminals," I reminded him, and felt a certain satisfaction when his scowl deepened. "And this isn't about the Revels, it's about the Countess."

"Whom you also went to see alone. You have absolutely no sense of self-preservation whatsoever. I told you I would take you after Serus."

"And I told *you* I wanted to go before. Why must everything I do here depend on you, or Master Tiberius, or Mistress Philomena, and not my own discretion?"

Elyan pinched the bridge of his nose with his fingers. "You really are the most exasperating person I have ever met."

"I took an umbra with me for protection."

"Who might've turned out to be no use to you at all should the need have arisen," Elyan snapped. "You have no idea what an umbra can do to a flesh-and-blood person, if anything at all!"

I opened my mouth to retort, my natural reaction, it seemed, to anything Elyan said, then closed it when I realized he was right. Which was infuriating.

"Fine," I conceded. "I shouldn't have gone alone. But I had to know about Vala Lirr's umbra and about the first. I couldn't wait, and now… And now she's dead. And *don't* say it's a coincidence. Someone killed her because of what she told me, because of what Vala Lirr told me."

"The Countess had a great many enemies, Briony." Elyan sounded exhausted, his voice strained and hoarse. "She did not become queen of her own little tower kingdom for nothing. In fact, did you not just say you attended the Melancholy Revels last night? Lady Ashwinder is the Countess's most vocal and emphatic adversary. Like as not, she and her repugnant husband wanted her room and the prestige that comes with it and she was taking too long to die."

"That's appalling."

"That's *life* here, Briony."

I flinched away at his cruelty. "I am inclined to believe a great many things about Lord and Lady Ashwinder, but I cannot believe them capable of murdering her in that horrible way. Besides, Thaniel told me that they coveted her jewels, but the contents of her room were destroyed in the fire."

Elyan waved this away dismissively. "Perhaps Lord Ashwinder was careless—he is not exactly the most proficient Mage among us.

Or perhaps they pocketed the jewels before they started the blaze. Who can say."

His words made sense, certainly, but they discounted perhaps the most crucial fact of all. "It cannot be a coincidence that Vala Lirr spoke the Countess's very words. Someone wanted her silenced."

"For what purpose, Briony?" he exploded in frustration. "There is no escape from Asperfell! The ravings of a lunatic and a shade cannot change that fact. Their words are worthless to you. Pointless, meaningless drivel! I can think of no one in this prison or in this world who would commit murder to stop a mad old bat from whispering in the ear of a Mage with little training and an aptitude of no consequence!"

It was as though he had struck me across the face.

For a long while we stared at one another in the deafening silence. Then I rose on shaky legs and left him without another word.

Back in my chamber, I tore the wreath of hellebore from my hair and flung it into the Magefire, where it caught and burned. I watched until it disappeared, then sunk to the floor and buried my head in my skirts. They reeked of smoke and bits of ash still clung to them, leaving dark smudges when I moved the pad of my thumb across the tulle. Another gown destroyed. Nothing, it seemed, could survive this place.

What an utter fool I'd been. Asperfell had hardened Elyan long ago against the possibility of escape and he'd made no secret of his disdain for hope. He had five hundred years of history in his favor, and all I had *was* hope; hope and the whispers of Mages long dead.

Perhaps as the years passed, I would become just as cynical, just as hardened, but not yet. Whatever magic coursed through my blood, it was my father's blood, and I'd promised him that I would have courage, that I would find the light in the dark. I would help Elyan escape this place if I could, even if he did not think it was possible. Even if he'd lost all hope.

All I had was hope, and I supposed I would have to be his.

There was nothing of the Countess to bury, but we held a funeral for her just the same.

Mistress Philomena carved her stone, and the few of us who had known and cared for her met in the bitter cold while Master Tiberius spoke words of comfort and hope that none of us believed.

I was shocked to see Lord and Lady Ashwinder in attendance, along with Lord Frobern, Lady Antonia, Brethwain, and Mistress Orial. They stood huddled together in velvet cloaks of all colors with filigreed clasps of gold and silver; illusion magic, no doubt. Beneath her hood, which was artfully placed in billowing waves, Lady Ashwinder's face was porcelain, frozen in beautiful, artificial grief. She must've felt my eyes upon her, for she turned, and our eyes met. Her chin dipped ever so slightly, the corner of her mouth tilted upward, and then she looked away. A warning?

I turned away, and my gaze fell on a tall, solitary figure, his dark hair blowing gently in the frigid air. Although his face was still ashen and there were dark smudges under his eyes, Elyan did look much better than he had the night before, which I noted with a quick glance before ignoring him entirely.

While it was true that *the first* could've been anything at all, I knew it must be something of some importance or significance for Vala Lirr to have said it before she vanished. She'd spoken of freedom, and although five hundred years of history and the barbed tongue of a prince told me otherwise, I was sure she meant a way out of Asperfell.

She'd told me to seek it, which meant that, whatever or whoever it was, it was here at the prison. There were countless lifetimes worth of history within the walls of Asperfell, and some of it had been written down. Perhaps the books and scrolls in the library in Master Tiberius's workroom held some clue as to the identity of the first.

Master Tiberius bowed his head, silence descended over our sorry company, and then it was over. The others pulled their cloaks about themselves and set off back toward the fortress, no doubt in search of a cup of hot wine and a seat by the fire.

I knelt and placed a bundle of rosemary at the base of the Countess's gravestone for remembrance, and when I rose to my feet, Elyan was waiting for me.

"Walk with me," he said, and offered me his arm.

"And why would I do that?"

He frowned; it had not occurred to him I might refuse him. "Because if you don't, you'll miss me making a spectacular fool of myself. I'm about to apologize to you, and as I'm sure you can imagine, I have very little experience with apologies." He offered his arm to me again. "Please. Walk with me."

I had half a mind to return to Asperfell, leaving him amongst the gravestones and the cold, but the idea of an apology from his lips was far too irresistible, and I found myself slipping my hand into the crook of his arm. He led me away from the gravesite toward the open moor. In the distance, the immovable Sentinels bent over their great swords, silent and waiting.

Rimed with frost, the dry grass crunched under our feet and our breath gathered in clouds as we walked. Inside of my boots, my toes were frozen, and my makeshift cloak did little to protect me against the chill, but my lungs drew in the cold like a balm, clearing my head and sharpening my thoughts.

"You mentioned a forthcoming apology," I reminded Elyan.

"So I did," he conceded, then sighed heavily. "Well, there's nothing for it; last night I behaved abhorrently, and I am sorry for it. Sorrier than you know."

I refused to look at him. "You said beastly things. Even for you."

"I know. I've thought of little else since. You must believe that whatever my reasons, or my state of mind, I did not mean them."

"Didn't you?" I stopped walking and pulled my arm from his. "You've made no secret of the fact that you find my skills lacking. Perhaps you meant the rest of it, too."

"Your skills *are* lacking," he pointed out, and as I opened my mouth to shout at him in outrage, he went on quickly. "Only because you are untrained. As for the rest of it, you frustrate me to no end with your need to save us all and to put yourself in the way of bodily harm to do so, but do not mistake me. It is courage, Briony. It is courage, and sometimes I wish I possessed half of yours."

I was not going to let him off that easily. "You told me my aptitude was little more than nothing."

He had the grace to look contrite. "That I regret most of all. I spoke in anger, and in fear, if I am being perfectly honest with myself. I thought by discouraging you, I might save you from your own damned determination. It was, needless to say, a horrible miscalculation on my part."

I found I could not speak after his entirely unexpected speech, and he took advantage by reaching for my hand and tucking it back into his arm.

"And what of the Countess's words?" I asked him as we walked, looking up at his sharp profile. "Or do you not believe them? Or me?"

"I do believe you," he said. "And Vala Lirr. It is too great a coincidence. But I do not like what it portends."

"Which is?"

"Whatever it all means, these whispers and secrets of the dead and whatnot, it was evidently worth killing an old woman over. It was exceedingly powerful magic that created the Magefire."

"And now she's gone, and Vala Lirr besides," I said in defeat. "And I have no one left to ask."

Elyan looked distinctly uncomfortable. "Yes, well, the truth is,

I may know of someone you could speak to, but the experience will not be pleasant, and the price may be more than you wish to pay."

"Who is this person?"

"Not a person," Elyan corrected me. "A Moriae. And a nasty one at that."

"I don't know what that is."

"Perhaps that is for the best."

My fingers gripped his arm resolutely. "Even so. If this… this Moriae can help me, I am determined to try."

"I should discourage you. Gods know I wondered whether to tell you at all, but there seems to be little I can do to deter you once you've made up your mind."

I smiled at that. "It's settled, then."

"Well go tonight," he said. "If you will it."

"Go where?"

"To the southwest tower."

I frowned. "The one that's abandoned? Is that entirely safe?"

"Not in the slightest," he answered. "But that is where the Moriae was bound, and that is where we will find him."

I met Elyan by the black oak tree just after midnight.

"Here," he said, shoving a small cup into my hands. I sniffed it, and my nose wrinkled. Laetha. "It'll fortify you for what's to come."

I took a small swallow, coughed, handed it back. Elyan downed the rest of it and set the cup on the ledge beside the tree.

"Ready?"

I nodded.

He led me into the staircase of the southwest tower and called Magefire to his hand to light our way. I followed closely behind, keeping my eyes firmly fixed on Elyan's back just in case Asperfell decided to rearrange its corridors and stairs. After twelve years, I imagined Elyan knew each and every way the castle tricked its inhabitants and would have no difficulty finding his way, but should the worst befall me, I would likely be found weeks later tangled in vines.

"Asperfell is ever so much larger on the inside than I'd imagined," I told Elyan, as we ducked under a pointed archway and emerged in a long hallway studded with doors. "Do prisoners reside in all these rooms?"

"Not anymore. Asperfell used to house many more prisoners than she does today. I imagine that is why this wing has been allowed to run wild."

And run wild it had. The vines with their delicate white flowers and pale tendrils had worked their way through even the smallest fissions in the walls and clung to the stone, spreading their deadly beauty.

"Master Aeneas used to say that it was the rise of enlightenment and education that led to the decline of the Gate," I said, recalling the afternoons I spent in my old friend's tower at the Citadel.

"In the first two hundred years after it was constructed, Mages were sent to Asperfell in droves, and for crimes that would earn you little more than a fine and a month's imprisonment in the Tower now. The dark ages of our kingdom exacted a heavy toll on those born with magical blood."

Elyan paused when we reached a set of winding stairs that disappeared into the black above and looked back at me, lifting the Magefire so I might better see his face and he mine.

"People will always fear that which they do not understand, and magic is particularly difficult to puzzle out for those who have never felt it deep within them, never used it. You might think that defeating Keric and restoring some semblance of reason to the kingdom will forever free us of the fear of persecution, but the fact that it was able to happen at all only proves that, at their core, people will always be afraid, and they will always find someone to blame. Someday, all of this will happen again. That I promise you."

I did not want to believe it, and yet I was standing in a prison a world away from everything I had ever known for no reason other than the magic I bore in my blood, magic I'd been born with, a choice I'd not made. And although I was not so naïve as to believe that every Mage in Asperfell was the victim of fear and not their own demons, there were many who should never have been here at all. Phyra was one. I was another, as was the man before me.

Elyan shook his head free of the shadows of his thoughts and I followed him up the stairs.

"How do you know how to find him?" I asked. "The Moriae, I mean." Elyan's movements during our journey had been precise and sure; he had obviously traveled this way before.

"We are old acquaintances, the Moriae and I," Elyan replied quietly. "Though I have not seen him since first I arrived and for good reason."

He did not seem inclined to speak any further, and I did not press him. Instead I followed quietly as he led me through a crumbling archway into an atrium filled with cobwebs and strange statues and oh so many vines. An umbra hovered in one dark corner, and his unsettling gaze followed our approach.

"Bloody Arlo," I heard Elyan mutter, as he inspected the damage to the stones above the door. "Gods, look at this mess!"

I did not know what Arlo Bryn had to do with it, but the vines really were tangled every which where, and Elyan uttered a number of choice curses as he worked with magic and Magefire to move enough of them aside that we could pass. While he worked, I made a study of the stone figures around us. They were carved by a skilled hand, but had succumbed to time and piles of crumbling stone lay at their feet. I approached the figure of a woman in a flowing gown that had slipped down over one shoulder, baring her breast. Stars had been carved upon her gown, and I thought she might be Thala. Her serene oval face rested against one hand in peaceful repose. The vines had come for her, too, winding their way up her legs and around her body. They formed a crown of sorts about her hair, and I moved them aside to get a better view of the diadem that she wore.

The vines sprung to life at my touch; tendrils shot out, wrapping themselves about my wrist, lacing through my fingers like a lover's hand. I gave a shout of surprise, shaking my arm furiously to be rid of them.

Elyan was at my side at once, cursing my stupidity and the vines in equal measure. He pulled them off of me and flung them back at the statue of the sleeping woman, where they retreated, coiling once more about her hair.

"Honestly, what were you thinking?"

"I'm sorry," I said, properly chastised. The vines had begun to squeeze my fingers unpleasantly before Elyan had managed to shake them off, and I winced as feeling returned to them. "Are they usually so enthusiastic?"

"No. But I find it best not to provoke them. Ah—that should do it."

He'd managed to reach the latch of a heavy wooden door. It opened only a few inches before it stuck soundly, and Elyan was forced to wrench it open with his bare hands, admitting us at last.

The room was utterly dark and smelled most unpleasantly of mold and decay. Magefire glowed in Elyan's hand, and he searched the walls until he found the hearth—or, rather, what had once been the hearth and now resembled little more than a small dark hole. He knelt and coaxed the flame into a roaring fire, and I looked about at our peculiar surroundings.

Vines had claimed the moldering bed long ago, curling and twisting around the canopy, a bower of white flowers now. There was no other furniture, only four columns, one in each corner of the room, that were carved with all manner of strange symbols. The same symbols were also carved on the floor in the center of the room, and it looked as though something dark had once been spilled there; the stones were stained a deep, rusty brown, and I had the horrible feeling it was blood.

"What do we do now?" I asked. "How do we find the Moriae?"

"Oh, he's already here," Elyan answered wryly. "We need to convince him to show himself."

I could not fathom this. The room was filled with nothing but stone and vines and shadows and fire. I could see no entrances other than the one we had passed through and there were few places to hide; behind the columns, perhaps, though I could not see how the Moriae could do so unless he was much smaller than I had imagined.

"How do we summon him?" I asked. Elyan did not meet my eyes right away. In fact, he seemed determined to avoid them. "Elyan?"

"Blood," he said. "Your blood."

"Oh. You might've mentioned that earlier, you know." It appeared that I was correct about the dark stain at our feet.

"I know," Elyan replied, drawing a dagger from his waist, a dagger that I had not realized until now he possessed. I watched the sharp edge of the blade with growing unease. "I feared you may not have come if you knew, but I felt certain you would agree once you were here."

"Is this the price?"

"No," Elyan said, his voice heavy with regret. "No, it is not."

He bade me lift the sleeve of my gown and laid the bright blade of his dagger against the skin of my arm. "I'm sorry," he told me. Then his fingers dug into my skin below my shoulder, and without warning, he brought the dagger down in a graceful arc, severing my pale skin. Bright red blood welled at the surface and streamed down my arm. I struggled, but he held me tightly, both with magic and his own strength. My blood dripped onto the floor below me, splashing on the symbols carved in the stone. When he had judged that enough had been spilled, he released me.

I wrenched myself away from him, my hand pressed against the wound on my arm. The shock had given way to a dull, aching throb, and I clenched my teeth and muffled the pained cry that rose up within me. Wordlessly, he passed me a handkerchief he'd no doubt brought for this very reason, and I pressed it against my skin.

"I *am* sorry," he said again. "Truly."

"He had better show himself." In dismay, I saw the handkerchief was almost entirely soaked through with my blood. "What now?"

"We wait."

I sat gingerly on the end of the ruined bed, and Elyan knelt before me and lifted the cloth from my wound. The blood had ceased flowing, but the pain was still frightful; he winced at my sharp intake of breath. I watched, fascinated, as he touched two fingers gently to the cut and closed his eyes. The tips of his fingers began to glow, and an answering light rose in my skin.

"I'm no Healer," he said, his brows drawn together in concentration. "But I can lessen the pain somewhat."

The pain was, in fact, receding with his touch, but it still caught my breath, made my head spin. "Tell me about the Moriae," I said, desperate for a distraction. "What is it?"

"You grew up at Orwynd," he said, and I felt the pad of his thumb moving in slow circles against my skin where he held my arm. "Surely you learned of the eldritch creatures who live in the Morwood?"

"As much as I was able given my aunt's aversion to them," I answered tightly. By the Gods, it hurt still.

"Breathe," he told me. "Slowly now. Do you know what they are?"

"The remnants of the Old Gods' servants in the mortal world."

"Most little more than fairy stories, so weak is their power now," Elyan said. "But some still remain to torment those of us who err. The Moriae is one such creature."

"But what *is* it?"

"Memory," he answered. "The Moriae is a creature of memory. It was said to have been sent by Bellus himself—to seek always those who had done great wrongs, to haunt them with the most horrifying things in their past."

"How did it end up here?"

"Moriae are drawn to those whose memories are strong, whether good or no. They haunt the dark places, seeking just such victims, and when they find them, they bind themselves to them, feeding off their memories to survive." He sighed deeply. "This one likely rode in with some unfortunate bastard long ago and, once the bastard was dead, found itself trapped here. Judging by the marks on the columns, the Mage tried to rid himself of it at some point and managed to contain it to this room. They are nearly impossible to banish altogether."

"Why was it necessary that we use my blood to summon it? And not yours?"

"He's already had my blood."

"And it was truly delicious."

The silky voice came from across the room, and as we both turned, a tendril of black smoke stole from the shadows and curled around the top of the column closest to the moldering bed, round and round again. Then down it flowed, no longer smoke but ink, rivulets of it, dripping down the carved stone until, from the puddle, black as tar, a figure rose: a head first, then shoulders, narrow and skeletal, and then impossibly long arms that ended in spindly fingers—far too many fingers. These impossible hands splayed against the stone of the chamber floor as it pulled the rest of its body up, the puddle rising with it to form the rest of its ghastly body. Elyan was an exceedingly tall man; this creature, this wraith made of ink poured over bones, stood three heads taller. As I rose, shaking, to my feet, it swooped down over me as if I were being inspected.

I was not ashamed at the trembling in my limbs as its skull tilted forward on its protracted neck, so stricken with terror was I at its nearness, but I kept myself perfectly still until, evidently satisfied, the Moriae withdrew.

"Well done," whispered Elyan in my ear, and I let out a shuddering breath.

"Welcome, Orare," the Moriae greeted me, though it had no mouth at all. The lazy, slithering voice, like the rasping of a snake's skin, echoed throughout the chamber, conjured from the air itself. "Why have you sought me out?"

"I've been told things," I began. "By umbras within the prison, and by... others. I've come to ask what they mean."

"The first, you mean," the Moriae answered slyly, as though it were thoroughly amused with me. "You want to know what it is and where you can find it."

"Yes."

It laughed then, and its laugh was truly terrible. Its skeletal body seemed to collapse upon itself until it was ink once more, and then it rushed across the stones in lapping waves that chased one another until they crashed upon the column opposite and became the same dense black smoke as when it first appeared to us. Wispy black tendrils rolled upward and spread across the ceiling until it was a puddle of ink—or was it tar?—once more. Fat drops of it fell to the floor at my feet, and I took a step back, nearly colliding with Elyan. Less than an arm's span in front of us, the skeletal wraith appeared once more, pulling itself from the grisly black stain to peer down at me.

"I am sorry to say I am forbidden to speak of them, Orare," the Moriae answered me. "Deeply sorry."

"Them?" My mind seized on this revelation. "They are more than one person?"

The Moriae did not answer me, but it tilted its head at a grotesque angle on its spindly neck.

"Why are you forbidden to speak of them?"

"We all are," came its answer. "Me, you, him." He lifted his chin at Elyan. "Every living thing in this prison and the dead besides are forbidden to speak of the first. But oh, they've been trying, haven't they? Now that there's someone come along who can hear them."

"Me," I whispered.

"I hear them in the dark, speaking in riddles," he said, drawing out the end of the word in a hiss. "They grow louder, more restless." One long, bony hand, glistening black, stretched out into the space between us, a mere hairsbreadth from my cheek. I stood rigid, waiting for the inevitable touch, fearing it, and fascinated by it despite my revulsion.

A moment passed, then another. Then the Moriae's hand flexed and I heard the sickening crunch of its bones before it withdrew.

"Their message," he said at last, "is not being received."

"That's why she's come," Elyan said. His voice held an edge that had grown increasingly sharp since the Moriae appeared.

"I have heard them," I told the Moriae. "I just do not understand what it is they are trying to tell me."

"As I said, I cannot tell you who the first is." The Moriae shrugged the spiny bones of its shoulders. "However, I suppose I *could* tell you where to look."

"Yes," I said without hesitation.

"Careful." Elyan's voice held a warning. "He will not tell you for free, and even then, what he tells you may not be what you want to hear."

The Moriae laughed, a high, cruel sound that bounced off the walls of the cavernous room, and the power in it, *god power*, was so deafening that I was forced to slam my hands over my ears and squeeze tight my eyes to ward it off.

When I gingerly opened them again, the black tendrils of the Moriae in its liquid form were oozing up the column to our left, chasing one another lazily to the ceiling. "Oh, your highness," it hissed. "You are much changed these twelve years. Such cynicism! Did I not uphold my end of *our* bargain?"

Elyan's jaw was clenched so tightly I could see his muscles straining. His hands were balled into fists at his sides.

"What *is* the price?" I ventured.

"Memories," Elyan gritted out. "His price is your memories."

I felt the floor shift beneath my feet, and I stared with growing horror at the stain the Moriae had formed above us.

"What sort of memories?" I asked hesitantly.

The Moriae pulled its head from the stain slowly, its many fingers splayed against the ceiling, and regarded me with its sightless eyes. "Strong ones," it said. "The sort that sustain you in your darkest hours. The ones that have a life of their own."

Then it dropped all at once in a gangling heap of ink and bones onto the chamber floor. I waited until it had collected itself once more.

"And what will you do with my memories?"

"He'll keep them," Elyan fairly spat out.

Anguish bloomed within me, a bitter flower. "You mean… I would cease to remember them?"

The Moriae answered me with silence. *Yes*, that silence told me. *Yes*.

"He cannot tell you who the first are. Like as not he cannot tell you where to find them, either. This was a mistake, and one I will gladly suffer through another apology for. We should go."

"Must you be so hasty?" The Moriae oozed toward us. "Your highness, you know very well the goods I offer are worth the price."

But was what I sought worth what I stood to lose? The truth was, I could not imagine parting with a single memory, for I was made of them; would I be unmade for lack of them? Would I cease to be myself entirely? I was afraid—oh, certainly I was afraid, but I'd come so far and the answers stood before me wearing the smile of my enemy.

"It's all right." I laid my hand on Elyan's arm. "I have many strong memories. I'm sure I can part with a few."

"Just so," the Moriae said, and a bargain was struck. I tried not to flinch as the Moriae descended upon me greedily. "Let's see, shall we?"

Its hideous fingers rose and took my face from chin to temple. I had but a moment to take a deep breath and draw upon all the courage I possessed before my vision went black—and then blazed to life in blinding, brilliant color.

The Moriae sifted through my memories the way one might flip through the pages of a book.

Images careened through my vision so fast I could scarce settle on one before he shuffled them again and again, pausing now and then just long enough for me to see the flash of a smile, smell a scent on the wind, hear a peal of laughter. The faces of those I'd known, those I'd loved blurred and melded together, then came apart again, populating the landscape of my life. My parents and sister, Cyprias, my Uncle Geordan, Master Aeneas, Mistress Eudora. I saw them all, and myself with them, and I ached with longing.

And although I would not have believed it possible, there were memories from Asperfell there, too, because I had been happy here. I saw the moment I'd first used my magic, days spent in the garden with Yralis, the night I had attended the Melancholy Revels with Thaniel.

And then I saw twinkling lights in a canopy of willow branches, and a smile that stole my very breath. It was the night I'd woven hellebore in my hair and danced with a prince beneath a starry winter sky.

Oh, please not that one, I begged. *Not that one!*

There was laughter in my head, and then I felt the Moriae release me.

The force of it sent me staggering backwards.

Elyan's hands reached out and caught me before my body met stone, and I sagged in his arms, disoriented and confused, pinpricks of light at the corners of my vision. My stomach roiled, and I turned and retched, bringing up nothing but bile that burned my throat and stung my eyes.

"Steady, now." Elyan laid one hand, large and warm and solid, on my heaving back and used the other to pull my hair away from my face, flushed. "Just breathe."

I obeyed, sucking in great gasps of air. Then, when I was sure I could manage it without collapsing once more, I turned to the creature who had caused me such torment.

Did I imagine it, or did the Moriae seem taller now, his limbs longer, and had his fingers grown extra joints?

"I paid your price," I said, my voice shaking terribly. "Now tell me where to find the first."

"And for that, here is what I can offer you." The Moriae leaned forward and I lifted my face to its words, desperate that I should not miss a thing. "Follow the roots to the foundations of bone."

I waited for him to continue, then realized with dull shock that there was no more to hear; this was all he intended to give me. "But that's nothing," I said slowly. "Just more riddles."

"It is as much as I am able to give you." The Moriae dipped one sharp, protruding shoulder in a shrug. "Do not blame me if it isn't entirely to your liking."

Exhaustion and pain and anger rose in me. "It isn't anything!"

"You *bastard*!" Elyan gritted out. "You slippery, lying bastard."

The Moriae drew away from us both, its arms spread impossibly wide. "I've said all I am allowed to say."

"What do you mean, 'allowed?'" I asked.

The Moriae swooped back down toward me with frightening speed, and I flinched as I was once more overcome by the nearness of it.

"We are all of us bound by the same enchantment, Orare. I can no more break it than you."

"What enchantment?" Elyan demanded. "Speak quickly, or I will use every ounce of power within me to not only banish you, but ensure that you suffer in the doing of it."

The Moriae paused at this. Foolishly, I'd not thought to ask Elyan if he could siphon magic from a messenger of the Old Gods, but evidently the Moriae believed he could, for he withdrew to a careful difference and watched us balefully.

"I told you, I'm bound," it said, and its voice sounded sullen. "Threaten me all you want, your highness, but there is nothing more I can tell you."

Elyan looked very much as though he was considering harming the Moriae, or at least finding out if such a thing were possible. He must've decided it wasn't worth the risk, because he turned his back on the eldritch thing and crouched down on the stone close to me.

"Can you walk?"

"I think so." In truth, I was not entirely sure. I was shaking quite badly, and nausea was rising in my throat. But I could not bear to spend another moment in the presence of the Moriae.

Elyan took my hands in his and pulled me to my feet; my legs did not seem to want to obey even my most basic commands. I took one shaky step, then another, and pitched forward as my knees buckled. Elyan caught me before I dashed myself against the hard stone and swept me up into his arms as though I weighed nothing. I wanted to protest, but I found myself so exhausted and dizzy that my head fell quite involuntarily against his chest and I had no desire to lift it again.

"I don't need your help," I told him wearily, as he carried me toward the door.

"Of course not."

"And I am only permitting you to help me because I am temporarily incapacitated."

"I would not have imagined otherwise."

Behind us, the Moriae called out: "I wish you both the very best of luck."

We did not look back.

22

The pale, watery light of the rising winter sun was spilling into the courtyard by the time we descended from the southwest tower, and Asperfell was waking. I did my best to ignore the curious stares of my fellow prisoners, no doubt surprised to see Elyan and me in a state of wearied dishevelment.

When we reached a silent corridor far from watchful eyes, he set me gently upon one of the stone benches and I stared off into the distance at nothing at all. I'd shed my blood and given up my memories, and all I earned for my troubles was a throbbing cut on my arm and another riddle clamoring inside my head. I was desperately weary and heartsick.

"When you went to see him, did he tell you nonsense, too?" I asked Elyan bitterly.

"I didn't go to see him," he answered, as he lowered himself onto the bench beside me. "I found him quite by accident."

When he first arrived, Elyan had been quite a novelty to the prisoners of Asperfell, who had never seen a royal before, let alone imagined one would be imprisoned with them. Even as a boy of sixteen and not fully trained in his aptitude, Elyan was a danger to them if provoked; yet they persisted, particularly a group of men devoted to seeing the young prince brought low. Skilled as he was, he was still only able to draw magic at the touch, and there were too many of them. He fought with wild desperation and was able to lay hands on two of the men, drawing so much magic from them that they fell unconscious and could not be roused for several days. The remaining three men, filled with humiliated rage, set upon Elyan with a vengeance.

They were relentless in their pursuit, and a panicked Elyan fled up into the dark recesses of the abandoned tower as far as his feet could take him. He was already bleeding from the assault, and when he reached the room at the top of the stairs and fell to his knees with relief at having outwitted his assailants, his blood dripped onto the floor and summoned the Moriae.

"I had no idea how I'd gotten there and didn't know how to get to the courtyard again," Elyan told me. "So, I made a deal: memories for the way out."

"Do you ever wonder what he took from you?"

Elyan's face darkened. "I don't have to; he told me himself."

"Why?"

"I imagine it was like rubbing salt in an open wound." He shrugged. "As an injured, angry, terrified boy I doubt that I was very diplomatic." I remembered that earlier Elyan had, in fact, threatened to kill the Moriae. "Thus, he took great pleasure in telling me that he took memories of my mother."

"I'm sorry." I would likely never know what the Moriae took from me, and I wondered if it was better that way.

He shrugged, and I felt him closing himself off as he sometimes did when I pressed too far. "It's done now."

"Yes, it's done now."

I drew a shuddering breath and blinked in the growing light of the morning. I wondered that I did not cry; perhaps Asperfell had wrung all the tears from me that it could. I doubted this was true. Somewhere outside, I heard birdsong.

"Elyan?"

He tilted his head. Golden light spilled over the planes of his face and any words I might have spoken were utterly stolen from me.

He must've understood somehow, because he shifted on the bench and lifted his arm so I could lean against him, tucking my head in the space below his shoulder. His fingers stole into the tangle of my hair, and I closed my eyes. The tears, when they came, slid over my lips, leaving trails of salt and sunlight.

I fell asleep fully clothed with my breakfast untouched the moment I returned to my chamber and did not rise again until well into the afternoon. After suffering obediently through a lecture by Mistress Philomena on shirking my duties, I met Elyan in Master Tiberius's workroom where we told him everything that had befallen us with the Moriae, including his infuriating riddle, the riddle I had paid for with my memories.

"Roots suggest a plant, or a tree." Master Tiberius stroked his beard thoughtfully, as he so often did. "But it could also mean the origins of something or someone, perhaps their heritage."

"Bones could be death," I ventured. "But how does one have a foundation of death?"

"A foundation is a base upon which something is built," Master Tiberius answered. "Death is a poor foundation for anything."

Elyan looked up from the tincture he was preparing for the cut on my arm. He'd added a few leaves from one of Master Tiberius's dusty old jars to a cup of something clear, and now it smoked and swirled and turned purple. "Do you suppose he means a grave, or is that too obvious?"

"I thought the same thing when you first said it," Master Tiberius replied. "Perhaps a specific grave."

I held out my arm as Elyan began to unwind the strip of cloth he'd used to bind my wound. Thanks to his magic, the cut was not nearly as awful as I imagined it would be, merely a thin, angry red line. I winced as he dabbed my flesh with a cloth dipped in the purple liquid. "But whose grave are we looking for?"

"The Moriae said 'the first' were more than one person," Elyan said. "Perhaps it is not simply one grave."

"He also said the entire prison was prevented from speaking of them," I reminded him. "How are we going to find the graves of people we cannot speak of?"

"If it is even a grave we are looking for."

I slumped back in my chair, feeling disheartened. I had known deciphering the Moriae's riddle would be a fearsome thing, but I did not expect that even the combined knowledge of Master Tiberius and Prince Elyan could not manage it.

From the archives we pulled as many scrolls and maps as we could find that contained information about the graveyard and the Mages buried there. We spread them out and anchored their edges with candles and bent our heads low to read the faded script, some so old that we would've had difficulty translating it were it not for Elyan's royal schooling, which contained ancient dialects.

Willow arrived bearing a meat pie and a jug of hot wine, and I realized then just how hungry I was. I wolfed down two whole pieces, licking the juice and tiny flakes of pastry off of my fingers when I was finished. If Mistress Precia had seen me, she would've rapped my knuckles soundly. I poured myself a cup of wine, and while Master Tiberius and Prince Elyan talked in low voices at the worktable, I looked out the window at the frigid winter afternoon already beginning to darken into evening. Icy filigree had begun to creep up the panes of the window despite the warmth of the fire within, and I touched the cold glass with the tips of my fingers. Across the moor, I could see the Sentinels, utterly still beneath a dusting of snow.

Had it really only been mere months since Master Aeneas had

conjured the Gate and Cyprias had thrust me through? It seemed a lifetime since I'd crossed into this world, so changed was my life from what had come before. It was as though I had gone through the Gate as one person and emerged as another entirely.

And then it came to me. "Elyan, the two men who first opened the Gate, who built the prison—what are their names?"

Elyan looked up. His mouth opened as though to reply, and then he stopped and cocked his head to one side, his brow furrowed. "Do you know, I cannot remember," he said slowly. "I studied them quite extensively in my youth, but now…"

"Master Tiberius," I said, my excitement growing. "Do you remember when I asked you the same question many weeks ago, and you could not remember their names either?"

"Nor could you, as I recall," Master Tiberius answered faintly. "Oh my."

With a shout of excited laughter, I dashed across the workroom and threw open the door to the library. The scholars within grumbled heartily at the interruption, one even going so far as to shake a wizened fist at me, and it did not help that in my haste I upset an enormous pile of loose parchment with my skirts, sending pages fluttering this way and that. But if there was anyone at Asperfell who could confirm what I believed to be the truth, it was the ancient Mages who now fixed me with decidedly hostile expressions.

"Gentlemen!" I announced. "I am so very sorry to disturb you, but it is of the utmost importance. Do any of you recall anything about the two men who first passed through the Gate and created Asperfell?"

A Mage with bottle green robes and pointed black eyebrows answered me irritably: "Of *course* we do, young lady. We are the keepers of all Asperfell's knowledge."

"Wonderful," I said. "What were their names?"

There was a great deal of muttering and shuffling and furtive glancing between the lot of them before the Mage in green cleared his throat. "Well, their names were…" he began, then frowned. "That is to say…"

"Exactly," I nodded. "And can any of you recall where I might find anything written down about them in your illustrious archives?"

They more resembled a room full of owls than Mages as they blinked at me, their jaws slack.

"You see?" I fairly shouted at Elyan and Master Tiberius. "Nobody can remember their names, and therefore nobody can speak of them—just as the Moriae said! And there are no records to be found, nothing to tell us what they may have done, or where their graves are now!"

"But why are we unable to speak of them?" Elyan asked, looking over at Master Tiberius. "An enchantment?"

Master Tiberius stroked his beard. "It is possible, I suppose. It would take a tremendously powerful Mage, far beyond any of us."

"But why do it at all? Why enchant the population of an entire prison against the memories of two men long dead?"

"Vala Lirr told me to seek them if I wanted freedom," I said, giving voice to my most desperate desire. "Perhaps the spell is to guard against prisoners discovering a way out by prying too deeply into the doings of its founders!"

Under ordinary circumstances, Elyan would've made a spectacular show of his annoyance with my talk of escape, but now he gazed at me thoughtfully. "The Moriae could not speak of them, either—except in riddles. Just as the rest of them have done."

"But how?" I shook my head. "How do they know?"

"All of them—the umbras, the Countess, the Moriae—they all said they could hear whispers." Master Tiberius's eyes glittered. "They've told you as much."

"And you think the whispers they've heard are meant for me?"

"Whatever the reason, someone is trying to speak to you, and they are using your aptitude to do it," Elyan said. "You are the only one who is able to hear them."

I stared at them. "Who? Who is whispering?"

"Who indeed," Master Tiberius said. "I believe that, my dear, is what you are meant to discover."

"There are thirty-two trees in the graveyard," Nollie told us the next morning, when we emerged from Asperfell clutching armfuls of maps. "And I've never seen anything about a—what did you call it?"

"Foundations of bone," I answered.

"Right. Well, I've never seen anything like that near any of the trees. And what exactly *is* this foundation of bone?"

"I have no idea, but we think it might have something to do with the creators of Asperfell."

Like every other prisoner, neither she nor Perkin could recall the names of the men, nor knew where they were buried, but she reasoned their graves would likely be amongst the oldest if they existed at all.

"We'll help you," Nollie nodded. "As much as we are able to, and provided that one doesn't inadvertently raise anyone." She jerked one stubby thumb at Perkin. He waggled his fingers back at her.

We set to work examining the oldest stones in the graveyard, starting with those in close proximity to trees. Most of the names had long since worn away despite any magic that might've been placed upon them; thus, it was fortunate we had Necromancers to tell us what our maps and our eyes could not. With their power, they probed beneath the frozen earth, seeking what secrets the bones below could tell them and found nothing to suggest that anything entombed in Asperfell's graveyard was out of the ordinary.

"The only bones I feel are the poor bastards buried here," Nollie told us after several bitterly cold hours crouching in the dirt and snow.

"Sleeping nice and tidy, they are," Perkin added. "Shame."

I sat back with a huff, my breath a cloud of white. "And the two men? The first?"

She shrugged. "Who's to say? But I would think their graves would have a bit more to-do about them, don't you?"

I looked up at Elyan. "Perhaps they are not buried in the graveyard."

"Perhaps they are not at Asperfell at all. They created the Sentinels, after all; perhaps they decided to strike out and see what lies beyond the forest."

"That cannot be. Why would Vala Lirr have told me to seek them if they were not here?"

"It's a wide moor," Nollie pointed out. "Maybe they chose to lie apart from the other prisoners."

A light snow was beginning to fall, and through the gently drifting flakes I gazed out at the impossible distance between us and the Sentinels. "If that is the case, however will we find them?"

Shivering and exhausted, Elyan and I thanked Nollie and Perkin for their help and trudged back to Asperfell in what I hoped was a temporary defeat.

"A grave seemed too simple a solution anyway," Elyan said, as we stepped into the courtyard. "Any sort of riddle worth its salt would not let us off so easily."

"Perhaps," I conceded. "Is there anywhere else we might find roots and bones?"

"I am loath to admit that I'm at a loss."

"As am I," I agreed, and stifled an unladylike yawn with the back of my hand.

"You look exhausted. Perhaps we begin our search anew once you've had some sleep."

I wanted to object, but I was so very, very tired. Elyan extracted a promise from me that I would find something to eat and then sleep as long as I could before seeking him out again, and so I trudged toward the kitchens. The evening meal was long past, but perhaps Willow would take pity on me. The hour had grown late and the darkness with it. I called Magefire to my hand, holding it aloft in the corridor.

I'd thought I was alone; even the two umbras who usually haunted the hallway outside the storerooms were nowhere to be seen, but somewhere behind me, and quite nearby, I heard a strange shuffling sound, as though something were being slowly dragged across the stone floor. "Mistress Philomena?" I called into the dark. "Willow? Is that you?"

The strange shuffling sound grew louder now, closer, and my heartbeat quickened apace. Hesitating, I glanced back the way I'd come, wondering if I should call Elyan. Likely he was too far away to hear me now. I gathered my courage and turned back.

A familiar face, ugly and scarred and snarling, rose up before me. "Grenn!" I gasped.

The Magefire slipped from my hand and vanished, plunging the corridor into near-darkness as Grenn's meaty hand grasped my arm. A scream tore from my throat and the force of the shield I conjured threw Grenn backwards into the wall, but neither made him rethink his assault. With a snarl, he fell on me again, his hands reaching for my throat.

"Grenn, stop!" My hands scrabbled against his, my nails gouging into his flesh. It did nothing to deter him; he squeezed, his scarred hands digging into the tender skin of my throat, his thumbs pressing against my windpipe. "Please!" I croaked. "Let go of me!"

He did not seem to hear me at all. In fact, his eyes seemed to stare right through me. And there was something very, very wrong with them.

His grip tightened, and I struggled against the black seeping into the edges of my vision. My magic rose within me, but there was no umbra to call out to, no one to control, no one to help me. And yet I felt a pull at the string, as I always thought of it; something was there, responding to my magic.

I screamed out to it, whatever it may be: "Set me free!"

The hands at my throat slackened and withdrew, and I fell into a heap at Grenn's feet, coughing and sputtering and gasping for air. Then I scrabbled away from him as fast as I could and stared. It was as though Grenn had turned to stone. His hands—only moments ago close to squeezing the life from me—were hanging limply at his sides.

What had I done?

I scarcely had time to wonder before Grenn's fingers began to twitch, and his head swiveled grotesquely toward me as though he was emerging from a trance. I gasped as his eyes met mine: they were completely and utterly white.

"Briony!" I heard Elyan's voice behind me and turned to see him running toward us, color high in his cheeks, his face like thunder. He thrust me behind him as Grenn shook off the last of whatever my magic had done to him, and with a deafening roar, he lunged at us.

He did not make it far.

Elyan's arm stretched out, and the glow of magic pulsed beneath the skin of his palm. Grenn crumpled to the ground with a sickening thud, his mouth going slack. Magic pulsed beneath his skin, an answer to Elyan's call; but it quickly faded as Elyan's hand grew bright, so impossibly bright that I shielded my eyes from it.

We stood utterly still for a long moment, Elyan's arm outstretched, Grenn's stolen magic playing under the skin of his hand. Elyan was breathing quickly, his shoulders rising and falling with the struggle of the foreign magic within him, the muscles of his back taut.

"Is he dead?" I managed to say in a strangled voice.

"No." Elyan knelt beside Grenn and flipped him over onto his back. "I didn't take nearly enough for that." His lip curled in distaste, and I thought perhaps he was disappointed that he hadn't.

"It wasn't like last time," I told him. "He wasn't trying to—" I swallowed hard. "His eyes were completely white, and I don't think he saw me at all. It was as though he wasn't himself."

Elyan bent over Grenn and pushed the lid of his eye up to reveal the same milky white nothingness I'd seen before. His breath caught in his throat. "There's some other magic inside him, not of his own blood.

"I felt it. I... spoke to it. It's why I'm still alive."

"Impressive," he whispered. I looked in his face for any sign of mockery, but found something closer to awe. He looked away and added, "I think someone else is controlling him, like a marionette."

"Is that possible?"

"Not by any magic I know of," he conceded. "I need to draw it out of him if we hope to question him about what happened."

I realized he was looking to me for consent and I nodded. I was no longer afraid of this lumbering thug, not with Elyan at my side.

Elyan dropped down beside Grenn, lifted one hand, and closed his eyes. I watched in fascination as Grenn's skin began to glow, softly at first and then brighter. Elyan's brows drew together and I thought I saw his lips moving silently, and then something strange began to happen to Grenn's face; shadows began to play beneath the surface of his skin, shadows that swirled and churned until, so agitated that they could not be contained, they rose into the air, mingling with the light of his magic, and Elyan's, and then they disappeared entirely, taking Grenn's face with them.

The face that remained was a stranger to me.

Elyan gasped. "That's not Grenn, that's Ajax."

I stared at him aghast. "But *why*? Why would anyone disguise this man as Grenn?"

Even as the words tumbled from my lips, I knew. Grenn had attacked me once before, of his own volition, and had been locked away below for it. Surely no one would question these renewed efforts but would see it as mere revenge and nothing more. Mistress Philomena would carve me a stone, I would never learn the true identity of the first, never discover the way out of Asperfell, and

Tiralaen's last hope would never return to claim his throne and free his people. It was simple, really. Efficient. And it may very well have worked were it not for my magic.

Elyan seemed to have reached the same conclusion as I. "It wasn't enough to kill the messenger. Whoever murdered the Countess wants you dead as well. What I don't understand is why they didn't just use the real Grenn."

I imagined Grenn locked away in his cell below, held by a chain to the wall, pacing back and forth only as far as the chain allowed him. "Because Grenn couldn't escape on his own. It would do them no good to set their strings to a puppet that couldn't get past his own locked door. Only Ajax would do."

"And only if they could put Grenn's countenance upon him. Who do you know in this prison with illusion magic?"

"Lady Ashwinder." The name tumbled from my lips in a whisper.

"Perhaps." Elyan tilted his head. "But this magic was... complex. Far beyond what I thought her capable of."

"There was a woman below," I said slowly, as the realization came to me. "An illusionist, and a powerful one."

"Ceris." Elyan nodded. "Yes, she is quite powerful, but why on earth would she send Ajax as Grenn to attack you?"

I shook my head. "Ceris did not seem to care much about me either way. And neither she nor Lady Ashwinder would know about the whispers, nor have any reason for wanting to prevent escape from Asperfell."

Elyan's dark brows drew together. "Someone does. And they have magic beyond anything I've ever known." He sighed and shook his head. Then he brushed my skin lightly with his fingertips and let them rest, the warmth of his magic seeping beneath my skin, singing to the magic in my blood. "Perhaps it's time to let this go," he said softly.

My hands reached out and took hold of the fabric of his shirt and

I held it tightly as though it would give me courage. "I can't," I whispered fiercely. "I made a promise."

"A promise that is not worth your life, Briony," he said, and when he shook his head, his dark curls spilled over his forehead and he looked so much like the young man he'd been before this place had taken him and held him against the whetstone and sharpened him so. "I would be a fool to let this go on."

I met his gaze squarely with as much stubbornness as I could muster. "You would be a fool to try to stop me."

Elyan laughed, a low, rumbling sound that made my breath catch suddenly in my chest, and he shook his head ruefully at me. "A fool I am not," he said. "But I'll not lose you."

He lowered his head until his forehead rested against mine, and I thought that perhaps if he took my shoulders and tilted me just so, if he leaned down ever so slightly, if I rose up on my toes just so, our lips might touch. But they did not; we remained as we were, not as we could be, poised with exquisite agony between wanting and having.

And then suddenly, just like that, the answer rose in my mind, and it was a tangle of black in a courtyard of stone, blood spreading across snow.

"Roots," I whispered.

Elyan's eyes narrowed in confusion. "What?"

"Roots!" I exclaimed, laughing, and gripped his hands excitedly. "Come with me!"

23

"It was never a grave," I told him, as we ascended into the light of the courtyard, my voice tight with excitement and certainty. "Graves do not have foundations, you see, but buildings do!"

The black oak of Asperfell rose before us, its limbs twisted into a canopy both beautiful and terrifying. The night I'd dreamed of a red stain spreading from the base of the tree, I'd heard whispers in that very same place, a thousand whispers that became one.

"Follow the roots to the foundations of bone," I said, and smiled. "These are the roots we're meant to follow."

It was madness, certainly. I had no proof of my convictions, only a feeling, but it was strong and sure, and I felt it deeply in the marrow of my bones, and in the magic in my blood. There was something below us, something that had been whispering to the umbras, to the Countess, to me, and it spoke of freedom.

"I suppose it does make a certain sense," Elyan agreed reluctantly. "But how do we proceed?"

I stared up at the warped branches of the black oak tree, at the mighty trunk that burrowed into the soil below and disappeared, beckoning me to where I knew not, and a knot of doubt tightened within me. How exactly were we to follow the roots? No doubt they delved deep into the soil and stone below, lost to human eyes.

"I've not actually thought that bit out yet," I confessed.

"I don't suppose you happened to bring a shovel with you when you went through the Gate?" Elyan asked drily.

"I did not."

"Right. We need a Naturalist, and a damned powerful one at that."

"Is there one such Naturalist here?"

"Yes," he answered, and glanced sidelong at me. "But you are not going to like who it is."

I possessed no invitation to the Melancholy Revels that night, and the man guarding the door nearly turned me away until his gaze slid over the top of my head and glimpsed Elyan's tall form in the shadows behind me. Without another word, he held the door open for the both of us.

It was lucky Elyan was afforded such deference even though the nobility did not care overmuch for him, because not only did he believe the Naturalist we sought would be present at the Revels that evening, but we would also be able to confront Lady Ashwinder about the illusion spell cast over Ajax.

"With subtlety," Elyan had warned me, and I had responded with sighs and laments that I could not rouse a group of umbras to terrorize the truth from her.

When we entered the Revels, the room went absolutely still. Every eye was upon us; well, I conceded, not *us*, exactly. Every single member of the society and their illustrious guests were starring with jaws gone slack at the man standing beside me. Games ceased, music trailed off, conversations fell silent, and those who had been seated rose at once; habit, no doubt, after years at court.

Across the room, Lady Ashwinder recovered herself and, grabbing her husband's hand, raced toward us as fast as her gown of gold silk would allow, Lord Frobern and Lady Antonia on their heels. When she reached us, Lady Ashwinder sank into the deepest, most prostrate curtesy I had ever seen; indeed, her forehead nearly touched the floor in supplication. The rest of the room followed suit, and though I rather suspected his irritation at it all, Elyan endured the attention with the grace and detachment cultivated in his youth.

"Your highness," Lady Ashwinder said breathlessly as she rose, her cheeks flushed and her eyes positively alight. "We are honored and humbled by your presence this evening."

Gone entirely was the derision with which she had spoken of Elyan so often in my presence; here was a loyal, adoring subject.

Elyan bowed slightly at the waist. "I thank you, Lady Ashwinder."

"And Mistress Briony!" Her smile slid to me. "How lucky you are to be escorted by his highness this evening!"

There was a time not so very long ago that the very thought would've sent me into a spectacular fit.

"Oh, yes," I told her. "I am most lucky."

Lady Ashwinder fluttered her hands about her. "But where are my manners? Would either of you care for refreshment?"

A silver tray appeared, and although my stomach turned at the sight of the clear liquid within dainty crystal glasses, I took one while Elyan deferred.

"Thank you," I told her, and opening my eyes wide in what I hoped was a worthy imitation of Lady Antonia, I added: "I met with some misfortune only moments ago and I am afraid I am still quite shaken." With the curious eyes of the gathering upon me, I took a dainty sip of Laetha.

Lady Ashwinder's eyes narrowed slightly, though in concern or suspicion, I could not say. She was far better skilled than I could ever hope to be at the art of deception. "Misfortune? Of what sort?"

"The worst sort, I'm afraid," I answered. "I was attacked in the corridor outside the kitchens. Had his highness not been nearby, I fear I would've come to grievous harm."

"Goodness!" Lady Ashwinder drew open the fan that hung from her pale, delicate wrist and fluttered it about her face as though this information quite overwhelmed her.

Lord Ashwinder, for whom our conversation had held little interest, now turned suddenly from Lord Frobern. "Attacked, you say?" he asked with a frown. "By what?"

"Indeed, not a what," I replied, and paused ever so slightly. "But a *whom*."

This revelation caused quite a commotion among those members of the society closest to us; whispers and titters of excitement and dread filled the air, and hands clutched at bosoms in exaggerated shock.

"Oh, who attacked you, Mistress Briony?" Lady Orial fretted, wringing her hands together. "Was it someone from below? Has someone... *escaped?*"

I met her eyes solemnly. "Yes. Someone from below has escaped."

This was, evidently, what they all feared, for a great cry rose up at my words and those Mages who had resumed their games and conversations looked up in curiosity.

"Damn it all!" Lord Ashwinder exploded. "I thought it was Thaniel's job to keep that riffraff locked away!"

"Oh, indeed it is," I said, nodding quite intently. An idea had been forming in my mind since Lady Ashwinder had greeted us, a way to ascertain her guilt without giving her cause for suspicion. *Subtly*, as Elyan had said. I plunged ahead. "But the swine attacked Thaniel, too, and four of his knights!"

I thought Lady Orial would faint dead away into the arms of Brethwait, who was wholly unprepared for such an occurrence as he held a full goblet of wine, utterly forgotten in the commotion. Lady Selwyn had taken hold of Lord Frobern, whose face was positively white.

"I say," Lord Frobern stammered, his usual swagger quite gone. "Why target you?"

"Oh, he wasn't targeting me," I answered. "I was merely in the wrong place at the wrong time, you see. He was searching for a Mage who had ensorcelled him into doing harm without his consent." I did not dare risk looking behind me at Elyan's face for fear what I saw there would cause me to give myself away. "He wishes to exact his revenge on this person—whomever he or she may be. And the worst of it is, even though we were able to subdue him, he escaped and is roaming Asperfell at this very moment, searching for the Mage who wronged him."

"Indeed," Lady Ashwinder said, and the tension that had gathered in her shoulders and about her mouth during my speech quite disappeared, and she smiled once more. "Well, I dare say he will not find such a person among my guests. Can you imagine!" She laughed, a high, merry sound. "Although I should chide you for scaring us so thoroughly, Mistress Briony."

Lord Ashwinder, Lord Frobern, Lady Selwyn, and Brethwait chuckled as if the whole thing were nothing but a pleasant joke, though Lady Orial still looked somewhat queasy.

I finally glanced up at Elyan, but his face betrayed nothing. I longed to ask him if he still believed her guilty, but knew better than to do so in the midst of such prying company.

"Well," Lady Ashwinder said, when they had all recovered, "I do hope you will escort me tonight, your highness. There are a great many people who would love to speak with you!"

"Regrettably, I am on urgent business this evening, Lady Ashwinder," Elyan answered, and I took a certain sort of pleasure in watching Lady Ashwinder's perfect oval face fall. "If you could be so kind as to point me in the direction of Arlo Bryn, I would be eternally grateful."

Lady Ashwinder thrust her fan out in the direction of the corner across the room. "I believe he's there," she answered. "If you do decide you have a moment—"

"You will be the first to hear of it," Elyan answered. Then he took her hand in his and pressed a kiss upon it. "My thanks."

I was both relieved and dismayed to see Arlo Bryn presiding over a game of Flesket at his usual table tucked away in the corner Lady Ashwinder had indicated. Of *course* he was a Naturalist; he exuded a life and vibrancy that, as much as I was loath to admit it, was intoxicating. It was, I supposed, why people flocked to him despite his roguish behavior; they could feel the pull of his magic within him, a connection to the living world that surrounded them, familiar and vital. It certainly explained the odd look that Arlo had exchanged with Thaniel the very first night I'd attended the Melancholy Revels; Alchemy was no doubt seen by many as a more distinguished and valuable aptitude than lordship over growing things. But Thaniel's mother had been a Naturalist. No doubt he understood well enough the value of such magic, even if it resided in the blood of a bitter enemy.

"If he's a Naturalist," I whispered to Elyan, "then why have I never seen him in the garden? Surely he would be a far greater help than me."

Elyan snorted. "Arlo Bryn would never stoop so low. He prefers to ply his aptitude on much more illustrious tasks."

"Such as?"

"Well, gambling, wine, and women aside, he keeps the flowering vines at bay, or tries to."

I frowned. "Didn't they strangle a man several months back?"

"I said 'tries to.'"

"Briony Tenebrae!" Arlo Bryn spread his arms wide and welcomed us with a smile and an incredulously delighted laugh. "And is that his royal highness himself? To what do I owe this profound pleasure— and it is profound, I assure you. Sit, sit." He waved to the two chairs opposite him, and the Mages there had no choice but to lay down their cards, the game now over.

We sat, and glasses of Laetha appeared before us.

Arlo Bryn listened, a self-assured smile playing about his wide mouth, as we told him why we'd come, what we wanted him to do. He already knew, of course, about the Countess's death, and Vala Lirr's umbra, but he did not know about the riddles, or the Moriae, and, just like us, he found himself at a lost when we asked him about the two men we believed to be the first, the two men who passed through the Gate before all others and built Asperfell.

"Fascinating." His eyes gleamed. "What *have* you stumbled into?"

I glanced at Elyan. "We aren't entirely sure. That's why we need you."

Arlo drummed his fingers against the tabletop. "Tell it to me again," he said. "Tell me what the Moriae said."

"Follow the roots to the foundation of bone," I repeated.

"That's the whole of it?"

"It's not much to go on, I'm afraid."

"It's nothing to go on," Arlo answered drily. "Well, it *would* suggest tree roots, as you've said, and I daresay you'll find plenty of bones below, but to what purpose?" He raised one eyebrow at me. "Do you not think if there were a secret Gate hidden in the dungeons, someone would've found it by now?"

"We don't know it's a Gate," I replied, bristling at the sarcasm laced in his voice. "But the umbra did say freedom."

"Yes, but whose?" Arlo tapped a finger against his temple, his gaze sliding past me to Elyan, who so far had spoken very little other than what was necessary to corroborate my story. "As intriguing as this all sounds, I don't do anything for free."

"You can't imagine us so naive as to assume otherwise," Elyan answered. "Tell us your price."

Arlo shrugged. "Well, coin is useless to me here. I traffic in favors, your highness, and one of yours could be quite useful. Will you be indebted to me?"

"No," Elyan said flatly. I did not blame him; it was unimaginable the sort of mischief Arlo Bryn might cause with the power of a Siphon at his command.

"No?" Arlo tilted his head. "Are you sure? No matter." Slowly he turned his gaze on me, and he smiled. "Perhaps I want a different sort of favor after all."

It took me a moment to realize what his words meant, what his sleek, predatory smile meant, and when I did, I flushed crimson with embarrassment and outrage. "How *dare* you—" I spluttered, and his damnable smile widened.

Beside me, Elyan had gone deathly still. "Lay a finger upon her and I'll relieve you of it, and more besides."

"Oh, is that how it is, then?" Arlo studied Elyan with sudden interest. "Well, that is unexpected. Still, as you've nothing I want, I believe we are quite finished here."

"Wait," I said quickly. "Please. There must be something else."

He shrugged, indifferent. "Everything I could possibly want, I have, and what I don't have, I can get elsewhere." He stood and straightened his finely embroidered coat. "Do enjoy yourselves."

As he made to leave the table, a thought born of desperation struck me and I realized there was, indeed, something he wanted that nobody else could give him; nobody but Elyan and myself. "We can get you out."

Arlo stopped, looked down at me. "There is no way out," he said, but there was a sliver of doubt in his voice.

"There may be," I answered, and I hoped I sounded more confident than I felt. "Vala Lirr said 'freedom.' What other possible freedom could she have meant than ours?"

"Conjecture." Arlo drew his brow together in a frown, but he sat back in his chair. "It likely does not mean what you think it does."

"Someone tried to kill me because of it," I told him. "That hardly seems like nothing."

"People try to kill me all the time," he replied, and pointed a finger at Elyan. "*He* tried to kill me once."

Elyan snorted. "I did no such thing."

"That massive stone just *happened* to fall almost exactly where I was walking?"

"Whatever this is, it is not nothing," I told him firmly. "I know it. There is something below, something important, and I cannot reach it without your help."

"And if it all amounts to nothing?" Arlo challenged. "I could lose much and gain nothing."

"You'll gain nothing if you stay," Elyan pointed out.

Arlo studied Elyan and me in turn, his face calculating, no doubt determining exactly the likelihood he would benefit from helping us. Finally, a decision reached, he thrust out his hand with a sigh. "All right, I'll help you," he said. "Though I may be damned for it. If I die down there, by the way, I'm becoming an umbra and haunting you both for the rest of your lives."

"In that case, I hope we die down there right along with you," Elyan replied, and it was done.

Arlo shook both our hands, a mockery of a solemn pact, and called for more Laetha, which I refused. "Now, then," he said, after he'd taken a long swallow from his glass. "When do we go?"

Because we had still not discovered who had used Grenn to attack me, we could not risk waiting. And so it was agreed we would go the following night. We had not yet told Master Tiberius of our discovery, and I was hopeful that even if I could not convince Phyra to lend her gift to our quest, Thaniel may agree to lend his. Elyan was a powerful Mage, and Arlo no doubt possessed some modicum of skill, in fisticuffs if not magic, but it could not hurt to have a warrior with us as well, better still one who could make enchanted weapons.

"Gods," Arlo said darkly, looking down at his empty cup. "I can't decide whether it would be better for me to stop drinking for the night or keep drinking because we might all die tomorrow."

And with that, we took our leave and left him at his table to decide his fate.

"You didn't have to do that, you know," I said, as we departed the Melancholy Revels. "Defend me, I mean. I could've done it perfectly well myself."

"I've no doubt," Elyan replied drily. "Though I am not entirely sure your methods wouldn't have resulted in us being bodily removed from the gathering. I can personally attest to how hard you can slap a man."

"Arlo Bryn is a scoundrel," I said. "He would've deserved it for what he said."

"I would give much to not have our success hinge on his aptitude," Elyan sighed. "I don't trust him."

I glanced sidelong at the sharp, beautiful edges of his profile in the shadows of the corridor. He'd called the success 'ours' rather than mine alone, and it was not lost upon me. I nudged him gently. "Did you really try to kill him?"

"What?" He looked down at me. "No. Not intentionally, anyway. Arlo Bryn is a wastrel and a rake, but he keeps well enough out of my way and I out of his."

"You know, you and Thaniel are very much alike," I told him. "You both have very high expectations for the moral exactitudes of criminals."

Elyan did not share Thaniel's quite unfortunate history with Arlo Bryn and could more easily forgive his loathsome behavior than the Alchemist could. I began to worry I would not be able to convince both Thaniel and Arlo to accompany me without bloodshed.

"That was quite clever, you know," Elyan said suddenly, and for a moment I stared up at him in utter confusion. "With Lady Ashwinder," he clarified.

"Oh!" Caught up in convincing Arlo Bryn to help us, I'd completely forgotten about it. "I was wondering what you'd make of it. You *did* say I had to be subtle, after all."

"Indeed. So long has it been since they've used their magic for anything but tricks and comforts, Lady Ashwinder would've been terrified at the prospect of one of the prisoners below hunting her down."

"But she did not seem terribly concerned, did she."

"She did not," Elyan agreed.

I nudged him gently in the side. "I told you."

"So you did," he admitted. "But perhaps it would've been better had it been Lady Ashwinder."

"Why in the world would you say so?"

His brow raised. "Because the alternative is far worse."

It was with this in mind that we emerged into the courtyard. The black oak rose before us in all of its twisted grandeur and I could not help the thrill that raced through me at the sight of it; how very soon we could be free of all this.

"Well, then," I said, "shall we to Master Tiberius?"

Elyan reached out and took my hand, pulling me gently toward him, and away from Master Tiberius's tower. "Not yet. Tomorrow, at dawn."

In the pale light of the moon spilling through the tall, thin windows that lined the colonnade, he looked far younger than his twenty-eight years, and I realized it was because his expression was open, guileless, and almost unsure, a jarring counterpoint to the angles of his face. There was a question poised at his lips, in his eyes, and I pressed his hand gently. "What is it?"

"There's something I need to tell you," he said, and his voice was very low. "But not here."

I thought he meant my chamber, or perhaps his own, and I flushed at the thought of either, but it was toward the kitchens that he led me, and then beyond them to a storeroom. He lifted two thick woolen blankets from a crate near the door to the garden.

"We're not going outside, are we?" I asked warily. The hour had grown late, and cold had been seeping into my bones since we'd left the Melancholy Revels.

"We are, as a matter of fact," Elyan answered, and I watched his fingers move on the surface of the cloth, imbuing it with warming spells far better than I could manage. "You'll have warmth enough, I promise."

He wrapped the blanket around me, tucking it under my chin, and I clutched it against myself as we stepped into the bitterly cold night. The newly fallen snow glittered in the harsh, clear light of so many stars, and we cut a swath through it silently as Elyan led me beyond garden and graveyard, keeping close to the walls of the great fortress. When at last he stopped and I looked up, there was the large, jagged crack in Asperfell's outer wall that I'd seen him repairing so very long ago. It looked as though he'd returned since, and many times; the crack was very nearly healed. Only a few inches remained, a hand's length, rising from the base of the wall. How much magic must it have cost him, I wondered, to have drawn the edges of the schism together and bind them.

"This is the last one," he said quietly behind me. "Or, at least, the last one in need of my ministrations. There are others, but none so deep nor as much a threat as this one."

I touched my fingers to the cold stone and felt the distant thrum of magic deep within the wall, coiling around the sundered stone, holding it fast, healing it. I'd felt this magic before, twice: when Elyan had used his magic to heal the cut in my arm when we'd faced the Moriae, and earlier that very day, when he'd eased the bruising Ajax's hands had wrought.

What he mends, he caused himself, Master Tiberius had told me. This was what he meant.

"You did this," I said at last, and my hand fell away from the wall as I turned to face him.

He looked not at me but at the crack as he crouched beside me, the blanket slipping from his shoulders as he reached out and rested his hand on the wall beside mine. "It was not purposefully done, but yes. I did this. And before we make the descent tomorrow, I must tell you why."

On the cold stone wall, my fingers found his. "Tell me, then."

Elyan conjured a Magefire for warmth, and we sat in front of the flames with our backs against the wall, huddled in our blankets. He spoke in a low, even voice, his eyes firmly fixed on the vast fields that stretched away from us toward the silent, snow-covered trees of the forest beyond.

"No doubt Master Tiberius has enlightened you as to my character when I first came to Asperfell," he began. "I was consumed with anger toward Keric, and toward myself, and I cared little for what happened on the other side of the Gate because I deserved to lose it all. And for many, many years while Keric was still a boy-king under the thumb of your father and other men, I thought justice served. Keric was a flawed king, but I thought myself much worse, and the kingdom better off rid of me."

"We weren't," I whispered.

"I know." He tilted his head briefly and met my eyes. "Stories began to reach us through the Gate, stories of Keric's cruelty, of the people's suffering, and at first I tried to shut it out because there was nothing I could do. As far as any of us knew, there was no chance of escape and five hundred years of evidence as proof. But Mages kept coming, and their stories grew darker and more vile. Finally, I decided that whatever my failings, even if they would not, *could* not accept me as king, they were still my people and everything that had happened to them was my fault. I had to find some way to escape and stand for them."

It was the first time I had ever heard him speak of the people of Tiralaen as his, or of himself as their king. We'd called him the Raven King of Asperfell in the years after his banishment, monarch of a twisted kingdom of thieves and murderers and traitors, his proper place. Likely Tiralaen still imagined him thus; not a one of them knew the truth. But Elyan had known it, even if he would not admit it to me, or to Master Tiberius, or even himself. He had still seen himself as their king, and them his people, his responsibility, his burden.

"I pored over Master Tiberius's accounts of Siphons who had pulled magic from several Mages at once, for I believed that to be the key to opening the Gate from this side. All I found were hundreds and hundreds of failures until I realized that, as a Siphon, I could pull magic from anywhere, not just other Mages."

What he mends, he caused himself.

"You mean Asperfell," I breathed, and the realization of what he meant took hold of my heart and held it fast with an icy fist.

"Yes," he said, and his face was drawn with sadness and deep regret. "Against the wishes of its Master and with very little consideration given to the people who called it home, I drew magic from the only thing more powerful than Mages themselves: an entire prison built to hold them.

"It was a spectacular failure, of course," he conceded, looking back out across the moor, soft and still and glittering in the starlight. "I was only able to hold so much magic within me, and for half a minute only, perhaps less. Not nearly enough time to open the Gate, but more than enough to burn me up from within. I should've let it kill me, but, coward that I was, I released it to save my own life, and nearly brought the entire fortress down upon us all. So would Asperfell have fallen were it not for Master Tiberius and Mistress Philomena. I slept for three days, and when I awoke, Asperfell was still standing, but deeply damaged."

He'd mocked me cruelly when I'd first arrived with my fool's errand, and I thought he believed me naïve and inexperienced and raw. I'd thought it cynicism—when all along it was failure, and shame, and guilt. This was why he'd closed himself off whenever I asked him about escape, why he believed so fully that it could not be done.

"I cannot help but hurt people, Briony, and my hubris knows no bounds," he said, and his voice was little more than a fraught whisper. "I told you before, my gift is a curse, and so am I. These people, prisoners though they may be, they are my people, too. Are their lives any less valuable than those on the other side of the Gate simply because they've erred? I thought little of them when I nearly brought the fortress down upon their heads, yet are they not my people, too?"

"Yes," I told him softly. "They are your people, too. *We* are your people."

So often since my arrival I had forgotten that the man who sat beside me on the cold hard ground, the man in whose arms I'd stood only hours before, was a king and I his subject. In Asperfell, where we were bound by suffering and by survival, I could pretend, and so often did without realizing it, that birth and power mattered less than our regard for one another. It was an inclination that would no doubt be quelled soundly if we ever did manage to return to Tiralaen. My family, however noble its blood, dwelt now in disgrace—bereft of its position, its wealth, and its patriarch. An exiled king on the march to regain his throne could not squander himself on a marriage that brought with it no allies, no soldiers, no coin, no advantage whatsoever. I could not help the bitterness that rose in me at the thought.

"For the last five years I have been siphoning my own magic into Asperfell," Elyan spoke in the silence, coming to it at last, what had brought us there that night. "Healing it, rebuilding it. Fixing yet another of my many mistakes. And I've done so believing I would never leave this place. And now you've come along, and although I still can't believe it could be possible, there may be a chance, and

I fear, Briony… I fear that without me, without my magic, this place may not survive."

"But without you, Tiralaen will not survive."

The terrible choice hung in the air between us, and in his eyes I saw fear, fear for the people of Asperfell among whom he had lived the last twelve years, who recognized him not simply as a powerful Mage, but their sovereign, to whom they owed their allegiance, and relied upon for their protection.

"I cannot stay," he said, his voice heavy with regret and sadness. "But I cannot leave them without knowing I've done all I could to reconcile the damage I caused."

My gaze fell again on the crack, very nearly healed. "You mean to finish, then. Tonight."

"Yes," he said, and he suddenly looked wary, almost apologetic. "But I do not believe I can do so with my magic alone."

I had already begun to wrestle out of my enchanted blanket as he spoke, and wincing against the onslaught of cold air, I pushed my sleeve up to my elbow and held my arm out to him.

He looked down at my skin, gooseflesh prickling the surface in the sudden absence of warmth. Then he met my eyes once more. "Are you sure?" he asked quietly, and I nodded with far more courage than I felt.

Elyan pressed one hand against the last remaining vestiges of the crack and took my own hand in the other, our fingers laced tightly together. "It might feel strange, the siphoning," he told me softly. "But no harm will come to you. I promise."

I nodded, and he began.

He was right: the siphoning did feel strange, but not unpleasantly so. I felt my magic stirring beneath my skin, rising to his call, and light blossomed and grew until I was all aglow, and so was he. My magic flowed from my body into his, mingling with his own, and he took our shared power and gave it to Asperfell. Coils of silver wrapped around the split stone, drawing the jagged edges together, and although they would never be as they were, never fit perfectly, our magic gave strength to the broken places and that would have to be enough.

Elyan let go of me and slumped forward against the wall, now healed and whole, bracing himself against the stone with hands still incandescent with our shared magic. A peculiar feeling of weightlessness was spreading through me, and I suddenly felt an overwhelming urge to lie down upon the frozen ground and sleep for an eternity. I blinked, and stars swam hazily at the edges of my vision.

"I feel strange," I told Elyan, whose head was bowed low, his breathing rough and uneven. "Ought I to feel strange?"

"It will pass," he answered hoarsely. With what looked like an extraordinary effort, Elyan pushed himself away from the wall and dropped to the ground beside me. He leaned his head back, eyes closed, and I watched the last traces of silvery light disappear back into his skin.

"Did it work?" I asked him. "Will the magic hold?"

Elyan's head lolled to the side, and he opened his eyes and gave me a weary smile. "I rather think it will," he answered. "Thank you."

"You're welcome."

He exhaled deeply, his breath a white cloud in the bitter cold and his eyes closed again. "You don't have to stay out in the cold," he said. "I'll be right enough soon."

It was absurd, the thought of leaving him alone in the dark, drained utterly of magic and exhausted. Instead I wrapped my blanket around me tighter and shifted until we were side by side. "What do you miss most?" I asked him.

"From home?" he asked me, and I nodded. "Books," he answered, without hesitation.

"Truly?" I could not help but smile.

"Truly," he said. "I think I've read just about everything in this place and I must tell you that most of the novels are just terrible."

I laughed. "They really are."

"Of course, my father always thought I read too much. As if a person could possibly read too much. He feared me too much of a scholar to wear the crown, seeking refuge in the library and not in the training yard."

"Your magic makes you warrior enough, does it not?"

"My father was always wary of my magic. The last Mage born to our house was three generations ago, and she never sat on the throne."

Of course she wouldn't have. She'd been a daughter, and not a son.

"Had I been a Battlemage, I suppose he may have felt differently," Elyan said with a shrug. "But as a Siphon, I was always somewhat of a mystery to him, a peculiarity in a long line of otherwise perfectly normal kings."

Perfectly normal kings who hunted wild boar and held tournaments and made politically advantageous marriages. Perfectly normal kings like Gavreth, rugged and handsome and vigorous, kings who rode into battle with armor shining and banners flying. Not a tall, serious young man with a sharp tongue and a frightening power who preferred a book to a sword.

"And you?" he asked. "What do you miss most?"

What did I miss most? When I'd first arrived, I'd missed everything. And then, as my world at Asperfell grew, my life before narrowed, and I dwelled only on the most beloved of my memories. "My parents," I told him. "And my sister, Livia, and Uncle Geordan. Master Aeneas, of course, and even my Aunt Eudora."

"And Cyprias," Elyan added.

I turned. "Who?"

He frowned, tilting his head in confusion, and his lips parted as though he meant to say something to me, but the words did not come. Instead, the most curious expression bloomed on his face, shock, and then what very much appeared to be anguish, but why on earth would it have been? He regarded me with such sorrow, such pain, I could not account for it at all.

"Elyan?" I whispered in confusion.

"It's nothing," he said at last, and his face shuttered and closed, a sign, I now knew, he would no further speak of it, whatever or whoever this Cyprias was. "Please, continue," he said. "You were speaking of your family."

"In truth, it has been many years since I've seen them, especially my father and mother," I admitted. "Sometimes I fear I will forget their faces."

"You may do," Elyan conceded. "But what they looked like is unimportant, is it not? Only that because of them, you are who you are. Thus, they live on in you."

He rested his head back against the cold stone wall and closed his eyes. I imagined it would be some time before he was ready to stand, to make his way back inside Asperfell.

"Elyan," I said, and tilted my head toward him. He lifted his head ever so slightly and regarded me, eyebrows piqued in question. "Did you know Master Tiberius has filthy poetry hidden in his workroom?"

His laugh, rich and deep and wonderful, echoed in the crystalline silence and filled me with a warmth greater than any blanket, no matter how filled with magic.

24

To my dismay and despite my protestations, Elyan refused to allow me to seek a bottle of Lyphril from Master Tibcrius's stores.

"Sleep is what I need," he told me, as we climbed the stairs toward his chamber. It was a slow affair as I could hardly support his weight, but his unsteady gait had me concerned he would careen into a wall at any moment.

"And a stiff drink," I said, remembering the night the Countess had died.

Laughter rumbled in his chest. "Gods, yes."

When we reached his chamber, I poured him a generous measure of Laetha, wrinkling my nose at the strong, astringent smell, and brought it to him where he sat on the edge of his bed ridding himself of his boots. He tipped it back in one swallow, and I brought him another.

He told me not to stay, to return to my chamber and sleep, to stop worrying over him, but I stayed until his eyes closed and his breathing evened and a modicum of color returned to his skin. And then I stayed a little while longer so that I might study him.

Just as when he smiled, his face was transformed utterly when he slept. He would never be rid of the sharp, beautiful angles that shaped his countenance, but they were softer somehow, the perpetual scowl between his brows smoothed away. An unruly lock of his dark hair had fallen over his eyes and I moved it gently, my fingertips lingering on his skin. Then, because I was sure he was asleep and because I simply could not resist, I trailed my finger gently down his cheek and across the sharp line of his jaw, shocked and breathless and delighted at my own daring.

And then he reached out and grasped my hand.

I froze in horror, complete and absolute. Oh, why had I not left when he'd asked me to? In weakness and in longing I had stayed, and now been found taking the most intimate of liberties. What must he think of me? Heat suffused my skin and I knew that when he opened his eyes, he would see my cheeks flushed scarlet.

But he did not open his eyes. Instead, he brought my hand to his lips and pressed a kiss against my feverish skin. My breath caught in my throat, and I waited, captured exquisitely between hoping he dreamt and wishing he did not.

"Go to bed," he told me, his voice rough with sleep. Then he released my hand.

I rose on unsteady legs and backed slowly toward the door to his chamber. With shaking hands I lifted the latch, and fled.

My ghostly soldier was waiting for me when I arrived, and so, too, was Mistress Philomena. She watched me with eyes of flint as I approached warily; her presence so late could mean nothing good, and I wanted none of it. The memory of Elyan's skin was still imprinted upon my fingertips, and my heart had become a stranger to me. I longed for nothing but solitude so that I might reckon with this unexpected enemy, but it seemed another waited to challenge me first.

"I take it he's told you, then," she said at my approach. "About the cracks, about what he's done to Asperfell."

"And *for* Asperfell," I reminded her.

"Which would not have been necessary if not for his ludicrous attempt at escape all those years ago," she snapped. "And now, it seems, you've convinced him to try his hand at it all over again."

"This is nothing like last time."

"But it *is* escape, is it not?" She folded her hands before her, and my eyes were drawn to the giant ring of ancient keys she always wore at her belt. "And it will end in failure just as before and worse. If Asperfell is weakened further, you will doom us all."

"Tiralaen is doomed if he stays."

"A kingdom that has abandoned us is no concern to me. But the people within these walls *are* my concern. And since you've come, since you've filled Elyan's head with nonsense about umbras and firsts and freedom, I've feared for them."

I bristled and fought to keep my voice from betraying the sharp sting that I felt at her words. "It isn't nonsense," I said.

She considered me, making little effort to disguise the disapproval on her face. "When first you came, you told me that you were innocent, that you'd done no wrong. I fear you will prove far more of a danger to Asperfell than anyone could've imagined."

"How is it a danger to free a man wrongfully imprisoned?"

"Because his freedom comes at too high a cost," she hissed. "There are more than two hundred souls within these walls. What do you think will happen to them if the absence of his magic causes the damage to revert?"

"Even so, he did not kill his father," I answered. "You cannot keep a man in prison for a crime he did not commit."

Her lip curled in distaste. "He made his choice years ago when he used Asperfell's magic to attempt escape. He was selfish."

"He feared for his people. Surely you can understand why."

"These are his people," she said simply.

She turned to leave me then, and this time I did not hesitate. "How did you come to be here?" I called to her.

Mistress Philomena stood still. She was almost completely shrouded in darkness, save the pearly glow of Logas beside me, and the threads of silver in her dark hair gleamed in the borrowed light. "You did not look in the archives?" she asked, turning her head ever so slightly toward me.

"No. I wanted to hear it from you."

For a moment stretched impossibly long, I feared she would yet again leave me with her silence. Then she turned, so very slowly, and folded her hands together primly in front of her. "If you must know, I was sentenced to Asperfell for the theft of a child."

I was not entirely sure I'd heard her correctly so absurd was the idea of Mistress Philomena stealing anything, let alone a child. But I'd also never known her to lie.

"A very long time ago I worked for a rich family in the Iluvien countryside," she began. "They had a vast estate and wished to build a hedge maze full of statues. I was young, but my talent as a sculptor was undeniable, and so they brought me on after my apprenticeship. I was happy there, at Symson Hall, and I might be there still if it wasn't for Elspeth."

"Who is Elspeth?" I asked.

Her expression softened and became wistful. "Elspeth Symson. She was the youngest daughter of the master. The loveliest child you ever set eyes upon, and full of sweetness. She used to sneak out to the gardens and bring me little presents tucked into her apron pocket."

Mistress Philomena smiled then, and I realized all at once why: "You loved her," I said. "Elspeth."

"I did," she answered. "As my own. She had an older sister whom I also cared for, but she was a quiet, shy thing who kept mostly to herself and did not speak much. But Elspeth was like sunshine."

"What happened to her?" I was afraid of the answer; nothing that ended with Asperfell could've begun well.

She pressed her lips into a thin line as she so often did when her thoughts turned unpleasant. "Once Elspeth turned ten, I began to notice a change in her that I could not account for. Her life at Symson Hall was a blessed one, and yet she grew quiet and withdrawn, almost fearful. Much like her sister. I began to inquire of the household staff whether they knew what might've occurred, but I learned nothing until Elspeth's sister, Aurelia, sought me out one day and told me the truth. I didn't believe her at first, to my eternal shame. Perhaps I could've stopped it sooner if I had."

"Stopped what?" My voice was little more than a whisper.

Mistress Philomena leveled her steely gaze at me. "Her father, Miss Tenebrae. Her father. The man who was supposed to protect her from harm was causing it instead."

"Do you mean—"

"He hurt her, Miss Tenebrae," Mistress Philomena said softly. "He hurt both of them. He began with Aurelia, and then when he grew bored of her, he turned to Elspeth. My sweet, golden child. I could not help her sister, but I could help her. So, I waited until the dead of night, and I took her from her bed, and fled with her to Dalgrave. From there I planned on traveling east to the desert lands where no one would ever find us."

But they'd not made it to the desert lands. If they had, we would not be standing together in the darkness.

"Lord Symson's bannermen apprehended us at an inn," she continued. "They took Elspeth from me and turned me over to King Gavreth's Mageguard. I appealed my sentence and begged for clemency, but Lord Symson was rich and influential, and afraid I would reveal the truth. And so I was sent here."

"That's horrific," I said, finding my voice at last. "Those poor girls."

"I should've known I could not help her by taking her away," Mistress Philomena replied. "I should've stayed and tried my best to protect her."

"And what of her mother?" I demanded. "Should she not have fought?"

Mistress Philomena's smile was cold. "You were a girl of privilege, Miss Tenebrae. You know very well what is lost to a woman when she takes a man's name. Lady Symson was a fragile thing before she was married. As a wife, she may as well have been an umbra for all that she was noticed and heeded by her husband. I suspect very much that she knew and allowed it to continue because she was too weak and fearful to challenge him."

"All the same—" I began.

"I knew the consequences should I be caught," she cut me off. "And still I did it. I should've known better."

"But does the reason matter not?"

"I should've stayed and tried to protect her," Mistress Philomena repeated. "And so should Elyan."

She left me without another word, standing alone beside my door, with helpless rage burning in my chest for a man I'd never met and, if I was honest with myself, for her.

I woke before the dawn. For a long time, I huddled in my blankets, squeezing my eyes shut and willing myself to sleep a few hours more, fortification for what was to come, but my body would not obey me. I bathed and dressed while the rest of Asperfell lay in dreams and slipped out my door just as the sun began to rise.

Logas was waiting for me.

"I may not return," I told him. "If I do not, know that I will be forever grateful." It was not enough; nothing I could possibly say would ever be enough. He bowed low, and I bowed in return.

I thought about waking Elyan, but he'd siphoned so much magic the night before and no doubt needed the rest. And so I decided to go to see Master Tiberius alone. There was no one about as I made my way to his workroom, not even Mistress Philomena, who was always about. I was not particularly keen to encounter her after last night, but the silence was unsettling.

"Master Tiberius?" I called, as I knocked softly on the workroom door. "It's Briony. May I come in?"

There was no sound at all on the other side and I frowned. The door was unlocked, and though I felt a momentary pang of guilt, it quickly subsided as I remembered why I had come. I turned the latch and let myself inside.

The Magefire in the grate had gone out, leaving the room shrouded in shadow and gloom, and there was no sign of the Master of Asperfell other than an empty cup and plate on the worktable beside a series of parchments spread out and anchored with polished black stones. I bent over them, and it took me a moment before I realized they were very old maps of Tiralaen. I traced my finger north from Iluviel, searching for Orwynd, or at the very least the tiny village of Rosmyr some two days' ride north, but there was nothing at all but wide swaths of forest. No doubt the map had been drawn long before House Tenebrae had built the house that would become their ancestral seat.

I studied the map further and found the long-conquered kingdom of Ulreth to the south still existed, including the village of Beheren, which was wrong because it was now Kithia, and I wondered how I knew that and frowned. Such a small, inconsequential thing, a village that once belonged to one kingdom and then passed to another. Shaking my head, I let the map be.

Resigned that Master Tiberius had not been to his workroom that morning and unsure when he might return, I made my way to Elyan's chamber. Standing at his door, my courage waned as I remembered the night before and I wondered if he, too, would remember what I had done, the touch of my fingers on his jaw, his lips against my skin. I hoped that he would and that he wouldn't in equal measure.

I gathered my strength and knocked. He must've just woken up for he wore a fearsome scowl and his hair was a wild, tousled mess, but he held the door open nonetheless. I ducked under his arm, grateful for the warmth of the Magefire in his grate.

"Master Tiberius is not in his workroom," I told him. "And I can't recall seeing him since yesterday morning. Do you suppose he's all right?"

"Undoubtedly so. He'll turn up. In the meantime, we must find Thaniel and Phyra."

He grabbed his breakfast from outside his door, and I was outraged to see that his royal station afforded him a thick slice of buttered toast along with his bowl of porridge. I waited until he'd left me to bathe before I seized and devoured it, washing it down with his cup of tea. By the time he returned, his dark curls still dripping, I'd very nearly fallen asleep in front of his Magefire.

"Hungry, were we?" he asked, after he'd shaken me fully awake.

"It is wholly unfair that you get toast and I felt I must remedy the situation."

"Gods save me from more of your scheming," he said, but this time he smiled. "If our excursion tonight is unsuccessful, I will ensure you receive toast each and every morning hereafter."

"And if we are dead?"

"Then for your sake I hope they have toast in the land beyond."

A consolation prize, to be sure, but I nodded nonetheless and shook the hand he offered.

Thaniel was still abed when Elyan pounded on his door, and from within I heard a muffled groan followed by a thud and the sound of glass breaking.

"Damnit!" Thaniel shouted, his voice thick with sleep. A moment later the door was wrenched open and he stood at the threshold in his nightshirt, his hair standing up on end. He glared at the both of us.

"Yes, what?" he asked irritably.

"We're sorry to wake you," I said. "But it really couldn't wait. We must speak to you, and Phyra."

Thaniel looked very much as though he would've liked to refuse us and return to the warmth of his bed, but he sighed and said, "Give us a moment." Then he shut the door and I heard a voice, a female voice, speak to him from inside his chamber. I recognized the voice immediately.

I turned to Elyan swiftly with wide eyes. "Phyra shares his chamber?"

"I imagine so, from time to time," he answered me with a diffident shrug.

I was familiar enough with the goings-on in Asperfell to know that coupling was frequent, and unless one counted the marriage that Lord and Lady Ashwinder had bestowed upon themselves, none of the participants in the prison were man and wife, nor did they often stay with the same paramour for long. I was not so much surprised that Thaniel and Phyra engaged in such activities as that Elyan seemed wholly unbothered by what in Tiralaen would've been a scandal worthy of ruination. Asperfell was a different world entirely, that much I knew, but surely it was not so far removed from societal rules that such behavior was so easily dismissed, particularly by a member of the royal family, held to a higher standard than any of the rest of us. Elyan was, after all, opinionated to a fault, and his judgments merciless, as I could attest.

At least it answered the question I'd wondered since the first day I'd met them. "They are together, then?" I asked Elyan. "As man and wife?"

A frown creased his brow. "No," he replied slowly. "Of course not."

The way he said it, and the expression on his face, made me feel as though there were something I ought to have known and didn't, and I felt the mild sting of being left out of a secret.

I never got the chance to ask him anything more about it, because Thaniel's chamber door opened again. He'd dressed and made an effort with his hair, though he still looked distinctly rumpled. In the shadows behind him stood Phyra in a gown of midnight blue, her dark hair hanging in a single plait over one shoulder.

"All right," Thaniel said. "You've got us, now what do you want with us?"

I shook my head. "Not here."

Mistress Philomena was likely about; it would not do for her to hear what we planned.

So, the four of us made our way to Master Tiberius's workroom, hoping he might be there at last, but the room was as cold and dark as before. Elyan lit a Magefire in the grate, and the four of us huddled around it.

"Now, then," Thaniel said. "Do you want to tell us what this is all about?"

Elyan deferred to me in the telling of it, and I spared no detail: the Countess, Vala Lirr, the Moriae, Grenn, and the builders of the prison whose names we could not say. When I spoke of Arlo Bryn, Thaniel gave a snort of derision, but otherwise they listened silently as I told them of our plan to follow the roots of the black oak of Asperfell and somehow locate the foundation of bone, leading to what we hoped was a path to freedom, a way back home.

"We could manage it, perhaps, with only ourselves and Bryn," Elyan said as I finished. "But it would be easier with more."

Thaniel leaned forward, resting his chin on his clasped hands. "So you don't know exactly where these roots lead? Or if there's anything at their end at all?"

"I'm afraid not," I replied. "But we have hope—"

"*She* has hope," Elyan interrupted. "I am not entirely sure we are all not going to die down there."

I glared at him. "We have hope that the umbras are leading us to freedom, as they've said. We know it's something important. Worth killing for."

"And that's another thing," Thaniel said. "Someone murdered the Countess and tried to murder you. Who?"

I glanced at Elyan. "We don't know that, either."

Phyra had until that point remained curled in her chair as though she was sinking into it and leaving us all behind. Now she turned her dark, fathomless eyes on me and said, "Someone in this prison doesn't want you to continue down this path."

"And you think I shouldn't?"

"No," she said. "On the contrary, I believe you must."

She looked over at Thaniel, and a look passed between them, one only they were meant to understand. Then Thaniel sighed heavily in resignation.

"I'll go," he said. "If only to save you from Arlo Bryn because that bastard can't be trusted."

"And you?" I asked Phyra hopefully. "Will you help us?"

She was silent for a long moment. "I will not raise the dead. I made a vow long ago that I'll not break."

"I understand," I said.

"Then I will go with you," she answered.

"And what of the Master?" Thaniel asked, frowning around at the empty workroom. "You've told him all of this, yes?"

Elyan and I exchanged an uncomfortable glance. "No," I admitted. "Not all of it. I tried to tell him this morning, but as you see…" I gestured weakly to the empty workroom.

"Is this usual for him?"

"No," Elyan admitted, his face troubled. "We've not seen him since Grenn, so he doesn't know about our suspicion about the roots, or our plans."

Thaniel's frown deepened. "Well, where can we find him? Do you know where his chamber is?"

Elyan did, and we left the workroom and followed him through labyrinthine passages to the south tower and up narrow, spiraling staircases until we reached the topmost room. Elyan rapped on the door and we waited. When no reply came from within, Elyan called out, "Master Tiberius? It's Elyan. Are you all right?"

Only silence answered us.

"Perhaps we should check inside," I said.

The large, airy room was surprisingly barren; nothing at all like what I had expected after seeing Elyan's chamber with its elegance and warmth. There was a large, threadbare rug that covered the cold stone floor, a modest four poster bed devoid of curtains, and a small, round table upon which sat a stack of books, a decanter of amber liquid, and a single glass.

"Goodness, he isn't one for finery, is he?" Thaniel remarked, as we moved hesitantly into the room.

"No," Elyan said. "He quite shuns it, actually, but he rarely spends time here. His workroom is his home." He frowned at the bed. The coverlet was folded neatly; there were no signs that anyone had disturbed it recently. "Although he does typically retire here to sleep at least."

"So where's he gone, then?" Thaniel asked, as Phyra perched on the edge of the bed. "And why?"

Unease had been growing within me since I'd seen Master Tiberius's empty workroom that morning. I'd not known him for long, not nearly as long as the three people standing in the room with me, but it seemed entirely out of character for the Master of Asperfell to up and vanish without a trace. All signs pointed to something sinister, and I knew surely that Master Tiberius's fate was tied to mine, and to Elyan's.

"Do you think the murderer could have been so bold as to target the Master?" I asked suddenly.

"He *was* deep in our counsels about the first," Elyan conceded.

"If you're right—and believe me, I hope you are not—we may not have much time."

We left the Master's room as we found it and descended back down into the prison in somber silence. If I'd been determined before, it was nothing to the fierce sense of purpose I felt now. Below lay secrets, yes, but any uncertainty I'd felt at the descent had evaporated like fog against the morning sun.

As we stepped into the courtyard, I saw the lone figure of Arlo Bryn standing below the black oak of Asperfell, his hands clasped behind his back, staring up at the gnarled branches. He turned at our approach and smiled widely.

"Ah! The intrepid adventurers here at last," he said, rubbing his hands together. "Shall we begin, then?"

I could not blame Elyan and Thaniel for the dour looks they gave Arlo, but having feared that he had decided sometime in the night that we were all quite mad and he wanted nothing to do with our absurd task, I felt relief upon seeing him.

"Phyra, is it?" Arlo said. He must've met her before, knew who she was, but there was surprise in his gaze, and curiosity behind his swaggering smile. "The Necromancer. Funny, I thought you didn't use your power."

"She doesn't," Thaniel snapped. "So whatever it is you're thinking, don't."

Arlo held up his hands innocently. "Peace, Thaniel. I promise to behave." He flashed a wide grin at Phyra.

She stared back at him, her dark eyes betraying nothing.

"Yes, well, let's get on with it, shall we?" Elyan interrupted them. I'd sensed a growing tension in him since we'd found Master Tiberius's workroom empty that morning. It was there in the set of his jaw, the bunching of his shoulders, the ice in his eyes. He'd known the Master of Asperfell longest, and he was far more than a teacher and guide; he was a friend.

I looked over at Arlo. "How do we proceed?"

Arlo turned his attention back to the black oak tree. He climbed up onto the stone platform and stepped carefully onto the circle of soil. Then he put out one hand and rested it gently upon the ebony bark, and bent his head close as though listening for something. His hand began to glow, and the tree answered in kind, silvery light rising to the surface. As we watched silently, the light began to spread across the trunk, snaking up into the knotted branches and down where tree met soil, until the tree was all alight with magic. At last, he lifted his head, releasing a shuddering breath, and then he looked down at us, his hand still firm against the tree, his magic still coursing through it.

"The roots run deep," he said at last, his eyes wide and slightly wild. I thought I smelled green in the air. "And they run in more directions than I'd imagined—it's almost like branches in reverse, a canopy of sorts." He made a sweeping motion with his hands. "I think I've found the deepest point, but there's something blocking it, something… unnatural."

"More unnatural than a jet black tree that never withers or flowers?" Thaniel asked.

"How do we get there?" I asked.

Arlo's gaze flickered to one of the archways off the colonnade and a stairway that led down rather than up, although—and I nearly sighed with relief—not into the well-guarded dungeons. "There," he said, pointing.

As our guide, Arlo went first, then Elyan, and then me. Phyra followed some ways behind, and Thaniel brought up the rear. As we passed under the archway and into the tunnel, blackness consumed us and Magefire bloomed in my hand. It did not chase the shadows away entirely, not even when my companions summoned their own flames, for Asperfell was made of shadows, and made shadows of us all.

As we walked, Arlo trailed his fingers lightly against the stone wall, seeking the way from the roots of the black oak all around us. He paused as we reached a divergence in the tunnel, then led us down a smaller passageway, its stones far less worn than the one we'd just left. At the end of the tunnel was yet another passageway to the left, and to the right a set of crumbling stairs that descended into darkness.

"Down we go," Arlo said.

I breathed in and out slowly to calm my racing heart as we descended. I kept my eyes on Elyan's back and tried not to think of the walls shrinking, closing in on me, trapping me forever in darkness. He turned to look at me over his shoulder from time to time, as if checking to make sure I was still behind him, that I'd not been swallowed up.

Thus we proceeded through several tunnels, pausing while Arlo walked slowly up and down, feeling the wall here and there, sending his magic beyond the stone until he received shimmering traces of an answer in kind, his brow furrowed and his lower lip caught in between his teeth as he struggled to make out the pattern, to see the path that would lead us to the end of our journey.

When at long last he chose the path we should follow, we followed him with our Magefire aloft, plunging farther into the depths of Asperfell, down yet another set of stairs treacherous with moisture, guided by Arlo's magic and our Magefire until I wondered if we were fated to wander the lonely tunnels of Asperfell forever. And then, at last, Arlo stopped.

"It's there," he said, lifting his handful of Magefire to illuminate a single path ahead: a tunnel taller and wider than all that had come before it. On either side of the entrance stood pillars carved to resemble the twisting black branches of the tree above. Within each was a hollow bowl that I knew at once was meant to hold Magefire. "The tips of the lowest roots are down there."

"Well, then," Elyan said, and looked to me. "Let us into the darkness."

He and Arlo lit the pillars at either side of the tunnel entrance, and then, Arlo leading us once more, we passed through the archway.

At once the Magefire in our hands dimmed, though we'd not commanded them to do so; it was as if the darkness in this place was different from all others; it devoured, and we were helpless to its appetite. How I wished my magic were stronger! The flame in my hand had shrunk to little more than that of a candle, and I could hardly see what lay before me. Then a hand took mine, large and warm and strong, and my Magefire grew, illuminating the sharp, beautiful angles of Elyan's face above mine.

"There it is," Arlo said, and I tore my gaze away from Elyan to see what it was he had discovered. "The end of our path."

Transfixed, I walked forward, my Magefire held high. Though I'd never seen it before, the moment my eyes beheld it, I knew it; it was a story come to life, utterly ridiculous that it should be real, and yet of course it was.

I whispered, quite unable to quell entirely the smile that tugged at the corners of my lips: "The black wall."

25

Upon further inspection, I realized what stood before us was not a wall at all, but roots—hundreds and hundreds of roots, thick and black and twisted, gleaming in the light of the Magefire. Woven together, they formed a mighty barrier that stretched the length and width of the corridor, and in their center was a woman; a woman carved from wood of the black oak itself, her eyes closed in sleep, or perhaps in death. Her arms stretched above her head, her fingers joining with the roots above her, her legs disappearing into the roots below, the tendrils of her long hair spreading around her head like a halo.

"By the Gods," Thaniel breathed. "It is true."

"Yes," I said, remembering suddenly the details of that particular story. "But where—"

There was a sudden burst of movement from the shadows, and with a hoarse cry, a bundle of rags launched itself at Arlo, who gave a great shout of fright and scrambled backwards. The bundle of rags, which I realized at once was a man with long, tangled white hair and a beard to match, carried a thick, knobby wooden staff that he raised above his head and swung at us wildly.

Luckily, Thaniel's reflexes were swift. He drew Maelstrom from the scabbard at his waist and raised it, preparing to block the man's next blow.

It never fell.

Rather, the moment the man saw Thaniel's sword, he froze, his feeble arms quivering under the weight of his staff. Then he lowered it slowly, his eyes never leaving the churning, mercurial steel in Thaniel's hand.

"That blade," he croaked. "Did you forge it?"

Thaniel gaped at him in surprise, then, evidently perceiving the old man as little threat to us, lowered his blade. "Yes," he answered. "I did."

"Beautiful," the old man said, and hobbled forward, leaning heavily on the staff he had just attempted to attack us with. Reaching out, he brushed his fingertips against the gleaming metal, and I watched in awe as it reacted to his touch, shimmering and churning. "Absolutely beautiful."

"I'm sorry," Thaniel stammered, quite agog. "But who are you?"

Indeed, it was a sentiment felt by every one of us, if the expressions around me were to be interpreted correctly. Could this be the spirit Thaniel had told me about who guarded the black wall? His clothing had long ago been reduced to rags, and they hung off of his emaciated frame, sending up clouds of dust every time he moved. His face, what little of it I could see under his unruly beard, was heavily lined with age, but his bright blue eyes were keen and sharp. In fact, they looked strangely familiar, as though I'd seen their like before.

"Yes," Elyan said, stepping forward. "Who are you?"

"Who are *you*?" the old man demanded, poking Elyan in the chest with the end of his staff.

Elyan could not have looked more shocked if he had tried. "I do not answer to you. Now tell us—who are you?"

"Oh, for pity's sake," I sighed, and pushed past Elyan and Thaniel to stand before the old man. "My name is Briony Tenebrae. We mean you no harm."

He turned swiftly at the sound of my voice, and his wrinkled face split into a wide grin. "Orare," he said, and his voice was rich and pleasant. "You are most welcome."

It was my turn to gape at him. "You know me?"

"Oh, yes," he answered. "I know who you are. And I know why you are here."

"Indeed," I answered faintly. "And who are *you*?"

His smile deepened. "I would've thought you'd worked that bit out by now." It almost sounded as though he was teasing me.

It was impossible, and yet I knew it must be true. I said slowly, "You are one of the first."

"I am." His eyes twinkled, and again I was reminded of someone, though I could not remember who. "My name is Master Rhowyn, and I was one of the two men who discovered the Gate and built Asperfell."

"You said your name!" I exclaimed.

"The moment you woke me from my long sleep, the spell upon my name was broken," he answered. "I have waited a long, long time for you, Briony Tenebrae. I knew what you were the moment you stepped through the Gate, even though you did not."

I frowned. "But Master Rhowyn built Asperfell five hundred years ago. You cannot possibly be that old."

"I am, as a matter of fact," he answered. "So, if you will forgive me…"

Leaning heavily upon his staff, he lowered himself onto the floor until he sat cross-legged before us. "Ah," he groaned. "That's much better." Laying his staff in his lap, he looked up. "Now, then. Where were we?"

"You were just explaining to us how it is you could possibly be five hundred years old," Elyan answered him drily.

"Well." Master Rhowyn shrugged his bony shoulders. "I *am* an Alchemist of rare talent, if you'll forgive the immodesty."

I frowned. "Yes, but I was told no Mage had managed to live

immortal, even the man who—" A sense of wonder spread through me. "Oh," I gasped. "Oh my."

Master Rhowyn nodded, his merry eyes alight. "Just so. Goodness, you are clever!"

"Would someone mind explaining what on earth it is you two are talking about?" Arlo said with considerable exasperation.

"I do believe we have the pleasure of meeting the owner of The Cat," Elyan said.

Master Rhowyn chuckled. "Oh, I have missed him! Is he well?"

"Very well," I assured him. "Though he does have quite a mind of his own."

"Wait a moment." Arlo held up one hand, his brow furrowed. "You're saying you're one of the two men who built this prison and you invented some sort of... *elixir* to prolong your life?"

"Yes," Master Rhowyn conceded. "And no. The elixir did prolong my life, but there is a curse that binds me to this place beyond death and I have waited centuries for someone to come along to break it."

"You're the one who has been whispering to the umbras," I said, unable to contain the excitement in my voice. "And the Moriae— you're the one who has been leading me here!"

Master Rhowyn chuckled. "As I said, I have been waiting for you for a very long time. I was dismayed to realize you had no idea of your gifts when you arrived, but you have come farther than I ever expected."

Behind me, Elyan spoke. "Have there really been no other Orares in Asperfell before?"

"There was one," Master Rhowyn said sadly. "Many, many years ago. I tried to whisper to him through the umbras, too, but his mind was too broken by the time he arrived. The voices of the umbras, their pain, their longing, were too much for him to bear. He jumped off of the top of the west tower." He turned his gaze on me. "But you have proven strong, Briony Tenebrae, and courageous, and you have surrounded yourself with worthy companions. I pray you all have courage left to do what must be done."

I sank down onto my knees before him. "I don't understand what it is I must do. What do your whispers mean? Why have you brought me here? I have so many questions."

"Not the least of which is, who is it that cursed you to endure in this place?" Elyan added.

Master Rhowyn's face darkened. "Evil festers at the heart of Asperfell and it's been left unchecked since the first prisoners were brought here. I am neither living nor dead, held fast in a curse, and all because I dared to challenge him."

"Who?" I asked. "Who cursed you?"

His brows rose in surprise. "Can you not guess?"

"The other man who discovered the Gate with you," I whispered.

"The very same," Master Rhowyn sighed. "My brother."

It was far too much for me to grasp so quickly and my mind fought against the impossibility of it all. "Do you mean that he yet lives?" I stammered. "Here, at Asperfell?"

"Oh, he yet lives," Master Rhowyn said darkly. "The dead keep the secrets of the living, or had you forgotten? I am the dead, he the living. And I've kept his secrets for five hundred years, but no longer."

"But if he is still living, surely we've all seen him at some point or another, haven't we?" Thaniel pointed out with a frown.

"Verily you have," Master Rhowyn agreed. "You've just not realized. He's made sure of that. He did unspeakable things, and, Gods forgive me, I realized too late." He fixed his bright eyes on me. "But now you've come, and you may yet be able to save us all."

"And who, may I ask, is *us*?" Elyan said.

Master Rhowyn craned his neck all the way back to stare up at him, and I thought I heard several bones crack unpleasantly as he did so. "You shall see, your highness," he answered. "Once you reach the foundations of bone."

"The whispers," I said. "They spoke of freedom."

Master Rhowyn nodded slowly, and there was such sadness in his eyes. "They did."

"But not ours."

"No," he answered. "Not yours."

I said, very softly: "There is no Gate, then."

"No," he answered. "But it does not end here, Briony Tenebrae. You may be sure of that."

I could not speak; my throat had constricted with tears that threatened to spill in torrents down my cheeks, and I was afraid that if I uttered one word, one single, solitary word, I would fall utterly to pieces right there on the floor. I could not bear to look behind me at the faces of those who had risked so much to help me only to discover here, at the end, the reward I'd been so sure was waiting for us was nothing at all. But I knew I must. It was with considerable effort that I rose unsteadily to my feet and turned to face them, searching for Elyan's extraordinary eyes amid the flame and shadow.

"I'm sorry," I told him, and my heart was sick and sore with it. "I promised I would free you, and you put your trust in me, and I was wrong." My gaze found Thaniel and Phyra standing close together and, beyond them, Arlo, arms crossed, leaning against the wall of the tunnel. "I am going ahead, if I am able, to help those Master Rhowyn speaks of. But none of you need go with me."

"Do you really think I'm going to let you go down there without me?" Elyan chided gently. "I've spent a considerable amount of time keeping you alive despite your best efforts, and I'll not have it wasted."

"I'm going with you, too," Phyra spoke up. And beside her, Thaniel nodded resolutely.

"There is sure to be danger ahead," I told them.

"Yes," Thaniel agreed. "And we'll not leave you to face it alone."

I glanced at Arlo, who had little reason to stay now that I could not uphold my end of our bargain. "And you?"

For an impossibly long moment I thought he would not answer me, and I believe Thaniel was quite ready to tell him he could turn back for all he cared when at last he shrugged and said, "Oh, what the hell. I've come this far."

I turned and looked down at Master Rhowyn, who seemed to be waiting for my answer, and I said: "Tell me what I must do."

Master Rhowyn's wrinkly face split into a grin. "Just so," he said. Then he grasped his staff and held one knobby arm out to me. "If you please, Mistress Briony."

I helped him rise unsteadily to his feet, and together we turned to face the carving of the woman in the roots. "Wake her up," he instructed.

"Pardon me?" I blinked.

"My dear girl, she is the gatekeeper! You must wake her if you are to reach the foundations of bone, for it lies beyond and you cannot pass without her permission."

"Who is she?"

Master Rhowyn sighed, a long, rattling sound like wind through the leaves of a quaking aspen. "She is my wife."

"Oh Gods," I whispered.

"My brother's cruelty knows no bounds. She resisted him as well, and this was her punishment. The black oak is an extension of her very self."

I remembered the night I'd fled the Countess and found myself before the black oak tree, listening to so many voices and then a single voice. It had been hers; I knew it as surely as I knew myself.

"You must work hard to find the magic within," he told me. "She has been dormant for quite some time, but she is still there."

I stepped forward until I stood below the black wall and Master Rhowyn's wife, and drawing a deep breath, I looked up at her face, smooth and austere in repose. Imagining as best I could that she was a living, breathing woman, I reached out with my magic, seeking the echo of hers. Magic was there within the black wall, certainly, and quite a lot of it, but I could not tell what was hers and what was the tree's, or were they one in the same?

Are you there? Can you hear me?

I felt an answer to my call, and though it was faint, fainter than anything I'd ever felt in an umbra, I seized upon it.

"*Awaken*," I said, and my voice echoed throughout the tunnel.

Nothing happened; nothing at all.

From behind me, I heard Arlo mutter, "Well, that was uneventful."

"We're quite far below, Bryn," Elyan growled. "Nobody would ever find you."

"Nor care to look, I'd wager," Thaniel added.

I looked helplessly at Master Rhowyn, and gripping his staff in both hands, he leaned forward encouragingly. "Try again."

I reached out once more, seeking his wife's magic, frustrated when I could not distinguish it from that of the tree. After a moment, I thought I felt her, just as before, and I grasped at the connection between us, however weak, and spoke to her again.

Can you hear me? Please hear me. I must speak with you!

Something stirred within her magic, and hope leapt within me, but before I could try once more to command her to awaken, her magic slipped away. Try as I might to grasp for it and hold it fast, it disappeared. "No!" I whispered, and my hand reached out and met the black roots of her prison.

"Again!" Master Rhowyn banged the end of his staff on the stone floor and again I reached out, and again her magic evaded me, and again, and again until I slumped back, exhausted.

"I can't," I managed to grit out. "I can't find her within the tree and every time I do, I lose her. It's as if she's forgotten how to speak, or who she is. If only—oh!" I exclaimed, for the answer had come to me all at once. I gripped Master Rhowyn's sleeve with sudden urgency. "What is her name? Your wife—tell me her name!"

"Eniara," he said. "Eniara."

This time, when I reached out with my magic, I began there: with her name.

Eniara, I said, and I felt her then; her magic stirred, responded to my call, reached out.

Eniara, I said again. *My name is Briony. I mean you no harm, but I must speak with you. Can you hear me? Do you understand me?*

I waited.

I reached within me, for the magic in my blood, feeling as I always did the exquisite warmth as it rose to the surface, wrapping itself around my throat, pouring from my mouth sweet as honey and strong as iron.

"Awaken!"

This time she heard me, and obeyed. The roots that held her fast began to writhe and slacken, relinquishing her at last. The moment her foot touched the ground, she was a statue carved of the black oak no more, but flesh and blood, the very same as she had been the day she was taken and made to guard this cursed place. She was very short, of a height with me, and wore a simple spun gown of white, the same color as the waves of hair that framed her wrinkled face. It was a regal face, a proud face, and yet a kind one as well, with pale brown eyes that looked upon me and then around at my companions before resting on the man beside me.

"Rhowyn?" she said, her voice low and brittle from so many years spent in silence. "Rhowyn, is that you?"

Tears coursed down Master Rhowyn's face, thoroughly wetting his beard.

"Oh, Eniara," he answered. "How I've missed you."

"I fell asleep waiting," she said softly, as he took her hands in his. "I've been asleep a long time."

"Five hundred years or more," he told her. "And you still look as beautiful as the last day I saw you."

Eniara rested her hand against her husband's withered cheek and gazed at him sadly. "So much time has passed."

"For us," he said. "And for them."

"So long they have suffered," Eniara whispered.

"That's why we've come," I spoke at last, loath to disrupt their reunion after so long, but unsure how much time we truly had.

As if she only just remembered I stood beside her, Eniara turned swiftly toward me. "Orare," she said. "The danger you face ahead is great, and once you pass the roots, we can no longer help you."

"I dare say she'll have plenty of help," Master Rhowyn interjected. "But you must hurry. They'll have heard you by now, and if they have heard you, he knows you are here. Come now, all of you—you must go. At the end of the roots you will find stairs; endless stairs. And then the door."

I looked up at the black wall. "How do we pass through?"

Eniara and Master Rhowyn looked sadly at one another. "I must rejoin the roots," she said. "For I am them, and they are me. Thus I shall allow you to pass."

"I'm so sorry," I whispered to them both. To have held one another again after five hundred long years, and then to be torn asunder once more was more than I could bear.

Eniara took my hands within her own, paper thin and fragile, yet so very strong. "All will be well, Orare," she told me fiercely, and her eyes blazed with such courage. "You are the first true hope we have known. Have courage, trust in yourself and your companions, and all will be well."

"I will," I promised, then turned to Master Rhowyn. "What will happen to you?"

"I am cursed to serve as a gatekeeper until he dies," Master Rhowyn answered. "And thus, I shall wait, and guard my Eniara."

"I understand," I said. "And if I can, I will come back and free you. I give you my word."

"Careful now," Master Rhowyn warned. "The word of an Orare is not to be given lightly."

I fixed my eyes firmly on his. "I give you my word."

Master Rhowyn and Eniara embraced, their fingers lingering on one another's faces as though desperate to memorize each and every slope and line and plane to sustain them through another long sleep.

Then Eniara stepped back toward the roots, and they reached down to receive her. Black tendrils wrapped themselves around her arms, lifting her, parting so she might join them once more. Her skin darkened, hardened, and the last glimpse I had of her true self was the glimmer of her eyes before they closed. Then, beneath her feet, the roots parted to reveal a passage through the wall.

"Go," Master Rhowyn said. "And be quick, Orare! I will try to buy you as much time as I am able, but his powers are vast."

"No one needs to tell me twice." Arlo ducked inside the passageway first, bolstered, no doubt, by his aptitude. "Come on, you lot!"

Thaniel pushed Phyra gently ahead. "I'll be right behind you," he told her, and they disappeared.

Elyan was at my side, and it was time to say goodbye. "Thank you," I told Master Rhowyn. "For everything."

His expression was grim. "Do not thank me yet, Orare. You may yet regret what comes to pass. I hope not. But who can say?" He shrugged, then reached for his staff and ambled back into the shadowy corner from whence he'd come.

Elyan rested a hand against my back. I took a deep breath and plunged ahead into the darkness of the tunnel of roots.

We emerged in a vestibule some thirty feet long with high, vaulted ceilings and tiny alcoves carved into the walls to hold Magefire. At the far end was a large, wide staircase that descended below; it was the only way forward.

"Gods, what *is* that?" Thaniel's face was twisted into a grimace of distaste. "Does anyone else feel that?"

"It's magic," Elyan answered. "But it's wrong somehow. Tainted."

I could feel it, too. It was hot and thick, a suffocating sort of magic that was quite unlike my own or, indeed, any other magic I'd felt before.

"There's something else," Phyra said softly behind me.

I turned and looked back at her. "What do you feel?"

"Death," she said softly.

"Oh *wonderful*," Arlo groaned.

Thaniel glanced swiftly at him. "You don't have to come, you know."

"Oh, I know," Arlo agreed pleasantly. "But how else am I going to get Phyra to fall in love with me without a splendid act of heroism?"

"Gods, you're insufferable."

The stairs seemed to go on forever, and the feeling of wrongness in the magic around us grew until the air felt thick with it, and cloying.

"Are you all right?" I heard Thaniel whisper to Phyra, and I wondered if the feeling of death was also growing stronger alongside the strange magic. If she replied, I did not hear her, but her footsteps did not pause.

"I can see the bottom!" Arlo Bryn shouted.

Moments later, we reached the end of the impossibly long staircase and Magefire roared to life around us, conjured by unseen hands. I looked around to see alcoves full of it, illuminating an antechamber not much larger than my own room. At the far end was a door made of jet black wood, and above, carved from the same, the immense torso of a skeleton was fixed into the stone, its arms outstretched as if to welcome us. Magefire danced in the hollows of the sightless ebony eyes.

"Oh!" I started in shock and horror, and I stumbled backwards, colliding with Elyan's chest, his hands reaching out to steady me. "What is that?" I could not look away from the grotesque figurehead.

Phyra moved forward until she stood directly below the carving of the skeleton and its outstretched hands. She tilted her head up and closed her eyes. "He's dead, and yet alive," she said, and pressed the heel of her hand to her head, her face contorted as though in pain. "Sleeping and waiting." She gave a gasp and a shudder. "There's death inside!"

Arlo turned from the door and fixed me with an incredulous expression. "You still want to go in there?"

"Briony," Elyan began warily, and I realized his hands still encircled my arms, holding me against him.

I wrenched myself free and turned to face him. "No," I said firmly. "No. We've come all this way—I have to finish it. I have to know."

It was as though the door itself had heard my desire and sought to fulfill it, for it opened.

I knew not what we would face, and for a moment my resolve weakened in the face of the open door and what lay beyond. But I felt Elyan's hand slip into mine, warm and solid, and he was beside me, looking down at me without a trace of doubt or fear.

"Shall we?" he said, and I remembered when he'd said those very words to me on Serus. Could it have only been mere days? It seemed a lifetime ago. I'd taken his hand then without hesitation, and I took it now, and we crossed the threshold of the door together.

Thaniel and Phyra followed us, and Arlo Bryn came last, muttering curses, and the black oak door closed behind us.

We emerged into a room like death.

There was no stone wall, no stone ceiling, only bones. Thousands and thousands of bones. The skeleton above the black oak door had been merely a taste of what was to come; this was the fulfillment of that promise. The room was a dome, held up by white bones and veins of shimmering red that pulsed and snaked and coiled and drew them together, held them fast in a horrifying still-life of distorted limbs and sightless eyes.

I had found the foundation of bone at last.

Phyra gave a low moan and covered her ears, her dark eyes wide and stricken, and Thaniel reflexively pulled her toward him. Arlo looked as though he might be thoroughly sick.

"Blood magic." Elyan's voice dripped with contempt. "By the Gods, I've never seen it like this before."

"Who are they?" Phyra whispered.

It was as if the room had heard her question and sought to answer it. A voice that sounded like thousands of voices speaking as one entered my head, and the words they said came from my own lips as they used their magic—and mine—to speak through me: "*We are the builders of Asperfell.*"

My companions stared at me with wide eyes and I shook my head in confusion, pressing my hands against my head. But still I heard their voices in my head, clamoring for my voice, demanding my magic. For five hundred years they'd been silent and now they would be heard, whether I was willing or no.

"Stop," I gasped. "It hurts—it's too loud."

Let us in and be our voice, Orare, they said. *Be our voice!*

"There's too many of you," I whimpered. "I can't—I can't!"

"Briony?" Elyan was at my side. "What is it?"

"They're trying to speak through me," I told him, my face contorted with the effort to keep them at bay. "They want to be heard."

"Then let them," Elyan said fiercely. "Let them in and let us be done with it."

And so I stopped fighting and I let them in. They rushed into me and moved through me, climbing over one another, screaming to be heard and gradually a thousand voices spoke as one, and told me their story.

"They were slaves," I said. "Slaves, and criminals, and men and women of hopeless debt. Five hundred years ago, two Mages came from the south and promised them that if they built their prison, they would set them free. They *lied*."

This last word was spat with such venom that I gasped aloud as my head spun with it: *Lied, lied, lied.*

"One of them tried to make amends, but the other was too powerful. He bound them with his blood and his magic, built the foundation of his fortress with their bones. And he feeds on them even now. After all of these centuries, he still feeds upon their magic, and on ours."

The pain and helpless rage in their words was so visceral that for a moment my vision swam red. Were it not for Elyan's steady grip on my arms, I would've fallen to the floor.

"Oh Gods," I choked. "He used them. He promised their freedom and took their lives instead." All around us, the veins of red that bound the bones of the builders throbbed and roiled, and five hundred years of desperation and helpless rage snarled and snapped in my head. "They are the reason he yet lives! He's used their magic to stay alive—he feeds on them, feeds on us!"

"Wait," Arlo interjected. "What do you mean he feeds on us? Who?"

"The other," Elyan said grimly. "Master Rhowyn's brother." And the voices in my head hissed at the very mention of him, a cacophony of rage and seething.

Yes, the builders spoke to me once more. *Here is the true purpose of Asperfell. Not a prison, but feeding trough. Tiralaen fills it with unwanted Mages, doomed souls, exiled and forgotten. And so he has cheated death for five hundred years. Our blood, our magic. Your magic.*

"By the Gods," Arlo said slowly. "You mean to say that all this time, our magic has been feeding this man? Keeping him alive?"

I turned and faced the bones of the builders. "Tell us how to free you," I begged them, all of them. "We cannot leave you like this."

Elyan shook his head grimly. "Blood magic can only be undone by the Mage who created the spell," he said. "And it is unlikely the originator of *this* particular spell would submit to our request."

Another way, another way! The voices clamored about in my head.

"*You are of Asperfell,*" I spoke for them, lifting my hand and pointing at Elyan. His eyes went wide. *"Your power is mingled with us, with his, within the very stones of Asperfell."*

"All the healing you've done, mate," Thaniel said, his voice an awed whisper. "All those broken places you fixed with your magic."

Yes! The voices said in triumph, and I echoed them. "They feel your power within Asperfell," I told Elyan. "But I don't know that it will be enough, and neither do they."

"Surely it's worth a go," Arlo said. "If it doesn't work, they're no worse off than they were before, yes?"

Elyan was studying the wall nearest him, running his long fingers across the bones and veins. "It's evil magic," he said, a grimace of disgust on his face. "I can see the way it twists and binds, but I can't unravel it. Not without him."

"Who?" I asked.

"Master Rhowyn's brother," Elyan said. "The Blood Mage. If I could siphon his magic, I might be able to unravel his spell."

"Well, now, we can't have that, can we?"

A familiar, pleasant voice spoke up from somewhere behind Elyan, and I had less than a heartbeat to ponder its meaning before Elyan gasped, a horrifying, gurgling sound that caught in his throat. I looked down numbly as the point of a blade emerged through his ribs, through his skin, through his shirt.

His wide eyes met mine, and his mouth moved as though he were trying to speak; blood bubbled at his lips, spilled down his chin, and then he crumpled to the floor.

Standing behind him, holding a long knife slick and dark with blood, was Master Tiberius.

26

It is a curious thing to realize the depth of your feelings for another whilst losing them in the same breath. It is a sensation both exhilarating and desolate; a surprise, aching and lovely, and a loss beyond surviving. Thus it was with Elyan. I loved him, and he died.

A scream exploded in my gut and clawed its way viscously to my throat, where it tore itself free, a long, horrible, guttural sound that took a part of me with it as it filled the air of the chamber of bones. I cannot remember if I screamed his name, or perhaps I made only sounds; raw, rending sounds like an animal, devoid of all thought and reason. I cannot remember.

Thaniel pushed Phyra behind him and, drawing Maelstrom, ran toward Master Tiberius with a face full of fury, a battle cry at his lips. But for all his rage and gleaming blade, he was no match for such power.

Master Tiberius calmly raised one hand, and Thaniel was blown across the room as if he were no more than a rag doll. His back collided with the wall of bones, and I watched in horror as the hands and arms of the slaves of Asperfell came to life, grasping at Thaniel, holding him fast in a hideous tableau of splayed limbs.

Arlo, abandoning all pretense of heroism, broke into a panicked run, but he'd only made it a few steps before Master Tiberius lifted his hand and he, too, was thrown against the wall, his arms and legs and neck held fast by grasping, bleached white bones.

"You son of a bitch!" Thaniel bellowed at Master Tiberius, before a skeletal hand closed over his mouth, muffling his desperate curses.

"That's better now," Master Tiberius said with satisfaction, as he surveyed his work. Through the skeletal fingers that grasped at Thaniel's and Arlo's faces, helpless rage frothed and churned in their eyes.

Beneath Elyan's broken body, blood was slowly spreading across the stone floor, and I could not go to him for the Master of Asperfell stood in my way. I glanced wildly about the chamber but did not see Phyra anywhere. I hoped that in the commotion she'd managed to escape.

There was no one left to help me. I was utterly alone.

"I must admit I'm touched that you put yourselves in harm's way to rescue me," Master Tiberius said amiably, as though we were settling in for a chat in front of the Magefire in his workroom. This time there would be no well-worn chairs, no dusty bottle of wine, no comforting smell of parchment and ancient wood. "But as you can see, I am in need of no such assistance."

"Elyan!" I called, my voice hoarse with tears and screaming. "Please, get up!"

"Oh, he can't hear you now," Master Tiberius told me pleasantly. "He's much too far away. And it's for the best, really. I must admit I always wondered if Elyan's connection to Asperfell, the presence of his magic within the walls, might give him some form of power over my spell, but my curiosity is not so overwhelming that I would risk my ruin."

"No," I stammered in disbelief, my eyes still fixed on Elyan's broken body. "No."

"He really was such a remarkable Mage," the Master continued. "Despite his recklessness, his insatiable need to play the king, even in this cursed place. And he has been a rich vein of magic all these years, nearly enough to sustain me, but there have been too few since." He looked up at me. "Even you, my dear, with your magic like a wellspring, new and fresh and untainted."

Something hovered just beyond my understanding, a papilem floating on motes of dust and light, but shrouded in shadow, out of reach.

"Why?" I whispered.

"My dear," he said, spreading his arms with a smile, "I am the Master of Asperfell. And, as you've spoken to my worthless brother, or what is left of him, you know that I have *always* been the Master of Asperfell and always shall be."

My mind reeled. "But what about all of the Masters in the archives? Centuries of names, of different handwriting—"

"Fictions. Counterfeits," he answered. "I use a new name with every generation. You couldn't expect me to use my given name, could you? And not just because it'd give away my ruse. No one may speak it, or think it, or dwell too long upon the person it signifies. Not even me."

"The enchantment," I said.

"A masterful spell, is it not?" He smiled at that, and my heart twisted painfully in my chest. "I suppose I could've simply killed anyone who became too curious, but I do find it is so much easier to create beautiful illusions, beautiful lies, and allow people to see what they will. For five hundred years I've lived thus, and will live five hundred more when you are gone."

His name, now free of its ancient bonds, rose unbidden in my mind.

"Viscario," I whispered. "You killed your own brother."

"I did a great deal more than kill him, as you've seen," he replied. "And it was well deserved."

"He was trying to save them, and you killed him!"

Master Tiberius's face darkened. "Do not mistake Rhowyn for a hero, Briony. He shared my vision—no, he was desperate for it! So desperate that he blinded himself to the truths of what it would take to make it a reality."

"He was your brother!"

"And he was weak!" Master Tiberius snarled. "We were building a kingdom together, an eternal kingdom, until he let that damned wife of his turn him into a sniveling, weeping coward. That harlot had no vision. She saw only what we were at that moment, not what we could be, the kingdom we could build."

My eyes glittered with furious tears. "On the backs of indentured servants to whom you promised freedom!"

"We are all of us built on the backs of those who came before," he told me. "The Citadel, your Shining City, all of your libraries and universities and marvels and innovations are built on the backs of those easily oppressed. You were a child of wealth, of privilege, and did you once offer a seat at your family's table to the indentured servants who scrubbed your privies, elbow deep in your excrement as they were?"

I wanted him to be wrong, wanted it desperately, but I could not deny that I'd given little to no thought for those who had built the gilded world I'd inhabited, and in that moment, I felt hot, sick shame spread through me. And, perhaps because of it, renewed determination.

"That doesn't absolve you of what you've done. You lied to them," I spat. "You lied to them and you stole their lives. Their deaths!"

A very ugly look crossed the face of the man I'd once trusted and admired, and I was afraid. "Those who can be made to serve *must* serve. And so, I have made servants of you all. These wretched creatures upon my walls, those aimless souls imprisoned above, they are all in my service. Highborn or low, noble or slave, it matters not. All of them have served me, and serve me still." Master Tiberius's eyes lighted upon Elyan's still form. "Here was a prince, and yet he served me like all the others. And why not? Even kings, *kings*, serve me! His brother serves me even now."

"Keric?" I asked, bewildered. "But he's—"

"A world beyond us, yes." Master Tiberius smiled once more. "But what is the distance between worlds but a Gate?"

It was as if the stones of the floor upon which I stood crumbled beneath me and I was weightless, adrift. "You've crossed the Gate," I breathed. "You've gone back to Iluviel."

"As clever as you are, and educated so much as a woman can be, you have no doubt noticed the number of Mages sent to Asperfell has dwindled in recent generations, and with it the magic that sustains me. I could not allow it to continue, and so I took matters into my own hands."

The night of my Trial, Elyan had told me how a Blood Mage had infected King Gavreth with deadly magic—an unknown Blood Mage of unimaginable power. His death had ushered in an era of paranoia and persecution. And it was all the fault of the man who stood before me. Every devastation, every agony, every dark and hopeless thing that had befallen Tiralaen since the moment Elyan had stepped through the Gate, it was his doing.

"*Why?*" The word was a ravaged whisper in my ruined throat.

"Why?" He cocked his head at me, as though he could not fathom why I would ask such a thing. "To live eternal, of course."

"You told me no Mage in living memory has ever done so."

The Master of Asperfell smiled. "Indeed. And there is no one yet living who remembers me. Well, except for Rhowyn, of course. And he isn't exactly living."

The Dead keep the secrets of the Living. They'd tried to tell me, Vala Lirr, the Countess, and, I realized too late, the voices of the men and women by whose bones we were surrounded; that night at the foot of the black oak, they'd tried to tell me in the only way they could.

In riddles I'd not understood until it was too late. For five hundred years, Master Rhowyn had been cursed to guard the door to the hell below us all, whispering to the umbras, the touch of a fingertip upon the water creating ripples that grew and spread and broke upon the shore of my untried magic. And the man before me, the man I'd thought I'd known, had tried to silence them.

"You killed King Gavreth."

"I did what needed to be done to revive interest in my neglected Gate. To spur the populace of Tiralaen into action. To bring Mages flooding into my kingdom as they once had done."

"You killed the Countess," I said. "And you tried to kill me as well."

"Oh, I certainly tried," he replied. "Had I succeeded, there would have been no need for this." He gestured vaguely at the crumpled body at his feet. "Pity. But of course, you have proven quite the surprise, Briony Tenebrae. Not the only Orare to come to Asperfell, but the only one to survive this long, and untrained as you are—I cannot deny I was curious to see what your power would make of you and you of it, but alas, our time is at an end."

"What do you mean?"

Master Tiberius folded his hands before him. "Surely you did not expect I would allow you to leave this place? No. You and your companions will join this esteemed company, and I will return above and convey the tragic tale of your misguided journey and eventual demise."

"You'll weaken," I told him. "Keric has no need for you now—he has his own Blood Mage and I only came to Asperfell by the grace of Master Aeneas. There will be no more after me."

Master Tiberius seemed entirely unbothered by this. "Keric will fall in line," he said. "I know your young king better than you think, my dear. I've visited him often, in one guise or another. And every visit has tilted him further and further into madness. A sad necessity, really."

"I won't let you succeed." My voice was shaking; indeed, *all* of me was shaking.

"But you will," he said. "Because you are nothing. A pitiful Mage with a pitiful aptitude and no one to help you. You are, my dear, entirely alone."

"She's not alone," a soft, lilting voice whispered in the darkness.

Master Tiberius turned.

Soaked in his own blood and white-faced with fury, Elyan rose to his full height behind him, completely and inexplicably alive.

Before the Master of Asperfell could move against him, Elyan's fingers, blazing with so much magic, were at his forehead. He reached out and slammed his other hand against the wall of bones and blood.

The magic that surrounded me, that filled the chamber of bones, was a duel between the light and the dark; between the twisted, evil magic of the Master of Asperfell and the pure, brilliant magic of its king. The sheer, raw power of it threw me back against the wall of bones with such force that my breath was stolen from me. I slid down to the floor in a tangled heap.

A scream cut through the roar of power that surrounded us—a high, hideous shriek of outrage. I could not tell if it was Elyan who screamed or Master Viscario, or if the sound came from my own throat because it was all around me, flooding my senses and seeping into the marrow of my bones. I covered my head with my arms, squeezing my eyes shut tight against the onslaught. Pressure began to build inside of me as my magic rose in answer to the threat of so much power until I feared I would come undone.

Then, with one final wrenching scream, a blinding, dazzling light exploded within the chamber of bones, and the last thing I saw before tumbling into darkness was the silvery glow of magic radiating from pale skin.

* * *

Somewhere above me, voices murmured low and urgent, and I fought my way toward them in the darkness. There had been a bright light, and a sudden, violent explosion of power, a collision of magic. Elyan's magic.

Elyan!

I was cradled by hands strong and sure, fingers tangled in my hair, and a face swam above me, a face of sharp planes and angles, beautiful and beloved, moving between light and shadow as I opened my eyes.

"You died," I breathed, reaching out a tentative hand to touch his jaw, as though he might prove to be a dream after all and fade away into nothingness. "I saw you die."

His hand covered mine, holding it fast against the warmth of his skin, and his eyes were full. "An experience I do not recommend."

I stared at him in wonder. "How?"

He turned his head and I followed his gaze to see Phyra. "He had not gone very far," she said softly. "He heard you calling."

So she had not escaped after all. She'd hidden, and he'd forgotten her entirely, forgotten that she walked with one foot in the land of the living and the other in death. Phyra had vowed never to use her power, and yet for Elyan, for me, for all of us, she'd done just that. She'd ventured into death and brought him back to me.

Fierce joy erupted within me, and with a sound that was half laughter and half sobbing, I threw myself with abandon into his arms, heedless of propriety, heedless of anything but that he was real and warm and alive.

He laughed, a deep rumble in his chest, and his arms came around me like bands of iron. "I'm all right," he murmured against my hair. "I'm all right."

So, too, were Thaniel and Arlo. The skeletal hands that held them against the walls slowly relaxed their hold, and they fell to the floor disheveled and bruised, but otherwise unharmed.

"Well, *that* was unpleasant," Arlo said with a groan, as he raised himself up on one elbow. "Remind me never to help any of you ever, ever again."

Thaniel had scarce risen to his feet when Phyra flew into his arms, stealing his breath as she knotted her skinny arms about his waist. "You did it," Thaniel whispered into her hair. "I knew you could."

"Yes, thank you for that, by the way," Elyan told her. "Though I would've preferred not to have been stabbed in the first place."

I drew back in his arms and looked wildly around the chamber. "Where is he? Where is Master Tiberius?"

"Gone," Thaniel answered me grimly. "Through the Gate, back to Iluviel."

"No!" The word rushed from my lips in anguish, and I turned my stricken gaze to Elyan. "We've failed."

He answered me softly: "We didn't."

From out of the shadows they came, drifting like fog, and their umbras glowed red, a testament to their enslavement, to the blood they bore, coveted so desperately and used in so vile a manner. Elyan and I rose on unsteady feet, and I stepped forward to meet them, the men and women who had been promised freedom in exchange for their magic and received an eternity of agony instead.

The figure of a man, tall and strong and proud, separated from the others and approached us. "My name is Kasam," he said, and this time, all of us who stood in the chamber could hear his words. "I speak for those who were enslaved and by your courage have been freed this day."

I looked over at Elyan, disbelief mingling with hope, and saw the ghost of a smile on his pale face. "You untangled the spell."

"A feat I could not have managed but for the magic I gave these stones over so many years," he answered, and there was pride, and peace, in his tired voice. "Without it, even what I took from Master Tiberius—Master Viscario, as it were—would not have been enough."

All around us, the veins of red that mingled with the bones of the builders were shriveling and turning black, rotting and falling from the walls, twisted, brittle twigs that littered the floor. Though the bones remained, they were diminished now, and I felt no fear, only regret, and deep, deep sorrow.

"What will happen to you now?" I asked Kasam.

"We will fade," he answered. "And rest eternal. But first, we wish to bestow upon you a boon, Briony Tenebrae, for without you, we would still be held fast by the evilest of magic."

I shook my head. "It was Elyan who unraveled the spell."

"And you who brought me here," Elyan said. "None of this would have been possible without you. The victory, such as it is, is yours."

Kasam smiled at me. "You have only to ask, Orare. If it is in our power to give you, we will."

I knew at once what to ask for. "Can you conjure the Gate to Iluviel?"

"That power remains with the Master of Asperfell and shall remain with him until his death," Kasam answered in a voice heavy with regret. "We cannot help you."

Master Rhowyn had told me clearly enough there was no Gate to be had in this place of death and suffering, and so I had not expected they could; not really. Still, I tasted the bitterness of disappointment in my throat and could not bring myself to look at Elyan.

"But there may yet be another way," Kasam said. "There is a place, a cave, far to the north through the forest. It is said the veil between this world and the other is thin there and can be pierced. If you can find the cave, you may be able to return to your world."

I looked up at Elyan in dismay. "Even if it is true, we'll never make it past the Sentinels. We'd need—"

An army.

I could not ask it of them, not after everything they had been through, and yet I also knew we had little chance of success without the aid of Kasam's company of red umbras. "Help us," I said. "Help us get past the Sentinels."

Kasam was silent for a very long time and I feared he meant to reject me, but at length he asked, "This is what you will?"

"It is," I said. "Help us escape them, and we will head north and seek this cave you speak of."

"We are no army," he warned me. "And in death we have not the magic we had in life. But we will help you such as we are, in thanks for our freedom."

I turned to Elyan. "I know you don't believe it can be done—" I began, but his fingers were at my lips, silencing me.

"But I *do* believe in you," he said. "And if it can be done, you will find a way."

"In the dead of winter," I said. "On foot. Gods, is it even possible?"

"One thing is certain," Thaniel spoke up behind us. "We cannot stay in Asperfell. Not anymore. So whether this cave is real or no, we have little choice."

"Agreed," Arlo said. "And the sooner the better. I'd rather not spend one more minute in the death room, thank you very much."

I looked once more at Kasam and he bowed solemnly. "We cannot remain tethered to this world for long. Do not delay," he said. Then he and the rest of the builders faded, leaving us alone surrounded by their bones.

"Right," Elyan said. "Let's go."

The way back through Eniara's prison lay open for us, but when we emerged on the other side, Master Rhowyn was nowhere to be seen. Had he come to harm delaying Master Viscario from reaching the foundation of bones? I would not believe it; I *could* not believe it.

"I won't forget my promise," I said, and hoped that, wherever he was, Master Rhowyn heard me.

With Arlo at the head of our company, guiding us by the roots of the black oak tree once more, we ascended from the hell deep inside

Asperfell. I held fast to Elyan's hand, loath to let him go, afraid he would slip away back into the darkness.

Mistress Philomena was waiting for us, white-faced and grim, when we emerged.

I stopped abruptly and gripped Elyan's sleeve. "Wait. What about everyone else? There are two hundred prisoners here, perhaps more. Do we leave them to Master Viscario?"

"No," he said, but there was regret in his voice. "But we cannot wait for them. We must strike out now for the Sentinels, and the cave."

"I know."

"By the Gods," Mistress Philomena whispered, as she took in our disheveled appearance; the blood soaking Elyan's clothes; our haunted eyes. "What *happened?* Where is Master Tiberius?"

"His name isn't Tiberius," I answered.

We had precious little time, but she deserved to know; all of them did. While Elyan hastened to his chamber to shed his bloodied clothes and Phyra, Thaniel, and Arlo took leave to prepare for our journey, I told Mistress Philomena everything I could. She did not want to believe me; denial and derision warred with doubt and reason on her face until, at last, resignation and acceptance won out.

She sagged, her jaw slack and her skin tinged gray. "I cannot believe it. How can this be? What are we all to do?"

"Leave," I said grimly. "Come with us. If you stay here, you risk his return."

"No." She shook her head. "Asperfell is our home. It is ours, and we must defend it, not abandon it."

"You cannot protect them against Viscario." I said fiercely. "I've seen what he is capable of."

"But I cannot leave them," she said. "If the Master is as corrupt as you say, and you are fleeing with the man who should be his successor, then they have no one."

"The choice must be theirs," I said. "If we can somehow render harmless the Sentinels and forge a path to the woods, they must be allowed to take it, if they wish."

"They are criminals," she replied. "Murderers and rapists and thieves, however rare the magic in their blood. They should never be allowed to go free!"

"They are as you say," I admitted. "But do you not think that banishment from Tiralaen was enough? They will never again see their homes, their families."

"And what of the two men you travel with? They committed murder in Tiralaen, you know this. Should they be allowed to return after what they have done?"

Over the long months of scheming and planning and hoping, I'd not considered that Elyan and I might have companions to aid in our flight from Asperfell. Thaniel and Arlo had taken lives however noble their cause and although I counted Thaniel a friend and Arlo a helpful nuisance, they were criminals serving a true sentence. By freeing them from the prison, was I no better?

The triumph in Mistress Philomena's eyes told me full well that she'd seen hesitation in mine and knew me conflicted.

"I don't know," I said honestly. "But you cannot deny that what Master Viscario is doing to them, to *us,* is wrong, and if you allow it to continue, then you are complicit in something monstrous. Think of Elspeth."

Mistress Philomena's face hardened to stone. "Do not speak of her."

I pressed on. "You took her from her home because what was being done to her there was far worse than what lay out in the world with you. It is the same for them."

"They are criminals," she repeated, though some of the severity had gone from her voice. "The decision to set them free is not ours to make."

"There is no one else to make it."

Elyan had returned. He was dressed in fresh clothes and carried two packs with him. "Here," he said, and thrust one at me, along with a cloak of rich green velvet. "Clothes and sundries from the workroom. I've sent Thaniel to fetch whatever can be spared from the kitchens."

"We haven't much time," I reminded him. "We've no way of knowing how long Kasam and the rest of the builders have."

"Then we'd best hurry."

I fastened the cloak around my shoulders; it was a far finer thing than my remade bedcurtain, but far too large for me, and Elyan performed a hasty mending spell that brought the hem up nearly a foot by my reckoning.

"Better?" he asked, and I nodded.

Thaniel and Phyra emerged from the kitchens with packs full to bursting, but there was no sign of Arlo Bryn.

"Abandon his empire of gambling and debauchery for a journey on foot through the woods in the dead of winter?" Thaniel scoffed. "Are you mad? He most certainly isn't coming."

"Wrong as usual, Thaniel."

We turned to see Arlo sprinting down the staircase, a bag slung over his shoulder, and Thaniel let out an audible groan.

"Loath as I am to leave my little empire, as you put it, I won't spend another minute in this castle letting that bastard leech off my magic." He hefted his bag higher on his shoulder, and I heard the unmistakable clink of glass within.

Thaniel's eyes narrowed suspiciously. "Now that wouldn't happen to be Walfrey's enchanted bottle of Laetha, would it?"

"Whatever gave you that idea?" Arlo winked.

I turned back to Mistress Philomena and took her hands in mine. "I know I've been a burden," I told her. "But I thank you truly. For everything."

"I've been a prisoner here twenty years," she said. "And it has been the only true home I've ever known, strange as that might sound to you."

"It's not strange." I pressed her hands. "Not strange at all."

"I'm just trying to protect them," she said, and I took heart at the steely resolve I saw in her eyes. She would need all the strength she possessed to keep the prisoners of Asperfell safe from their Master should he ever return. Then she pulled her hands from mine and stepped away from me. "Good luck, Briony Tenebrae."

"Perhaps we will meet again someday," I said.

The corner of her lip quirked in a wry smile. "For your sake, I hope we do not."

My last glimpse of the inside of the fortress that had been my home and so much more besides was Mistress Philomena standing beneath the black oak of Asperfell, her hand raised in solemn farewell. I lifted my own in return, and the doors shuddered and closed behind me.

27

We stood together in the snow and faced the only thing left between us and freedom: the Sentinels. I'd not come near them since I'd arrived, and they'd remained unchanged, kneeling silently over their swords in wait. Beyond them, the forest, and farther, the possibility of home, however small.

"You sure your army is coming?" Arlo Bryn rubbed his hands together and glanced around us at the vast, empty expanse. "I've no plans to die today."

"Indeed, none of us do," Thaniel added.

Phyra pointed. "Look."

They appeared all around us, the red umbras of the builders, as if conjured from the air itself. Kasam had claimed they were no army, but they certainly looked fearsome enough, though I doubted that would be enough to stop the Sentinels. Indeed, I knew very little of their capacity to fight, or even to touch the physical world around them.

I was no warrior; neither was Phyra. I knew almost nothing about what Arlo Bryn was capable of, but I had to imagine, given the daring of his attempted rescue of his wife, that he had some modicum of skill as a fighter. Thaniel possessed skill and an extraordinary blade, and Elyan was the deadliest man I knew. Still, we seemed rather a ragtag band, the five of us, with a legion of shades that could understand my words only.

"We'll need to take out at least two of them to clear a path to the forest," Elyan said. "And hope that once we're gone, they won't pursue us."

"And if they do?" I asked.

"Run like hell," he answered grimly.

It was far from reassuring. I looked around me at the translucent figures that dotted the landscape, ready to earn the rest they so richly deserved. Kasam met my eyes and nodded solemnly at me.

"They're ready," I told Elyan.

We marched across the frozen landscape with the red company behind us, a ghostly horde against the pure driven snow. The journey I'd begun when Master Aeneas sent me through the Gate to free Elyan from Asperfell might very well end that day on the moor, but I would not yield until I had spent the last of me.

As we drew close to the Sentinels, Elyan turned to me, his hands heavy on my shoulders. "Stay back and try not to do anything foolish," he murmured, his voice low. "If it should go badly, turn and run back to Asperfell and don't look back. Do you understand me?"

I had no intention of leaving him to face danger alone, but I was far too clever to say so out loud. And besides, there was something I had wanted to tell him for some time and I could not wait. I'd waited before, and he'd died. I'd not miss the chance again.

"On the night the Moriae looked through my memories, I could see them as clearly as it did," I said, the words tumbling from my mouth urgently. "And I made up my mind that I would not protest whatever he took, but then I saw the night we danced at Serus and I couldn't let him take it; I *begged* him not to take it. And I wanted you to know."

I expected him to chide me for thinking thus when my mind should've been undivided from our desperate task, or, worse still, say nothing at all and leave me in wretched suspense, but he did neither. Instead, he took my face between his hands, and kissed me.

Of that kiss all I can say is that I understood all at once why my sister set such store by such things. His lips demanded of me that which I knew nothing of, but I was filled with a fierce and sudden joy at the discovery of it. I must've smiled, or perhaps I laughed, and I felt him respond in kind, his arms tightening around me and his forehead lowered to meet mine.

All at once there was a deep rumble as the ground shook beneath our feet, and Elyan and I turned. The Sentinel directly ahead of us had begun to move slowly and deliberately toward us, its blade raised in challenge.

"We'll need you, Orare," Kasam told me, as the red umbras gathered behind him. "Your commands must be strong and sure."

"I've never seen a battle," I told him, and I wished my voice had not shaken as I did. "All I know of strategy I learned from books."

"I was a carpenter before," Kasam answered, and the voice in my head was gentle. "I know nothing of battle, either. We shall learn together."

The night I arrived through the Gate, I'd woken a Sentinel by coming too close; mere feet only. Now, the hulking stone statue that stood directly between our party and the forest stepped forward slowly, deliberately, until we were no more than inches beyond the reach of its sword.

Arlo Bryn stepped forward. "Allow me," he said with an insufferable wink.

Then he pressed his hands to the ground and closed his eyes. Hundreds of roots broke free of the frozen soil at the Sentinel's feet and began to wrap themselves around its legs, pulling its massive body down to the earth.

Elyan rushed toward the hulking, struggling figure and stretched his hand out, magic rising in his fingertips. The Sentinel had no voice with which to shout in outrage, but watching it fight against the roots that coiled and squeezed and pulled as its magic was drained from it, I could well imagine what it might sound like. I heard a sickening snap, then another and another, as the roots bearing the Sentinel to the ground began to strain and break with the struggle.

"Hold it down!" Elyan shouted to Arlo. "I need to get close enough to touch it!"

"I'm trying!" Arlo's face had gone red with the effort of channeling his magic and sweat stood out on his brow. "That thing's bloody strong!"

The Sentinel broke free at last of its bonds and struck out at Elyan with one massive stone fist. He conjured a shield, but the force was still enough to bring him to his knees. My heart leapt into my throat. He gained purchase, pushed himself once again to his feet, and rushed at the Sentinel again.

He needed help; I knew at once how to give it.

I turned to Kasam and the red company, my magic rising at my silent call. "Help him!" I commanded them. "Climb the Sentinel—stop its legs! Blind its eyes!"

They possessed no physical bodies, but there were hundreds of them, and they converged on the Sentinel like a swarm, climbing up its massive stone legs and wrapping themselves about its head to render it sightless.

Their distraction gave Elyan the time he needed. Hand met stone, and he fought to hold on as the Sentinel began to stagger about, its hands passing through the umbras of the builders as if trying to tear them away. The Sentinel went down on one knee with a crash and dropped its blade as Elyan siphoned its magic, his skin shining as brightly as I'd ever seen it.

So intently had I been watching him, I'd not noticed that a second Sentinel had joined the fray. It ran at Elyan, its footsteps shaking the very ground upon which we stood, and it lifted its blade high.

Elyan was ready. He let go of the first Sentinel and turned, his fist ablaze with stolen magic. The new Sentinel's stone blade cracked with the force of Elyan's first blow, and the second split the sword in two, sending chunks of rock raining down onto the frozen moor. The stolen magic spent and seeping from him in tendrils of light, Elyan collapsed; he only just managed to scramble backwards as the Sentinel swung its empty fists into the ground.

"Again!" I bellowed, pointing at the second Sentinel. "Before it stands!"

Their glowing red forms converged on the Sentinel's back before it had risen to its full height, and I watched, breathless, my heart hammering in my chest, as they bore it back to the ground. They had some ability to weigh down the living statue, it seemed, and so were not entirely formless. Elyan rose, magic racing beneath his skin, and lunged forward, clamping his hands around the Sentinel's bowed head.

As its magic began to seep from it, setting Elyan alight as it filled him, the Sentinel grew still.

"Bind it, Bryn!" Elyan bellowed. "While it's still down!"

Roots burst from the frozen ground, sending a shower of snow, soil, and stone into the air, and began to wrap themselves about the Sentinel's neck, shoulders, and arms, holding it fast against the earth below.

Elyan, possessed of its magic, turned on the first Sentinel, now recovered from his siphoning, and brought his hands together. The blow was deafening; the Sentinel was thrown back by the force of it and crashed to the ground in a heap of stone, utterly still.

Wielding Maelstrom, Thaniel began to hack and chip away at the stone body of the second Sentinel, darting to and fro below it at astonishing speed so that each blow fell before the Sentinel had a chance to recover from the one before. As a shower of rock and dust tumbled to the ground from the Sentinel's leg, I had an idea.

"A little help, if you please!" Thaniel shouted to Arlo.

The Naturalist gritted his teeth, his fingers scratching the surface of the frozen dirt in desperation, searching for a conduit. "Gods, why did we have to do this in deep winter!"

He found what he was looking for at last, and a tangle of roots exploded from the ground and took ahold of the Sentinel's legs.

"Get the sword! Get the sword!" Arlo shouted.

"I'm trying, you ass!" Thaniel growled back.

He struck the Sentinel's sword-hand again and again, Maelstrom gleaming in the blinding winter sun. When the Sentinel ducked to avoid him, Thaniel let out a great shout and jumped, scrambling up onto the Sentinel's back and shoulders, where he continued to rain down blow after blow.

The Sentinel reached up with one immense stone hand and flung Thaniel off; he landed among the dirt and snow, bleeding profusely from a gash on his head.

A cry of anger erupted from somewhere behind me, and I turned to see Phyra running toward the Sentinel, even as it advanced upon her fallen protector. My heart leapt into my chest. There were no dead to raise here; how could Phyra's gift possibly help us?

"No!" Thaniel ground out at her, raising his head with considerable effort. "Stay back!"

But she did not slow, and I knew that, whatever it was she was planning, she would not succeed without help.

"Kasam!" I shouted. "I need you!"

The red company was fast fading, and those who remained were considerably weaker than they had been at the onset of the assault. Evidently, their time was nearly at an end. Those left looked to Kasam, awaiting his instructions; *my* instructions.

"Shield her from view!" I commanded him. "Keep her safe!"

The builders swarmed around Phyra and around the Sentinel's face, concealing her and distracting it in the same breath. Phyra lifted one hand, and suddenly I knew what she meant to do. In the places where Thaniel's blade had pierced stone, where it was weakest, Phyra's touch brought time upon it, causing it to crumble as though a hundred years or more had passed in an instant. As pieces of its legs and torso began to decay and tumble down to the ground below, the Sentinel staggered, then fell, Phyra only just able to avoid being utterly crushed.

"It will not last long!" she called to Thaniel, who rose, blood streaming down his face, and took up Maelstrom once more. The blade gleamed as he brought it down upon the crumbling stone of the Sentinel's flanks.

The Sentinel bound by Arlo's roots was beginning to stir as the effects of Elyan's siphoning wore off. I watched in horror, unable to summon the magic in my voice fast enough to bid the builders help him. Stone connected with flesh, and the Naturalist was hurled back, his body landing with a sickening crunch near the feet of the Sentinel engaged with Elyan some distance away.

"Bryn!" Elyan shouted. "Can you stand?"

The magic he'd siphoned was spent, the glow fast fading from his skin, and his movements had become slow and chaotic. A spectacular bruise was already forming below his left eye, and he turned his head and spat blood into the snow and dirt.

Facedown on the ground, Arlo lifted one weary hand.

Only a few of the red company remained, and their efforts to distract and detain the Sentinels grew weak with their fading. Phyra had warned her magic would only last so long; the Sentinel she and Thaniel had held at bay was already beginning to stand, the stones and rubble that had fallen to the earth with her magic returning as time and nature reconciled themselves once more.

Thaniel rose unsteadily to his feet and wiped the blood from his face before he took Maelstrom once more in both hands. The two Sentinels stood and faced them once more, lifting their swords indifferently, ready to strike down those who dared passage. Beyond, the forest beckoned, farther now, it seemed, than when the battle had first begun.

"We're not going to make it, mate," Thaniel said to Elyan. "Nothing is bringing them down and our ghostly company is fading fast."

"We don't need to bring them down," Elyan answered. "We just need to get past them."

"A distraction, then?" Arlo suggested. "The rest make a run for it."

Thaniel glared murderously at him. "And who is meant to be the distraction? Anyone but you, I imagine."

There was movement behind me, and I wrenched my gaze away from my friends, standing wounded and weary against men of stone who did not bleed or tire, their hope fast fading.

A third Sentinel had abandoned its post, its sword raised, ready to aid its companions. As I watched in horror, it began to gather speed, bearing down upon my friends, helplessly caught between enemies they could not hope to defeat. Oh Gods, was my fate truly to watch the man I loved die once more before my very eyes?

Elyan had seen; he began bellowing at Thaniel, Arlo, and Phyra, telling them to run back to Asperfell while he held the Sentinel at bay for as long as he could. But they stood their ground beside him, awaiting the onslaught on both sides.

He looked to me, then, across the moor, with such desolation in his eyes. He was desperate for me to flee, outraged that I did not.

Too many years of my short life had been wasted in waiting; now the moment was upon me at last. I was not strong; my hands had never wielded sword nor bow nor staff. I knew rudimentary spells only, and my aptitude...

There is power in a voice such as you cannot imagine.

I wanted it to be true so very, very desperately, but I may as well have been screaming into the wind for all the good my voice could do me here. Only a handful of the red company still remained; they could do nothing to stop the Sentinel, and there was no other magic near me to command. The third Sentinel was but three steps away from where my friends fought on against the others—then two steps, then one. Its massive sword was held high, ready to crash down upon them.

No other magic…

It was impossible; oh Gods, it was madness!

I'd not lose him again.

And so I threw my hands out in front of me and screamed with all that was within me: "Stop!"

It was as if time itself stood still.

The Sentinel froze, its blade hovering in the air, and I could not breathe as my magic coursed through me, a thread of power shining and sure that connected us, stone and flesh. I did not know if the Sentinel possessed language, if it could speak to me, but it understood me well enough, and had obeyed my command.

"Withdraw your blade," I ordered, and when I felt resistance, I reached out with my magic, sent it barreling down the thread. My voice was thunder, filling the moor and shaking the frozen ground beneath me. *"Withdraw your blade!"*

The Sentinel slowly raised its sword up and away, waiting, I realized, for further instructions.

And he was not the only one.

The other two Sentinels had stepped back from my friends and raised their swords, waiting in perfect stillness. All resistance was gone from them; they held no will of their own, only mine.

I moved on trembling legs toward Elyan, and I collapsed in his arms in relief and exhaustion. "It's all right," I assured him. "They will not harm us."

"How?" he breathed. "How is this possible?"

I could not begin to explain it myself, and so I merely looked up at him and said, "Well, am I an Orare or aren't I?"

Phyra, Thaniel, and Arlo had joined us, and as much as I wanted to stay safely ensconced in Elyan's arms, I did not know how long my magic would hold the Sentinels. I withdrew and faced them.

"I know you can understand me," I said, and my voice echoed with power. "My name is Briony Tenebrae, and I am an Orare. The Master who bound you has left Asperfell. He has power over you no longer. You will allow us to pass safely to the forest. And you will allow any others from the prison to do the same, should they wish it."

They did not want to let us pass; I could feel their rebellion in the taut thread of our connection, and I knew it came from the ancient and terrible magic that had bound them to the task for centuries.

And then, in my head, there was a voice—an ancient, harsh gurgle—and I realized it was the voice of the Sentinel, such as it was. It was trying to speak to me. *You may pass, Orare. You, and only you.*

No, I answered. *The prisoners of Asperfell must be allowed to go free. If they wish it.*

It cannot be, came the Sentinel's low rasp. *Only you.*

If there could only be one, I already knew I would give up my place to Elyan; it was not me Tiralaen needed, but her king.

But I was not ready to concede quite yet.

Let me take my companions, then—those who stand before you only, I said. *Let them pass with me, and we will depart and leave you be.*

There was nothing but silence in my head and I feared I'd miscalculated horribly.

Then, at last, the Sentinel before me went down on one knee slowly, so very slowly, and stretched one hand out toward the forest.

Go. And do not return.

I turned and faced my companions. Elyan, Thaniel, and Arlo were covered in filth and blood, and they looked so exhausted their legs might give way at any moment. They watched me half in fear and half in hope. Phyra stood some distance away, and all around us what was left of the red company waited.

They were waiting for me, I realized. They'd not heard what the Sentinel had said.

"We may pass," I told them. "But only us." My eyes found Elyan's; he knew what it cost me to say it.

"It is not defeat, Briony," he said, and his voice was very low. "There may yet be a way to save them. Just not today."

"By the Gods, what are we waiting for?" Arlo Bryn was already hefting his pack onto his shoulder.

Thaniel placed a weary hand on Phyra's back, and together they followed Arlo past the kneeling Sentinel.

Kasam stepped forward. Already I could see the shape of him growing less distinct, his features fading. "We have fulfilled our promise."

"You have fulfilled it wonderfully," I answered, and smiled at him—smiled at them all through grateful tears. "Thank you."

"Tell our story, Orare," Kasam said. "With your voice, bear witness to what has been done here."

"I will," I promised. "I will never forget you, or what you did here today."

Kasam lifted one hand, and then he and the rest of the builders of Asperfell faded with the wind. *Bear witness*, his voice floated back to me, a sigh.

I looked back across the moor. In the distance, Asperfell was an ancient and immovable ballast against the bleak winter sky. It had stood thus for five hundred years and might stand five hundred more. Within, Mistress Philomena would need every ounce of strength she possessed to protect the men and women in her care, criminals such as they were; criminals, and yet victims, too.

And standing tall and still, his dark hair blowing softly about his face, was the man who should be king of Tiralaen and the man who should be the Master of Asperfell, and they were both Elyan; Elyan with his extraordinary eyes filled now with resignation, and with sorrow as he looked on the place he had called home, unworthy as it was, for nearly thirteen long years. Did he regret his choice, I wondered? Did he regret me, who had forced him to make it?

He sighed deeply. Then he turned and took my hand, and together we walked away from Asperfell, past the kneeling Sentinel, and into the forest.

Epilogue

We trudged through the snow and underbrush of the forest, putting as much distance between ourselves and the Sentinels as we could before nightfall, wary even in victory that they might decide to hunt us down and return us to Asperfell. Our steps were heavy, weighed down with injury and exhaustion, and more than once we turned to look behind us until we could no longer see the gray towers of the prison in the distance.

When at last the sun began to set and Elyan was sure we had not been followed by Sentinel or umbra or Mage, we collapsed below a tree whose thick and gnarled roots were as much above ground as below.

"This will do," Arlo said with a gleam in his eye. "This will do nicely."

He rubbed his hands together, then laid them gently, almost reverently, against the tree's great roots. They came alive at his touch, rising and stretching from the soil, and wove together to form a domed shelter, large enough for us all to fit within.

"What do you know?" I said, as I inspected the tightly knit roots. "You may not be so terrible to have around after all."

Thaniel looked up from his pack. "Don't encourage him."

We lit a Magefire inside and saw to the grim task of cleaning and bandaging the wounds we'd sustained that day, both on the field of battle and in the depths of Asperfell. Dirt and blood were banished with magic, and strips of linen served as bandages. Elyan was far too weak to siphon any more magic, and so Arlo uncorked the bottle of Laetha and passed it around to dull the pain.

When I bade Elyan shed his shirt so that I could inspect the gash on his chest, I could not help but stare at the place where Master Viscario had stabbed him. If I'd not seen the knife, seen his blood, I'd have thought I'd dreamed it; his pale skin was smooth and clear; not even a scar remained.

Death magic was far more powerful than I'd ever imagined.

We melted snow in a pot pilfered from the kitchens to cook our simple supper. Elyan caught a rabbit, and Phyra added greens and, to my dismay, parsnips from our stores at Asperfell to the pot. We rested while it simmered, and then I ladled the soup into bowls. We ate in spent silence and passed the Laetha between us until we were sated and warm, though shadows still lingered in our eyes. I looked around the fire and wondered if my face was as ashen and drawn as those that looked back at me.

I sat beside Phyra, huddled deep inside her cloak, and together we stared into the depths of the Magefire. There were smudges of purple under her eyes, and her normally rich skin was pale and wan. She looked exhausted.

"I'll be well again soon," she told me with a faint smile, as though she'd sensed my concern. "I've not walked with Death in a very long time."

I looked across our woodland shelter at Elyan. "I don't know how to thank you for what you did for him today."

"Not just for him," she answered lightly, and I knew well enough her meaning.

"How did you know you could do it?" I asked her. "After so long."

She turned, and her eyes were dark and troubled. "I didn't.

In fact, I feared Death may cast me out so long have I shunned him, but he was of a mind to forgive."

"You saw him?"

"I saw his envoy," she told me, her eyes fixed on the fire. "Death rarely comes himself."

"And will he be all right?"

"I don't know. He'd not gone far and came back with me willingly and without struggle. But it *is* Death, and none among us ever really know what passes between Death and those he welcomes into his arms, and what they leave behind when they are taken back."

"What did it look like? The place where you met Death's envoy. I read once it looks different to each Necromancer."

"Water," she answered softly. "Endless water shrouded in mist. That is all."

At length she grew weary and laid down in her cloak in front of the fire; Thaniel hunched nearby, watching Arlo with narrowed eyes, though he needn't have bothered. The Naturalist had drunk a vigorous amount of Laetha to dull the pain from his injuries and hardly seemed interested in anything untoward.

I glanced back to the opening and saw Elyan had disappeared. Leaving Phyra to drowse by the Magefire, I drew on my cloak and stepped outside.

I found him in the darkness of the clearing with his hands clasped behind his back. His head was tilted back as he took in the black expanse above us, glittering with so many stars, the white clouds of his breath rising to join them.

"When I first arrived, I made a thorough study of them," he said, his eyes still fixed on the sky above. "They change with the season, as ours do, form the same shapes, even fall in the same way ours do, and yet for all that, this world is not our own, nor will it ever be."

I slipped beside him, and he lifted his arm so that I could tuck myself into his side. "We'll find the cave," I said softly.

He looked down at me. "You know, this may be the most ambitious of your schemes thus far."

I smiled. "Is that so? I rather thought facing down three Sentinels with nothing but an army of umbras was rather daring."

"Well, yes, that too." He turned and drew me against him, his hands brushing my errant curls from my face, lingering at my jaw, my neck. "The journey will not be easy, nor what will come after should we return to Tiralaen."

No, it would not be easy. We were but five, seeking a place we knew not where, in a land not our own. Even if we were to encounter no danger at all, which seemed entirely at odds with every moment that had passed since I'd stepped through the Gate, there was the matter of surviving in deep winter with nothing but a few meager supplies and our magic to help us; to say nothing of the havoc Master Viscario might at that very moment be wreaking in Tiralaen and beyond.

We'd exposed him and broken the enchantment that granted him eternal life through the blood of the builders; his desperation was bound to be ruinous. Even if he could not exact his revenge this side of the Gate, he would no doubt be waiting for our return. And he knew about Keric's Blood Mage. I feared Tiralaen's suffering would be unimaginable.

"We'll manage," I said softly. "Somehow we'll manage."

"Will you ever grow to doubt, I wonder?" His thumbs moved gently against the skin of my jaw and I leaned into his touch. "Will hope ever fail you? There is darkness in this world as surely as there is darkness in ours, and hope is a perilous thing."

"It is not in me to yield, no matter how dark," I said, remembering my father.

Elyan smiled ruefully. "I've learned well enough not to doubt you when you've set your mind to a task, no matter how impossible it may seem."

Snow began to fall around us gently, and yet I was warm in his arms and safe. He smiled at me, that slow, sweet smile that had stolen my breath on a night such as this, and then he kissed me long and deep and all around us was snow and stars and magic.

THE FOREST KINGDOM

Book Two of the Asperfell Trilogy

Coming in 2021

ACKNOWLEDGEMENTS

The act of creation is made possible not simply by the plying of talent and skill, but by the opportunities that proper support and encouragement provide. In this, I have been blessed with an embarrassment of riches.

To my husband of nearly fifteen years, know this: You are my favorite. You are my best friend. You have always believed in me so fiercely, and because of that, I have learned to believe more fully in myself. By encouraging and supporting my creative endeavors, you show our daughter how valuable the contributions of women are to the world and inspire her to expect the same in her future. There is no greater gift you can give her than loving me the way you do.

To my parents, who always wanted me to teach English and write stories for a living: Although it took me perhaps longer than I should have to know myself as well as you knew me, I got there in the end, and I could not have done it without all that I am, and all that I am, is owed to you.

To my daughter: Your courage, your kindness, your compassion, and your imagination inspire me each and every day, and I am so lucky to be your mother.

And, finally, to all those who came before me: I am only the latest in a long line of women who used their pens to inspire change, and that I am able to do so is a testament to their courage, their passion, and their commitment to demanding *more* for future generations.

I hope I have acquitted myself the same.

There is evil in this world, and it is allowed to fester and grow when we stand still, and when we say nothing. I urge you all: find your voice and use it, for there is power in a voice such as you cannot imagine. Do not doubt it.

ABOUT THE AUTHOR

A certified Language Arts teacher and classically trained opera singer, Thomas lives in Wenatchee, Washington, with her husband, daughter, two enormous dogs, and two mischievous cats. She aims to smash the patriarchy one novel at a time, creating characters and worlds that inspire, empower, and elevate women.